JENNIFER S. ALDERSON

The Lover's Portrait

An Art Mystery

Second edition

ISBN: 9789083001111

This book was professionally typeset on Reedsy.
Find out more at reedsy.com

To Philip and Cherie, for all your love and support

Contents

1

Two More Crates

June 26, 1942

Just two more crates, then our work is finally done, Arjan reminded himself as he bent down to grasp the thick twine handles, his back muscles already yelping in protest. Drops of sweat were burning his eyes, blurring his vision. "You can do this," he said softly, heaving the heavy oak box upwards with an audible grunt.

Philip nodded once, then did the same. Together they lugged their loads across the moonlit room, down the metal stairs, and into the cool subterranean space below. After hoisting the last two crates onto a stack close to the ladder, Arjan smiled in satisfaction, slapping Philip on the back as he regarded their work. One hundred and fifty-two crates holding his most treasured objects, and those of so many of his friends, were finally safe. Relief briefly overcame the panic and dread he'd been feeling for longer than he could remember. Preparing the space and artwork had taken more time than he'd hoped it would, but they'd done it. Now he could leave Amsterdam knowing he'd stayed true to his word. Arjan glanced over at Philip, glad he'd trusted him. He stretched out a hand towards the older man. "They fit perfectly."

Philip answered with a hasty handshake and a tight smile before nodding towards the ladder. "Shall we?"

He is right, Arjan thought, *there is still so much to do.* They climbed back up into the small shed and closed the heavy metal lid, careful to cushion its fall. They didn't want to give the neighbors an excuse to call the Gestapo. Not when they were so close to being finished.

Philip picked up a shovel and scooped sand onto the floor, letting Arjan rake it out evenly before adding more. When the sand was an inch deep, they shifted the first layer of heavy cement tiles into place, careful to fit them snug up against each other.

As they heaved and pushed, Arjan allowed himself to think about the future for the first time in weeks. Hiding the artwork was only the first step; he still had a long way to go before he could stop looking over his shoulder. First, back to his place to collect their suitcases. Then, a short walk to Central Station where second-class train tickets to Venlo were waiting. Finally, a taxi ride to the Belgian border where his contact would provide him with falsified travel documents and a chauffeur-driven Mercedes-Benz. The five Rembrandt etchings in his suitcase would guarantee safe passage to Switzerland. From Geneva he should be able to make his way through the demilitarized zone to Lyon, then down to Marseilles. All he had to do was keep a few steps ahead of Oswald Drechsler.

Just thinking about the hawk-nosed Nazi made him work faster. So far he'd been able to clear out his house and storage spaces without Drechsler noticing. Their last load, the canvases stowed in his gallery, was the riskiest, but he'd had no choice. His friends trusted him—no, counted on him—to keep their treasures safe. He couldn't let them down now. Not after all he'd done wrong.

2

Bedtime Routine

July 18, 2015

With an acquiescent sigh, Konrad Heider turned on his computer, pushing the power button firmly in with one of his long, manicured fingers. Leaning back into his wingback chair, he wondered—like most nights—why he still bothered after all of these years. Yet his evening search had become part of his bedtime routine, like a glass of warm milk or hot lemon tea to help soothe his soul and lull him to sleep. Without going through the motions of looking for his family's stolen paintings, he would never be able to drift off no matter how hard he tried.

So much of his uncle's artwork had disappeared during the war. The precious few paintings and sketches he'd managed to save now hung above his own desk as a source of inspiration, a constant reminder of why he had to keep searching. Where were the rest? Could they really still be tucked away in someone's attic or basement, just waiting to be found? Intellectually he knew that was unlikely, given the sheer number and high quality of the lost works. Yet caches of missing art were still being found all over Europe. One never knew. One had to have hope.

In the past ten years, research into the provenance of artwork acquired in the 1930s and 1940s had become routine at most major art museums. No one wanted to be accused of hanging stolen works on their walls. He knew he should be thrilled that so much more information was now available, but the prospect of scouring through all of those catalogs, publications, and collection databases was sometimes overwhelming.

He clicked open a web browser and entered his username and password. Moments later, the latest search results from his many Google alerts appeared on the screen. After scanning the list, he closed the browser, almost relieved there was nothing new to sift through.

As he shifted in his chair, a sharp pain shot up his leg, taking his breath away. His joints ached; his bones were becoming increasingly sensitive to the changing seasons. And the winters seemed to be getting harsher, longer, colder. *Or am I just getting older?* he mused, massaging his knee, then thigh.

If only there was someone else he could share his secrets with. A younger someone who could take on the hunt, as he did for his uncle all those years ago. But no, he'd never married or fathered a child, at least not that he knew of. He'd never fancied long-term relationships—too many questions, prying eyes that wanted to know him intimately, to be privy to all of his secrets. He'd never wanted anyone that close to him. But now, alone in this big house, he understood the need for offspring, for an heir, someone he could trust his secrets to.

Regret would get him nowhere, he told himself, shaking his head as if to force the thought out of his mind. No matter. He would carry on to the bitter end, as his uncle did, if he had to.

3

Stolen Objects

Zelda Richardson's knees knocked slightly as she waited for the project manager to summon her. Despite the fact that this was an unpaid internship—thus essentially nothing more than volunteering—she was more nervous now than she had ever been for a job interview back home. But then there was more riding on this internship than just a peek into the world of art curation and exhibition design.

She tried to distract herself, tilting her head back so as to better admire the darkly stained rafters of the exposed attic ceiling crisscrossing above. The Amsterdam Museum's reception area was nestled under the rooftop. Seated behind a counter to her left were two women with headsets on, quietly chatting as they waited for something to do. On either side of the small, windowless space were narrow hallways leading to the staff offices that occupied the uppermost floor of the building, leaving the three lowest levels available for the museum's public displays dedicated to different aspects of Amsterdam's expansive history.

Not that the museum's staff had to worry about running out of exhibition space anytime soon; the building was massive. Four galleries, each a city block long, were built around an open courtyard, connecting at the corners to form a large square. The chronologically arranged exhibitions were spread across the labyrinth of hallways and corridors, joined together by hidden staircases and sky bridges. Just thinking about the museum's varied collection brought a smile to Zelda's lips. It was the only historical museum she'd ever been to that featured fascinating displays about legalized prostitution, squatters' rights, marijuana use, and gay marriage.

And here she was, about to become one of those lucky few who created exhibitions worthy of this very museum. She wanted to jump out of her chair and dance around in joy, but the receptionists' presence kept her seated and silent. A year ago, she never would have dreamed that working for a museum as a curator or exhibition maker was a realistic possibility.

It was thanks to the support and encouragement of Professor Marianne Smit that she'd dared to apply for the museum studies master's program last month. Smit was one of the three historians leading the Art History of the Low Lands course at the University of Amsterdam. She and Zelda had spent a lot of time chatting during the group's biweekly train trips to museums around the Netherlands and Belgium. In the past six months, Marianne had become more than a teacher; she was Zelda's mentor and confidante. Marianne knew about Zelda's past as a website developer for big corporations, as well as her reasons for wanting to switch careers. Instead of making her feel inferior because of her previous profession, Marianne inspired Zelda to believe she could, in fact, do something different with her life.

Getting into the museum studies program was a long shot, but landing this internship would change everything. It really didn't matter what her tasks would be; she just had to do her best and prove to both her mentor and the university's selection committee that she was serious about pursuing a career in the cultural sector. Without this master's degree, no museum would ever consider hiring her.

A buzzing sound interrupted her thoughts. One of the receptionists spoke quietly into her headset before clearing her throat and saying in perfect English, "Mrs. Dijkstra will see you now." She pointed to the hallway on the right. "It's the fourth door down."

Zelda nodded in acknowledgement, casually wiping her sweaty palms across her skirt as she rose, leaving wet streaks on both sides of her hips.

When she knocked on the project manager's door, a deep voice called out,

"Please come in."

Bernice Dijkstra smiled up at her from behind her desk. "Zelda Richardson. Marianne said you would be coming by today."

Bernice rose, patting her tightly cropped afro as she did. Reading glasses dangling from a cord around her neck bounced on her ample bosom as she strode towards the door. She was shorter than Zelda's five-foot ten-inch frame and rather wide-hipped. Bernice was also the first person of any color other than white that she had met working in a Dutch museum, Zelda realized, as her boss-to-be crossed the room and offered her a hand.

"Bernice Dijkstra. It's nice to make your acquaintance, Zelda. Marianne has told me quite a bit about you. It seems you have a real passion for art history."

Zelda was surprised but pleased to hear her mentor had spoken so highly of her. Like most Dutch people she had met in Amsterdam, her mentor was quite reserved, her true feelings usually hidden behind a mask of slight bemusement. It was so hard for her to see what Dutch people were actually thinking; compared to her overbearing American ways, they seemed downright secretive.

"Please sit down." Bernice pointed to one of the two overstuffed chairs in front of her desk. Zelda took in the room for the first time, unsure of the best way to reach her seat. Bernice's office floor was a maze of portable archive cabinets, rolling bookshelves, and open cardboard boxes, all overflowing with paperwork. Stacked up between them were more piles of books and documents waiting to be boxed up.

"Thank you for coming to meet with me on such short notice," Bernice said as she wriggled her way around the desk. "You will have to excuse the mess. Now that the *Stolen Objects* exhibition is about to open, we can begin archiving all of the paperwork associated with it."

Zelda looked around wide-eyed. Was so much documentation really necessary for one exhibition?

"How much do you already know about this project? What has Marianne told you?"

Pretty much zilch, she wanted to say but bit her tongue instead and tried to recall the tidbits of information her mentor had emailed her. Marianne had only told her about this internship four days ago, saying her old friend Bernice was in a bind and needed help getting a website online on time—a task Zelda was uniquely qualified to do— and that it would be a fabulous way for her to see firsthand how an exhibition was created. The exhibition's title alone, *Stolen Objects: Unclaimed Paintings and Sculptures in Dutch Museum Depots*, piqued her curiosity, so she'd said "yes" via email immediately. Unfortunately, they hadn't had a chance to meet and discuss the proposed internship in detail, meaning she knew almost nothing about her potential tasks or the exhibition.

"Well, *Mevrouw* Dijkstra," she began, so proud of how she pronounced the Dutch word for "Mrs." that she almost forgot what she was going to say.

The project manager interrupted her. "Please call me Bernice."

"Oh, okay. Bernice." Zelda forced herself not to wipe her hands across her lap again. "I know the Amsterdam Museum is about to open an exhibition of paintings and sculptures that were taken from Dutch citizens by the Nazis during World War II, but have not been returned to their rightful owners. Some objects will be displayed, though most will only be viewable online via a collection database listing all of the stolen works of art. The Dutch government initiated this exhibition in the hopes that families will recognize artwork as their own and claim them." She looked to Bernice expectantly. That was all she knew for certain.

The project manager leaned back in her chair, the wooden frame creaking in protest. "Okay, let's start at the beginning. Approximately thirty-five thousand works of art were entrusted to the Dutch government after the Second World War ended, almost all of which have been returned to their legal owners. Yet ten years ago, there were still three thousand unclaimed paintings and sculptures stored in museum depots across the Netherlands. The secretary of state for education, culture, and science assembled a team of researchers from twelve Dutch museums and research institutions and tasked them with reconstructing the provenance of these remaining unclaimed pieces, in the hopes of finally locating the owners or their heirs."

Bernice paused and looked to Zelda. "Do you know what provenance is?"

"It is a record of the changes in ownership of an individual painting or sculpture," Zelda responded quickly.

"Yes, that's correct," Bernice said, seemingly more relieved than impressed that her potential intern recognized the term. "Our researchers have access to databases and archives containing historical documents pertaining to the sale or exchange of artwork all over Europe. It's an arduous, time-consuming task, scouring through all of the available records, hoping to find a mention of one of the unclaimed works. Unless the piece was pictured in an exhibition catalog, sold at a large auction house, or purchased via a reputable art dealer, it can be very difficult to find a clear paper trail that tells us who the owners once were. Even after ten years of searching, our researchers were only able to reconstruct the complete provenance of approximately half of the paintings and a handful of sculptures. The other fifteen hundred pieces, several of which will be displayed in our upcoming *Stolen Objects* exhibition, remain a mystery." Bernice wrung her hands as she talked, clearly riled up by the less than fruitful results of the team's efforts.

Zelda could feel her forehead creasing in confusion. "If there is no documentation associated with these orphaned objects—"

Bernice cut her off, continuing in a calmer tone, "We hope that by holding this exhibition, we can generate interest in these objects and hopefully find someone who recognizes a piece as their own. Many of those who fled the Netherlands before or during the war took their purchase contracts and title transfers with them, even if they had to leave the actual artwork behind. There have been several cases in the past of children—and even grandchildren—who have found documents in a forgotten storage space or safety deposit box and successfully claimed their family's artwork. Who knows what this exhibition will stir up; anything is possible. But if no one knows that the artwork is here in the Netherlands, then we will never find the owners or their heirs."

Zelda nodded, finally understanding why this exhibition was being held. There was a small chance someone would recognize their parents' or grandparents' painting or sculpture. It had apparently happened before and could always happen again.

"That's why our marketing department is launching an international media campaign to promote the opening, and why the website's extensive database listing information about all of the stolen art is also available in English. In fact, we organized a conference for a number of American and Canadian museum directors last week, to help generate publicity and interest in our project."

"Why North America?" Zelda asked.

"Four *Stolen Objects* exhibitions have been held since the war ended, but they were only publicized in Europe. Because so many Dutch nationals fled to Canada and the United States in the late 1930s and 1940s, we suspect the owners of many of these unclaimed works live in North America. We do realize that some may have already passed on, but hopefully their heirs will recognize paintings taken from their families. That is why this exhibition, the international advertisements, website, and conference are so very important to helping locate the legal owners of these works, before it is truly too late."

Zelda was awed by the enormity of this project. More than a thousand pieces of art still unclaimed after all of these years and even the experts didn't know where to look for the potential claimants. She felt privileged to be part of such a noble project, no matter what her role was. But did Bernice and her team seriously think this exhibition was going to succeed, that someone would actually remember what pieces of art they or their parents once had hanging in their house, seventy-odd years ago? And would they have the documents to prove it?

4

Deflated Expectations

Bernice rooted around her desk for a notebook as she continued explaining the *Stolen Objects* exhibition to Zelda. "Though the Amsterdam Museum is hosting the exhibition, several Dutch museums have worked jointly on every aspect of it. I've asked one of the exhibition's organizers, Huub Konijn, to join us in the conference room. He is a senior curator at the Jewish Historical Museum working out of our IT department until the opening next month. Huub will be able to tell you more about the website; he and his team were responsible for designing it, as well as writing the descriptions of the unclaimed artwork. We are using the same copy in both the catalog and website."

Bernice leaned forward and mindlessly thumped her pen on her desk. "In many ways, the website is even more important than the exhibition, simply because we cannot exhibit all fifteen hundred objects in one building, yet we can disseminate detailed information about all of them online."

Zelda couldn't help but get excited when Bernice began to talk about the importance of the website. Even though she still didn't know what her specific role in this extensive project would be, she figured it must be something to do with the multimedia side of things. Her mentor Marianne had seen her resume; she knew quite well what Zelda was capable of.

"I will ask one of the secretaries to get you a press packet and catalog, as well as a copy of the exhibition proposal and handbook. Those last two documents are written in Dutch. Marianne said you could already read Dutch quite proficiently?" Bernice looked to Zelda for confirmation.

"Yes, reading comes quite easily, though holding a conversation is still difficult for me." Encouraged by her Art of the Low Lands instructors to familiarize themselves with the local language, Zelda and several fellow students had signed up for a conversational Dutch course shortly after arriving in Amsterdam. She enjoyed the challenge of learning a new language, but was finding it extremely difficult to replicate the oddly guttural sounds needed to properly pronounce so many Dutch words. It felt like she was gurgling saliva instead of speaking a foreign tongue.

"That is often how it goes when you learn a new language. It is not a problem that you can't really speak Dutch yet; everyone working on this project is quite proficient in English."

Zelda could feel herself going red. *That is exactly the problem,* she thought. Every Dutch person she'd met in Amsterdam could speak English so well she rarely got the chance to practice her newly acquired language skills. She was proud she could read most newspapers, understand television shows, and even write simple sentences in Dutch after only six months of classes, yet she wondered whether she'd ever learn to speak the language properly.

"You will have to excuse me for not being so prepared. That conference tapped our resources to the extreme. And with my personal assistant away on vacation, it has been very hectic around here." Bernice stood up. "Would you follow me, please?"

She rose obediently, following Bernice out of her office and down a short flight of stairs at the end of the narrow hallway. When Bernice pushed open the door, Zelda gasped reflexively. She had never seen a conference room quite like this one before. Art deco wall lamps—complete with stained glass shades—bathed the room in a soft, warm light. Wooden paneling and ornate floral paper covered the walls and ceiling. Filling the room was a long table made of mahogany, its slight red hue accentuated by the lighting. A narrow band of sunlight streamed through the windows lining the left side of the room, lighting up parts of the floor and table.

She followed Bernice to the far end of the room where an older man was already sitting. Absorbed in his laptop, he didn't even bother to look up as they moved towards him.

Bernice began the introductions regardless. "Huub, this is Zelda Richardson, the American Marianne told me about. Zelda, this is Huub Konijn, senior curator at the Jewish Historical Museum."

As Zelda rounded the long table, the curator finally glanced in their direction, dutifully standing up to offer her a hand. She tried not to gawk as he unfolded his long body from the conference room chair. Huub Konijn was one of the thinnest men she'd ever met, with a shock of white hair gelled back in a pompadour. Not a single strand seemed to be out of place. Though she knew little about men's fashion, even she could tell his tailored gray suit and brown leather shoes were quite expensive. He forced a smile as she grasped his hand.

"Great to meet you," she said. "Marianne said you needed some help with the website."

The curator let her hand drop.

"Actually, Huub and his team have already created the online database containing information about all of the stolen objects still in the government's care, available in Dutch and English. I was hoping to show it to you now," Bernice stated calmly, nodding to the curator. He turned the laptop towards Zelda.

Her grin collapsed into a grimace. She couldn't bring herself to look at the screen. Marianne Smit had specifically mentioned the website and collection database in all three of her short emails; Zelda had assumed that her expertise as a website developer would be essential.

"Then what do you need me for?" she asked, trying hard to keep the confusion out of her voice.

Huub glared at the project manager, almost daring her to continue. The hostility emanating off of him was palpable. *Why is he so angry? Does it have anything to do with me being here?* Zelda wondered.

The project manager let her hands fall to the table before continuing in a warm, upbeat voice. "Several important American and Canadian museum directors, curators, and trustees were able to attend the conference last week. Our aim was to build up interest within the upper ranks of these leading institutions in the hope they would add links and information about our exhibition to their websites. We also handed out several copies of the English language exhibition catalog during the conference. As I mentioned before, the same text appears in both the catalog and database."

Bernice cleared her throat, looking slightly uncomfortable as she shifted position. The curator turned to gaze out the windows; the bright sun lit up his profile.

"Unfortunately many mistakes were pointed out to us during the conference, many grammatical errors...." Bernice gestured tiredly at the computer screen. "In fact, we are still getting emails about them."

Zelda eyed Huub slyly as the project manager explained their predicament. His face remained a mask of chiseled stone. She could only wonder what kind of meetings had taken place before she'd been called in and what kind of grief the curator had gotten for delivering such a faulty product.

Bernice sighed heavily. "There has been so much criticism that the director believes it prudent to have the text edited by a native speaker before publishing the final version of the English language catalog or officially launching the website." She looked directly at her potential intern as she spoke, clearly gauging her reaction. Zelda did her best to mimic the curator, keeping her face as neutral as possible and her mouth shut.

"It is essential to this project that the information presented is clear and accurate if heirs are to be certain a piece once belonged to their family. Here, let me show you what I mean." Bernice pointed to the screen in front of her.

Zelda finally let her eyes focus on the website. She could hardly believe what she was looking at. The database's home page was nothing more than a search engine floating in the middle of a light gray background. *With all of this artwork at their disposal, this is the best they could do?* she thought.

Bernice typed "Jan Brueghel I" into the blank field, and six small images appeared. To the right of each was a brief description of the painting's subject matter as well as its size and material composition. Next to two of the paintings was a short description of the documentation the museums' researchers found during their ten-year investigation.

As Zelda scanned the scant information available, she could feel her enthusiasm for this noble project fading by the second. The museum would be lucky if anyone came forward, based on the meager data listed on the screen in front of her.

Before Bernice could elaborate, the curator jabbed a finger at the laptop. "My team and I translated these texts. Three of them studied in London; their English is impeccable." He spit the words out as if they were venom. Zelda wasn't sure whether his poison was directed at her or Bernice, but either way it was obvious Huub really did not want her help.

"Yes, Huub," Bernice replied curtly, "you've said that many times, yet here we are. Unfortunately, we listened to you when we still had room in our budget for professional translators, otherwise we wouldn't be in this mess."

Though Bernice was speaking in Dutch, Zelda was able to understand every word. *What am I getting myself into?* she wondered again, realizing she had little choice but to grin and bear it if she wanted to stay on in Amsterdam. Without this internship, the university's selection committee would never take her application seriously, and her study visa wouldn't be extended.

She forced herself to read through the descriptions visible on the laptop's screen. There were a few glaring grammatical errors and odd word choices, but for the most part, they were perfectly understandable. Nodding her head slowly, she replied cautiously, "Yeah, it looks pretty good."

Huub exploded, spewing Dutch at Bernice like daggers. Though Zelda could understand basic conversations, he spoke far too fast for her to be able to keep up.

Ignoring his tirade, the project manager focused her attention solely on Zelda. "The exhibition opens in one month. At the conference, we promised to have the final version of this database available for perusal by the museums' own staff—as well as the international press—one week before the official opening. That way curators and museum directors can begin generating publicity among their donors and board members, and the North American media have a chance to learn more about objects featured in the exhibition before it begins. Hopefully some of them will cover the opening in their newspapers and magazines."

Bernice broke eye contact before continuing, Zelda suspected out of embarrassment. "That means we need to have all of the texts re-edited within the next three weeks in order to meet our deadline. Marianne mentioned you the other day over lunch, and I hoped, because of your familiarity with online databases and being a native English speaker, you would be willing to assist us."

The project manager grinned broadly, clearly avoiding Huub's piercing gaze as she addressed her potential intern. "What do you say? Would you do this for us?"

Zelda kept her smile plastered on, suppressing the need to cry out in frustration. *This can't be happening,* she moaned in her mind. This is why they needed her help so badly, editing text? She was applying for a master's degree in museum studies, not linguistics.

"How many objects are there again?" she finally managed.

"One thousand five hundred and thirty-seven, to be exact."

"You want me to check the descriptions of fifteen hundred objects within the next three weeks?" *Are you kidding me?* she wanted to scream at Bernice. She was going to be spending a lot of time in the museum, but stuck behind a computer.

Bernice must have noticed the panic on Zelda's face. "Yes, I know it is a lot to ask, but we would really appreciate your help. We hope this site will be seen by a large English-speaking audience, and it would be a shame if someone didn't make a claim because of a confusing or even faulty translation," she explained patiently.

Zelda looked at the two museum professionals before her—one glaring tersely at the other—and wondered whether working for them was such a hot idea after all. Office politics had never been her strong suit. She didn't relish the idea of being put in the middle of these two bullheaded professionals, and it sure seemed like that would be her role. And the work itself was not at all what she expected it to be.

On the other hand, if she bowed out of this project now—thereby offending both Bernice and her mentor, Marianne Smit—how many more chances would she get to work *inside* a museum? None. Marianne was the

16

most senior person on the university's selection committee; if Zelda stayed on her good side, she was almost guaranteed one of the twenty available seats. But if she backed out now, she could kiss her chance at getting into the master's program goodbye. And then what choice would she have but to go back to Seattle and build websites? If she could even find a job again. She hadn't kept up with the latest developments in computer technology since arriving in Amsterdam nine months ago. Considering how fast software changed, it might as well have been nine years.

Though a knot was forming in the pit of her stomach, she nodded enthusiastically. "I'll see what I can do. I'm happy to help, in any way I can." She had to make this work, she just had to. And who knew? If all went well, Bernice might, in the future, have some more work for her that was actually related to exhibition design or collection research.

"Wonderful. I'll forward you all of the corrections I've gotten since the conference. Please don't get frightened off when you see how many emails there are." Bernice beamed at Zelda before turning towards Huub Konijn. His icy expression wiped the grin right off of her face. She cleared her throat and leaned forward on one elbow, shutting him out of her direct sightline.

"I've reserved one of the workstations in the museum's library for you to use, starting next Monday. It's quiet in there, so you should be able to work relatively undisturbed, which is important considering the number of objects involved. I will also email you a list of books to read in order to gain more insight into the exhibition and our research project."

Bernice closed her notebook and pushed back her chair. "Now, Zelda, if you don't have any more questions, I will show you out."

5

Think On Your Heart

Bernice walked slowly back to her office, sure Huub had already fled the conference room. The last thing either one of them wanted was another pointless confrontation. What was done was done. Zelda Richardson had said "yes," as Marianne assured her she would. They were lucky Marianne mentioned her; Bernice hadn't expected to find a qualified volunteer on such short notice. At least she hoped Zelda's being a native speaker would be enough to satisfy Leo de Boer, the director of the Amsterdam Museum; the girl didn't have any official training as a translator or editor.

Not that they had a choice; there was no time or money left to do it any other way. She'd warned Leo from the start that Huub's team wasn't sufficiently trained to translate all of those texts; they should have hired a professional translator months ago. If Huub wasn't such a control freak, Leo would have been less inclined to agree with him.

Since being named head curator of the *Stolen Objects* exhibition, Huub had become obsessed with every aspect of it, far more than any other curator on the team, even volunteering—no, demanding—to lead both the collection research and website project groups. If Bernice hadn't known about his past, she might think his obsession was bordering on unhealthy. Yet it was his family history and previous accomplishments that granted him a level of trust no other curator had enjoyed, so far as she could remember in her twenty-seven years at the museum.

Well, this time even Leo had to admit he hadn't been critical enough. Her blood pressure began to rise just thinking about their current predicament.

"Think on your heart," Bernice mumbled. She stopped in the empty corridor and inhaled deeply, feeling the calm flowing back through her ample body as she exhaled. As the second breath slowed her pulse, Bernice tried visualizing the clear blue skies and dark green leaves of the Suriname River's jungle-encrusted banks, visible from the veranda of her second home on the outskirts of Paramaribo, as her doctor had taught her. She'd already submitted her request for early retirement due to medical reasons; Leo should approve it before the end of the month. Only five more projects to go and she was free. Her heart wasn't going to let her grow old, not if she let Huub and the others continue to get under her skin.

When her pulse returned to normal, she continued on to her office. She still wasn't sure Zelda was the right person for the job, but she'd done all she could to get them out of this mess, as any good project manager would.

Bernice closed the door behind her, resolving to forget about Huub and the faulty translations for now. She grabbed an empty box and set to work organizing the mountains of paperwork cluttering up her usually pristine office.

6

Flying Drones Across Museumplein

"What did you say?" Friedrich asked distractedly as he picked up his remote-controlled Cessna 182 Sky Trainer from the patchy brown lawn covering most of the Museumplein and intently examined it for signs of damage.

Zelda stretched her lean body out on her blanket, soaking up the warm summer sun and taking in the views as she waited for him to finish checking the plane's flaps and gears. The ship-shaped weather vanes and decorative spires mounted atop the Rijksmuseum—and several of the richly decorated mansions surrounding the square—shimmered and sparkled like stars on the horizon on clear days as this, outshone only by the enormous golden harp adorning the Concertgebouw, drawing her eye to the far left end of the square. In the middle of the grass, a group of schoolchildren playing soccer screeched in delight as they raced up and down the makeshift field, while tourists smoking joints watched from under a cluster of elm trees.

Since she'd moved to Amsterdam, this unattractive field of grass had become one of her favorite haunts. Not because of the square itself, but three of its more famous residents. Rolling onto her stomach, she was momentarily blinded by the sun's rays bouncing off the Van Gogh Museum's tall glass windows. Strange to think inside that gray, moon-shaped building hung some of the most expensive artwork in the world. The imposing red-and-white brick building next to it—the Stedelijk Museum—seemed a more appropriate place to house an art collection. The recent addition of a giant bathtub to the backside of the nineteenth-century structure was meant to remind visitors it was home to postwar and contemporary art. However, the institution that attracted the greatest number of tourists was just behind her: the Rijksmuseum, home to the nation's most cherished paintings, sculptures, ceramics, jewelry, and furniture. It even had seventeenth-century dollhouses on display. Most of its visitors, though, came to admire some of the best Rembrandts and Vermeers in existence.

Many an afternoon Zelda had spent blissfully roaming the halls of those three treasure troves, dreaming of one day working for them. If she managed to get into the master's program, that is.

She turned back towards Friedrich. Judging from his relaxed smile, his plane must have survived its short flight without incident. Figuring she had his attention again, she finally replied, "I said the internship isn't what I was expecting it to be. They want me to check some texts for translation errors; that's it. I mean, with all my knowledge and experience building websites, you'd think they would want me to redesign their site for them. I don't know what kinds of visitors they're hoping to attract, but it's the antithesis of appealing," she fumed.

"Aw, poor little Zelda." Her skinny blond friend chuckled as he spoke. "Those mean old curators don't realize what a talent they have within their midst! They won't let you redesign their website after being inside the museum exactly two days? Are you serious?"

"But Marianne made it sound like that was exactly what they wanted. Why would she say it if it wasn't true?" She still couldn't accept that her mentor only recommended her for this internship because she was a native English speaker.

"Marianne doesn't work there; who knows why she said what she said. Perhaps she figured it was the best way to get your attention."

"Or maybe they don't know what they need, or what questions to ask. I could add a flash animation to the database's home page so visitors would see some of the artwork when they open the site. It would only take a few minutes to create, and I'm sure Bernice and Marianne would be impressed with my initiative."

21

"But would Huub? It sounds like he doesn't want your help with the texts, let alone the website's design."

"Yeah, but—"

"No buts, Zelda. Do what they asked you to do and you'll probably be able to stay in Amsterdam a while longer."

Zelda shot Friedrich a dirty look. She'd known him for five months, but most days it felt as if they'd known each other forever.

Knowing they wouldn't be able to agree, she nodded towards his Cessna as she stood up. "Are you going to take her up again today?" She shook the grass out of her blanket before shoving it into her backpack.

Friedrich examined the wings once more before shaking his head slowly. "No, the wind is getting pretty strong. Plus some cops just entered the square; I'd better put her away."

Zelda followed his gaze towards two gigantic horses clip-clopping their way across the grass, police officers perched high atop their wide backs. Even though flying remote control aircraft was strictly forbidden in Amsterdam's parks and squares—due to the potential danger to innocent bystanders—Friedrich took one of his many planes for quick spins here most days of the week. As of yet he'd caused no bodily harm, and, as with most things in Amsterdam, the police were pretty relaxed about his short, low-level flights.

He wiped the model plane off with a soft cloth before carefully placing it into its hard-shell case. "You want to get a coffee before I have to go to work?"

"Sure, I've got nothing better to do. Well, read more of the books on Bernice's list, but that'll take me at least another week. Let me help you." Zelda slipped her backpack onto her shoulders before grabbing Friedrich's, grunting with effort. "Geez, what are you teaching yourself this week?"

"Portuguese and Catalan. I still can't decide whether I want to go to Lisbon or Barcelona during the winter break." Friedrich's choice to work at the University of Amsterdam's media lab had everything to do with his love of languages. His bag was always filled with DVDs and books about foreign tongues and lands, and almost never about his own study. Despite

22

his protests to the contrary, Zelda knew he'd only enrolled in the psychology program to please his family, not himself.

"Winter vacation is only two weeks long, and I'm pretty sure most people speak a little English in both cities—they are touristy hotspots, after all."

"Perhaps, but I learn so much more about another culture when I understand their language. Besides, it's fun."

"Fair enough," she said, wondering how many other travelers would bother to learn a new language for such a short trip. "Oh, I almost forgot; I've got your latest column with me. I guess editing your writing is good practice for the internship," she quipped, fishing a piece of paper out of her backpack before handing it to her friend.

Friedrich glanced over her few corrections of his latest blog post about drones and nodded before folding it up and shoving it into his pocket. "Thanks, I can post this later tonight."

As they walked across the Museumplein, the puffy clouds racing across the summer sky reminded Zelda of the Dutch old masters housed in the Rijksmuseum looming before them. The massive structure always conjured up visions of Camelot in her mind. It looked like a castle on steroids with its eight medieval towers jutting up above the skyline. Stone statues of knightly looking artists, brightly colored coats of arms, and story-high tile tableaus were woven into the extensive façade. A long gable-arched passageway running through the center of the building completed the effect. Only a drawbridge and moat were missing.

The illusion was somewhat tainted by the enormous story-tall letters of the iconic "I Amsterdam" structure placed between a small reflecting pool and busy bike path leading into the museum's belly. Friedrich and Zelda dodged irritated cyclists and oblivious tourists clamoring for a place on the giant letters as they made their way into the arcade. The presence of this unusual architectural feature had baffled Zelda completely, until she'd learned that such a tunnel was a prerequisite of the planning commission back in the 1880s, meant to connect "old" Amsterdam with the new neighborhoods being built behind the Museumplein.

Now the passage functioned as both a popular bike path and the entrance to the museum. Once they'd passed through to the other side, they were immediately confronted by a cacophony of horns and bells created by the many bicycles, motorcycles, and automobiles racing along the Stadhouderskade, a busy thoroughfare running along the back side of the Rijksmuseum. Before them lay Amsterdam's historic city center, distinguished by the ring-shaped canals on which richly decorated houses had been built in the seventeenth and eighteenth centuries. They stopped by the pedestrian crossing, waiting for the traffic light to change. Ahead of them was a bridge leading to the Spiegelgracht, a street famous for its many galleries and antique dealers.

Friedrich glanced shyly over at Zelda. "So, how's Pietro?"

"He's doing great, as always," she responded excitedly, her eyes lighting up as she thought of her lover. "But it sounds like his grandmother is really sick, she might be dying. It's good he went back to visit her; you know how Italians are so family-oriented."

Zelda looked up to catch her friend rolling his eyes. He didn't think much of Pietro, but then he would think poorly of any of her suitors, she suspected. Ever since their first meeting, she'd had the feeling he was smitten with her. But she knew the feeling would never be mutual; Friedrich was more like a brother than a lover any day of the week.

She looked over at her gangly friend, her mind slipping back to their first official meeting five short months ago. She needed a Dutch language tutor, and he wanted help with his English. They'd met through the message board in the media lab Zelda's teachers had encouraged her class to use. Friedrich had acted so goofy and awkward during their first meeting that she'd almost walked away before finishing her coffee, figuring she could try again. If he hadn't been so grateful to finally have someone respond to his note, she probably would have. And she'd needed a Dutch tutor so badly.

By the time she'd figured out he was Swiss, it didn't matter anymore. Friedrich was a master at languages. Born in Bern, he grew up speaking German, French, Italian, and English. During high school he'd taken extra classes in Spanish and Russian, just for fun. After their second meeting, it was clear to her that she needed his help a lot more than he needed hers.

24

If he wasn't such a perfectionist, he could see for himself that his monthly columns reviewing remote-controlled aircraft were better written than many penned by native English speakers.

Despite his gift for regularly shoving his foot in his mouth, she was glad they'd become friends. He was the most real person she'd met in Amsterdam so far. But that was what made his critique of Pietro painful. Maybe he had a point. No, she reminded herself, Friedrich was good at flying planes and learning languages, but he was socially inept and certainly knew nothing about being in love. From what little personal information she'd been able to wheedle out of her twenty-five-year-old friend, it sounded as if he'd never had a serious girlfriend. His own feelings for her were just clouding his judgment, she reckoned.

"But Pietro is still planning on coming back in September, a few days before his art history classes begin. He said it's what his grandmother wants him to do. In fact, he called again last week to ask if he could stay at my place for a few more months. Assuming I get in, of course." Unlike Zelda, Pietro had already been admitted into the art history master's program, where he would be specializing in contemporary Dutch painters. She secretly wished he had tried for the museum studies master too, so they could spend their days together, as well as their nights.

"So you're going to let him freeload off you for another semester then?"

"He's not freeloading; he cooks most of the meals."

"Yeah, with food you buy."

"Stay out of it, Friedrich. We're in love, get used it. Besides, after I get into the master's program this fall, we can get a bigger place together."

"Have you shared your fantasy with Pietro yet?"

"Piss off," Zelda snapped, shaking her head, upset with herself for letting Friedrich get to her. He'd hit a nerve by verbalizing her deepest fear, that Pietro was just using her. She refused to let the thought take hold in her mind. No, Pietro was in love with her and she with him. That was that. The serious housing shortage in Amsterdam had nothing to do with their relationship.

Sure, they'd only been together for three months before he'd gone back to

Italy for the two-month summer break. But Zelda already knew he was the one; she'd never met anyone as wonderful, funny, or caring as Pietro before. So what if he didn't pay for the groceries or chip in with the rent?

But lately, every time she mentioned her Italian lover, Friedrich acted like a total jerk. He was supposed to be her friend; she didn't have time for his jealous shenanigans, not with everything else going on in her life.

"You know, I don't think I'm up for coffee today. I have an awful lot of history books to get through," she said, tossing his backpack onto the ground, trying to keep her voice from cracking in anger.

As she stormed off, Friedrich called out, "Oh, okay. See you Saturday. *Tschüss!*"

"Yeah, whatever," Zelda mumbled, knowing full well she'd see him then.

7

Searching For Stolen Masterpieces

Another day over, another search begun. As Konrad Heider waited patiently for an auction catalog to download, he rocked his drink gently, relishing the sound of the ice cubes clinking against the crystal. His enjoyment was cut short by a computerized ping alerting him to an incoming message. Wondering who would be emailing him at this late hour, Konrad clicked on the flashing icon. Edward Cutter, an old friend and senior curator at the Museum of Modern Art in New York City, had sent him a message. Though the full moon shone through the window of his study in Düsseldorf, dusk was just beginning to creep over the skies of America's East Coast.

Edward was one of the few people he looked forward to seeing at the tedious opening parties and galas that lined the agendas of New York's social elite. The same ones he was always invited to, thanks to his sizeable donations to the city's many museums and cultural funds. He abhorred the schmoozing and one-upmanship but attended them anyway, hoping his vast network would one day provide him with a lead—any lead—to the whereabouts of his family's possessions. He knew that if anyone had suspected the true motive behind his apparent generosity, they would never have allowed him to penetrate their inner circle, no matter how much he donated to their causes. No, they would have denied having ever known him.

After a few short sentences filling Konrad in on the latest gossip, Edward quickly turned to the business at hand.

> *I think I recognized one of your family's pieces at a conference about stolen artwork in Amsterdam a few weeks ago, a drawing by Henri Matisse of a reclining nude. The project manager let me take a snapshot of it hanging in the depot, without a flash unfortunately. I told her I'd get in touch with you and let you verify it, instead of giving them your name. I know how much you value your privacy. A beta version of their website is active, though not complete. Here's a link to it so you can check the provenance yourself. Let me know when you're going to be in New York next and we'll do lunch. Yours, Edward.*

Konrad's heart raced as he closed his eyes and allowed himself to imagine it was true, that the sketch he was about to see was in fact one of the three hundred and twenty-two pieces taken from his uncle during the Second World War. And that this Matisse would somehow lead him to the others.

He wanted so badly to believe the paintings were still out there, waiting to be found. Yet after all these years of searching, he often wondered whether he hadn't wasted his life looking for artwork destroyed in bombings or fires long ago.

Konrad opened his eyes and clicked on the photograph. A few seconds later, a blurry image of a dimly lit art depot filled the screen. Paintings of various sizes and styles were suspended on a large mesh rack. In the center of the photograph was the Matisse Edward had so kindly brought to his attention. A sigh escaped Konrad's lips. Even at this poor resolution, he could tell it wasn't his uncle's piece; this nude was looking over her left shoulder, not straight at the painter. He'd memorized his family's most important works many years ago. He knew every brush stroke, line, and smudge like most men knew the body of their lover. This was not one of his.

He zoomed in on the Matisse anyway, if only out of a sense of duty to Edward. As the image sharpened, another part of the screen caught his eye. He'd been so focused on the reclining nude that he hadn't really looked at the other paintings hanging on the story-tall mesh rack. To the left of the Matisse was a beautifully rendered pastoral landscape, a single cow dominating the foreground. A Paulus Potter, no doubt. But the canvas on the left was something totally different. It was unknown to him, yet so familiar.

He zoomed in again. When the painting filled the screen, he sprung out of his chair, gasping for air. His eyes were deceiving him, he was sure of it. Yet even with the streaking colors and bad lighting, he recognized the shapes of the woman and flowers immediately. *But how could that be?*

His eyes shot over to a framed photograph on the left of his desk: his uncle as a young man dressed in his uniform, standing proudly in the middle of his grandly furnished living room. Paintings and sketches in gilded frames covered the walls behind him. Above one shoulder hung the only modern piece in the room, a small canvas depicting a young woman sitting next to a vase of irises. The same painting now hanging in the Amsterdam Museum's depot.

He clicked on the museum's website address, opening up the database containing information about the stolen art in the government's care. His hands trembled so badly he had trouble typing the artist's name into the search engine. A single canvas appeared on the screen. He gazed in awe at the young woman staring back at him. The image was unmistakable; there was no question in his mind they were one and the same. After all these years, he had finally found one of his family's paintings.

He wiped away a tear before breaking down and weeping uncontrollably into his folded hands. Everyone told him his uncle had been crazy to keep searching, that his art collection could not have survived the war unscathed. The paintings were gone; Konrad should stop looking and start living. But his uncle had dedicated his life to finding his stolen masterpieces and had, with his dying breath, urged him to keep looking. Konrad had no choice but to honor the older man's wishes and take up the hunt. He owed that much to the man who'd raised him. And tonight, he'd found his first.

After decades of searching, his family might finally have the chance to reclaim what was rightfully theirs. As he looked at his uncle's portrait, the

8

Girl With A Vase

"Are you insane?" Huub Konijn locked eyes with Zelda, staring at her with such intensity she couldn't help but shiver.

"No, not that I'm aware of," she shot back.

"What were you thinking then?" The curator gestured dramatically towards the project manager's computer monitor. "You were asked to correct the English language text, not redesign the website. Why did you think it was okay to add this animation to our home page?"

Zelda wondered whether he'd ever considered a career in theater. She did her best to scowl back at him, sure she was not in the wrong. "To enhance its visual appeal. I used to create websites for a living, you know," she retorted.

"Obviously you never stopped to consider the months of work my team put in to get this database ready. Not to mention the countless project meetings needed to gain a consensus on how it should look and function. We designed it in a *specific* way for a *specific* audience. It is a resource for investigators, museum curators, and legal teams doing serious research into missing works of art, not for every Jan and Janneke to peruse. Visual appeal is *not* a priority." The curator pounded on Bernice's desk to emphasize his point, wincing as his bony knuckles hit the hard surface.

"Wait a second. I thought you wanted the owners and their families to search through the database as well, not only researchers and lawyers." Zelda couldn't stop the words from pouring out of her mouth, yet she instantly regretted speaking them aloud.

"You evidently know nothing about this kind of research," Huub growled, his skin tone reddening by the second. Zelda was afraid his head was going to explode. "Most families hire private detectives, independent researchers, or lawyers to search for them. Very few claims are submitted by the owners or their family members."

Bernice Dijkstra gazed at the curator over the rim of her reading glasses, a puzzled frown on her face. "Huub, I don't understand why you are so upset by this one animation. What's the harm in adding a few images to the database's home page? It takes up very little space and adds a touch of color to an otherwise dull page. Perhaps seeing these paintings will help generate interest with a wider audience."

Zelda covered her smile with her hand, happy to finally have the project manager's support. When she'd proposed adding some images to the home page last week, Bernice had treated her like a real employee, listening carefully to her idea and ultimately responding positively to her suggestion. So why was the curator dead-set against her tiny addition?

"Did you even look at the paintings she selected before allowing her animation to be added to the site?" Huub asked sullenly.

"Of course I did. And I rather like her choices, especially the first one, the Wederstein. It's such a colorful, modern piece. The broad paint strokes, subtle shading, and that girl's gaze—it's simply arresting."

Huub rolled his eyes at the project manager, opening his mouth to respond when Bernice quickly added, "Don't forget, all the works in the depot are important to someone, regardless of who painted them."

"Oh please, Bernice, stop dancing around the fact the first thing visitors see when opening our website is Lex Wederstein's *Girl with Vase*." The curator's tone dripped with arrogance. "That portrait does not have the international allure we want to project. And her other choices are indeed colorful, yet created by artists no one's ever heard of. You know as well as I do our depots are filled with unclaimed masterpieces worth hundreds of thousands of euros, as well as canvases whose only real value is sentimental."

Huub turned to face Zelda, only beginning to dish out his wrath. "If you're going to choose visual showpieces for our site, don't pick the most unknown works in the database. Why didn't you use the Koekkoek, Van Ruysdael, Frans Hals, Van Gogh, or Jan Steen in your animation? If any paintings are featured, it should be these. I thought you were here to study art history; have you even heard of any of the famous artists I just mentioned? Now any reviewer visiting our site will take one look at the Wederstein and think they've stumbled across some shoddy auction house or provincial museum's website and move on. It makes us look very unprofessional."

Zelda was too shocked by his dressing down to respond verbally. She hunched up her shoulders slightly and looked down at the floor. One more comment and a flood of tears would burst loose. In her enthusiasm to impress Bernice—and thus Marianne and the university's selection committee—she hadn't considered the work Huub's team had already done to get such a large site up and running. Nor how many toes she had stepped on by circumventing him and going straight to Bernice with her idea for the animation. Even Friedrich had tried to warn her, and she'd blown him off. She had a lot to learn about working in a museum, where exhibitions were created through group consensus. She was so used to leading projects and setting their parameters that she'd forgotten what it was like to work as part of a team.

Huub stared at the computer, shaking his head as he spoke. "Bernice, I still don't understand why you didn't call or email me last week before you changed my team's design."

"You were presenting a paper at that conference in Portugal and I saw no reason to disturb your trip." The project manager's voice was calm but stern. "Besides, I like Zelda's animation. You know I was not in favor of your somber design."

"But it loads faster."

"It is a visual database containing more than a thousand works of art. People can't expect it to load instantly. I like the animation, and so does Leo de Boer."

The curator looked like a little boy caught peeing in a swimming pool. "Leo? Why did you get him involved?"

"After your email outburst demanding Zelda's head on a stick, I thought it prudent to ask him what he thought of her animation. He is, after all, the director of the museum and by default the head of every project we take on."

"And?" he asked through gritted teeth.

"He likes the idea of an animation but agrees with you, Huub; works by more important painters should be shown. And the images should be larger and spread across the top of the page as a banner. Agreed?"

Bernice pressed on before the curator could respond. Her tone obviously indicated that she was done debating this; Leo de Boer had spoken, and she was simply relaying his message. "You can pick out the artwork yourself and have your team create the new animation before the end of the week, when the site is officially launched. Considering Zelda made this one in a matter of minutes, I assume it will not be a challenge for you to meet this deadline."

Zelda felt like a pawn being expertly played by the project manager. No wonder Bernice had been so receptive to her idea; she'd wanted to change the database's home page all along and used Zelda's suggestion as an excuse to do it.

"But Bernice," Huub protested, "the site has been live since the conference. And today, advertisements are appearing in art magazines all over America. The website's address is listed on our publicity materials. We can't prevent the general public from looking at it. We need to take the animation down right away, before the media sees it."

"There's no reason for panic. Have your team remove her animation from the site now and replace it with a new one later this week. I doubt anyone has seen, or will see, her version. The advertisements list the opening of the exhibition as this Saturday. Most people won't bother to look at the site until then."

Huub gave Bernice a tight-lipped nod.

She nodded back before clearing her throat. "Zelda."

The expression on the older woman's face told Zelda things were about to go from bad to worse.

"Thank you for your help," Bernice said. "We appreciate your enthusiasm." She started to rise. "I'll be sure to tell Marianne what good work you've done for us; creating the animation was a fine idea."

Zelda knew she should be thrilled they were going to use her concept, regardless of the fact that Huub was going to redesign it. Yet she felt more embarrassed than triumphant. Was editing some English language copy really enough to wow the university's selection committee?

She tried desperately to think of a way to stay involved a little longer. "The official opening is this Saturday, right? Do you still need volunteers to greet guests and check their invitations? I'd be happy to help out."

"We have enough volunteers already. You are welcome to attend the official opening as our guest; I'll have an invitation mailed to your home." Bernice leaned over her desk and stuck out her hand.

"That would be great!" Zelda knew her time was up, yet remained planted firmly in her chair, unable to accept her role in this project was truly over.

"We'll see you Saturday, okay?"

Bernice's hand was still extended, looming over her wide desk. Zelda knew there was nothing to do but shake it and walk out. She nodded slowly, tears welling in the corner of her eyes, telling herself to keep it together. Most Dutch people couldn't handle open displays of emotion, and breaking down now would only make her look stupid.

One of the museum's receptionists knocked on the door, then stuck her head inside without waiting for a response. Sheepishly glancing at the group before apologizing for interrupting, she said in Dutch, "Mrs. Dijkstra, there's a telephone call for you from America that sounds rather urgent. Her accent is so strong that I'm having trouble understanding her, but it sounds like she's saying she 'won't wait forever.'" She pronounced the last three words carefully in clipped English.

The project manager picked up her telephone and sunk back into her chair.

"Yes, this is Bernice Dijkstra." As she listened, a frown creased her forehead. "Could you please speak more slowly. I don't understand—a girl with a face?"

Her perplexed expression turned to surprise as she bolted upright in her seat. "Did I hear you correctly? Please repeat." Listening intently, Bernice grabbed a pen and began scribbling wildly while her face drained of color. "Of course. Yes, that would be possible. If you want to. Really? That is wonderful news. What? Yes, we look forward to meeting you, too."

Bernice let the phone drop from her hand, keeping her eyes focused on the notepad in front of her. Slowly, she found her voice. "Huub," she whispered, "we have our first claimant."

The curator's expression switched from irritation to euphoria in a millisecond. "That is wonderful news! Was that one of the curators from the conference calling? Which piece is it?"

The project manager continued to stare at her notepad, avoiding eye contact with the other two, plainly still in shock. "No, a woman saw her father's painting on our website. You were right, Huub; the advertisements are already out in America."

"Well, which one is it?" he asked, impatience creeping back into his voice.

"Lex Wederstein's *Girl with Vase*. She recognized it immediately, from Zelda's animation on the home page."

9

Irises

Zelda was practically dancing with impatience. In a few moments, the owner of a painting once stolen by the Nazis would be walking through the conference room door. What would she look like? Or sound like? Zelda closed her eyes, imagining the claimant to be tall and elegantly dressed with a slight European accent, probably the sort who wintered on the Costa Brava or the French Riviera. All she knew for certain was that Rita Brouwer was flying in from Columbia, Missouri, via Chicago and London—a grueling flight itinerary to be sure.

Her jangling knee bumped against the conference table, waking the laptop humming in the middle of it. She couldn't help but smile when she glanced at the screen and saw the *Stolen Objects* database already open. Thanks to her own naiveté—as Huub Konijn had so kindly put it—they had their first claimant. After all of the curator's ranting and raving about what an unimportant piece it was, she couldn't help but feel vindicated at how the "worthless" Wederstein had been recognized first.

Zelda looked over at the painting, now resting on an easel in the corner of the conference room. She was entranced every time she looked at it, the way the woman looked so directly—almost defiantly—at the painter. Yet there was the slightest curve to her lips and a sparkle in her eye, as if she knew something the viewer didn't. Even the way it was painted was mysterious. The artist used a minimalistic approach, an almost abstract way of painting, yet the girl's delicate features and the irises' purple blossoms were so clearly defined, it was as if he'd copied the image from a photograph. The broad strokes of color and sturdy lines defining the shapes seemed to dance off the canvas. That was why she'd placed it at the beginning of her animation: so when the database loaded, the user would be as captivated as she was. Of course *Girl with Vase* was no longer featured on the home page. As soon as humanly possible, Huub's team had replaced her animation with a larger version rotating through works made by internationally known artists.

Despite the curator's dressing down last week, Bernice Dijkstra had asked Zelda to come back and take notes during their meeting with the museum's first claimant. Huub was not pleased, but Bernice was insistent. It was standard practice to have someone take notes during such meetings, and as practically everyone working for the museum was on vacation for the rest of the summer, they had no other choice, she argued. When Bernice asked whether she would be interested in helping them out once more, Zelda's heart began to sing. She didn't even mind that she was only there to take notes or that Huub was glaring at her; she was just thrilled to still be inside the museum and technically part of the project team. And to have the honor of meeting the first claimant, naturally.

Excitement crept into the project manager's voice as she explained how Zelda should write down everything that was said by all parties, verbatim if possible. Bernice's twinkling eyes and trembling voice reminded her how important this meeting was going to be.

A knock on the door brought silence to the conference room. One of the museum's receptionists popped her head inside. "*Mevrouw* Dijkstra? Rita Brouwer has arrived."

"Fantastic; show her in, please." The project manager rose to greet their mystery claimant. A pudgy, badly dressed woman in her late seventies entered the room.

"Howdy folks, it sure is nice to be here today." It sounded like John Wayne's sister had entered the room. Rita Brouwer stopped inside the doorway and looked around through her coke-bottle glasses, whistling softly once she spotted the painting in the far corner. Zelda could tell from the older woman's expression that she recognized *Girl with Vase* immediately.

Despite her girth, Rita was across the conference room in a heartbeat, stroking the surface of the Wederstein painting as if caressing a lost love. Zelda thought she heard the woman whisper, "Well I'll be, it is irises," but couldn't be sure.

"What are you doing?" Huub rushed over and slapped her hand away. "Step away from that painting; we do not know if it is truly yours yet."

Rita turned to face the curator, hands on her hips. Before she had a chance to chew him out for being so rude, Bernice jumped in between them.

"Huub," she scoffed, while gesturing towards the chair next to her own. "Mrs. Brouwer, please have a seat. Would you care for some tea or coffee?"

"I want to sit here, where I can see my painting. I did just fly twenty-threehours to enjoy that privilege, you know." The older woman plopped herself down at the head of the table, in the chair closest to the Wederstein painting. As she settled in, Rita hid a gaping sigh with the back of her hand. "I apologize in advance for yawning the whole time. It's the jet lag, not that meeting you all is a bore!" Huub winced as Rita guffawed. Zelda was waiting for her to slap her knee. "I sure could use a strong cup of black coffee. That'll keep me going a while longer."

Bernice poured her a cup and set it down on the table before her.

"I tell you what; I never thought I'd see her again." The old lady gazed lovingly at the painting, absorbing every detail while a grin spread across her face. "She's a bit dustier than I recall, but I'd still recognize her anywhere."

The project manager smiled politely, while the curator's frown seemed to deepen. Huub's apparent discomfort with her uncouth behavior made Zelda warm to the old lady immediately.

Bernice cleared her throat, signaling the official start of the meeting. "Thank you for making such a long journey to be with us today. I must say, your telephone call took us by surprise. We were still putting the final touches on the website and collection database when you phoned. How did you happen to see it so quickly?"

"I volunteer at my local library two days a week. Good for the body and mind, staying active like that. During my lunch break, I was flipping through one of the new art magazines that had just come in and saw your advertisement for an exhibition of stolen artwork. It got me thinking about my daddy, so I asked one of the girls who work there to help me look up the Internet link listed in your ad. Boy, I just about fainted when I saw Daddy's painting right there on the home page!" Rita chuckled. "Those girls at the library were worried I was going to have a stroke or something worse! One of them even drove me home once I got to feeling better, bless her."

"Now you've seen the painting in person, do you still believe it to be your father's?"

Rita responded immediately. "I know it's his, no question about it."

"But how can you be so sure? It was seventy years ago. Perhaps..." Huub started to ask.

"You really think I wouldn't recognize my own sister anymore? I may be old, but I'm not senile."

"Sorry?"

Rita pointed to the young woman in the painting. "That's a portrait of my oldest sister Iris, painted just before she turned eighteen."

Huub and Bernice exchanged glances. "Do you know the name of this piece?" the project manager nudged gently.

"*Irises*."

"Excuse me?"

"*Irises*. That's the painting's title. Well, technically *Irissen*." Rita pronounced the Dutch word carefully. "Excuse my pronunciation. Once we moved to America, my mama stopped speaking Dutch with us; she wanted us to become real Americans, not stay foreigners."

Bernice looked puzzled for only a split second before a warm smile settled on her face once again. "Okay, this is a good start. In our database, this piece is known as *Girl with Vase*, not *Irises*."

Rita stared at the project manager for a split second before her snorts of laughter filled the room. "No self-respecting artist would give such a dumb name to such a colorful painting. No, it's called *Irises*, because of my sister's name and the flowers. I should know, I heard the artist say it himself when he gave it to my daddy."

40

Huub's eyebrows shot up as Bernice's jaw dropped slightly. Zelda could hardly believe they'd found someone who had known both the artist and its original owner. Surely this would make Rita's claim a cinch.

"The artist, Lex Wederstein, he was Iris's first steady boyfriend," Rita said. "They met when she was sixteen years old. That would have been in 1938. If the war hadn't broken out, they would have gotten married, but that's neither here nor there. He was a really talented artist. There might still be some of his paintings stored at the Rijksakademie—that's the art school where he studied—although that Nazi general ransacked Lex's studio and probably destroyed any artwork he found. And there should be two pieces in the Stedelijk Museum's collection—one with a hole in the middle where that Nazi's boot went through it! Though I wouldn't be surprised if that general ripped those two paintings to shreds, right then and there."

Zelda was making notes as rapidly as she could, even though she felt as if she was hearing only part of the conversation. When she glanced up at the project manager, she saw Bernice was intrigued by what Rita Brouwer had to say. The curator, on the other hand, was resting his chin on his folded hands, listening as if he was hearing a fairy tale for the first time. She could hardly believe how rude he was being.

Why is he so skeptical? she asked herself. As Huub had repeatedly said before Rita arrived, this was an insignificant painting with no real monetary value. Why would this little old lady lie about being the owner of it? Sure, he'd also said some people wanted to find their family's missing treasures so badly that they claimed a piece and convinced themselves it was the long-lost artwork of a long-dead relative. But Zelda could not believe Rita was making any of this up. Based on the older woman's emotional response alone, she wanted to throw the canvas in her arms and tell her to keep it.

"Before we talk more about the artist, perhaps you can tell us what you remember about this particular painting. When did Mr. Wederstein paint this portrait? Was it commissioned by your father? What is your father's full name?" Bernice asked, once Rita's laughter subsided.

"Philip Verbeet was his name. Lex gave it to him at Iris's eighteenth birthday party on February 4, 1940, three months before the war started. It

41

was as much a present as a way of paying him back for some frames Daddy had made him. He owned a frame shop on the Stadhouderskade, only a few doors down from our house. It was also real close to the art academy where Lex studied. That's how he met Iris; she used to help out in the shop on Saturdays."

"That was generous of your father, to accept this painting in lieu of payment," Huub interjected.

The curator's sarcasm didn't slow Rita down at all. "Daddy wasn't really giving Lex special treatment. He traded paintings for supplies with lots of young artists; that's how he built up his collection. Daddy would have loved to have earned a living as a landscape painter, but he didn't have the talent for it. Not that he didn't keep trying, mind you. He'd stink up his shop with his oils when things were a bit slow." Rita smiled at the memories, wriggling her nose as if she smelled her father's paints and turpentine once again.

"What collection?" Huub asked.

Rita grinned wickedly, tapping her temple twice before plopping her large purse on the table. "I thought you all would want to see this," she said, while wrestling a large and very old book out of her bag. Its spine had cracked open, and the black cover was curling up at the edges. Still, it held together as Rita carefully opened it.

"My mama was always crazy about photo albums; right up to her death she was constantly gluing them together. This one has pictures of our last days in Amsterdam, when our daddy was still alive. Most of his artwork hung in our house, at least until we ran out of wall space and he had to store some of it in his frame shop. He'd switch his paintings around every few months so we could enjoy them all."

She tapped the first photograph on the page with a stubby finger as Huub and Bernice moved to either side of her and peered over her shoulder. "This is our street, the Frans Halsstraat. And that's our house. The bottom two floors and garden were ours."

From across the table, Zelda could see what they were looking at, albeit upside down. The photo showed a long row of terraced houses running the length of the street. Rita was pointing at a door in the middle of the block.

Her old family home was actually an apartment consisting of the lower half of a narrow four-story building. It was a simple-looking brick structure, distinguishable from its neighbors only by a wide metal beam decorated with five rosettes, which stretched across the façade. Their front door was on the street level; next to it was a short flight of stairs leading up to their neighbor's home.

Rita gently turned the page. "Here we are," she chuckled. A large photograph of five girls in identical dresses filled the right-hand page. They were seated on a long couch in what appeared to be the living room. Hanging on the wall behind them were several paintings encased in ornate gilded frames.

"That's my sister Iris there. She was the oldest," Rita explained, pointing to the girl on the far left of the couch. Zelda was captivated. With her long black hair, almond eyes, and wide lips, Iris could have easily been a model. "Next to her is Fleur, Viola, and Rose, and that's little ol' me there on the end. My first name, Margriet, means Daisy. My father loved his garden so much he named us all after flowers." Rita laughed at her younger self, an adorable little girl dressed in a navy blue dress with a sailor's cap resting on a bed of ringlets. Zelda could hardly believe that she'd become the pudgy woman with thinning hair and thick glasses now sitting before her.

"Let's see here." Rita bent down so her glasses were almost touching the paper. "The handwriting's pretty faded, but it looks like Mama wrote 'February 1940' next to this picture. I would have been eight years old. Look at us girls! Not a care in the world." Rita's voice was tinged with sadness. "How things changed a few months later when the Nazis invaded the Netherlands." She pointed to a painting in the photograph hanging above Fleur's head. "There's *Irises*."

Zelda squinted to make out the composition from her chair. As her eyes focused on the small rectangle, she could see this was unmistakably the same piece of artwork now resting on an easel across from her.

"My father took most of these pictures." She flipped slowly through the album, revealing more family photos of the children and parents playing and posing in their modest two-bedroom apartment. Rita's mother was tiny in every sense of the word. A delicate lily, Zelda thought, wondering whether Rita's father called her that. Judging from the few photographs of Philip Verbeet they'd seen so far, Rita took more after him than her mother. He was a stocky, barrel-chested man with a large mustache and bowler hat. His smile was infectious, and Zelda could feel her lips turning up at the edges just by looking at him.

Most of the pictures had been taken inside the family's home. The rooms were simply furnished and quite sparse considering five children and two adults lived in such a small space. But the walls made up for it. Every square inch was covered in paintings, sketches, watercolors and etchings, most fitted with broad, intricately-carved frames.

"This is the photograph Lex took, the same one he used to make the portrait. He was madly in love with Iris, you know." *And she with him*, Zelda thought. Iris's coy smile and laughing eyes were aimed towards the camera, at her lover behind it. After seeing this picture, she could easily believe Lex had a future as an artist. The resemblance between the photograph and painted portrait was almost uncanny.

Rita's audience watched attentively as she slowly flipped through the album, pointing out a sketch here or a painting there. Huub Konijn appeared slightly puzzled, as if he couldn't quite believe what he was seeing. Zelda couldn't place his emotions or interest level until Rita turned the page again, revealing close-ups of the living room walls. A large canvas hanging above the dining table caught her eye. She recognized the artist, but couldn't think of the name. She'd visited so many museums and learned about so many painters and sculptors during her six months of art history classes that all of their names were jumbled together in her head.

Before she could finish scouring her brain for the answer, the curator let out a sharp gasp. "Is that a Toorop?" he asked, pointing at the same painting Zelda was trying to place.

"Yup, my daddy had a few of her pieces. I was never really a fan of her work, all those dark colors and grim faces. I'm more partial to Jan Sluijters. The pieces he gave my daddy were so colorful; I used to beg him to let me hang them in our bedroom instead of there." She pointed to a photograph of their stairwell, in which three large canvases hung above the handrail.

"Charley Toorop? Jan Sluijters? Is that a Karel Appel? Where did your father get these pieces? How could he afford them?" Huub asked, obviously flabbergasted to see works by several of Holland's most famous modern painters hanging in the Verbeets' modest dwelling.

Rita laughed loudly, slapping her knee. "Oh, the look on your face! Don't you worry; he didn't steal them or anything like that. Even the Appels and Sluijterses of this world had to start at the bottom. Not all of the painters my daddy bartered with got famous; I'd bet even you wouldn't recognize most of the artists in his collection."

"Is that a Carel Willink?" Zelda wasn't sure whether Huub had heard a word Rita said, he was so engrossed in the photographs before him. "I don't recognize this piece. It must have been painted by a student trying to imitate his style," the curator said.

"No, that was definitely painted by Carel Willink. My mama admired his work so much she gave him pots of her homemade jam whenever he came by the shop. He lived around the corner from us, on the Ruysdaelkade."

"I studied his oeuvre extensively last year while working on a retrospective of his work, and I do not recognize this painting. And none of Willink's canvases are listed as missing or stolen." Huub's determined expression wavered as he studied the photograph again. "Though it does look quite similar to some of his earlier works."

"That's because it *is* one of his earlier works. Look, here's another one of his, and one from Sluijters, two more of Appel's, and Daddy's only Corneille."

Huub's face softened slightly as he looked over at Rita with a glimmer of respect. "These paintings would help document the early changes in style and technique of some of the Netherlands' most important painters." As he bowed to inspect the pictures once more, skepticism crept back into his voice. "If they were really painted by the artists you say they were, that is."

Before Rita could respond, the curator pushed on. "Tell me, Mrs. Brouwer, why hadn't your mother submitted a claim with the Dutch government years ago? All of these important artists, surely your family must have been interested in finding out what happened to your father's collection?

If these paintings are indeed by Appel, Sluijters, and the rest, well, they would be worth a lot of money," Huub said, gauging her reaction as he spoke of the paintings' potential value. "You say young artists studying at the Rijksakademie frequented your shop; many famous Dutch artists taught there, including Jan Sluijters. Perhaps these pieces were made by students who were copying their teachers' styles?"

Zelda wondered whether Huub was testing Rita or just being a total prick. Before she could find out, Bernice jumped in to save the conversation. "Tell me, Mrs. Brouwer, how is it you still have this photo album?"

"My mama squeezed it into our suitcases before we went to the farm."

"Before you went to which farm?" Bernice asked. She was clearly not having trouble understanding Rita's southern drawl, but was running out of patience with the old lady's long-winded explanations.

"We had to leave Amsterdam because of what happened to Lex at the Stedelijk Museum. So my mama and us girls spent the last three years of the war on my aunt's farm in Venlo."

"What exactly happened at the Stedelijk Museum?" Huub asked.

"In May 1942, Lex got asked to be part of a group exposition at the museum, the most important place for working artists to show their work back then. After Hitler's troops invaded Poland in 1939, he had the good sense to start using his mother's maiden name—Welsh—as his own. He even re-signed most of his old canvases so he could get them displayed in galleries. It made Lex so mad he couldn't use his real name, but he understood it was too big a risk. I guess that's why he signed *Irises* with 'Wederstein.' That portrait was never meant to be sold."

"Do you mean to say Lex Wederstein pretended not to be Jewish?" Huub asked, clearly dumbfounded.

"He considered himself to be Protestant, like his mama. But his daddy was a full-blooded Jew, and that meant Lex was too, according to the Nazi regime. Even though Lex wasn't even Jewish according to the Jewish religion! It's one of those matriarchal religions; if your mama's not Jewish, then you're not either." Rita paused for a moment to collect her thoughts, giving Zelda a chance to catch up. Taking notes was turning out to be much more difficult than she'd expected it to be.

"When Lex's daddy got fired from his job in 1940 because of his religious persuasion, he was worried he would get shipped off to one of them work camps in Germany. He wanted to take the whole family into hiding and wait out the war. Back then no one could have known Amsterdam would be occupied for so many years; most people figured it would all be over in a few months. So Lex refused to go with them. He was finally starting to get exhibitions in galleries; there was even a review in an important art magazine about his first solo show, saying he was an artist to watch. My sister Iris was real proud of that. Being able to make his living as an artist had always been his dream, and he'd be damned if the Nazis would take that away from him, too."

"That seems particularly brave, or incredibly stupid," Huub interjected.

"It wouldn't have surprised you if you'd known him," Rita maintained. "It helped that Lex didn't look Jewish. He was tall, blond, and blue-eyed—just like his mother. That's probably why he got away with it for so long, hiding out in plain sight. He was a beautiful boy, so full of life. He survived two years, living the way he wanted, right under their noses. If only he could have controlled that temper of his…" Her voice faltered. She gazed at the painting of her sister before adding softly, "He never stood a chance."

Zelda used the momentary silence to gauge the museum professionals' reactions. Bernice showed no obvious sign of being moved by the older lady's narrative. Two chairs down, Huub stared out the window at the courtyard below, seemingly lost in thought. *Has he even been listening to Rita?* she wondered. Before she could catch his eye, Bernice spoke up. "What happened to Lex Wederstein, Mrs. Brouwer?"

"Lex betrayed himself at the exhibition," Rita said, a deep sigh escaping her lips. Her eyes clouded over, and she fell silent again.

"Would you like more coffee, Mrs. Brouwer? Or perhaps to go back to your hotel? We can always meet again, once you've gotten better adjusted to being in a different time zone," Bernice asked, concern evident in her voice.

Rita looked up at the three people sitting around the table as if she was seeing them for the first time. *She must have transported her thoughts back to*

47

the 1940s, Zelda thought. The older woman shook her head slightly, as if to return herself to the present. "No, thank you. I'm fine. It's just, well, I haven't really talked about any of this for a very, very long time. Frankly, I feel like I'm describing someone else's life to you all."

She slapped her palms on the table before breaking into a forced laugh. "Listen to me rambling on! Where was I? Oh yes, the exhibition at the Stedelijk Museum. Hours before the opening, Lex got word his family had been arrested by the Gestapo. They'd been hiding in a neighbor's attic, a few doors down from where they lived. Lex and his brothers used to play with their children, and his mother was always going over to their house to help make jam, bake pies, or chitchat over coffee. Lex's parents had every reason to trust them. Unfortunately, in those days, the Nazis were offering good money for information on the whereabouts of any Jewish persons still in the city and on those hiding them, as well. Can you imagine that? Paying people to snitch on their neighbors and friends? But there was no work, and people were starving and freezing to death because they couldn't afford to buy food, clothes, or oil for heating—when there was any to be had. Those were very desperate times. Apparently the friends hiding Lex's family got worried that they were going to get arrested, so they turned his family in to the police themselves. To beat their neighbors to the punch, so to speak." Rita shook her head in disgust.

"Lex came to our house as soon as he found out. I was only ten years old at the time, but I remember how angry he was. Nothing Iris or my daddy said or did seemed to console him. A while after he arrived, he stormed out without even saying goodbye. Iris wanted to go after him, but Daddy wouldn't let her. Lex needed some time to cool off, he'd be back when he was good and ready, he said. Of course we didn't know where Lex would go or what he might do. None of us thought he'd go to the opening, not in the state he was in. After he left, Iris was inconsolable. It was as if she knew she'd never see Lex again."

Rita wiped away a tear. Zelda blinked away one herself, imagining the overwhelming sense of helplessness and accompanying rage Lex certainly must have felt. His entire family arrested and deported, despite having done

48

everything they could to hide their existence from the Nazis, even living like mice in a dark attic for two long years.

"The next day, some of Lex's friends came to our frame shop. He had gone to the opening after all. They said at first Lex appeared normal, laughing and carrying on like nothing was wrong. It was only after he started to get drunk that they noticed something was eating at him. He made sarcastic remarks about a group of SS officers in the gallery and even tried goose-stepping across the hall. Before his friends could get him out of the museum, Lex saw a SS general admiring one of his paintings. He ran over and shook the man's hand before screaming at the top of his lungs that he was the artist—and a Jew. Apparently everyone thought he was joking at first, but Lex kept insisting he was Jewish, even screaming his real name over and over again: 'Wederstein, Wederstein, Wederstein!' When that general finally realized Lex wasn't joking, he ripped the painting from the wall and put his boot through it. Lex flipped out. He jumped on the general's back and tried to choke him."

"Lex was immediately arrested for attacking an officer, not wearing his star, sneaking into the museum, and participating in the exhibition under false pretenses. That night there was a raid on his street, and everyone was arrested, even the supposed friends who'd ratted his parents out to the Gestapo. A few days later, Lex, his entire family, and several of his neighbors were shipped off to Auschwitz. None of them came back." Rita sounded so bitter. "He didn't just commit suicide the night of the opening. He murdered almost everyone he'd ever known and, in a way, my daddy. He was such a naive boy."

"What happened to Lex's family and neighbors is atrocious, but I still do not understand: how did his actions force your family to leave Amsterdam?" Huub asked, his arms folded firmly across his chest.

Is he made of ice? Zelda wondered. How could Huub react so indifferently to such a heart-wrenching story?

Rita sat up straighter in her chair before answering, her tone defiant. "My daddy heard that the general had torn Lex's studio apart and found photos of him and Iris together. He'd been asking around the art academy, trying to find out who the girl in the photograph was. My daddy knew most of the artists and teachers at the Rijksakademie and trusted them, but like I said before, the Nazis were paying for information, and money was hard to come by. It was probably only a matter of time before someone talked. Even though that general didn't have a legitimate reason to arrest Iris or harass our family, my daddy was so shaken by what he'd done to Lex he shipped us off to stay with my mother's sister the very next day. June 14, 1942, to be exact. We could stay on her farm in Venlo until the war was over. We would all be safer there, my father thought."

"If it was so dangerous, why did your father not go to Venlo with you?" Huub asked.

"He stayed behind to sell what possessions he could and store the rest with friends who were determined to stay. It wasn't our furniture or clothes he was worried about, but his art collection and the tools and supplies in his frame shop. He couldn't bear to leave it all behind for the Germans to take. The Gestapo wasn't even looking for him—only Iris—so he had nothing to worry about, he said."

Rita paused to take a long sip of coffee before resuming her story. "After we got to the farm, we hardly noticed there was a war going on. My aunt had five boys a few years younger than us girls, so we had a hoot chasing them around. There was plenty of meat, eggs, and vegetables, even with so many mouths to feed. It was almost idyllic, except for the fact that my daddy never arrived."

"What do you mean?" Bernice asked.

Rita gazed at her sister's portrait. In a soft voice, almost a whisper, she said, "A week after we got to the farm, he sent a letter saying he'd sold his equipment and supplies to a fellow frame maker and that he'd paid the rent on our house for another five years. Hopefully we'd all be home by then, he wrote." She smiled at the memory, before her forehead creased up.

"Mama always found that strange because she said they'd decided to leave Amsterdam for good and immigrate to America as soon as it was safe to cross the Atlantic."

"So, he wrote to your mother that he'd sold his art collection to a fellow

50

frame maker, yet you are here submitting a claim on it?" Huub asked, incredulity apparent in his voice.

"No, only his frame making tools and the inventory in his shop. At the end of the letter, he wrote that he'd found the perfect place to store his art collection and his paintings would be safe there until this bloody war ended. I don't know if he left them with that frame maker or someone else. But he did not sell them to anyone, I'm sure of it!"

"And where did he go after he stored his most precious possessions with these unknown friends?"

"I don't know. He ended his letter by saying he hoped to be leaving Amsterdam in a few days and he couldn't wait to see us." She wiped away another tear before adding in a resigned tone, "That was the last time we ever heard from my daddy."

10

Proof Of Ownership

Bernice Dijkstra bowed her head silently. Zelda wasn't sure whether she was praying for Rita Brouwer's father or whether she needed time to process everything the older woman had shared with the group. A few moments later, she cleared her throat and began to speak, her tone formal once again. "Thank you so much for flying over to talk with us. You have provided important new information about this painting, a piece we knew very little about."

She paused again, almost as if she was unsure whether to ask a question that was plainly still weighing on her mind. "Mrs. Brouwer, I realize you were a little girl when you last saw this painting, but do you remember seeing any identifying marks on the back or frame?" she asked.

Rita looked over at her quizzically and slowly shook her head. "I can't say that I do."

"Does 'F. Halsst 14' mean anything to you?" Bernice asked, writing the text onto her notepad before holding it up for Rita to see. "It is written on the exposed wooden bars the canvas is stretched over, in a black ink commonly used in fountain pens. It is the only legible marking on the painting or frame."

Rita seemed momentarily puzzled before her face lit up in recognition. "Why sure, that was the address of our house, Frans Halsstraat 14. Wait, did you say it was written on the back?"

"The text is quite faint, but still visible with the naked eye."

Rita's brow furrowed in concentration. "That doesn't make sense. Daddy used to glue a little label onto the back of each of his new paintings as soon as he got them. But it had the address of his frame shop on it, not our home. I'm sure of that."

"Maybe the label fell off," Huub offered.

"Then why did he write our home address on the back, instead of the shop's?" Rita wondered out loud.

"How should I know? He was your father," the curator retorted.

"Mrs. Brouwer," Bernice broke in again, attempting to salvage the mood, "did you bring any official documents stating that your father was the last legal owner of this painting?"

"Excuse me?" Rita huffed, crossing her arms over her ample bosom. "My daddy was the only legal owner."

"How can you be so certain he didn't sell it? You said yourself that no one in your family knows what happened to his collection after you left for Venlo," Huub interjected.

"He never would have sold that painting, not in a million years. It was a gift from his future son-in-law and a portrait of his own daughter. And as far as who he might have left his collection with, well, I'm as baffled as you are. Where did you find *Irises* anyway? Whoever had it must have the rest of my daddy's collection," Rita stated, obviously fed up with the curator's attitude.

"*Irises* and several other paintings were found in a house on the Vermeerstraat, close to the Museumplein, in which a high-ranking German officer resided for at least part of the war. Most Nazis didn't see the capitulation coming and had to flee Holland quickly, often leaving their possessions—and those they'd stolen from Dutch citizens—behind. In the summer of 1945, homes and offices used by the German army were cleared out, and any salvageable artwork, furniture, or antiques found were turned over to the Dutch government so they could be returned to their rightful owners," Bernice explained in a soothing voice. "But we don't know how *Irises* ended up in that house. We were hoping you might know why it was found there."

"I'm as confused as you are. Maybe that crazy Nazi general did find my daddy and steal his artwork. Lord, how I wish I knew his name. Iris is so forgetful these days, I doubt if she'll remember it, but I'll be sure to ask her." Rita pulled a handkerchief out of her bag and blew her nose. "Were the rest of Daddy's paintings there, too?"

"If you can provide us with a list of his artwork, we can check our database for you."

Rita rustled through her purse again, this time pulling out a thin manila folder. "In November 1945, we immigrated to Boston to live with my mama's brother and his wife. Some friends of theirs told her about how people whose artwork had been stolen during the war could file a claim to try to get it back. She wrote a letter to the Dutch government right away, explaining what had happened. She also included a list of all the pieces she could remember. Daddy never wrote up an inventory list, so far as we know. When he got a new piece, he'd stick his label on it, find a place to hang it up, and that was that."

She opened up the folder and began shuffling through the documents inside, most yellowed with age. "I have the list Mama sent to the Dutch government here somewhere..." she said, humming as she searched. "Aha." She pulled out a single piece of paper and laid it on the table.

Huub grabbed it and scanned the list of missing paintings. "No, this is impossible. There should be some mention of these pieces in the artists' biographies. I already told you I found no mention of missing Carel Willink paintings. Yet there are three titles on your list attributed to him that I have never heard of." The curator was quiet for a beat before asking, "Do you have any of your father's notarized titles of ownership? Or his business ledgers, which would prove he actually made frames for these artists?"

"I know he had been collecting art for as long as he had his frame shop, more than thirty years. So far as I know, Daddy didn't have an official contract or title declaring him the owner, just the record of supplies he'd traded with the artist as proof of his purchase. I have no idea what happened to his business records after we left Amsterdam. Mama didn't take any paperwork with us to the farm, only her photo albums and some clothes."

"So, you have no proof that these pieces were really painted by the artists you say they were?" Huub said smugly, his unspoken accusation hanging heavily in the room.

Zelda was stunned to hear disbelief in the curator's voice.

"Why would my mama lie?" Rita asked.

"My research staff will investigate this list further, after the summer vacation is over." His body language and tone made it clear he didn't believe a word the old lady had said.

"Well, what I'd like investigated is how *Irises* ended up in this *Stolen Objects* exhibition when the Dutch government told my mama back in 1946 that they didn't have any of our paintings. It's the tenth one on that list right there," Rita shot back, though her trembling voice betrayed how shaken she was by Huub's comments.

"What do you mean?" the project manager asked.

Rita reopened the folder and thumbed through the documents. "None of my daddy's works got returned to the Dutch government after the war. At least that's what I think this piece of paper says. Though I do admit, my Dutch is pretty rusty."

"May I?" Bernice asked.

Rita slid the letter towards her.

After reading it through, the project manager nodded in confirmation. "Indeed. This does state that there was no record of any of these paintings having been returned to the government. Your Dutch must not be as rusty as you thought." She smiled as she pushed the sheet of paper back across the table.

"I do admit it's puzzling," Bernice said, lightly tapping her pen against her notebook. "After the war, our government received thousands of works of art from the Allied forces. And that was in addition to the hundreds of pieces found in Dutch homes and offices used by the German army during the occupation. I'm afraid it took years to catalog everything. There's a very good chance that *Irises* had already been returned to the Dutch government, but had not yet been registered, and thus the employee who wrote to your mother could not have known it was there. Perhaps if she had tried again a few years later, she would have had better luck. I am sorry to have to tell you this."

Rita nodded her head thoughtfully. "I was afraid of that. So, my mama gave up too soon. Well, it doesn't matter now. And anyway, we got *Irises* back. I'm pleased as punch that anything from my daddy's collection has resurfaced. That gives me hope the rest are still out there, somewhere." She shot an evil glare in Huub's direction. He rolled his eyes but remained silent. "What a miracle, that out of all his pieces of art, *Irises* turned up first. My sister has been so ill for so long, it sure will be wonderful for her to see it again."

"Tell me, Mrs. Brouwer, do you still have the letters your father wrote to your mother while you were at your aunt's farm in Venlo?" Huub asked.

"If any of us girls have them, it would be Iris," Rita said through gritted teeth, obviously done with the curator and his steadfast disbelief.

"Is she looking for these documents?" Bernice asked.

"Well no, not exactly. To be honest, I haven't told her I'm here yet. I didn't want to get her hopes up if there was nothing to get excited about in the first place. She broke her hip last year, and it won't seem to heal up. And with the arthritis, well, let's just say she's having trouble getting around these days."

"Do you think it will be possible for her to search for them if she is so ill?"

"Heavens, no!" Rita laughed. "She can't go to the toilet by herself anymore. But her son lives real close by. I'm sure he'd go take a look for me if I asked him to. Heck, now that I know this painting really is *Irises*, I'll fly on out to Phoenix and take a look myself. Iris will want to know everything that's happened, every last detail. She won't believe it when I tell her!"

"If you do find any more documents, photographs, or letters that support your claim, please let us know," Bernice said.

"Any more photographs? What do you mean?" Rita asked, exasperation seeping through her voice. "I really don't know how many more pictures we have of *Irises* hanging in our old house. Besides, haven't I shown you enough to prove this painting is a portrait of my sister? And that it hung in our house until we left Amsterdam on June 14, 1942?"

56

"I understand your frustration," the project manager replied, her tone pacifying. "If the name of the man your father entrusted his collection to is in those letters, it may help our research staff discover what happened to the painting after your family left for Venlo. Do you have a lawyer?"

"Lawyer? Never had any use for one."

"You may want to retain legal counsel to assist you with the claims process, but the choice is yours."

"How long will this whole thing take anyway?" Rita demanded.

"After you've filed all of your documentation with the Restitutions Committee, two researchers will follow up on any new leads generated by the information you provide. They will revisit national and local archives to see if they can find out more about what happened to *Irises* between June 1942 and August 1945, when it was turned over to the Dutch government. Due to your sister's age and ill health, we will do our best to prioritize this case, but it will take several months to round out the investigation. On the basis of the researchers' report, the Restitutions Committee will then rule on the validity of the claim. If they determine your father was indeed the last legal owner, they will then advise the secretary of state for culture to return the painting to his heirs. If he chooses to adopt their advice—which he's done in the past twenty-two claims—then the painting will be returned to you and your sisters. It is a long process, yet once it is completed, you can be sure no one will be able to contest your ownership. I hope you understand."

"Yeah, alright. You'll have to show me all the paperwork I need to fill out before I fly back to the States," Rita replied curtly.

"I would be happy to. But first, I would like to inform the museum director and board of trustees that we have a claimant. I'm sure they will want you to join them at the exhibition's official opening this Saturday as their honored guest."

"That's mighty nice of you. I'd be tickled pink to attend."

Huub was obviously surprised by Bernice's invitation, yet remained silent.

"Give us a day to absorb all of this new information and discuss it with the Restitutions Committee," Bernice said. "Perhaps we can make an appointment for this Friday, in two days' time? We can fill out the first batch of paperwork then. I'm afraid there is a lot to go through."

"Friday sounds fine. I'm booked in at a little hotel close to the Museumplein for a whole week, so I'm yours when you need me."

"Wonderful. Perhaps Zelda can show you around tomorrow, assuming she has time? It sounds like you haven't been back to Amsterdam for quite a while."

Zelda's pen ran across the page as her head jerked up. *What did Bernice just say?*

"Wouldn't that be nice? I sure am looking forward to seeing the old neighborhood again. Do you know where the Pijp District is, Zelda? You're right, Bernice, I was just a little girl when we left Amsterdam. I don't remember the layout of the city anymore. To be frank, I never really wanted to come back. Too many painful memories. It'll be good to face my demons with a little company."

Zelda tried to wipe the panicked expression off her face as she found her voice. "Sure, I'm free. I'd be happy to show you around. Unless you'd rather catch up on your sleep, after such a long flight?" She smiled diplomatically, not really relishing the thought of playing tour guide.

"I've got all night to rest up. I can't wait to see my old neighborhood again. We're going to have such a hoot tomorrow, just you wait and see!" Rita howled, as she slapped Zelda's knee.

Zelda kept her grin plastered on and tried not to wince.

11

Covering Their Losses

Huub Konijn excused himself from the conference room as soon as Rita left and ran to the nearest bathroom. After he'd thrown up his breakfast, he wiped his mouth off with toilet paper and leaned back on his haunches. He couldn't get the image of his sister—gaunt and pale after years of mental and physical anguish, pleading for the return of their family's home and possessions—out of his mind. How she'd described every object in that house, even the frames that once held their family photographs, now long gone, replaced with the memories of another. Just as their home had been.

The new owners had showed no understanding, remorse, or shame. More embarrassment that Margo had dared to knock on their door, reminding them of the horrors of the war. Their family home and its antique furnishings had become one of the unintended spoils. All she got for her efforts was to be kicked out of the house, thrown onto the curb as if she was a bag of garbage. His sister, always so resilient, reduced to a pitiful heap, sobbing helplessly on the sidewalk. It was one of his earliest memories, one he couldn't repress or rid himself of, no matter how hard he tried.

According to the current owner's mortgage contract, the house had been purchased only six months after Huub's family went into hiding. As his father hadn't thought to prepay his property taxes, the bank sold it to cover its "losses"—furniture and all. Only their family's extensive collection of artwork was missing, stolen by neighbors or the Nazis before the bank could seize it. If only his father had given Margo a few paintings or sculptures to take with them to the farm. They wouldn't have had to suffer so.

Margo had been such a strong girl; she'd had to be to survive as long as she did. Ten years older, she had been more of a mother to him than a sister. He had no memories or photographs of his parents; he was a baby when the war started, and they sent him and their oldest daughter to a distant cousin's farm, believing it would be safer there than in a cramped attic.

The cousin grudgingly took them in, making them sleep in a dilapidated shed in a field far from his farmhouse and fend almost entirely for themselves. The unwavering belief that their family's extensive wealth and high social standing would be restored once Holland was free again was the only thing that kept Margo alive.

That horrible afternoon in June 1945 destroyed her completely. After that, she was destined to die in poverty, leaving Huub behind to fend for himself in that overcrowded orphanage.

Huub loved and hated his sister with the same intensity; the emotions were so intertwined he could hardly tell the difference between them. Rita's threadbare clothes and badly cut hair reminded him of what his once proud sister had been reduced to at the end of her short life—a lowly maid in a dingy hotel forced to prostitute herself for food.

It wasn't until he reached high school that Huub learned his family was not the only one whose homes and possessions had been sold or stolen while they were in hiding or after they'd been shipped off to concentration camps. It was then that he'd decided to dedicate his life to reclaiming what was rightfully his.

Huub wiped the spittle off his chin and rose. He wasn't weak. He had done what was necessary to take back what was his—not through pleading or begging—but through calculated action. As his sister should have done.

12

Burden Of Proof

When the early morning sun broke over the mansions lining the Museumplein, Rita Brouwer was already sipping tea in her hotel's breakfast room. A pile of empty muffin wrappings covered her plate. Rita hadn't slept a wink. Instead, she'd spent her first night in Amsterdam tossing and turning as she tried to figure out how she could persuade Bernice Dijkstra and Huub Konijn to give her *Irises* before she flew back to the States. If the opening was as big a deal as they claimed it would be, there should be plenty of reporters present, she reckoned. She'd have to have a condensed version of her family's history and sister's illness ready, just in case. Maybe if she got the media on her side from the get-go, those museum folks would be more inclined to return the painting to her sooner rather than later.

Why weren't the photographs proof enough? Why did she have to go through this bureaucratic nightmare simply to get back what was rightfully hers? *If only Mama had fought harder, she could have provided us with a better life. Instead, all of us girls had to work our fingers to the bone to survive, as she'd had to,* Rita thought, bitter tears streaming down her cheeks. "No, don't you dare think like that," she reprimanded herself, using a cloth napkin to dab her face dry. *It wasn't her fault she had to raise us alone. If only Daddy had come to the farm, like he promised.*

Well, now it was her chance to change their family's fortune and recoup at least one of their paintings, if not all of them. Today she would pump

Zelda for information; as an intern, she was privy to Huub and Bernice's expectations as to proof of ownership. Rita knew the curator was the one she needed to convince. He'd made it plain as day he didn't believe a word she'd said. *If more proof is what he wants, that's precisely what he'll get,* she thought, a devilish grin spreading across her face.

If sappy news articles about Iris's poor health or their daddy's mysterious disappearance didn't pressure the museum into giving her *Irises* right away, her daddy's letter might. With a little practice, she'd be able to write like him, at least enough to fool the museum's researchers. If Huub wanted a name, by golly he'd get one. There was no way she'd let a little thing like the truth get in her way, not when she was so close to getting *Irises* back.

13

Haunting Memories

"I get it already, I'm done with computers!" Zelda screamed as ceiling tiles crashed down all around her. She dove under her boss's desk seconds before another seismic wave rolled through the plush carpet floor, tossing her body around like a bean bag. Office supplies and CDs hurtled through the air as a computer slid off the bureau above her and crashed into a potted palm tree. Pottery shards and wet soil spilled onto the floor, burying the employment contract her boss had handed her to sign, mere seconds before the earth started to shake.

She could almost feel the tectonic plates pulling apart under her feet as the Puget Sound widened. Was this Seattle's predicted "Big One," finally breaking loose? Could one earthquake really decimate the Pacific Northwest, as experts loved to theorize it would? Gripping the thick metal legs of her boss's desk with all of her might, she rode the bucking earth, screaming her vow to make a change—as long as she survived.

Zelda jolted awake, sweaty sheets twisted around her legs, her heart pounding. Her eyes rapidly scanned her bedroom; nothing appeared to be swaying. The incessant beeping was just her alarm clock. And the earthquake was only a memory, she reminded herself, a memory of a real event still sketched too vividly onto her psyche. It had been almost a year since Seattle's one and only recorded major earthquake struck, changing her life forever. She hadn't dreamed about that day for almost a week.

How many more months would it be before that fateful morning stopped invading her dreams?

She picked up the glass of water on her nightstand, sloshing it onto her bare skin as she brought it to her lips. Her body was still trembling—the terror she'd felt during the earthquake rushing back through her like an unwanted adrenaline kick. For Zelda, that awful morning had been a wake-up call: life was too short to spend your time doing something you despised.

Four years before the earthquake, she'd tried to leave the computer industry behind for good, without success. After working eighty-hour weeks for months on end to meet impossible deadlines imposed by her employers, she'd suffered from massive burnout. The remedy had been to quit her job and fly to Kathmandu to volunteer as an English teacher for two months. It was her way of breaking free from her demanding work routine and materialistic shackles to try to figure out what would really make her happy in life.

After a turbulent time in Nepal, she'd backpacked around Vietnam and Thailand, only returning to Seattle when her travel funds had run out. She'd seen and done so much on that amazing journey that she felt like a different person, one who was more adaptable and resilient than her former self. All she wanted to do when she'd gotten back was throw her old life aside and begin anew.

At first she'd refused to go back to her old profession, certain she could apply her vast array of computer and project management skills to another vocation. Yet everything that interested her required extensive formal training or long, unpaid internships she couldn't combine with a full-time job.

After her fifth rent payment brought her savings account to an all-time low, she'd sent her resume off to a placement agency and had a job as a website developer within a week. Less than a month later, she was experiencing the same levels of boredom and stress she'd felt before she'd left for Nepal. But she'd stuck with it, saving as much as she could, telling herself she could always take another long vacation if work got to be too much again.

Three years later, she was skimming an online brochure for a month-long kayaking trip around Belize when her boss popped into her cubicle to see whether she'd be interested in a full-time contract.

If Seattle hadn't gotten its rumbling of the Big One, she probably would never have dared to quit her well-paid job to study art history in Amsterdam. It was a decision that changed her life in more ways than she could ever have imagined, so far only for the better.

Zelda closed her eyes and took three deep breaths, ordering herself to relax. As the tension dissipated, she looked around her small apartment again, taking in the tiny sink, two-person table, and one-person bed squeezed into the attic of an old canal house, and smiled in satisfaction. Sure, her entire studio was roughly the size of her old bedroom, but she didn't mind. Right now this cramped box represented a newfound freedom and endless possibilities.

Even after living in Amsterdam for nine months, she was still enamored with her new hometown. How the early morning sunlight shimmered off the canals' rippling surface as she biked to the university, a cool wind often twisting through her long brown hair. The simple pleasure of eating a chocolate-filled croissant underneath the Westerkerk as its carillon bells chimed out modern melodies most afternoons. Or the intense joy she felt wandering through the city's plethora of museums and galleries. She was definitely not ready to leave yet.

Kicking the covers off her bed, she turned off her alarm clock and stood up. Through her postage-stamp window, she could see two broad wooden boats chugging up the Singelgracht as they passed by the Heineken Brewery's headquarters. She watched until the boats glided out of sight before slipping into her bathrobe and heading off to the communal shower, two stories below.

"Well, good morning to you, young lady!"

Despite Zelda's early arrival, Rita Brouwer was already downstairs waiting for her in the hotel lobby. The older woman's scuffed shoes were highly polished and her threadbare clothes perfectly ironed. She obviously took pride in her possessions, though she had little money to spend on them.

"Come on, I'll sneak you into the breakfast room. For the prices they charge, the hotel staff can't really complain." Rita's hearty laugh and warm smile melted Zelda's reservations about the day almost immediately. There was something so likeable about the old lady, in spite of her lack of glamour. Her quick sense of humor and no-nonsense way of looking at the world reminded Zelda of her own grandmother, or at least what she could remember of her. That similarity made it so much harder to spy on the old lady.

Well, spying was probably too harsh a word to use. But Zelda had promised Bernice Dijkstra she would keep her ears open for any new information Rita provided that could help the museum prove—or disprove—her claim. Not that she expected to learn anything more about the missing paintings during their walk around Rita's old neighborhood. More likely she'd spend the day patiently listening to long stories about "the good old days," nothing more.

"No thanks, Mrs. Brouwer, I've already eaten breakfast. Shall we leave, or do you need to go…back to your room first?" Zelda almost asked if she needed to go to the bathroom before they left. She'd have to watch that; Rita wasn't her grandma, no matter how similar their personalities, and she shouldn't treat her as such, she chided herself.

"Young lady, Mrs. Brouwer was my mother-in-law, God rest her soul. You can call me Rita," she said, looping her arm through Zelda's and propelling her out the front door.

Rita turned right at the first intersection, onto a street lined with mansions. As they crossed over the tramlines and stepped onto the Museumplein, the old lady stopped in front of the reflecting pool. The wind was so still that the tourists climbing up the red-and-white "I Amsterdam" structure positioned at the end of the pond were mirrored in the water, the majestic Rijksmuseum soaring up behind them. The overpowering smells of ice cream, hot dogs, and grilled hamburgers wafted up from the food tents lining both sides of the pool.

"How I loved to skate here." Rita was positively glowing. "I was just a little girl—even for my age I was small—but I could skate all by myself by the time I was three. A natural talent, my daddy used to say."

"Oh, did the pool freeze by itself back then? Was it cold enough?" She'd heard stories about the brutally cold winters and frozen canals of the past, but global warming seemed to have put a halt to that some years ago. In fact, Zelda remembered watching how a chilling system involving tubes and a generator turned this same pool into a mini-ice rink last winter, weeks before a single snowflake had fallen.

"This little pond is new to me. As are most of those buildings over there." Rita gestured to their right, towards the Van Gogh Museum and Albert Heijn supermarket. "Back then there were no fancy lighting systems or pathways crisscrossing the square; only grass and trees. The city's ice skating association paid to have the entire field flooded every winter, and nature did the rest. After a good freeze, the whole square would be filled with kids and adults skating and sledding."

Rita sounded so happy as she got lost in her memories of better times. "It was so much fun seeing all of your friends out on the ice like that. At least it was, until the German army confiscated most of the buildings on the square. Heck, their embassy was right over there." Rita pointed to a large house at the far left-hand side of the Museumplein.

Zelda blinked in confusion, pointing at the same building just to be sure. "You mean the one on the end? Are you certain?"

"Sure I am," Rita chuckled. "I didn't expect to see our embassy there either."

Zelda shook her head in disbelief. She'd been inside that mansion, now the home to the American consulate to the Netherlands, a few weeks ago to renew her passport.

"The last winter we lived in Amsterdam, that would have been 1941, my daddy wouldn't let us kids skate here anymore. All the big Nazi party rallies were held here. Most of the buildings, including the Rijksmuseum, had those red banners with the swastikas hanging off of 'em. It gave him the creeps. As a matter of fact, he didn't want us going anywhere near Museumplein after the Nazis came to town. There were too many of them hanging around, trying to recruit the boys and pick up the girls. Later they put barbed wire around the whole square, for security reasons, they said. That was after we'd already left for Venlo. But there were still bits of it strung up when we came back to Amsterdam after the war had ended."

"Barbed wire fence? Here?" Zelda stammered.

"And bunkers with anti-aircraft guns mounted on top of them set up on each corner."

Zelda looked around the peaceful field of grass filled with lounging locals and picnicking tourists. She could hardly imagine how it must have been during the war with concrete bunkers jutting out of the earth and German soldiers standing guard, fortified to the teeth.

"But why? Because of the German embassy?"

"The Gestapo and SS had their headquarters here, and most of the high-ranking SS officers took over the houses close to the square," Rita said, referring to the large homes lining the streets around the Museumplein. "It was an important target for the Allies."

"But weren't people living in those houses when the Nazis arrived? Or were they offices back then, too?" Almost all of Amsterdam's free-standing houses were located in the direct vicinity of the Museumplein, making it one of the most prestigious—and expensive—neighborhoods in the Netherlands. Nowadays, only law firms, notaries, and small corporations could afford to buy them, save the odd millionaire who'd set up house.

"Yes, they were, but by rich folks who'd had lots to lose once war broke out. I imagine most of the families who'd been living here used their wealth to flee Amsterdam before the Germans arrived."

Zelda didn't know what to say. She knew so little about the city's wartime past. And after a visit to Anne Frank's house, she hadn't wanted to learn more. It was all too depressing.

"So, how do you like working at the Amsterdam Museum?" Rita asked.

Relieved the older woman had changed the subject, Zelda swiftly responded, "I'm not really working there. I'm an intern for the summer."

"Are you studying art history or Jewish religion?"

"Neither," she sighed. "It's a long story."

"I've got the time." Rita smiled encouragingly. "We've got a little ways to walk before we get to my old neighborhood."

"Well, I'm trying to get into a master's program in museum studies at the University of Amsterdam. It's a combination of art history, exhibition design, and museum management. With this master's degree, I could work as either a curator or exhibition designer at any museum I wanted to, or really any other place that presents objects or ideas to the public."

"A curator, that's wonderful. I always wanted to do something like that but never had the chance. I married young and had a baby before our first anniversary," Rita chuckled, adding, "Good for you."

"Well, thanks," Zelda mumbled as she studied her left shoe intently.

"You think I'm pulling your chain, but it's true. I've always been interested in art history. That's how I found my painting; I read all of the new art magazines as soon as they come into the library where I volunteer. It's such a wonderful way to keep up to date." Rita sighed wistfully.

"If all goes well, I should be starting this September."

"A master's degree is a two-year study, right?" Rita asked.

"Yeah, well, eighteen months of classes and a six-month internship."

Rita nodded slowly. "You know, for so many years my mother, sisters and I, well, we all pretended it wasn't important to know what had happened to my daddy's art collection. It was missing, just like he was, and that was that. But having *Irises* turn up after all of these years made me realize I do want to know why he never came to Venlo, and finding his paintings may help us figure that out. I've tried to tell myself it doesn't matter anymore, he's dead either way. But it does matter. To know how he died or even where he's buried would offer some sort of relief to both me and my sisters."

Zelda could feel her eyes tearing up. How difficult it must be, not knowing what happened to a loved one—especially a parent. She couldn't even imagine the depth of Rita's pain.

"I still don't understand why *Irises* was found in that house close by here, but it's the only new piece of information we've heard about in many years. Me finding *Irises* was pure dumb luck. With only my little pension and Social Security, there's no way I could hire some fancy art investigator to try to hunt down the rest of his paintings. But I do have my mama's list, with all of the titles and artists' names. Maybe you could check some of the local archives and see if you can't find any mention of the rest. My sisters and I would be happy to pay you for your time and troubles. It would be easier for you to find new leads here in the Netherlands than it would for me back in Missouri. Heck, I still can't check my email without one of the girls from the library helping me out, let alone search all those electronic databases they have nowadays," Rita laughed.

Zelda could hardly believe her ears. What a wonderful opportunity, she thought, money or not. It would be fun to play detective and see what she could find. "I'm honored you asked. I'd be happy to help, in any way I can." She squeezed Rita's arm affectionately. "To be honest, I don't really know where to begin either. But I can search through the exhibition's database and the national archives for you and see what I find."

Rita stopped in her tracks and pulled her in close for a great big bear hug. Zelda was afraid the older woman was going to smother her with kisses, too. "Why, that would be more than kind of you to try!" After releasing the younger woman, she rummaged through her purse, quickly producing a single sheet. "Here's a list of all his paintings, or at least those my mama tried to claim."

Zelda took the paper from Rita's outstretched hand and quickly scanned the names before shoving the list into her bag. As she did, her hand slid over a thick envelope.

"Oh, I almost forgot to give you this." She handed the older lady the envelope. "Rita Brouwer née Verbeet" was written in gold letters on the front.

"Looks fancy. What is it?"

"Bernice Dijkstra asked me to pass this on to you. It's your official invitation to the opening this Saturday. You did say you could attend, right?"

"Like I told your bosses, I'd be pleased as punch to attend. I already changed my flight so I can tell Iris the good news in person and see if we can find those letters Daddy sent us. I'm not flying to Phoenix until next Tuesday. That'll give me time to see more of Amsterdam before I go."

"I'm sure the museum's board of directors is going to love showing you off at the opening, you being their first claimant and all," Zelda said, as Rita glowed with pride.

They soon exited the square, following wide tree-lined streets filled with expensive mansions until they came upon the Boerenwetering. A small metal bridge rose high over the canal, connecting the Museumplein with the Pijp neighborhood. On the other side of the water, the terraced houses were substantially smaller and the streets narrower, busier, livelier.

"My old neighborhood," Rita exclaimed, pausing at the top of the bridge to take it all in. "I still recognize it after all these years."

Zelda figured the older woman would want to rest a moment and catch her breath, but Rita charged on, eager to tell her about every building and business they passed.

"Simone lived in that green house with her aunt and uncle. She was always losing her mittens. That was where Marianne lived; I used to play there every Tuesday. See that house with the blue trim around the windows? That's where Samuel the butcher lived with his brother. He used to save the best pieces of beef for my mama." There was a new spring in her step and lightness in her voice as Rita was transported back seventy years in time. Zelda expected her to leap into a game of hopscotch at any moment. She just hoped the old woman didn't break her hip doing it.

Rita grew quiet as they approached the next street, slowing to a stop as she gazed up at its name in wonder. "The Frans Halsstraat. This was where we lived. Frans Hals was a far better painter than Rembrandt van Rijn. At least that's what Daddy used to say."

She pointed straight ahead. "The Rijksakademie is a few blocks that way, and our house is around the corner." Rita blinked as she slowly lowered her arm. "Sushi? Well, I'll be," she tittered, adding, "That used to be our frame shop," as she nodded towards the "I Love Sushi" bar.

Rita charged on, rounding the corner onto the Frans Halsstraat at full speed, only to stop abruptly and gasp in horror, "Oh no, this can't be!"

Zelda followed her gaze down the block towards an unusual opening in the long row of terraced houses. At least two had been demolished and the lots stripped clean. Tied to the rickety metal fence was a billboard announcing there were still apartments available to buy, though there were no construction workers or machines in sight. Large wooden beams were placed at ninety-degree angles against the sides of the neighboring houses to keep them from caving in. She felt sorry for the homeowners on either side; not only did they have all the construction noise to contend with, but their privacy had also been seriously infringed upon. Their normally shielded backyards were clearly visible from the sidewalk, thanks to the large open space in the otherwise block-long row of connected homes.

Rita hurried down the street; Zelda sprinted to catch up. As the older lady approached the open lots, she paused momentarily, looking around in confusion before exclaiming, "Thank goodness, number 14 is still standing!"

She rushed over to the brick house situated to the left of the construction site, its façade painted a deep brown with dark green trim around the windows and door. Zelda immediately recognized it from Rita's photo album. She looked over at her companion, now standing on the doorstep of her childhood home, tears streaming down her face.

"This was our house," Rita said, her voice a whisper. As if in a trance, she began gently stroking the green-painted wood, murmuring to herself. Zelda looked around in a panic, sure someone walking or biking by was bound to call the cops, thinking the old lady had gone crazy. To her surprise, none of the passersby seemed to notice them. *This is Amsterdam,* Zelda reminded herself, *Europe's sin city. Stranger things happen here all the time.*

Soon enough, Rita composed herself, standing up straighter and taller. "Let's see if anyone's home."

Before Zelda could restrain her, Rita pounded on the door five times. "That should get somebody's attention," she said with a smug smile of satisfaction.

More like the whole neighborhood, Zelda thought.

A woman in her late thirties threw open the door. Her hair was pulled back in a ponytail and there were stains all over her T-shirt and sweats. "Yes?" she demanded in Dutch. In another room close by, a baby was crying.

"Hello, dear. My name is Rita Brouwer, and I used to live here. I was hoping to come inside and see the house again if—"

All of a sudden, the baby's cries turned to howls.

"My son, I must go to him." The home's owner sized up the older woman and her younger companion for a moment before racing to her child, leaving the door open. "Come inside," she yelled back as she jogged down a short hallway into the kitchen.

Rita took off after her as if she still owned the place with Zelda trailing slowly behind.

The screaming receded. The woman soothed her baby with kisses until he stopped crying enough to notice the two strangers approaching. He looked up at Rita and Zelda with open curiosity, smiling a toothless grin.

"Who did you say you were again?" the apartment's current owner asked, as she returned her baby to his high chair and began shoveling applesauce into his open mouth.

"Rita Brouwer, although back then I was Margriet Verbeet. This here is my friend Zelda Richardson. I lived in this house when I was a little girl. I haven't been back to the Netherlands since the war, you see, and walking along the Frans Halsstraat again brought back so many memories of my family, especially my daddy, God rest his soul. I had to see my old home again. You do understand, don't you?"

Zelda started inching back towards the door, sure the Dutch woman was going to throw them out. Instead, she gazed lovingly at her infant son—now happily smearing applesauce onto his high chair—then up at the old woman standing before her, grinning from ear to ear.

"Of course, you must come back and see where you grew up. How do you Americans say it, to see your roots?" She wiped her baby's mouth and hands off with a wet rag before taking him into her arms once again. Then she turned to Rita and offered her a hand. "I am Eva, and this is Cor. Why don't we start our tour in his room? It's time for his nap."

Zelda, flabbergasted at how easily Rita had gotten her wish, followed silently behind.

"How long have you lived here, Eva?" Rita asked, after the baby was tucked into bed.

"Klaas and I bought it a year ago, a few months before Cor was born. It was a rental unit before then and had not been taken care of properly," Eva explained as she guided them back towards the living room. "We spent quite a lot of money renovating and modernizing it after we moved in."

As they walked around the small house, Zelda began to recognize the rooms from the pictures Rita had shown them. Eva and Klaas had torn out a few walls, but in general the house looked the same.

"This is where my daddy started his frame shop, right here in this living room. He didn't have a family back then. After Iris was born, he moved his shop to the end of the street, where that sushi place is now."

After showing them the ground floor, Eva led them up a steep flight of stairs to the second story. To the left was a bathroom and storage closet, but most of the floor was taken up by the master bedroom.

"My parents slept downstairs, in your cute little boy's bedroom. This was our room." She stopped by the door's opening, almost afraid to go inside. A wash of emotions crossed over her face as she slowly raised her hand. Finally, Rita pushed open the door, exclaiming, "Goodness, it all looks so different now."

A queen-sized bed was placed diagonally across the large space, night-stands positioned on either side. His and hers armoires stood against one wall. French doors opened onto a small balcony, and rays of sunlight spilled through their uncovered windows, warming the sparsely furnished room.

"We took out the built-in closets last year. It really opens up the space," Eva said with a touch of pride.

"There weren't any closets back then. All five of us girls slept up here. My daddy built bunk beds on both sides of the room, and Iris's bed was set up in the middle." Rita crossed over to the French doors and opened them. The tiny balcony was filled with plants and two folding chairs. Rita stepped out and looked down into the garden.

"Oh my," she said, aghast, clutching the balcony's railing for support. Zelda ran to her side and grabbed her arm, afraid something was wrong with Rita's heart. She glanced down to see what had upset the older lady so. All she saw was a concrete shed in Eva's garden below, its crumbling walls in bad need of repair, surrounded by a patch of brown grass. The neighbor's yard on the left was equally disheveled. Along the right side of Eva's property ran two strands of barbed wire, the only thing separating her garden from the construction site. From the balcony, she could see the lot had been leveled and a few holes had already been dug out for the pillars on which the foundation would be built.

Eva joined them at the window. "Terrible sight, isn't it? If that project developer goes bankrupt, I'm afraid those lots will stay empty for years. Living next to an open pit is not going to help our property's value." She clicked her tongue in irritation.

"Our shed, it's so dilapidated!" Rita cried, her eyes locked onto the structure below.

"Oh, that. Klaas is planning on demolishing it one of these days, but he's so busy with work I don't know when he'll have the time. Besides, the walls are so thick he can saw and drill without disturbing the neighbors. You can't hear a thing, so long as the door is closed."

"My daddy sure would be disappointed to see it in such a sad state of disrepair. He was such a good carpenter; he could make anything with those hands of his," Rita sighed as she sat down on Eva's bed, her girth sinking deep into the mattress. For the first time since Zelda had met her, Rita looked worn out and fragile, like the seventy-nine-year-old woman she really was. Seeing that shed in its run-down state seemed to have sapped the life from her.

"I don't suppose the dollhouse is still there?" Rita asked, a tremor in her voice.

"Dollhouse? I'm sorry, I don't understand this word." Eva seemed to sense the change in Rita's mood as well, touching her hand to the older woman's forehead. "Would you like a glass of water or something to eat? You do not look well."

"No, I'm doing fine." Rita smiled weakly at her host. "I almost forgot seventy years have gone by. Of course things aren't the same as they were back then, when we lived here, when my daddy was still alive. Nothing is the same as it was."

"But this dollhouse?"

"My daddy built one for us girls, out there in that shed. It was like a miniature house, but with no roof or exterior walls so you could move the dolls and furnishings around inside."

"Oh yes, *een poppenhuis*. I have seen those in the Rijksmuseum before. They are very beautiful."

"We thought so, too. Our friends loved to come over and play out there. It was so big it covered most of the floor. But Daddy was so clever; he built it in an L shape along two of the walls so he could still get to his root cellar. He used to make wine from the grapes he grew in our garden. If there were enough raspberries, he'd make schnapps. And my mama liked to make preserves out of her strawberries and rhubarb. That's where they kept it all, in the root cellar. I'm sure that's all gone, too. Though it would be a hoot to find one of Mama's jams or Daddy's wines on a shelf down there."

"A root cellar under the shed? The real estate agent did not mention one. And there is no opening in the floor; it's made of a heavy, concrete tile. It must have been filled in years ago."

"I'm sure you're right," Rita said pensively. "There's not much use for root cellars nowadays. Nobody makes preserves or wines themselves anymore, do they? And with the Cold War finally over, bomb shelters are out of fashion, too."

Zelda could see Rita was trying to make light of the situation even though it was undoubtedly painful for her. She couldn't imagine the emotional turmoil Rita must have been experiencing since she'd set foot in her old family home and been confronted with all the changes that had taken place since the Second World War. With nothing tangible left for her memories to grab onto, Rita had to face the fact that all she had left were the photographs and stories of how her life once was, when her father was still alive.

The older lady rose from the bed, grabbing onto Zelda's arm for support. "You know, I think the jet lag's finally catching up with me." She tried to grin, unsuccessfully. "Maybe you could walk me back to my hotel?"

Zelda nodded.

Rita turned to her host. "I sure do appreciate you letting me see my family's home, Eva." She wrapped her arms around the Dutch woman before she could respond and squeezed her tight.

As she dislodged herself from Rita's embrace, Eva said, "It was a pleasure meeting you and hearing more about the history of my home. Are you sure you are feeling well enough to walk back to your hotel? I can call a taxi for you."

"Heavens, no. A walk will do me good." With a sad smile, Rita started down the stairs towards Eva's front door, Zelda following close behind.

14

Who Can He Trust?

Oh, how cruel the fates can be! Finally finding one painting after a lifetime spent searching, only to have it snatched away from him by another. Konrad Heider glared at his computer screen, cursing the photo of the Amsterdam Museum's board of directors huddled around Rita Brouwer as she held her father's painting tight. News of the sensational discovery had gone viral immediately, with most European and American news sites using this photograph to illustrate their story.

In light of the coverage her claim had received, he was surprised Edward hadn't mailed again to ask him about the painting. But then again, someone like Edward would only remember the masterpieces; the Wedersteins of the world were easily forgotten.

Konrad racked his brain, trying to come up with another way to acquire what was rightfully his. *Think, man; what would your uncle have done?* As he ground the stump of his cigar out, an idea popped into his head. He turned it slowly over in his mind, contemplating every angle before a broad smile spread across his face.

With a little help, he could probably sail around the other claimant and get the museum staff on his side in one fell swoop. But who could he trust to help him? And could he get all the documents forged in time?

Konrad opened the humidor and took out another Montecristo.

15

An Unexpected Development

Zelda snapped open *Het Parool* and leaned back in bed, a smile on her lips as she carefully re-read this morning's front-page story. The photo of Rita's tiny round face beaming as she held *Irises* up high was priceless. From her ecstatic expression it was clear the museum's first claimant was pleased, honored even, to be the center of attention. The Amsterdam Museum's board of directors was crowded around her, their joy rivaling Rita's.

Saturday had definitely been a night to remember for all involved, herself included. Thanks to the free champagne and knowledge that one painting had already been spoken for before the exhibition officially opened, the party ended up being an extremely joyful and drunken affair. She hadn't talked with Rita since, but she hoped the older woman had seen the Dutch newspapers this morning. After all, it was because of her family's heart-wrenching past that the media had covered the exhibition's opening so extensively. She would have to buy some extra copies for Rita, just in case.

She took a long sip of coffee, spilling a little on her blanket when her phone began to ring. *Speak of the devil*, she thought. Wiping the dribbles off her only afghan with one hand, she answered her phone with the other, fully expecting to hear Rita's southern drawl on the line.

"I'm glad I caught you at home," an altogether different person said. It was Bernice Dijkstra, and she sounded stressed out.

Zelda glanced at the clock; it was just after eight in the morning. She was surprised to hear from the project manager at all today; Zelda figured both she and Huub Konijn would take a few days off as payback for their hard work on the exhibition and website.

"There's been an, umm, unexpected development."

Zelda sat upright in bed as the project manager struggled to express herself. It was the first time she'd ever heard Bernice fumble her words. *Something must be really wrong to have rattled her so badly*, she thought.

"Could you possibly come to the museum? We could use your help."

"Okay, sure. Do you mean today?"

"I mean now. Are you available?"

She'd made no real plans, except to meet up with Friedrich later for a coffee. "I'm free for the day."

"Tell Susan at reception I'm expecting you. She'll bring you to me."

"Is anything wrong?" Zelda asked.

"I'll tell you everything once you arrive." Bernice hung up the phone without waiting for a response.

What in the world is going on? she wondered as she sprung out of bed and dressed in record time, running down the four flights of stairs and out to her bike. *Why was Bernice being so vague? Did something happen to the painting? Or, worse, to Rita?* Visions of the seventy-nine-year-old claimant having a stroke or heart attack as a result of all the excitement Saturday night popped into her head. When Zelda had left at two in the morning, Rita had looked pretty tired but had been enjoying herself so thoroughly that she'd refused to leave until the party was well and truly over. *If something had happened to her, Bernice would have told me over the phone, wouldn't she? What else could have freaked her out so badly?* A plethora of scenarios raced through her mind as she willed her legs to pedal harder over the bike paths and bridges connecting her apartment to the Amsterdam Museum.

Susan knocked loudly on the conference room door, in spite of the angry voices coming from within. Seconds later Bernice threw it open.

"Thank you for coming so quickly," the project manager said, as she gestured for her intern to sit down next to her. Huub was seated across from them but refused to meet either woman's eye as they took their places at the table. The project manager looked pale and withdrawn, while the curator's cheeks and neck were bright red. Zelda's arrival had obviously interrupted a heated conversation. *What the heck is going on here?* she wondered for the umpteenth time since Bernice had called her at home, thirty minutes earlier.

"We find ourselves in an embarrassing situation. Late Sunday evening a lawyer contacted Leo de Boer." Bernice's voice trembled, capturing Zelda's full attention. "He claims *Irises* was actually the property of a Dutch art dealer who was killed during the war. He represents the man's granddaughter. Last night he and his client flew in from New York City. They should be here any minute."

"Leo de Boer wants you to take notes of this meeting for us. From his conversation with the lawyer, it's clear his client is upset that Rita Brouwer was presented as the legal owner at the opening, before we had verified her claim. We will be recording this meeting as well, but it is important to have someone take notes in case the recorder malfunctions. Your being a native speaker makes you a natural choice. Would you be willing to do this for us?" Bernice was practically begging her to say "yes."

A second claimant? She could hardly believe her ears. *Does that mean Rita Brouwer lied to us?* Recalling the old lady's sincere joy at seeing *Irises* once again, she couldn't believe she'd lied about anything. She had to hear this second claimant's story for herself. "Sure, I can take notes for you."

Bernice turned back to Huub, apparently resuming the conversation Zelda's arrival had interrupted. "Let us not forget to remain open to the information we are about to hear," she said in Dutch. Zelda wondered whether the curator had forgotten that she could understand far more Dutch than she could speak.

"I told you before, I don't trust Rita Brouwer," the curator protested.

"Again, I urge you to wait until after we've heard what this new claimant has to say before you judge the validity of Mrs. Brouwer's claim," Bernice replied sternly, looking relieved when he nodded slightly.

"Zelda, may I remind you that you are only to take notes during this meeting, not participate in it," the project manager added in English.

Zelda knew this was for Huub's benefit so she nodded solemnly. "Of course," she said, trying to look humble as the project manager handed her a notepad and two pens.

The conference room's telephone buzzed, Bernice picked it up on the first ring. "Okay, send them up." She looked over at the curator. "They're here; Susan is escorting them upstairs." Moments later a knock on the door brought them all to their feet.

"Come in," Bernice called out.

As the door opened, cinnamon-tainted perfume wafted into the room. A tall, thin woman in a fur coat and five-inch heels sauntered in, a distinguished-looking older man trailing closely behind with a large black case in one hand. Her makeup was catwalk ready, her hair swept up in a loose bun with just the right amount of strands falling playfully around the nape of her neck. Zelda hated her immediately.

"Karen O'Neil," the new claimant stated, as she looked down at Bernice and offered her a limp hand. "And this is my legal counsel, Konrad Heider." The woman waved vaguely in her lawyer's direction. A brief smile passed over her lips as she turned to shake Huub's outstretched hand. Apparently aware Zelda was only there to take notes and therefore not important, Ms. O'Neil ignored her completely, setting her purse at the head of the table before walking over to the painting, once again resting on an easel in a corner of the conference room. The lawyer, however, offered his hand and business card to all three. Zelda glanced at it before taking her seat: "Konrad Heider, Founding Partner of Heider, Schmidt & Weber Law Firm," it read. Under his name and title were addresses listed for offices in Düsseldorf and New York City.

As the new claimant leaned down to examine the painting, Zelda saw no look of love or even recognition in her eyes, only a cold, business-like calculation. Without a word, the woman picked up the painting, flipped it over and scratched her manicured nails across the back of the canvas then around the frame, staring intently at her handiwork.

"What are you doing? Put that painting down!" Bernice Dijkstra shouted.

Karen slowly placed *Irises* back on the easel. "I was simply checking to see if my grandfather's stamp was on the back, that's all. The painting obviously hasn't been cleaned properly in quite a while." With a pout on her lips, she settled into her chair, her lawyer already seated on her right-hand side. She dug a nail file out of her tiny purse and began flicking bits of dirt from under her fingernails onto the table.

"Well, we would appreciate it if you would ask before picking up the painting again. It is not your property, at least not officially," Bernice said, adding, "There are no gallery stamps or markings on the back, only the address of Rita Brouwer's father."

"Oh yes, *her*," Karen said with disdain. "How dare you announce to the press that you've found the rightful owner without even verifying her claim first! Some media stunt." She continued, going for the jugular without batting an eyelash, "How are your newspapers going to react when they hear my side of the story? How is your museum going to look then?"

"First of all, we didn't know you existed until yesterday. Our research team was unable to find any official records concerning this painting's provenance. We had no reason to suspect it had been sold to an art dealer during the war. And secondly, we had no reason to doubt Rita Brouwer, given the documentation she provided."

Huub looked over at the project manager as if to interrupt; one glance at Bernice's expression and he held his tongue.

Continuing in a more composed voice, the project manager added, "Today we hope to learn more about your grandfather's gallery and his purchase of the Wederstein so we can fill in this painting's history." Bernice made eye contact with both the lawyer and his client, waiting for them to make the next move.

"You'll have to excuse my atrocious manners. I know you're just doing your job. I do apologize for jumping all over you," Karen purred, more to the curator than the project manager, batting her eyelashes and leaning forward so he had a better view of her surgically enhanced breasts. "You can't imagine what a shock it was to finally find my grandfather's painting, then to see it in *that* woman's hands."

Her performance achieved its desired effect. Huub rushed to her defense. "It is an understandable reaction," he said in a subdued tone. "We are glad you came forward so quickly."

"You are here now, and from what Mr. Heider said on the phone," Bernice broke in, gesturing to the lawyer as she spoke, "you have a valid claim on this painting. Let us start with your proof of ownership. You believe this to be one of the pieces taken by the Nazis from your grandfather's gallery during the war. His name was Arjan van Heemsvliet, is that correct?"

"Yes, that's right. Galerie Van Heemsvliet on the Spiegelgracht, number 7. My grandfather Arjan van Heemsvliet was the owner. I have all of the documentation with me: his inventory lists, ledger books, and a few bills of sale."

"How did you find out the Wederstein painting was here in Amsterdam?" Bernice asked. Zelda was also curious how such an unknown work had come to the attention of this jet-setter.

"How could I not have known about it? Thanks to that woman's sappy story, that photograph has been reprinted in every art magazine and newspaper I read. Though the title is different, the dimensions, materials used, and description matches the Lex Wederstein painting described in my grandfather's inventory ledgers perfectly."

"And what is the name of this piece, according to your grandfather's ledgers?" Bernice asked as Zelda held her breath.

"Irises."

Huub glanced over at Bernice, a twinkle in his eye, and smiled sweetly.

"According to his ledger, *Irises* was purchased directly from Philip Verbeet on June 16, 1942," the lawyer chimed in.

"June 16, 1942," Bernice repeated, locking eyes with Huub. *Two days after Rita and her family went to Venlo,* Zelda realized. She glanced at the museum professionals before her and sensed they were thinking the same thing. Was Arjan van Heemsvliet the mysterious friend Rita's father mentioned in his last letter? But if Arjan was only meant to store the art for Philip Verbeet, why did he include it in his gallery's inventory list?

Ms. O'Neil picked up where her lawyer left off. "There's no gallery stamp on the back of the Wederstein painting, but then my grandfather must have only had it in his possession for a few days before he was killed. No matter." Karen signaled to her legal aide. "This proof of sale was also found among my grandfather's papers, proving he paid good money for Philip Verbeet's entire collection."

The lawyer dug through his case, quickly finding what he sought, before handing his client two sheets of paper, who in turn passed them on to the curator. Bernice had to lean over the table to read along. After they both examined the pages, Huub looked up smugly at Bernice, saying, "This receipt states that Rita's father received ten thousand guldens for his entire collection."

Zelda glanced up in shock, momentarily losing her place on the page. Ten thousand guldens—why hadn't Rita mentioned this before? Was it because she hadn't known her father had sold his artwork—or was there another reason?

"Do you have these ledgers with you?" Huub asked.

Karen glanced over at her lawyer, who immediately removed a stack of books covered in paisley-print cloth from his satchel and laid them on the table before his client. Karen drummed her fingers on the pile as she spoke. "These ledgers comprise my grandfather's inventory list, detailing the paintings he bought or sold in his gallery since its opening in 1932. Each book contains roughly five years of transactions. He listed everything he knew about the canvases and their provenance. He also noted the price he sold each piece for, as well as the name of the new owner, until 1940. After that, the details of both the buyer and seller become sketchier."

"This last ledger," she said while handing it to the curator, "begins in 1939 and ends in June 1942."

As the curator flipped it open and began to read, she added, "He specialized in modern and contemporary artwork, predominately impressionists, fauvists, and cubists."

Huub gazed down in wonder at the inventory list before him. He responded slowly, while still absorbing the list of paintings bought and sold by Arjan van Heemsvliet, "Cézanne, Kirchner, Renoir, Chagall, Braque,

Léger, Van Gogh, Matisse, Picasso; your grandfather certainly had an impressive selection of paintings in his possession when he died. Most of the artists listed in this book were the *crème de la crème* of modern European painters working in the early 1900s. He must have been successful and well-connected to have bought and sold so many high quality pieces. Any one of these paintings would be worth a fortune on today's market." He spoke the last sentence so softly Zelda wasn't sure whether he meant to say it out loud.

Karen nodded in satisfaction. "As you can see, most of the pieces in this last ledger were never sold, thus were still in my grandfather's possession when he died. All of these paintings are now mine, of course," she stated, her tone leaving no room for doubt.

Huub's expression grew more intense as he scanned the list, flipping through the pages at an ever slower pace.

"Do you see any indication that the pieces listed in that book were sold, or to whom?" Bernice asked.

"I told you already—" Ms. O'Neil interjected with a huff.

"What are these numbers, written here next to some of the titles?" Huub asked, tapping at the page with his finger.

"We don't know for certain, though our investigators believe they may have indicated where the painting was stored. We have determined that Arjan van Heemsvliet could not have had all of these canvases hanging in his gallery at one time. There were simply too many."

Huub was silent a moment, taking in Konrad Heider's explanation. He continued to flip through the rest of the inventory book, quickly reviewing the information Van Heemsvliet had recorded before finally answering Bernice's question. "Most of these paintings appear to be part of his unsold stock; at least there is no indication they were sold or to whom. However, after May 1940, very few details are listed about either the buyers or sellers; in most cases he's only recorded the titles, dimensions, and materials used. Many of the artists' names are missing, as well."

The lawyer opened his mouth to speak, but Huub continued nonetheless. "I can think of two reasons why he may have done this. The styles of art that you say Galerie Van Heemsvliet dealt in were considered to be '*entartete*' or 'degenerate' by the Nazi regime. Dutch museums and art galleries were forbidden from displaying—or selling—these sorts of works after the war started. By leaving certain information out of this ledger, he may have been trying to protect his inventory from being confiscated and destroyed."

The smile that crossed Karen's face disappeared quickly as Huub went on. "Or your grandfather was purchasing artwork from Jews forced to flee Amsterdam and he was trying to protect himself and any potential buyers by not including the seller's names in his inventory books. If this proves to be the case, your claim would become far more complex. Any transactions between 1938 and 1945 that involved the purchase or seizure of artwork owned by Jewish citizens are now considered a 'forced sale,' rendered null and void after the war by way of royal decree."

"But in case of the Wederstein painting, Rita Brouwer cannot claim her father was forced to sell anything," Karen's lawyer countered. "According to several of the newspaper articles about the exhibition's opening last Saturday night, her father—Philip Verbeet—was Protestant, not Jewish."

"Are you certain Arjan van Heemsvliet actually purchased all of the pieces listed here?" Huub asked. "He must have had over three hundred works in his possession when he died, and most of them painted by renowned artists. It was common for galleries to take in artwork on commission, meaning they were never really the property of the gallery, but technically on loan from its owner—the potential seller—until the work was sold," the curator explained as he glanced over the inventory list before him. "That way the gallery owner would profit from the sale without having to spend a large amount acquiring the piece first. In return, the potential seller would receive a higher percentage of the selling price."

Karen erupted, "Why else would he have listed these paintings in his inventory ledger if they didn't belong to his gallery? Was it common for gallery owners to do that?" she sneered.

"The Verbeet collection was the last entry in that ledger," Karen's lawyer calmly stated. "May I?" he asked, gesturing to the book in Huub's hands.

Konrad Heider flipped through the ledger until he'd reached the middle.

"Here, the Verbeet collection of thirty-six paintings begins on this page. As you can see, *Irises* is part of it; the artist, dimensions, and description of the canvas all match. Considering no documentation was found with the painting after the war, it is not surprising it was cataloged as *Girl with Vase*. See this date? That means Arjan van Heemsvliet purchased the collection from Philip Verbeet on June 16, 1942. For a small fortune, I might add, ten thousand guldens was quite a large sum of money back then, especially for 'degenerate' art in wartime Amsterdam."

"If you had all of this documentation at your disposal, why didn't your family file a claim with the Dutch government in 1945?" Bernice asked.

"I didn't even know my grandfather's collection existed until quite recently. Before my mother, Isabelle Kershaw, died a few months ago, she told me about a box of paperwork stored up in her attic; I have most of its contents with me today. In addition to some personal letters, I found my grandfather's business documents inside."

"Why had your mother never mentioned him to you earlier?" Bernice asked.

"She'd always been ashamed of her past, and it wasn't until she'd been diagnosed with terminal cancer that she decided to tell me the truth. When my grandfather was killed in a bombing raid in June 1942, my grandmother was four months pregnant. The Nazis cleaned out his gallery the next day, taking all of the paintings and documents inside. As soon as she found out what had happened, my grandmother packed all of the paperwork and artwork still in Arjan's study and fled to her family's home outside of the city. After the war, she moved to New York and married an American business acquaintance of her father's. Her new husband raised my mother as his own child. He was an extremely successful businessman and the son of a prominent steel magnate. Neither my grandmother nor mother wanted anyone to know that he wasn't her biological father.

"It's taken me months to sort through all of his paperwork, but I now have a good idea of the type of business he was running and a list of the paintings he had in his possession when his gallery was ransacked. A few weeks ago, I hired a team of private investigators to locate all of the missing works.

My mother may have been ashamed of her past, but I am not. Once you read through his inventory list and ledgers, you will see that my grandfather was a successful businessman with a wonderful eye for art. I want his name resurrected and his paintings reunited so everyone can see that for themselves."

"We will have to verify all of the documents included in your claim, but the ledger and bill of sale do seem to prove your grandfather was the owner—albeit briefly—of *Irises* before he died," Huub stated self-assuredly, his tone implying further research was unnecessary.

Zelda could hardly believe her ears. *Huub is loving this,* she thought. He had taken an obvious dislike to Rita Brouwer the first moment he laid eyes on her, even though the painting obviously had enormous sentimental value for both her and her family. To Karen O'Neil, it was nothing but a piece on a list, and not even one of the more valuable ones. It just didn't seem fair.

"I have bills of sale for several other collections listed in my grandfather's 1939-1942 inventory ledger, though not all of them. Obviously my grandmother wasn't able to take all of his business papers with her when she fled, only those stored in his study," Karen said.

How convenient that the Verbeet collection was one of the bills of sale Karen's grandmother did manage to grab, Zelda thought, scribbling furiously.

Her lawyer jumped in with, "Ms. O'Neil's investigators are currently searching for the rest of the unsold paintings listed in Galerie Van Heemsvliet's inventory, but if your museum has information about any of these canvases, we expect to be informed right away."

Bernice looked at him as if he was crazy. "Without having read through the entire list myself, I could not possibly tell you *right away* if any other works belonging to Arjan van Heemsvliet were entrusted to the Dutch government after the war," she said, her voice dripping with sarcasm. "Your investigators are welcome to search through the database of unclaimed works on our website, though I *can* tell you most of the paintings are eighteenth- and nineteenth-century pastorals and portraits, not modern pieces."

Seemingly unfazed by Bernice's tone, Karen's lawyer nodded in acknowledgement before clearing his throat. As if addressing the court with his closing argument, he gestured towards the books and documents laid out on the table before them as he spoke. "As you can see, we have sufficient evidence to prove beyond a reasonable doubt that my client's grandfather was the last legal owner of Lex Wederstein's *Irises*. This afternoon I am going to ask your director to expedite this process by signing an official letter to the secretary of state recommending Karen O'Neil be granted title to the painting, effective immediately."

Bernice shook her head resolutely. "That is not possible, especially in light of the claim being submitted by Rita Brouwer. And frankly, her story raises many questions as to the circumstances under which this painting came into Van Heemsvliet's possession. Both your client and Mrs. Brouwer will need to go through the official claims process so we can verify all of the documentation provided by both parties."

"Please," Karen snorted. "I've shown you my grandfather's inventory ledgers and bill of sale. What more can I do to prove that *Irises* is mine?"

Heider interrupted his client's outburst, continuing more smoothly, "Ah yes. Rita Brouwer. We've read about her tragic story in the newspapers. It's unfortunate for her—and this museum—that she chose to leave out the fact that the painting had been sold to an art dealer by her father. Apparently you did not need to verify her claim before presenting her as the owner of *Irises* during the exhibition opening last week."

Bernice ignored him. "I agree with Huub that the inventory list and bill of sale appear to solidify your claim, Ms. O'Neil. However, you will still need to formally submit your documentation for review before we can proceed officially. Only after the entire process is complete will *Irises* be returned to either you or Mrs. Brouwer."

"After the embarrassment you caused my client, we will have no choice but to explain our side of the story to the media, unless your museum's director signs that recommendation."

The project manager eyed him defiantly. "Though we may have been premature in presenting Rita Brouwer as the rightful owner during the exhibition's opening, in point of fact she has not been given the painting.

Nor shall she—or your client—be allowed to take *Irises* out of this museum until ownership has been officially awarded to one party. And as far as expediting your client's claim, both Huub Konijn and I would also need to sign this recommendation, even if our director is willing to draft such a letter. And at this time, I am not inclined to do so without first having done more research into this painting's provenance."

The lawyer stared back at Bernice, his steel-blue eyes glistening. "We will be staying at the Amstel Hotel for the next two weeks and expect to be kept abreast of your findings," he stated dismissively before gathering up his client's documents and ledgers.

It was Bernice's turn to snort. "As our director will soon tell you, it takes months—sometimes years—to go through the claims process, even when there is but one claimant. In light of the fact there are two, I expect no one will be granted the title to this painting for many years to come."

"We'll see about that," the lawyer responded coolly. Nodding to his client, they both rose from the table and walked out without saying another word.

"Can you believe the nerve of that woman?" Bernice exploded as soon as the door fell into place. "Threatening us like that. Trying to blackmail us with bad publicity if we don't give her the Wederstein."

"I knew there was something about Rita Brouwer's story that didn't ring true," Huub retorted with the same ferocity. "She probably knew her father sold his art collection all along, but tried to dance around that fact by using her sick sister to make us feel sorry for her. I knew it was a mistake inviting her to the opening before we verified her story! The media are going to crucify us when they find out about this. Years of hard work wasted because the board of directors couldn't pass up a single PR moment. Worse of all, we've shamed the whole idea behind the exhibition: of reuniting paintings with their *rightful* owners, not just any owner."

"Huub, you know we had no reason to doubt her. I still believe her father was the original owner of *Irises*. Besides, who would have thought out of all the unclaimed paintings in our depot, the Wederstein would be subject to two claims in one week's time? I was as flabbergasted as you when that lawyer produced those inventory books and bill of sale, but it doesn't mean Rita knew her father sold his collection to Arjan van Heemsvliet. The transaction was dated two days *after* her mother took them to Venlo. And she wasn't lying about the rest of her father's collection. Did you see the list of paintings her father supposedly sold Van Heemsvliet? It's almost identical to the one she provided us with," Bernice said.

"Rita Brouwer doesn't really matter anymore; all of the pieces listed in that inventory book are clearly the property of Karen O'Neil," Huub responded, with the same level of conviction. "It's unfortunate for Mrs. Brouwer, but her father selling the paintings to help his family flee the Netherlands, or at least to get through the war, makes the most sense. Don't forget he paid the rent on their house for five years and Mrs. Brouwer can't explain where he found the money to do so. Philip Verbeet could have used part of the ten thousand guldens Arjan van Heemsvliet gave him. The rest of the money must have been with him when he died. *If* he died—his own daughter doesn't know what happened to him." Huub was on a roll, convincing himself of the old lady's treachery as he spoke.

As she thought back to Rita's cramped old home and the five children sleeping in one room, all Zelda could do was wonder, Why would Rita's dad pay rent on a tiny apartment he wasn't living in and claimed he didn't want to go back to, instead of using the money to help his family start over somewhere else, after the war?

"Why do you suppose Karen O'Neil is demanding immediate possession of the painting?" Bernice wondered out loud. "Are we certain this Wederstein is only worth a few hundred euros? Maybe she knows something we don't?"

"I already asked Sonja at the Stedelijk Museum about *Irises* and Lex Wederstein. The painting itself is worthless—however, she thinks its status as a recently reclaimed piece once stolen by the Nazis will help drive the price up into the low thousands," Huub said.

"Then I really don't understand why that lawyer is pushing so hard to expedite her claim; he must know it can take years before such complicated cases are resolved. And Karen O'Neil only found out about her grandfather and his gallery a few months ago. Why are they putting so much pressure on us to resolve this claim so quickly?" Bernice mused.

"To ensure her claim is expedited. Considering how badly we embarrassed his client, she has every right to be angry," Huub quickly answered, as if Bernice was refusing to accept the obvious. Like Zelda, he must have noted the look of outrage on Bernice's face, because he swiftly added, "Bernice, twelve of the most prominent museums and Jewish organizations in the Netherlands worked together to create this exhibition. We've got all our reputations to think of. I'm going to recommend to Leo de Boer that we give Karen O'Neil her letter. Once his recommendation has been sent to the secretary of state, Ms. O'Neil will have no reason to go to the media."

"No, Huub. We have to treat the claims as equally valid until we get to the bottom of this mess. And before we go making recommendations to the director, we need to talk with Rita Brouwer again. Perhaps she remembers Arjan van Heemsvliet. If he was a family friend, then that would support her assertion that her father gave his collection to Arjan to store, not sell. The ten thousand guldens might have been a loan to help tide over his friend's family during their time in Venlo."

Bernice turned to Zelda for the first time since Karen O'Neil had stepped into the conference room. "Do you know when Rita Brouwer is flying back to America?"

"Tomorrow night," she said.

"You're wasting our time, Bernice," the curator growled.

"I will call her hotel and see if she can meet with us again later today. Huub, we need to hear what she has to say about this bill of sale and her father's relationship with Arjan van Heemsvliet. It's worth a few hours of our time, especially if it helps us discover the truth." Bernice gazed intently at the curator as she spoke, making it clear she left no room for disagreement.

Huub nodded in confirmation, but Zelda could see he was still smoldering.

The project manager turned to her former intern once again. "Could you come back and take notes for us later? Until Rita Brouwer arrives, you can use a computer in the museum's library to type up the notes of this meeting. If you get hungry, ask my secretary for a pass to the employee lounge."

"Sure, yeah, that's a good idea, to do it while the conversation is still fresh in my mind," Zelda agreed.

16

Faulty Memories

Huub Konijn slammed his office door shut, startling the only IT guy not on vacation. *"Excuses,"* he muttered reflexively, though he did not feel sorry for his actions. On the contrary, throwing the door closed released some of the anger pent up inside.

"How could Bernice and Leo be so foolish?" he mumbled. How could they have invited Rita Brouwer to the opening and let her talk to the press, before verifying her claim?

He knew better than most how important family photos were to such an investigation, but as a starting point, not as definitive proof. If photographs alone had been enough to reclaim his family's artwork, he wouldn't have had to spend seven years of his life in stuffy archives and depots, crisscrossing Europe in search of official documentation.

He'd found his family's artwork by scouring four decades of newspapers and magazines, searching for any mention of his wealthy family. Their collection had never been lent to museums or open to the general public, which meant there were no published records or catalogs indicating his family's ownership.

Once he'd assembled a short list of titles and artists' names from a handful of photographs and articles, he'd set out to retrace the history of those works. Through years of archival research, he was able to ascertain the complete provenance of several paintings, ending with verifiable purchases made by his father and grandfather before him.

But not all of them. Huub knew better than Bernice or Leo how faulty memories of a happier time could become warped by unimaginable traumas. Three of the canvases he'd found mentioned in society columns, he'd remembered Margo describing during those long, winter nights in the shed when it was too cold to sleep. One of them had even hung above his crib when he was a baby, according to his sister. Yet his own research proved that all three had been sold by his grandfather for a handsome profit—via a respectable art dealer—in 1938, two years before he was born.

Why couldn't Rita accept that her family's paintings had suffered a similar fate? Instead, she was going to destroy their reputations for naught.

He respected Philip Verbeet for being proactive enough to sell his collection in order to help his family, in contrast to his own father, who could have done so much more. If only he'd had the foresight to give his titles of ownership and inventory ledgers to one of his many trusted gentile friends, Margo wouldn't have died penniless and he wouldn't have ended up in an orphanage. Proof of ownership, that was all that mattered.

He'd dedicated the past ten years of his life to helping others who had suffered as he did, to reclaim what they'd lost. Karen O'Neil had presented more than enough evidence to prove that *Irises* and the rest of Arjan van Heemsvliet's collection belonged to her. She even resembled what Margo should have become, had their family's collection of paintings and sculptures survived the war intact, Huub realized, momentarily visualizing his sister as a gracious and sophisticated socialite, moving in the same circles as Karen.

Karen deserved to have *Irises* returned to her family, just as his sister had deserved to see her possessions returned to her, Huub thought, silently vowing to do everything in his power to help Karen's claim.

17

Damn this War!

Arjan van Heemsvliet wrung out the silk handkerchief a third time, wanting to get every drop of blood out. His eyes fluttered shut as he squeezed. He knew he should sleep, if only to prevent himself from contracting the same horrible sickness as his patient. Yet he hadn't allowed himself a full night's rest since Gijs's first bout of chest pain and vomiting began four days ago.

If only he had been able to find the right kind of antibiotics! But even his extensive wealth and social network couldn't help him acquire the correct cure. Without it, Gijs would have little chance at beating this bout of pneumonia. It had been in his chest too long; the blood-laced mucus he continually coughed up attested to that.

Arjan's hands tightened around the silk cloth until his knuckles began to ache. Rose-colored water streamed out of his fist. Damn this war! Six months ago he might have gotten lucky; infections like these were rare in the warmer months. Since winter had settled over the Netherlands, too many medicines had disappeared entirely, unlikely to be seen again until peace was a fact.

How many more months would it be before the Allies could free the Netherlands from its Nazi captors? Arjan looked down at the red-tinted water filling the basin; a tear rolled off his cheek and rippled its surface. Gijs didn't have months, he realized. Perhaps a few days, if his lover was lucky.

18

Plain Lying

"I missed my boat trip to Marken for this? There is no way on God's green earth my daddy sold his collection to anyone, for any amount of money. I don't care what this Karen O'Neil says. There must be some sort of mix-up. Or she's just plain lying." Rita Brouwer slammed her fist on Bernice Dijkstra's desk so hard that her cup of tea rattled in its saucer.

Rita was on the verge of tears, but Huub Konijn kept up his assault, in spite of her emotional state. "We have seen the bill of sale. Ten thousand guldens in 1942 is equivalent to nearly eighty-four thousand dollars today. Considering how most of the artists in your father's collection were still unknown when he acquired pieces from them, and the majority of his artwork was modern and therefore considered 'degenerate,' he would have been lucky to have received half that amount from any other art dealer."

"My daddy was no fool. He knew his paintings would be worth more money the longer he held onto them. He followed the artists whose work he had and kept tabs on the ones who were getting gallery exhibitions and selling works to museums. He told my mama repeatedly that his art collection was going to pay for our educations; ten thousand guldens would not have gotten all five of us girls through college. And besides, where did all that money go? He certainly never sent it to us or deposited it in any bank account my mama knew about."

"You said yourself you don't know how he paid the rent on your family's apartment in Amsterdam," the curator pointed out.

"I also told you he'd sold his frame making supplies. He never deposited that money either. Besides, five years' rent for our tiny apartment couldn't have cost ten thousand guldens," Rita protested.

"Perhaps your father took it with him?" Huub paused before adding, "Are you certain he died during the war?"

"Are you suggesting my daddy took the money and ran? That he intentionally left us girls and our mama to fend for ourselves? If you really think that, then you didn't hear a word I said last week. He would have never left us behind; he loved us too much." Her voice quivered as she spoke, and tears trickled down her plump cheeks.

Finally Bernice joined the conversation, gently continuing where Huub had left off. "I am sorry to have to put you through this, Mrs. Brouwer, but the documents Ms. O'Neil provided are quite convincing. It does appear your father sold his collection of paintings to a dealer named Arjan van Heemsvliet two days after you and your sisters left Amsterdam for your aunt's farm in Venlo. Are you sure his name means nothing to you?"

Rita took off her coke-bottle glasses and wiped at her eyes with an embroidered handkerchief. "No, it really doesn't. But I was just a little girl. My sister Rose might remember him; she used to have a memory like an elephant. Though she is getting up there in years. Daddy might have mentioned this Arjan fellow in one of his letters." Rita paused a moment before exclaiming, "Wait a minute, you said this Van Heemsvliet was an art dealer; maybe my daddy made some frames for him?"

"That could very well be, but without your father's ledgers, it will be difficult to verify. If they did have a business relationship, it could explain why your father turned to Mr. Van Heemsvliet when he wanted to sell his collection. And if they were friends, that would clarify the large sum paid," the project manager said.

"I'm telling you straight, my daddy would have removed the paintings from their frames and stuffed them into a suitcase if he couldn't find a friend to hold onto them, but he never would have sold them or left them behind for the Nazis to take. They were far too important to him. Besides, he said in his last letter he'd found someone to store them for him—not buy them. Why would he write that if it wasn't true?"

"Are you sure that's what he wrote?" Bernice asked delicately. "It's been so many years; perhaps you've forgotten his exact words?"

"My mother read and reread his last letter to us girls so many times that every word of it is ingrained in my memory." The old lady shook her head resolutely. "No, there is nothing you can say that would convince me to withdraw my claim. *Irises* was a gift to my daddy from the artist. It's a picture of my sister, for goodness' sake! What does this Karen O'Neil person want with it anyway?"

"She's submitted a claim because she is the legal heir to Arjan van Heemsvliet's entire collection, which, according to the documents she's provided, includes all of your father's artwork," Huub stated.

Rita began to sniffle again. "I only phoned my sister last night to tell her the wonderful news that we were finally getting *Irises* back after all these years. What am I supposed to tell her now? That a woman we've never met claims to be the rightful owner? It'll break her heart. It should be returned to us, and I bet the Restitutions Committee will agree with me," she sobbed.

Unmoved by her tears, Huub retorted, "As it stands right now, Karen O'Neil's claim—from a legal standpoint—is quite convincing. As painful as it may be, you must accept that your sister may never see *Irises* again. Perhaps you can purchase it from Ms. O'Neil, but that is entirely up to her."

"Buy back a painting we never sold? Ridiculous! I'm flying to Iris's house in Phoenix tomorrow. Once I find those letters, you'll be able to see for yourself my father didn't sell anything to anybody."

Despite Bernice's attempts to calm the old lady down, Rita stormed out of the office, cursing as she went.

"I told you this meeting was a waste of time," Huub said, with evident satisfaction.

Bernice looked troubled. "Huub, what if Rita's father did give his artwork to Arjan van Heemsvliet to hold, not sell?"

"Then why did he write up a bill of sale for the collection and record all thirty-six pieces in his gallery's inventory ledger?"

"I don't know. But I have a feeling we are missing an important piece of this puzzle." Bernice stared off into the distance, speaking slowly as she turned her thoughts into words. "We know almost nothing about this art dealer or frame maker. Until we do, I suspect we won't be able to resolve this matter expeditiously."

"What more do we need to know? Karen O'Neil still has the bill of sale and inventory books. Bernice, you know I believe in the claims process; without it I wouldn't have any of my father's paintings back. If my sister had had the same documents Ms. O'Neil does, I wouldn't have had to spend years tracking down records in archives all over Europe. We must trust the facts, not give in to our emotions. Frankly, I don't care what Rita's father wrote to her mother or why he chose to sell his paintings to Van Heemsvliet. I suspect we will never know. Personally, I think he did the right thing putting his family above his possessions. Things can always be replaced. Perhaps if my father had tried..." Huub stopped midsentence and stared off into the distance. The bitterness seeping through his voice confused Zelda as much as the references to his family's artwork.

"I, for one, would rather resolve this mess as quickly as possible so we can avoid any bad publicity," the curator continued moments later, in a stronger voice. "There is no reason to destroy our reputations for the sake of one painting."

"What happened to giving the painting back to the rightful owner, not just any owner?" Bernice chastised. "What if Van Heemsvliet was working with the Germans? Or if Philip Verbeet was forced to sell his artwork? Either scenario would impact this claims process significantly. Thanks to the information provided by Ms. O'Neil and Mrs. Brouwer, our research staff finally has a starting point for investigating *Irises'* provenance. Until we have a better idea of the types of persons Van Heemsvliet and Verbeet were and of the businesses they were running, I will not sign any formal recommendation—even if our director stands behind Ms. O'Neil's claim. And to say that you can and will, Huub, is unprofessional in my opinion."

Zelda saw the daggers shooting from his eyes; if Bernice did too, they didn't stop her from rushing on anyway. "If Karen and her lawyer really do demand resolution within two weeks, then we had better prepare ourselves for bad publicity regardless. We can't even begin the research phase that quickly; our entire scientific staff is still on vacation. Well-deserved, I might add, after all the hard work and extra time they've put in these past ten years getting the exhibition and website ready. I cannot possibly put my job on hold to do the necessary legwork. Or are you going to hunt through all of those archives yourself, Huub?"

"Of course not, I have other projects too, you know," the curator pouted.

The project manager put her head in her hands, moaning, "This is our worst nightmare. I cannot, with a clear conscience, officially recommend Ms. O'Neil be granted ownership before we do at least a semblance of research. Yet, we can't just sit back and wait for them to go to *Het Parool* either. If the media gets ahold of this story, we'll be the laughingstock of the museum world. We've worked so hard; we can't let her destroy that."

Suddenly she looked up and locked eyes with Zelda, a strange smile spreading over her face.

Huub, seeming to sense what she was about to say, cried out, "No, no, no!"

"What other choice do we have?" Bernice snapped at the curator. "Zelda, we could really use your assistance again."

With those eight little words, Bernice Dijkstra made Zelda Richardson the happiest girl on the planet. "Anything you need, I would be thrilled to help with."

Bernice winced at her enthusiastic reaction but carried on anyway, "We need you to visit a few archives and search for information pertaining to Arjan van Heemsvliet, Philip Verbeet, and their businesses."

"Okay," Zelda responded cautiously. "What exactly should I be looking for?"

"Huub and I will compile a list of local and national archives you will need to visit, as well as a list of keywords to search for. I'll email it to you later today. Perhaps you can start tomorrow?"

"Bernice, I must object! Letting a foreigner carry out such an important task is unthinkable. She can't even speak Dutch properly."

"It's not as if she has to read the documents, just look up the keywords we give her and make photocopies of any records she finds. It will be *our* task to sift through the documents she collects and see what we can find out about Galerie Van Heemsvliet and the circumstances that led Philip Verbeet to sell his collection, before Karen O'Neil's lawyer goes to the media," Bernice snapped back.

"I still think we are wasting our time. The inventory list and bill of sale are enough proof for me. We should recommend Karen O'Neil be awarded the title and be done with this, before it turns into a publicity nightmare for all the institutions involved."

Bernice exploded, "I am not going to hand *Irises* over to that woman simply because her lawyer is an arrogant pit bull. We have two weeks before they do anything. I say we investigate these claims as fully as possible within the time remaining and then make our own decision as to what happens next, based on the documents Zelda finds for us." She glanced over at her intern apologetically. "You'll have to excuse us. This sort of situation—two strong claimants for one painting—has never happened before."

Zelda nodded as she stared back wide-eyed, suddenly aware of the gravity of the task at hand. She'd never done archival research before, at least not on this scale, and definitely not in another language. And to top it off, there was the pressure to find something—anything—that might show them who the real owner of *Irises* was so that all twelve institutions and the Dutch government could protect their reputations. Suddenly unsure of herself, Zelda gulped loudly, wondering whether she shouldn't just say she agreed with Huub, that this was a bad idea.

Sensing her hesitation, Bernice added in a reassuring tone, "We aren't asking you to draw any conclusions, simply to make photocopies of any information you find and bring them to us. Archivists are usually very knowledgeable as well as helpful; if you show them our list of keywords and names, they should be able to locate any relevant documentation in their archive for you, or direct you to another institution that does have the information we're looking for. If anything else, your photocopies will give our research staff a head start once they return from their vacations. Shall we make an appointment for this Friday at three o'clock? You can hand in whatever information you have found this week to Huub and me then. That way we can go through it all next week."

"Let me emphasize again what Bernice just said," the curator cut in brusquely. "You are not to *investigate* anything, simply look up the records we ask you to and copy them. That is all; understood?" He looked to Zelda for confirmation.

"Understood," she agreed, wondering whether she would be able to keep her word.

19

Different Social Circles

"I don't understand why you're complaining so much. It sounds like you found a lot of new information in the past two days. I'm sure Bernice will be pleased," Friedrich responded, while fiddling with the Red Baron's wiring. He was so engrossed in getting the new remote control for his plane to work properly, Zelda was surprised he'd heard what she'd said.

Not that she really minded how distracted he was. It felt so good to be outside again after spending the past two days shut away indoors, sifting through fifteen years of old Dutch newspapers, searching for anything written about Arjan van Heemsvliet or Philip Verbeet that might give the museum more insight into the types of men they were and the businesses they ran. She breathed in the fresh air, thankful she could now enjoy the warm summer evening with her friend, guilt-free. Per usual, Friedrich was already flying one of his many remote-controlled planes around the Museumplein's vast field when she'd arrived.

"True, I have found out a lot of new stuff about that art dealer, but I still haven't found a clear connection between him and Rita's dad. They moved in totally different social circles. And that bitch's grandma is a total mystery."

"You mean Karen O'Neil, wife of one of the richest real estate developers in New York City?"

"The recent widow of, God rest his soul." One look at the disapproval on Friedrich's face made her blush. "Maybe I should stop calling her 'the bitch.'"

"Indeed, before you slip and say it to her face."

Zelda reddened at the thought. That would surely get her fired from her internship, effective immediately.

"Let's go over what you found again," Friedrich finally laid his World War I fighter replica down on the blanket next to him and gave Zelda his full attention. "You said the art dealer was a real socialite, right? He was photographed at several galas and charity events?"

Zelda thought back to the pictures she'd found of the young art dealer. Arjan was plain in every sense of the word, almost indistinguishable from his fellow socialites in dress and stance. Fashion dictated the identical black suits, waistcoats, and white shirts with wide standing collars. Even their hair was similarly styled, either slicked back over their skulls or with a sharp parting on one side. The only visible difference between Arjan and the rest was the constant presence of a pocket watch, attached with a thin chain to his waistcoat.

"Based on the articles I found in the Dutch national newspaper archives, I'd say he was. It's as if he'd been invited to every important event held in Amsterdam between 1932 and his death ten years later. And he was either a trustee of or major donor to at least twenty charities, primarily soup kitchens and orphanages run by religious organizations of all denominations. On top of that, he was on the board of directors of six different cultural organizations. I don't know how he managed to find the time to be so involved." Zelda shook her head, imagining how harried his schedule must have been.

"Considering the sort of business he ran, all that volunteer work would have been a great way to network with those who had expensive tastes and substantial means."

"That's true."

Friedrich stretched out his skinny legs and flipped his long blond braid back over his shoulder. "You said earlier that Karen O'Neil's grandmother, Annette Schuppe, also came from a wealthy family. Maybe they met at a charity event."

"Perhaps they did," she admitted reluctantly. "Her father, Geert Schuppe, owned a construction company that helped build the Rijksmuseum and several other monuments in Amsterdam. Though I couldn't find a single mention of Annette in the society pages until 1939, and only then as the escort of another, much older man. She was eighteen at the time."

"There you go." Friedrich nodded in satisfaction. "She ran in the same social circles as Arjan van Heemsvliet and was attracted to rich, older men. Sounds like it runs in the genes," he laughed, referring to Karen's marriage to Samuel O'Neil, a real estate tycoon who had died the previous year at the ripe old age of ninety-five, leaving his fifty-year-younger bride one of New York's richest widows.

It sounded so easy the way Friedrich laid it out. But something was still bothering her. "I guess. It's just, in all the pictures of Arjan at galas and events, there's not a single shot of him with a woman. Even at the parties he gave at Galerie Van Heemsvliet, he's always surrounded by men." Zelda rushed to get her words out before her friend could scoff at her. "Of course, most of the time he was photographed with museum directors, trustees, or other philanthropists..."

"Who were predominately men back then, and even today despite all the hubbub about equal rights in the workplace."

Zelda nodded, knowing he was right—unfortunately. Newspaper articles and society columns only told so much. There were all kinds of explanations for Arjan van Heemsvliet's lack of female companionship, in photographs anyway. He and Annette could have met at a charity event but weren't photographed together. Or maybe his girlfriend was camera-shy. Though in all those society columns she had plowed through, there was not a single mention of a lady in his life. But then, the society pages in the 1930s and 1940s were more concerned with reporting the names and titles of those attending high-profile parties, detailing what their wives were wearing and whose daughter was engaged to whose son, but certainly not the sexual escapades of the Dutch elite. Modern tabloids and gossip columns seemed downright sleazy in comparison. And in reality, Arjan and Annette only had to have been together once to create their daughter, and not necessarily in a long-term relationship that would have been reported on by the press.

"And you found no connection whatsoever between the art dealer and Rita's father?" Friedrich asked, surprise in his voice.

"Nothing—not one mention of Philip Verbeet in the newspapers or society pages, only a few small advertisements he'd placed throughout the 1930s announcing a broad selection of frames at reasonable prices. The ads must not have cost much, and they only appeared a few times a year."

"Arjan van Heemsvliet was an art dealer; what if he got his frames made there?"

Like I hadn't thought of that already, Zelda huffed to herself, frustrated he was drawing the same conclusions she'd had and not offering new insights. How she wished she could talk to Pietro about everything that was going on. They'd had so little contact these past few weeks; his mobile phone was always switched off and he rarely had time to check his email because he was perpetually by his dying grandma's bedside. Despite her momentary irritation, she had to admit that Pietro's dedication to his family was sweet. And having so little contact only made her want him that much more. Until university resumed next month, she'd have to be content with his sporadic electronic messages telling her how much he loved her and how he couldn't wait to be with her again in September.

"Arjan could have gotten his frames made at Philip Verbeet's shop," she replied evenly. "Unfortunately, I haven't been able to find any records indicating they ever did business together. Hopefully tomorrow, in the city's archives, I'll be able to find out more about both the gallery and frame shop." She sighed. "If only Rita still had her dad's business ledgers. That would have been the easiest way of finding out if they ever worked together."

"Well, it sounds like you're doing the best you can."

"Bernice said she's getting a lot of pressure from the museum's board of directors to just sign the official recommendation effectively giving Karen full title to the painting. I guess they're afraid Karen's lawyer is going to show up with a television crew one morning and ambush them. And now she wants to have her own art conservator examine *Irises* so he can write up a condition report and tax it. Can you believe that? She doesn't even have the title yet, but she's already preparing to sell it."

"Some nerve."

"Got that right. It's such a shame. Bernice, Huub, and the others created this exhibition with such good intentions." Zelda sighed as she looked across the grassy field towards the Van Gogh and Stedelijk Museums. "Anyway, it's become a point of honor for Bernice not to turn *Irises* over to Karen or grant her conservator access until I've had a chance to check the archives on their list."

She lay back on the blanket and rested her head on her folded arms so she could gaze up at the cloudless blue sky. "Bernice wants a status report Friday afternoon so she can prove to Karen they're taking her claim seriously, in the hopes she won't go to the media before the two weeks are up. I guess she expected me to have found a stronger connection between Arjan van Heemsvliet and Philip Verbeet by now."

"Come on, you're doing this research by yourself, and for free I might add. Normally they'd have a whole team of professionals working on these claims. You said so yourself. Bernice can't expect miracles. Besides, she just wants to see if any new documentation comes to light, not to necessarily prove one way or the other whose painting it really is."

"I know. It's just I really wanted to figure this out for her, to be the one to solve the mystery, even if it does mean Karen O'Neil is the real owner. Of course I still hope she's a fraud and Rita gets to keep *Irises*. She's the one who will actually cherish it."

"Wait a second, solve the mystery? Your assignment is to gather information for Bernice and Huub to sort through, right? You aren't supposed to draw conclusions of your own."

"No, of course not," Zelda quickly replied, as she propped herself up on one elbow. She knew better than to tell her friend she'd made two copies of all the documents and records she'd found so far: a set for herself and another for the museum. Sure, her assignment was to photocopy any relevant documents and let her bosses decipher them, nothing more. Yet neither of her superiors really had time to read through everything she'd found so far. If she could piece together the truth before Huub and Bernice did, she would surely be guaranteed a place in the university's master's program.

"There's one thing still bothering me about Karen O'Neil," she added, hoping to change the subject.

"Just one thing?"

"*Irises* is an unknown work made by an unknown artist. Even if she sold it, the painting wouldn't bring in enough to pay for one night at the Amstel Hotel, let alone two weeks. On top of that, she's got the private investigators' and lawyers' fees to think of. Karen's spending tons of money to claim this 'worthless Wederstein,' as Huub Konijn calls it. It's just odd."

Friedrich shrugged. "Who knows why? Perhaps she's trying to set a precedent for future claims on the rest of the paintings in her grandfather's ledger. You know, scare other museums into giving in. You said several pieces on Arjan's inventory list are worth a small fortune. Or it could be she's bored. She is super rich; perhaps tracking down and claiming her grandfather's artwork is simply something to keep her occupied. Couldn't find a charity she liked, so she started up this crusade."

"That's probably it," she said, forcing a chuckle. Deep down she knew there was something peculiar about Karen's claim. But without proof, Friedrich would never believe anything derogatory she said about the New Yorker, maintaining that Zelda's dislike of the woman was seriously impairing her judgment. She knew it was more than that. But for now, she had to let it go.

"Could you get the remote control to work?" she asked, pointing at his Red Baron.

Friedrich nodded enthusiastically. "I think so. Shall we find out?"

"Sure," Zelda said, turning to face the warm summer sun as her friend prepared his little plane for takeoff.

20

The Missing Link

Karen was so easy to manipulate. Love struck since their first *rendezvous* in New York City five years earlier, she'd been hounding him relentlessly since her husband's death nine months ago. Konrad Heider knew she would be perfect for the job at hand: pliable, completely self-absorbed, and greedy as only the absurdly rich could be. She'd been so gob smacked by the contents of Arjan van Heemsvliet's inventory list she hadn't even heard him explain why he needed her help claiming it. Not that he expected her to check and see whether the artwork really belonged to his childless godfather. It didn't matter what she believed, as long as she went along with his plans and didn't ask too many questions. Callous as she was, he knew she wouldn't stand by his side if she discovered the real reason why he couldn't claim *Irises*, or any of the other paintings listed in Van Heemsvliet's inventory book, himself.

After slipping his horn-rimmed glasses back onto his nose, his thoughts turned again to their meetings with the exhibition's project team and Leo de Boer, director of the Amsterdam Museum. They had definitely not gone as he had envisioned. He had counted on De Boer caring more about his museum's reputation than one insignificant painting created by an unknown artist.

But no. The museum's director was even less receptive to Karen's demands of immediate restitution than Bernice Dijkstra and Huub Konijn had been. Despite his deep regret at the emotional trauma Karen had been subjected to,

De Boer had said, under no circumstances would the painting be returned to anyone before both claims could be fully investigated.

"Damn it!" Konrad swore aloud in his native German. He had to get his hands on that blasted Wederstein, no matter what the cost. It *must* be the key to finding his family's treasures. His uncle had become convinced *Irises* was the missing link, that somewhere hidden in its frame or canvas was a clue to the whereabouts of the rest. Why else would Arjan van Heemsvliet's cohort have packed *that* painting in his suitcase, instead of one of the many masterpieces in the art dealer's possession?

If only his uncle had taken *Irises* with him. A wistful sigh escaped his lips as he thought of how his life might have been, without this wretched search dominating it. His uncle was lucky to have escaped Amsterdam at all after the Nazis' unexpected surrender, only a week after Adolf Hitler's reported suicide. And he did manage to carry a few pieces back, Konrad reminded himself, smiling as he thought about the etchings hanging in his study.

Leo de Boer had ten days to sign the official letter recommending that Karen be awarded sole claim to the Wederstein; after that, he'd be forced to steal it. There was no way he was going to wait for the Restitutions Committee's researchers to decide the painting's fate. He was pleasantly surprised that the documents Karen had presented to the exhibition's project team passed their initial scrutiny, but he knew he wouldn't be so lucky once professional researchers and documentation experts got involved. Only an official recommendation signed by the museum's director would get him around that hurdle.

He had Karen keeping up the pressure on the museum's staff, demanding the right to drop in to see *Irises* at a moment's notice and nagging them to allow her own experts access to it, to ensure they wouldn't be able to put the Wederstein back in long-term storage anytime soon. So long as Karen was in Amsterdam, *Irises* would remain in the easily accessed restoration department, housed in a crumbling old building across the street from the museum itself, rather than in a tightly secured climate-controlled bunker.

While contemplating his short-term options, Konrad rose from his wingback chair and poured himself a bourbon from one of five crystal decanters lining the hotel's version of a mini-bar. Going to the media posed its own risks. It only took one nosy journalist to find out the truth about Karen and doom her claim. Until he could organize a break-in, the threat of scandal was still the most effective pressure point. With a little luck, the museum's director would get sick of Karen's constant meddling and give in to her demands before the two weeks were up. It wasn't as if that intern Zelda Richardson would be able to find any damaging evidence; she was just a student, and an American one at that. And while she was bumbling around looking for clues in far-flung archives, the museum was losing precious time.

No, it was better to give Bernice Dijkstra and her team their two weeks, let them come up with nothing, and then humiliate their director into turning the painting over to Karen. After a lifetime of searching for any sign of his uncle's treasures, waiting another ten days hardly mattered.

If Leo de Boer still refused to give in, he should have everything in place by then. An underpaid security guard or two might get injured during the robbery, but that was a risk he was more than willing to take.

He was so close to finding his masterpieces, he could feel it in his bones. The Wederstein was the key, the missing link—it must be. And once he finally had it in his hands, he would find the rest, museum be damned.

21

A Ray Of Hope

"Wim, you mean to tell me you can't find any more records or documents linked to Galerie Van Heemsvliet, either here or in Den Haag?" Despite her increasing frustration, Zelda couldn't believe how helpful the archivist at the Amsterdam City Archives was being. Obviously motivated by a passion for his profession, Wim Boxtel seemed as interested and eager to find out more about Arjan van Heemsvliet as she was. But in spite of his best efforts, there was almost nothing in the city or national archives pertaining to Arjan's gallery or business transactions.

"A copy of his business license and the application form is all I've been able to find. No records indicating which paintings he had in his inventory or who his clientele were," Wim murmured, gesturing towards the search results displayed on the screen before them. They were sitting at one of thirty computers with direct access to the city's vast digital archives, set up in front of the two-story-high windows lining the back of the building. On either side, other researchers were discussing their findings in equally hushed voices. Behind them were a marble-covered information desk and the entrance to the building.

Zelda hadn't known what to expect when she'd entered the city's archives for the first time. The massive, block-long building on the Vijzelstraat, easily recognizable by the dizzying red and gray patterns woven into the ten-story-tall brick and granite façade, was so imposing she was almost afraid to enter. In contrast, the publicly accessible resource center situated on the ground floor felt surprisingly light and airy thanks to the high ceilings, many windows, and large skylights running down the center of the rectangular structure.

"The fact that almost none of Arjan van Heemsvliet's business documentation can be found in our vast archives is not really unusual," Wim continued quietly. "If he died during the war and had no business partner—as we suspect—then there was probably no one left to donate his business records to either our city archives or the national art history archives stored in Den Haag. And from what you said earlier, it sounds like his wife, Annette Schuppe, may have taken much of it to New York with her after the war."

Zelda was getting pretty flustered. She had pinned her hopes on this appointment with the Amsterdam city archives' World War II specialist, but after searching through a wide variety of records and databases, Arjan van Heemsvliet was still a mystery. Having exhausted most of the keywords and names on Bernice and Huub's list, she was running out of ideas.

"At least we know he was not a known profiteer, otherwise his name would have been flagged. Several Dutch art dealers and gallery owners suspected of working with the Nazis were investigated after the war, and the results of that research were coupled to their personal record card. Of course, our list is probably incomplete. Art dealers were usually only investigated if there was a compelling reason. As far as Galerie Van Heemsvliet is concerned, we have hit a dead end. Let's see what his personal record card says," Wim said, typing as he softly spoke.

A scan of an old yellow note card with several typewritten names and dates on it filled the screen. In the top left-hand corner was Arjan van Heemsvliet's name.

"Every adult who has lived in Amsterdam has a 'personal record card.' Recorded on it are their full name, birth place, and religious persuasion, as well as the names of their parents, spouse, and any children. All of the addresses they have ever lived at should also be listed here, though if an individual moved often, it might not be complete."

Wim translated the document for her, using his finger to point out the

Dutch text he was reading aloud. "He lived in a single-family residence, Johannes Vermeerstraat number 76, from August 1932 until September 1942. That's quite an affluent neighborhood. Hmm, that's odd. The names of his wife and child are not listed."

"Maybe we're looking at the wrong file. Did we spell his name correctly?" Zelda asked as she compared her notes with their search query.

"I believe so," he said, typing in the name again.

The same card appeared on the screen, confusing her even more. "They were married in 1942. Perhaps it didn't get recorded, because of all the transportation and personnel problems brought about by the war?" Zelda asked.

"It is true many of those working for the city were deported to German work camps or went into hiding in 1940. And in combination with all of the diseases and the lack of heating and food so prevalent then, most government offices would not have been fully staffed during the war. But in 1942 all of the city's courthouses and archives were still open. If they got married in Amsterdam's city hall, a record of it should be in our files." Wim thought for a moment before adding, "However, if they got married in another city, it is possible the information was not recorded on this personal record card. Even though it should have been."

"And if the baby was born in another city?"

"Again, it should have been noted here, especially if they all lived on the Vermeerstraat in Amsterdam. But the war did cause all sorts of delays, and sometimes mail got lost or destroyed. It is irregular, but not unheard of," the archivist grudgingly conceded. "Let me search the national archives and see what I can find out about his wife, Annette Schuppe."

A few moments later, Wim stared at the screen in bewilderment. "Annette Schuppe was born in Alphen aan den Rijn in 1921 but never married nor had children while living in the Netherlands. She immigrated to New York City in August 1945. I recognize her father's name, Geert Schuppe; he was a successful businessman."

Zelda was more baffled than enlightened by this new piece of information. "This doesn't make any sense." She put her fingertips to her temple, willing herself to slow down and think through all the facts. "Okay, so Arjan van Heemsvliet was killed in a bombing raid in June of 1942. If he had gotten married a few weeks before he died, would that have messed up the registration of his marriage license? Would the birth of his daughter have been added to his personal record card at the city's archives if he was already dead?"

"A bombing raid in June 1942; are you sure?"

"Yes, well, that's what his granddaughter said happened."

"Strange. Wait here a moment, please." Wim sprung out of his seat and disappeared into the inner offices of the archives, returning quickly with a single document. "This is a map of occupied Amsterdam. The locations of the bombing raids and airplane crashes that took place in the city—those caused by the Allies and Germans—are listed here, by address and date. So far as I can see, there were no bombing raids recorded in June of 1942. In fact, according to this map, none took place in 1942, at least not in Amsterdam."

Zelda was at a loss for words. Was Arjan van Heemsvliet even killed during the war? Is that why the paintings disappeared, because he fled the country with them? But why would his granddaughter think he died in 1942? Could it have been a simple white lie told to comfort a child, Annette Schuppe letting her daughter believe her biological father was dead, instead of having to hear she was unwanted?

"Perhaps she has the wrong year," the archivist offered.

"Maybe." So many possibilities were running through Zelda's mind.

Wim fell silent, contemplating their options. Seconds later, he typed in a new search query. "Let's see if there's a death certificate in our archives. That may clarify things. Here's a link to it." Wim quickly read through the document before translating it for her. "It was applied for by his father, the Reverend Johannes van Heemsvliet, in October 1945. And no cause of death is listed."

"His father? I don't understand. Why would he have to apply for a death certificate for Arjan?"

"If his son was killed during the war but his body was not identified, then there would be no death certificate. Unfortunately, after the war ended, many parents and children had to file paperwork with the government to have their missing loved ones officially declared 'deceased,' if only to stop bills from coming in, to close businesses, or to pay off debts—that sort of thing. Otherwise no one else has the right to act on the missing person's behalf."

"How incredibly sad."

"This was truly a dire period for the Netherlands, and all of Europe really. I could tell you so many heartbreaking stories—" Wim stopped midsentence and turned back to his keyboard. "That gives me an idea."

Wim typed in Arjan's last known address, and another scanned-in document appeared. "This is an 'address card.' It lists all of the known occupants of a single address. According to this, a man named Gijs Mansveld also lived at Johannes Vermeerstraat 76 between March 1936 and February 1942."

"Gijs Mansveld; who could that be?" Zelda wondered out loud.

"Well, he's not Arjan's business partner. At least, there wasn't one listed on Van Heemsvliet's business application. If he'd added one later, his business license would have been amended automatically." The archivist leaned back in his chair, thinking. "Gijs Mansveld could have been his manservant or butler; a single man with a large residence would have needed several servants to keep his house clean and cook his meals. Having live-in staff was common in the 1930s."

Wim typed Gijs's name into the search engine and brought up his death certificate. "He died on February 24, 1942, of a bronchial infection."

The archivist switched back to the address card. "See that star? That means the house was occupied by a German officer, starting in September 1942. That was pretty common during the war. Mansions and other large homes were snatched up first, mostly by those holding a higher rank. Especially those in the Museumplein area. And Vermeerstraat is just around the corner from it."

He stared at the screen contemplating this new information. "German officers were known for frequently switching residences. They would trade up anytime a house became 'unoccupied,' mostly due to their Jewish owners being shipped off to concentration camps. Sometimes they didn't even wait until one was available. We've found instances of generals, colonels, and even majors in the SS ordering homes to be 'emptied' of their legal occupants simply because they wanted to live there."

"That's insane!" she exclaimed.

"That sort of abuse of power happened more often than you think," he replied grimly before tapping the screen once again. "Let's look up Arjan's parents. Before moving to Amsterdam in 1932, Arjan van Heemsvliet lived in Urk, the same town he was born in. The Urk city archives should have scanned in all of their family cards by now."

Wim opened a new browser window and began typing away. A few seconds later, he called out, "Found it."

Again he translated the Van Heemsvliet family card for Zelda. "He was indeed born in Urk in 1910, the oldest of three children, all boys. His parents were the Reverend Johannes van Heemsvliet and Meike Goes. Both deceased, in 1953 and 1948, respectively. Jacob, the middle brother, died in 1988. But the youngest brother, Gerard, is still alive and lives in Urk."

"That's good to know," she replied half-heartedly. "I guess we're finished with Van Heemsvliet. There's still Philip Verbeet. I know you couldn't find out much about his business, but could you show me his personal record card?"

"Coming up." Wim helped her translate the bits of information available, but after a few minutes of reading, it was clear there was nothing new to learn about Philip Verbeet in these archives. At least Zelda now knew that Rita's memory was perfectly fine; the names and dates she had given Bernice Dijkstra all matched up with the city's archival records.

"Well, Zelda, I guess that's it for now. If you come up with more search terms you want help looking up, give me a call."

"Okay, thanks. Could I get two copies of all the documents we've been looking at?"

"Of course. Ten cents a copy, the printouts will be waiting for you by the information desk in a few minutes." He turned to the screen and began printing off the records they'd viewed.

Zelda racked her brain, trying to figure out what she should do next. They'd gone through all of the names and keywords on Bernice and Huub's list, yet she still had no real leads to follow. And her research results seemed to raise more questions than provide answers. Why was there no record of Arjan's marriage to Annette Schuppe or the birth of their daughter? Who was Gijs Mansveld, and why was he living in Arjan's house?

If only she could talk to someone who knew Arjan, then she might gain some insight into the type of person and businessman he was. *Fat chance,* she thought, *everyone he knew or worked with is certainly dead or demented by now.* She frowned, before a glance at Van Heemsvliet's family card—still open on the computer screen—offered a ray of hope. Gerard van Heemsvliet, Arjan's youngest brother, was alive and in his late eighties. He might be able to remember something relevant about his brother, his gallery, or even Annette Schuppe. Right now, he was her only real lead. If she was going to impress Bernice tomorrow, she had no choice but to track Gerard down tonight. She glanced at the name of the town again.

"Excuse me, Wim, do you know how far Urk is from Amsterdam?"

22

Convoluted Lineage

"Tell me again why this is so important it couldn't wait until Saturday," Friedrich grumbled, as he deftly maneuvered through the thick evening traffic at full speed. The normal drive time from Amsterdam to Urk was an hour, but with her friend behind the wheel, Zelda figured they would make it in forty-five minutes. They were on the A6 freeway cutting across the reclaimed land of the Flevoland polder as it circled Lake IJssel. The countryside was dominated by cornfields, roaming livestock, and a smattering of young trees. The only two towns they passed through, Almere and Lelystad, were composed of ultramodern architecture rising out of the middle of nowhere.

She dug her nails deeper into the passenger seat and tried to ignore her friend's Indy-style driving by focusing on the landscape flying by her window. "I have that appointment with Bernice tomorrow afternoon. It's important I talk with Gerard beforehand, in case he has any information relevant to the museum's investigation. Even if Gerard was fifteen years younger than Arjan, I'm sure he'll be able to tell us something about his brother's wife and their daughter."

"But you weren't supposed to do any investigating yourself," Friedrich reminded her.

Zelda shrugged her shoulders. "If I'd found more records in the archives this week, then this trip wouldn't be necessary. It's still not clear what kind of business Arjan was running, when or if he married Annette Schuppe, why his daughter's birth wasn't recorded, or how he knew Philip Verbeet. Why did Rita's father sell all his paintings to Arjan, instead of any of the hundreds of other art dealers in Amsterdam? Especially after repeatedly telling his family he would never sell them, but was going to give them to a friend to store during the war."

She continued, "Then there's Gijs Mansveld; we still have no idea who he was or what he was doing living in Arjan's home all those years. Was he a manservant? Or a silent business partner? That would throw a wrench in Karen O'Neil's claim if he was." She was on a roll, thinking up more and more conspiracy theories as she went along. "And if Arjan was working for the Nazis, then her claim would be rejected completely. Maybe Gerard remembers something useful. Bernice will be proud of me for showing so much initiative."

"From what you've told me, that curator she works with won't. How many times did Huub Konijn remind you that you were only to photocopy relevant files and pass them along?"

Zelda ignored him, choosing instead to stare out the window at a passing wind farm. She could play it safe, turn in her pile of photocopies, and leave it at that. If the museum's professional researchers wanted to interview Gerard later, they could easily do so. But she couldn't bear to show up at tomorrow's meeting empty-handed. And so far, she was no closer to helping the museum verify one claim or the other than when she began three days ago.

The more she'd learned about Arjan van Heemsvliet, the more confused she'd become about the type of man he was. He seemed to be a generous philanthropist with a thriving art gallery, but she couldn't help but wonder whether his charity work wasn't a ploy to find discreet buyers and sellers for ill-gotten goods. If Gerard could provide any new information, it would give her a chance to shine. And if Bernice saw how hard she was working on this research project, she might ask Zelda to continue helping them with the investigation. If that didn't impress the museum studies program's selection committee, she didn't know what would.

Zelda prayed fervently that Gerard would let them into his home tonight. According to the route planner, they should be there by 7:15 p.m. Hopefully he'd still be awake when they arrived. Gerard was almost ninety years old, and she had no idea what sort of physical or mental state he was in. Maybe she should have called first, as Friedrich had repeatedly suggested, but she was afraid her Dutch would sound so jumbled on the phone that he wouldn't understand what she was trying to ask. As long as he could understand basic English, she should be able to explain herself properly. Most Dutch people could, but not all, and especially not the older generation. Before World War II, French and German were the languages Dutch children learned at school, not English. Zelda looked over at her speed-demon friend, glad he was willing to drive her to Urk at the last minute. Not only did he have a car, but he also spoke perfect Dutch and could always translate if necessary.

"Do you really think he'll remember anything useful?"

"That is a great question," she mumbled, knowing she shouldn't get her hopes up; Gerard was a teenager when his brother died. But she still wanted the painting to be Rita Brouwer's and hoped this meeting would provide her with a solid connection between Arjan and Philip Verbeet. Anything that could explain why Philip would have given the art dealer his collection could help Rita's case. If Gerard had never heard of Philip, then *Irises*—along with the rest of her father's collection—would undoubtedly go to Karen O'Neil.

The car's diminishing speed snapped her back to the here and now. They were entering the horseshoe-shaped village of Urk, its houses and shops built around the harbor that formed the heart of the small fishing community. She watched silently as Friedrich followed the GPS's directions, driving past the marina and onto a narrow street leading away from the water's edge. A few minutes later, he turned onto a cobblestone street and parked.

"Gerard's house should be around the corner," he said, before stepping out to feed the parking meter.

Zelda remained seated as a wave of uncertainty rolled over her. What was she doing here, intruding on this old man's life like this? His brother's death was probably a painful subject, and here she was dropping in and asking about it like a neighbor asking for a cup of sugar. Not to mention she was about to tell him he had a rich American great-niece. Did he even know Arjan had fathered a child? Or was that going to be a surprise, too?

Friedrich tapped on the passenger-side window. "Hey, Zelda, are you going to get out of the car, or are we just taking a tour of the Dutch countryside?"

Throwing open the door, she climbed out, mumbling "Let's do this" under her breath. She examined the first two house numbers they passed before pointing down the street. "His is number 29; it should be a bit farther up on the left."

They walked slowly, searching for Gerard's address in the early summer twilight. Two-story houses on tiny plots of land butted up against each other, most with well-groomed flower patches in front and small gardens around back. Through the manicured trees, Zelda could see couples drinking wine in the evening sun and, behind them, boats rocking gently in the village harbor. Bursts of laughter and catchy folk music rang out from open windows, and clouds of barbecue smoke scented the air.

Halfway down the street, she saw the number 29 partially hidden by a thick carpet of ivy climbing up the front wall of a small whitewashed house. She strode up the short walkway and rang the bell, Friedrich in tow.

As a series of chimes rang throughout the house, Friedrich moaned, "Why did I let you drag me into this?"

"Because you love me, that's why," she teased.

Friedrich's face reddened instantly, and he refused to meet her gaze. Zelda could feel herself going crimson as well. *I meant like a brother; why did I say that?* She'd never met anyone so open and honest as Friedrich before, and she really enjoyed his company. She didn't want to lose him as a friend, but she wished he would accept they would never be romantically involved. Before she could think up a witty comment to lighten the mood, footsteps became audible behind Gerard van Heemsvliet's front door.

"Yes? Who is there?" An older man's voice yelled out in Dutch as the porch light came on, momentarily blinding them. Through a small opening, the home's owner peered out at the strangers on his doorstep. After one look at the pair, he yelled, "*Aan de deur wordt niet gekocht!*" and slammed the peephole shut.

Zelda looked at her partner in crime, confused by the unexpected turn of events. "What did he say?"

Friedrich shrugged, saying, "He thinks we're trying to sell him something," as he knocked on the door again.

"Excuse me, sir," he called out in his most formal Dutch, "we aren't salespeople. We are here in connection with your brother Arjan. We have a few questions about his art gallery and family."

"Arjan is dead. Since the war," came the reply through the door, this time in English.

"Sir, please, I know this is a strange request, but we came all the way from Amsterdam to ask you about your brother's wife and child. Can you spare a few moments to listen to what we have to say? We promise not to stay long," Friedrich pleaded.

Gerard opened the peephole and took another long, hard look at the two strangers on his doorstep. A few seconds later, the lock turned, and he opened the door. "My hearing is not so good anymore. You'd better come inside," he said in slightly accented English.

Gerard van Heemsvliet had once been a tall man and perhaps even good looking, but time had not been on his side. His back was so curved he could barely tilt his head up high enough to look them in the eye. He leaned heavily on a thick wooden cane, his thin legs shaking under the weight of his large belly. Yet under a shock of white unkempt hair, his baby blue eyes were still clear, and his voice was strong.

Despite his poor physical condition, Zelda's heart skipped a beat. They were being let inside! "Thank you so much, sir. We just need a few minutes of your time. And might I say, your English is fantastic," she babbled as she and Friedrich followed the old man inside.

"Two decades of missionary work," he said dismissively. "Shall we sit here?" he asked, gesturing towards his living room. Friedrich and Zelda sat next to each other on the well-worn couch as their host slowly lowered himself into an easy chair.

The old man switched on a table lamp and examined his guests once more before asking, "What is this you say about my brother's wife and child? Is there something the matter with Ana or Abraham?"

"Ana or Abraham?" Zelda asked.

"My brother Jacob's wife and son. That is who you were asking about, correct?"

It took her a second to place the names. Jacob was the middle brother and had died of a stroke several years ago, leaving behind his wife and child. "No, we mean your oldest brother, Arjan. He ran an art gallery in Amsterdam."

Gerard shook his head. "There must be some mistake. He had no wife and certainly no child."

"How can you be so sure?" she asked.

The old man simply chuckled. "Tell me, why do you think these things?"

Zelda told him everything she knew about Karen O'Neil's grandmother and mother; how Annette Schuppe immigrated to New York City with their daughter, Isabelle, soon after the war ended, and how Karen came to know about Arjan van Heemsvliet's existence only a few months ago.

Gerard stared vacantly at the family photographs above his fireplace as she spoke. After she'd finished, he remained silent for a full minute before finally clearing his throat. "I have not yet offered you tea or coffee."

"A cup of coffee would be lovely, thanks," Zelda said, as Friedrich nodded in agreement.

As Gerard shuffled off to the kitchen, her friend whispered, "He really seems shocked to hear about Karen."

"Yeah, like he didn't even know Arjan's wife or child existed. But if his brother was expecting a baby, wouldn't he tell someone in his family about it?" she asked, just as the old man made his way back into the room, pushing a small trolley filled with cups, saucers, cookies, sugar, and milk.

"Take whatever you want," Gerard said as he sat back in his chair, watching his visitors fill their cups. After Friedrich and Zelda had both taken a sip, he asked, "This American claiming to be Arjan's grandchild; what proof does she have of her parentage?"

Zelda squirmed in her chair uncomfortably; she hadn't expected Karen's lineage to be an issue. "She told us your brother and her grandmother Annette were married on March 4, 1942, a few months before their daughter—her mother, Isabelle—was born. Are you certain no one in your family was invited to the wedding?"

"No, we were most certainly not. And that is what surprises me. If my brother was to marry a woman—especially if this woman was pregnant by him—I should think he would have told my father straightaway. He would have been welcomed back into the family, something my brother longed for." Gerard shook his head. "That is why I am so surprised to hear someone is claiming to be his offspring. What is her proof that my brother was her biological grandfather?"

"She has a number of your brother's business documents and ledgers."

"This makes no sense to me. She has documents that belonged to my brother? How did that woman get Arjan's things?" Gerard asked, visibly upset by all he was hearing.

"She said his wife, her grandmother Annette, took all the business documents she found in Arjan's study with her when she fled Amsterdam after he'd died," Zelda patiently explained. *Why was Gerard having so much trouble accepting that his brother had a wife and daughter?* she wondered.

"What was her name again?" he finally asked.

"Karen O'Neil is your niece."

"No, the woman my brother supposedly married."

"Oh, Annette Schuppe."

"That name means nothing to me."

"What about Philip Verbeet? Does that name ring any bells?" she asked, hoping against hope that he did.

Gerard's forehead creased in concentration. "I don't think so. Who was he?"

"He was a frame maker and perhaps a business acquaintance or friend of your brother's. We're still not sure how they knew each other, or even if they knew each other."

"I was never interested in art, and Arjan knew that. He didn't talk about his business or clients much in his letters."

Zelda's face fell. If Gerard didn't know anything about his brother's gallery or business dealings, then this was a wasted trip. Even the news that he had an American niece seemed to have backfired; the old man seemed determined not to accept her as his own flesh and blood. She wondered what Arjan had done to make their father mad enough to disown him, but she didn't dare ask Gerard straight out, afraid to offend her guest even more.

Instead, she blurted out, "Maybe your brother never said anything because he was afraid your father wouldn't approve of the bride, or the fact that she was pregnant. Perhaps if Arjan had lived longer he would have introduced you to them."

Gerard slowly shook his head. "The sin of premarital sex was much less offensive than what my brother had done to shame our family name. Our father would have gladly forgiven Arjan for getting a woman pregnant, especially if they were to be wed. Tell me, what does this woman want exactly? Just the one painting you'd mentioned earlier, *Irises?*"

"Well, no, she's claiming a long list of artwork, all of it much more valuable than this one piece. The Wederstein is the first painting she's found, though she does have a team of private investigators searching for the rest. Your brother possessed a valuable collection when he died in that bombing raid."

"Bombing raid? That's the first I've heard of that." Gerard's face clouded over. "We never knew how he died, only that he had been on the missing-persons list since August 1, 1942. A few months after the war ended, my father had him declared legally dead so he could close Galerie Van Heemsvliet and settle the business's outstanding debts. I'm not sure how much money our father had to pay, but I do remember him complaining about how many debtors Arjan had. When we went to Amsterdam in the fall of 1945 to collect my brother's things, his gallery had been turned into a café and his house stripped clean. If Arjan had left any artwork or other possessions behind, it had all been taken long before we got there."

Gerard looked off into the distance, shaking his head softly. "Perhaps Arjan did marry and father a child without telling us. It seems so unlikely given my brother's past. We all change, I suppose." With a loud grunt, Gerard pushed himself forward so he could reach the coffee pot and poured himself a cup. Once he'd gotten comfortable again, he said, "After Arjan moved to Amsterdam in 1932, I never saw him again. Other than the occasional letter, we had almost no contact. He never came back to Urk; it was too painful for him, the thought of running into our father or family friends on the street."

Zelda's curiosity finally overcame her politeness. "What did your brother do to offend your parents so deeply?"

Gerard stared at his wedding photograph as he took a long sip of coffee. Only after he set the cup back down did he respond. "My father was a reverend in our village. I attended seminary school, then worked in missions around the world until I met my wife. After we married, we moved back to Urk, to this house. When my father retired, I took over his church."

The old man paused again, choosing his words carefully. "I am very surprised to hear about this Karen O'Neil because of why my brother was banished from our family. Arjan was my oldest brother, fifteen years older in fact. When he was twenty-one, he was arrested for having sex with a man in a park close to our house. It was a known cruising spot for homosexuals, and the police raided it one night, arresting everyone they found."

"When one of the officers told my father what had happened, he went to the jailhouse and confronted my brother. I suppose he expected Arjan to deny it as lies. But my brother said it was true, he was attracted to men, not women. My father told Arjan that he was dead to him and to the rest of our family. He stormed out of the jail and had my brother's things boxed up and sent to the police station that same night. It broke my mother's heart, but there was nothing she could say or do to change his mind. Back then, homosexuality—or at least sodomy—wasn't only illegal; it was also socially unacceptable, especially in religious circles. Because my father was a respected religious leader in our community, he couldn't have anything to do with his homosexual son, at least not without offending most of his parishioners. And without the church, my father's life would have been meaningless."

Zelda couldn't believe her ears. Arjan was gay! Karen O'Neil couldn't be his granddaughter, which meant Rita's claim was still in play. Her exuberance rapidly dissipated as new questions formed in her mind. If

Arjan was homosexual, would Gerard have a claim on his gallery's artwork, as next of kin? Who was Karen O'Neil really, and why was she trying to get her hands on the Wederstein? Zelda was so lost in her own thoughts that she barely noticed Gerard had started speaking again.

"After Arjan paid a fine, he was released from jail. Two days later, he moved to Amsterdam. He'd always had an eye for art and a knack for selling things. Opening a gallery was perfect for him."

"But Holland is so progressive," she murmured, knowing full well that despite the country's open attitude towards homosexuals, even in liberal Amsterdam, some people had difficulty being tolerant and accepting of any lifestyle other than a traditional conservative one.

Gerard snorted. "In the 1930s, homosexuality was something to be ashamed of, at least in the smaller towns and communities like the one we grew up in. I am not asking you to agree, just to accept that is how it was."

Zelda dared only to nod in agreement.

"If Arjan did take a wife and have a child, he would not have been the first gay man to do so, especially back then. There was so much social pressure to conform," he speculated. "But I cannot believe he would have gotten engaged and not told our mother, even if it was a ruse. We still did receive an occasional letter from him. But he never mentioned a woman in his life. On the contrary, Arjan was quite open about the fact his male lover lived with him for the last several years of his life. I'm sure his name is in the letters."

"Is it Gijs Mansveld?" she asked.

"I am sorry, I really don't remember. It's been too many years since I've read them." Gerard used his cane to push himself out of his easy chair once again. "But they may be of use to your investigation. Let me get them for you." The old man gradually made his way upstairs, his body creaking almost as much as the staircase.

Friedrich and Zelda sat in stunned silence for a moment before she blurted out, "I told you there was something fishy about Karen O'Neil. If the art dealer was a homosexual, then she's a fake."

131

"Don't get too excited yet. Maybe Arjan had a fling with Karen's grandmother to get back in the good graces of his family, but died before he could spread the news," he replied.

"Come on, she's lying. I've felt it since day one."

"Then why does she have Arjan's inventory ledgers and other documents? Gerard was just a boy when the war started. Maybe something else happened between Arjan and his father, something his parents didn't want Gerard finding out about, so they made up a story about him being homosexual?"

Before Zelda could respond, the old man came lumbering back down the stairs with a dusty shoebox in his hands. After sitting down, he balanced the box on his knees. "There is another reason I do not believe my brother married or fathered a child. A few months before he disappeared, Arjan started writing much more often than he ever had before. He was scared and felt someone needed to know what was going on, in case something happened to him, but he didn't know who to turn to. We'd been close when he'd lived at home, closer than he was to Jacob in any case."

Gerard drew in his breath as if he was trying to suck up enough energy to carry on. "Arjan was being blackmailed by a colonel in the SS who'd recognized him leaving a nightclub for homosexuals. The Nazi knew Arjan was an art dealer and wanted paintings—lots of them—in return for his silence. Otherwise he would turn my brother over to the Gestapo. Who knows what would have happened to Arjan if he'd been arrested—forced castration, hard labor, concentration camp?"

Zelda could feel her jaw dropping. If Arjan was being blackmailed because he was gay, then Karen's lawyer had some explaining to do.

"My brother didn't see any other way out but to give the Nazi what he wanted. I counselled him to flee, leave all of his things behind and use his connections to get to the South of France. There he could get passage on a ship to America. The blackmailer would never be satisfied, he would always want more than my brother could give him. But Arjan refused. He wanted to stay in Amsterdam for as long as possible. He'd worked hard to build up his gallery and had seen firsthand how other shops were gutted as soon as their owners fled. Besides, no one thought the war would last as long as it

132

did.

"In one of his last letters, he seemed to realize he had to leave the Netherlands, only he was having difficulty taking the first steps. He didn't know what to do with his gallery or artwork; there was no one left in Amsterdam he could entrust it to. Maybe marrying this Karen O'Neil's grandmother was part of his plan to stay in the city. I honestly do not know. If Arjan was married and about to become a father, that would deny the Nazi his leverage over my brother, forcing him to stop the blackmail. So far as I can remember, Arjan never mentioned such a scheme, but it's been many years since I've read through all of his letters." Gerard patted the box gently. "It's possible there's something in here that will help you discover the truth."

Zelda couldn't believe her eyes or ears—Gerard was giving them their first real lead and documentation to support it, exactly what she'd yearned for. Bernice Dijkstra was going to be so proud of her.

"If this Karen O'Neil really is his granddaughter, I should like to meet her," he added shyly.

Confronted with the old man's genuine emotion, Zelda felt ashamed for hoping the New Yorker was a fraud. She took Gerard's hand. "I will tell her about you. Thank you for everything. I will make sure these letters are read and you're kept informed."

23

Breaking The Trust

March 22, 1942

Arjan downed his double vodka in one gulp. He was not accustomed to drinking hard liquor; the booze burned his esophagus and stung his stomach. Somehow it felt right, though. He deserved to feel pain. He'd always been so careful, ever since his arrest in Urk all those years ago. *How could I be so weak?* he wondered for the thousandth time. All of those friends who'd entrusted their most precious possessions to him, and he had let them down for one night of companionship.

I thought I was being clever, sneaking out of Grote Geerts through the back door while the Nazis were breaking down the front, Arjan thought. Until I tripped over that stupid dog's leash as it was relieving itself against a tree stump at the end of the alleyway. If only I'd left a few seconds sooner—or that little bitch had urinated a block earlier—how different my life would be, he howled silently, forcing himself to relive the events of the previous night.

He looked to the mantelpiece and gazed lovingly at the largest photograph he had of Gijs, already gone a month. How he missed his lover's perfect chin, gentle manners, soft caresses, and listening ear. They had been together a decade, and without him, Arjan felt helpless and off-kilter.

If only their real friends—those few he and Gijs could be their true selves with, who knew about and accepted their relationship—were still in Amsterdam, he never would have ended up in this predicament. Those trusted few had already left the city, fleeing when the Nazis began raiding gay bars and arresting anyone who was on the Amsterdam police books as a "known homosexual." Especially once it became clear that even the rumor someone was gay was enough reason for the Gestapo to knock on their door.

He and Gijs had kept their relationship secret since their courtship began eleven years ago, knowing most of Dutch society didn't approve and would avoid his gallery if they were open about it. Gijs only moved into his mansion after Arjan had gone through the charade of advertising for and then interviewing several potential live-in manservants, before officially offering his boyfriend the position.

"Oh Gijs," Arjan cried, no longer able to look the framed photograph in the eye, "if only you were still here, I never would have been so foolish. I just wanted to talk to someone without having to worry if every gesture or choice of words gave my sexual preference away."

Arjan sunk deeper into the wingback chair and stared at the hearth, his only reliable source of heating. The fire was already in need of more fuel. He'd soon have to start burning the old frames and broken furniture stored up in his attic. Hopefully it would be enough to get him through this savagely cold winter; true firewood was almost impossible to come by these days. Most of the trees lining the city's canals and parks had been chopped down branch by branch before the snow began. He briefly contemplated what he should throw on the fire first, before giving up and pouring himself another shot. As the booze rolled down his throat, he closed his eyes and began to speak aloud. Sitting like this, it felt as if he was telling Gijs about his day, the day the blackmail began.

"With trepidation I unlocked the gallery door this morning, still unsure whether I should flee or act normally. Of course I couldn't leave all the artwork behind; too many people are relying on me to be cautious and survive the war. What other choice did I have than to open up shop? The minutes dragged into hours, but no one came crashing through my windowsill. No police sirens disturbed the drone of the shoppers shuffling up and down my street. Only as I turned the sign from 'open' to 'closed' did I notice a man across the street, watching me. A fedora and scarf covered up most of his face, but that hawk nose was unmistakable."

"Gijs, I knew in an instant it was the man with the dog. I've seen him in the newspapers, photographed while speaking at those horrid National Socialist rallies held throughout the city. He'd even been inside my shop a few months earlier, insulting me with demands he be given an exorbitant discount on a Van Ruysdael because he was a high-ranking SS officer within the Reich Culture Chamber—Colonel Oswald Drechsler."

24

CSI: Amsterdam

"Ms. O'Neil asked to be kept up-to-date on the research we are doing into her claim," Bernice Dijkstra said, as a way of explaining to Zelda why her progress report was being witnessed by Karen and her lawyer. "And I promised the director she would be, at least for the time being," the project manager added gruffly, glaring at the claimant as she spoke. New York's richest widow smiled sweetly back.

Zelda was sure Ms. O'Neil hadn't asked but demanded to be included in this meeting. Why hadn't Bernice warned her first? She was nervous enough about presenting her more controversial findings to her and Huub, let alone Karen and her nitpicky lawyer. Her original plan was to tell them about Arjan van Heemsvliet being gay first, but she hesitated in light of these unexpected guests. Besides, her initial excitement was tempered by the fact she'd grossly overstepped her bounds. By going to Gerard's house and talking with him, she'd acted in direct subordination of the curator's specific orders. She only hoped Bernice would understand that she had done it for the museum, to save them time and possibly their honor, no matter what Huub's—or Karen's—reaction might be.

Before she could begin, Bernice's secretary walked into the conference room and handed her boss a large stack of photocopies.

"Thank you, Susan." Always the consummate project manager, Bernice immediately handed Huub, Karen, and Konrad Heider a thick packet of paper.

"Here are copies of all the documents Zelda has found this week. Before we read through them, perhaps she could share with us some of the highlights of her research?" She nodded in her intern's direction, encouraging her to speak.

Deciding to keep her surprises for the end, Zelda began with her search through the national newspaper archives, recounting what she had found out about the growing success of Galerie Van Heemsvliet, the many charities Arjan supported and the gala events he attended.

"Though I could not find any concrete information about the types of buyers and sellers he worked with before or during the war in Amsterdam's city archives, the archivist did confirm that Arjan is not considered a war profiteer, meaning there has been no documentation found that proves he traded or sold illegally acquired artwork to the Nazis or their sympathizers. They have a whole list of art dealers who were known profiteers; it's kind of scary how many did try to—"

"I knew it," Karen O'Neil squealed with glee. "My grandfather was a respectable, successful art dealer."

"The archivist did add that since Arjan was listed as missing in 1942, he and his business practices have never been fully investigated, as many of his colleagues' were. So his name not being on the city's list of known profiteers does not necessarily mean he didn't buy from, or sell to, the Nazis," Zelda swiftly added.

Karen's eyes narrowed as she pursed her lips. Before she could retort, Bernice asked brusquely, "And further, Zelda? Did you find any possible connection between Arjan van Heemsvliet and Philip Verbeet?"

"No, unfortunately not. None of their business records have been donated to any Dutch archives—"

"That's because whatever documents my grandmother didn't take with her were most certainly stolen by the SS, along with all of my grandfather's artwork when they looted his gallery," Karen butted in.

"So no, I couldn't find anything linking them privately or professionally. Maybe when Rita finds her father's letters—"

"Yes, yes, let's see if she can even find them first before we speculate further. Anything else?" Bernice cut in abruptly. She was acting as if she wanted to adjourn the meeting already.

Zelda took a deep breath; it was now or never. "The archivist in the Amsterdam city archives was quite helpful, as you said he would be. He found a few interesting records in other provincial and national archives, ones you didn't specifically ask for but are related to your keywords. I thought they might be relevant to this investigation so I printed off copies of them as well," Zelda said, making clear these documents were the results of the archivist's initiative.

Huub looked up at her quizzically. "And what exactly did this archivist find?"

"Well, for starters, he found Arjan's death certificate." Zelda's eyes automatically flickered over to Karen, who was still more interested in her mauve nail polish than what she was saying. Konrad Heider, however, did sit up a bit straighter in his chair.

"According to the official death certificate, Arjan was reported as missing on August 1, 1942, but only declared legally deceased in October of 1945 at the request of his father, the Reverend Johannes van Heemsvliet."

"Not by his wife?" Bernice asked, surprise in her voice.

"No, it was definitely his father," Zelda said, while rummaging through the photocopies before her. She stopped halfway through the pile. "It's this one; see the signature?"

"My grandmother was fleeing for her life! She'd have had no time for paperwork. Besides, it was the Dutch police who told her Arjan was killed in a bombing raid and that his gallery had been plundered by the Nazis."

"Until Arjan had been officially declared deceased, she would not have had the right to take care of his business affairs," Bernice commented, clearly baffled by Zelda's findings and Karen's reaction.

"But why would she want to? She married Robert Kershaw a few months after landing in America. He was one of the richest men in New York City; why would she have wanted to bother with an art gallery in Amsterdam? Especially as she'd told no one that Arjan was my mother's biological father.

Kershaw couldn't have children. He raised my mother as his own flesh and blood."

"But she took his business papers with her," Bernice hounded.

"She took a lot of paperwork with her when she fled Amsterdam. You've seen some of it—that which is relevant to our claim," Karen retorted. "The rest have nothing to do with this painting."

"Wait a moment, there's no cause of death listed on this certificate," Huub said, tapping his pen against one of the documents now spread out before him on the conference room table.

"That's right," Zelda replied, watching Karen as she spoke. "According to the city's archives, no bombing raids took place in 1942, at least not in Amsterdam or the direct vicinity."

"I never said he was killed in Amsterdam. All my mother said was 'a bombing raid'—it could have been anywhere in the Netherlands. She was dying when she told me; I didn't really have the opportunity to ask her lots of questions. My grandfather was an art dealer; I'm sure he would have traveled all over the country to meet potential buyers and sellers," Karen protested.

"What else have you found out, Zelda?" Bernice asked, while intently studying the New Yorker.

"More like what I couldn't find. There's no record of Arjan being married or having fathered a child, not in Amsterdam's city archives, or any other Dutch archive for that matter."

"We tried to obtain notarized copies of these documents before coming to meet with you," Konrad Heider said, smoothly jumping into the conversation. "Their marriage and the birth of their daughter, Isabelle, took place in Alphen aan den Rijn, at Annette Schuppe's family home. Unfortunately, their city's archives burned down in 1980, long before digitizing records was in fashion." Turning to Zelda, he added, "You should have asked us first; it would have saved you some time."

"It was no trouble." She smiled back serenely.

"And no, there were no copies of either document among my grandmother's papers," Karen said.

The project manager frowned. "That is troubling. It would have been the quickest way of verifying your parentage. The Restitutions Committee will certainly require that," she said, locking eyes with Huub, daring him to contradict her. "Perhaps Van Heemsvliet's name is listed on your mother's application for her American passport? Otherwise family photographs, personal letters, anything that connects your grandmother and mother to him will be necessary. Or we can try DNA testing."

"DNA testing? Are you serious? What is this, *CSI: Amsterdam?*" Karen laughed.

Her lawyer interjected, "Her mother's passport application is a good starting point; I will have our New York office look into this matter immediately. Finding documents to substantiate Ms. O'Neil's ancestry should not pose a problem, but it will require more time. We had not expected her mother's birth certificate to be necessary, in light of the substantial documentation we have already provided," he chastised.

Bernice looked to Zelda. "Anything else you want to share?"

"There was one more thing…" Zelda said hesitantly.

Karen let out a sigh of frustration, muttering, "For the love of God…"

Words sputtered out of Zelda's mouth as she tried to figure out where to begin. "I, um, didn't make copies of all of the documents I found this week. Last night, when I met with Gerard van Heemsvliet, he showed me a box of—"

Huub held up a finger. "Excuse me, you *met* with Gerard van Heemsvliet? Who is he exactly?"

Zelda held up Arjan's personal record card. "He is Arjan's youngest brother. I found his name and address at the Amsterdam City Archives yesterday and thought he might know more about Galerie Van Heemsvliet." She rushed to get her words out, hoping Huub wouldn't explode before she could tell the group about her discoveries.

The curator's eyes glowed in anger as he growled, "We'll discuss your specific assignment later. What did he have to say?"

"He didn't tell me anything new about the gallery or his brother's business practices, but he does have a shoebox full of letters Arjan sent him during the war."

All four looked up at Zelda with intense interest.

"I didn't have time to read them last night, but Gerard remembered quite a bit about what Arjan had written to him about his, um, personal life."

Without knowing exactly how to phrase it, she blurted out, "Gerard said Arjan was gay, one hundred percent homosexual, and the letters prove it."

"Gay? Please! Your little research trip has turned into a witch hunt, hasn't it?" Karen yelled. "I've had enough of this farce and your absurd accusations." The New Yorker directed her fury at Huub and Bernice. "I come to you in good faith with conclusive documents proving I am the legitimate owner of a piece of artwork stolen from my grandfather by the Nazis, and yet you treat me as if I'm on trial! Your intern has got a lot of nerve, insulting me and my family like this," Karen hissed in Zelda's direction. "And why is she investigating me, anyway? I thought she was supposed to be reconstructing *Irises'* provenance, not researching my family history."

"I assure you, this was not our intention. We had given Zelda a specific list of names and keywords to search for, and none were related to your ancestry," Huub said while glaring at the intern.

"Maybe they should have been," Bernice mumbled under her breath.

Karen waved her off. "Birth certificates, marriage licenses, you're just wasting my time."

"If I may," Konrad Heider interjected. "Just because someone was engaging in homosexual activities does not mean he did not also have a wife and child. In the early 1900s, it was quite common for homosexual men to marry and have families as a way of conforming to societal pressure and hiding their true identity. And once Adolf Hitler came to power, it became a matter of life or death—homosexuality was not tolerated by the Third Reich. I must again stress that my client and her ancestors are not on trial here. She has substantial, well-documented proof of her family's claim on this painting and the rest of Van Heemsvliet's collection."

"Gerard said Arjan had lived with his male lover for the last few years of his life. Besides, if he wasn't a homosexual, why was a Nazi colonel blackmailing him for artwork?" Zelda replied.

"What are you talking about?" Bernice snapped.

"Arjan wrote to Gerard about a colonel in the SS who had discovered he was gay. The Nazi threatened to turn him over to the Gestapo unless he gave him several oil paintings hanging in Galerie Van Heemsvliet. Arjan didn't know what to do and had no one else to turn to for advice."

"Are you absolutely certain?" Bernice asked.

"That's what Gerard said. It's all in the letters…"

"Which you have not read," Huub finished her sentence for her.

"True, but why would he lie?"

"To get his hands on what's rightfully mine, that's why!" Karen screeched. "If Arjan had no offspring, then he would inherit all of my grandfather's paintings. The nerve of that man!"

"Where are these letters now?" Karen's lawyer quietly asked.

"Gerard still has them, a whole shoebox full. I told him a researcher from the museum would be coming around to collect them later," Zelda quickly lied, not wanting to get into more hot water with Bernice and Huub. In actuality the letters were in her backpack, now resting against her leg. Considering Huub's reaction, it would be better to return them to Gerard and let the researchers pick them up in Urk. If she gave them to Bernice now, Huub would probably accuse her of tampering with them. Besides, she doubted he would let her near them again. Keeping them an extra day would allow her time to photocopy them all. Who knew, perhaps Arjan had written about Philip Verbeet or included other information that would be helpful to Rita's claim.

After she'd copied them, she would have to beg Friedrich to drive her back up to Gerard's as soon as possible. He'd probably be able to find time to take her to Urk if she promised to give him some gas money and buy him a nice lunch.

"Well, Zelda, you have exceeded our expectations," Bernice said, rather grimly.

Zelda wanted to weep. She'd envisioned a short round of applause or at least murmurs of approval once her findings were revealed, yet Bernice was acting as if she'd only caused them more headaches. Nothing about this meeting had gone as she'd expected.

"Your results have proven to me that we must investigate both claims fully. Ms. O'Neil, neither Huub, myself, nor the director can recommend you be awarded the title to *Irises* before our research team has first had a chance to do their jobs. From what Zelda has told us today, I would not be surprised if Gerard van Heemsvliet also wants to submit a claim on his brother's paintings."

Huub groaned as Karen sprung out of her chair. "This is absurd!" she shouted. "Despite all her unfounded accusations, I've heard nothing in Zelda's report that contradicts my claim."

"At the very least, our researchers will need to read Arjan's letters. Who knows what kind of information we'll find? He may have mentioned your grandmother or mother in them, which would help verify your parentage and claim. But we have to insist the investigation be done properly."

"Preposterous! You're only wasting time—yours and ours. *Irises* and the rest of my grandfather's collection are my property. We'll see what your newspaper and television reporters think of how you're treating the rightful heir to artwork stolen by Hitler's goons." Karen grabbed her purse and stormed out of the room.

Her lawyer jumped up to follow, pausing in the doorframe to add, "We will be taking this matter up with your director."

Bernice sighed as he slammed the door shut. "Let them go running to Leo. He won't want to give the Wederstein to anyone either, not before we've had the chance to sort this mess out. At least now we can tell the board of directors we have valid reasons for wanting to see the claims process through to the end. This Nazi blackmailer, Gerard's possible claim on the paintings, and Karen's ancestry—there are too many unknowns to make a definitive decision."

"Why are you doing this, Bernice? What about the media's reaction to Karen's story? All of our reputations will be tarnished beyond repair once the newspapers get a hold of it."

"I don't think so, Huub. Until Karen has found clear proof of her lineage, I don't think she would dare contact the press."

"What if she does? First we present Rita Brouwer as the legal owner of *Irises* without verifying her story. Then, when Karen O'Neil brings documents that do verify her claim on the work, we treat her like a pariah. There could be a major backlash for all the museums and institutions involved if our ineptitude becomes public knowledge. Funding could be stopped, future exhibitions could become uncertain, people could lose their jobs. And for what? So you can have more time to prove what we already know, that the paintings in that inventory book belong to Karen O'Neil? She was right, you know—whatever Zelda may have found out about Arjan van Heemsvliet's sexuality, it does not change the fact that she has his inventory books and a bill of sale. That's all that really matters to the Restitutions Committee."

"Is it? Let's pretend for a moment that he was gay and being blackmailed for artwork because of it. If he'd married or fathered a child, surely the blackmail would have stopped."

"But why would Karen's mother lie to her? She has Arjan's inventory books, Bernice. How else would she have gotten ahold of them, if not from her grandmother?"

"I don't know, but I would like to try to find out before we give the painting to the wrong claimant. If Arjan did not father a child, then his brother Gerard is most likely the rightful owner. Don't you think we should talk with him first and read the letters his brother sent him, before making another rash decision?"

He nodded begrudgingly. "Okay. Our researchers can make Gerard their first priority. We don't know what kind of person he is or what Arjan actually wrote. For all we know, they didn't get along and he's made up this story about Arjan being gay as a sort of revenge."

"Then why would he tell Zelda about the letters in the first place? Until we can talk with him at length, there's no point in continuing this conversation."

The project manager suddenly turned to her intern, as if she'd just remembered she was still sitting at the table. "Thank you for helping us out of a bind, Zelda. You really have dug up some interesting information and in only a few days."

"I would be happy to keep investigating Arjan's background if you want. I know the professional researchers are still on vacation for another week."

"You've done enough already," the curator barked. "Bernice and I were very clear in our instructions. Why did you go to Gerard's home? He should have been interviewed by professionals who know what kinds of questions to ask and have the equipment to record it properly. Because you didn't videotape your interview, we have no way of knowing if your questions were leading or what he actually said. We only know what you say he told you."

Zelda's lower lip began to quiver. Bernice attempted to soothe her. "What Huub is trying to say is that it would have been better if you had brought Gerard's existence to our attention and left it at that. Aside from that mistake, you have done a great job this week. I will be sure to tell Marianne that you've got a knack for doing this kind of research."

"Thanks," Zelda mumbled gloomily, before hastily adding, "That would be great," remembering that the research she'd done this past week would impress the university's selection committee far more than her copy editing skills.

The curator looked as if he wanted to say something nasty, but Bernice cut in first. "Now, if you don't mind, Huub and I have much to discuss before we meet with the director. Again, we all appreciate your hard work. Good luck with the selection committee; I'm sure you'll do fine." The project manager smiled warmly at her as she pushed her chair back from the table.

There was so much more Zelda wanted to say and do. Instead, she bit her lip and silently followed Bernice to the door.

25

Change Of Plan

It should have been so simple, claiming an insignificant painting created by an artist no one had ever heard of. But what a nightmare this was turning out to be. In hindsight, he should have stolen *Irises* straightaway and not bothered trying to claim it legally. And now that stupid intern was accusing Karen of all sorts of things. How much longer before the project manager or her researchers figured out the truth: that Karen O'Neil was most definitely not the granddaughter of Arjan van Heemsvliet?

Today's meetings proved that all of his efforts were for naught. Considering the intense scrutiny Karen's claim would be receiving from specialists and researchers, it was extremely unlikely his fake documents would pass their scrutiny. He had no other choice but to steal *Irises*, yet in a way that couldn't be linked back to either Karen or himself. Once Bernice presented Leo de Boer with the documents and information Zelda had found, Karen would certainly lose her preferential status at the museum and with it her instant access to the Wederstein. *Irises* would be back in the museum's long-term storage facilities by the end of the week. The furrow in Konrad Heider's brow deepened as he wondered whether any thief he knew could get the job done on such short notice, and how exorbitant their fee would be.

Unfortunately, that nosy intern had created another, more pressing problem, one he would have to deal with personally. After picking up his notes from their meeting with Bernice Dijkstra and Huub Konijn, he reread the passages he'd highlighted only moments ago. Gerard van Heemsvliet. Had his brother Arjan really written to him about being blackmailed? Worse yet, had he named his Nazi blackmailer?

It was of the utmost importance that Gerard be silenced and the letters destroyed. Without them, the museum would never find out the truth. It would be the intern's word against Karen's. That girl Zelda wasn't even a native Dutch speaker; it would be easy enough to argue she had misunderstood Gerard or the content of Arjan's letters. He was not proud of what he had to do. But after all these years of searching, in light of all he and his uncle had sacrificed, causing the death of an elderly man was easy enough to live with.

26

The Parakeets Of Vondelpark

"Look out!"

Zelda, lost in thought, registered the warning only seconds before a tiny winged thing buzzed alongside her head, practically scratching her cheek with its minuscule blades. "Damn it, Friedrich! You know I hate it when you do that," she shouted, swatting at her friend's latest acquisition with her backpack.

"Hey, stop that!" he yelled, landing his plane before she could knock it out of the sky. "I really didn't mean to get that close to your head. I guess I still haven't gotten the controls synced up right," Friedrich admitted sheepishly while cradling his remote-controlled craft like a newborn. Zelda scowled at him before doing a double take. His new toy was definitely not like any of his other planes. Its six-inch-long hull was shaped like a helicopter, but instead of having one rotor on top, thin blades were mounted on four arms extending out from its base, forming a deadly square when airborne.

"What is that?" Zelda asked.

"An AR.Drone 2.0 quadrocopter," Friedrich responded proudly. "I finally splurged and bought one. It maneuvers better than any of my other helicopters, or it should once I get the hang of it."

"Cool." She stretched out on the lush grass, happy he was willing to meet in Vondelpark today instead of Museumplein. He'd already set himself up towards the back of a small open field, his backpack resting against

Pablo Picasso's *Figure découpée l'Oiseau*. To Zelda, the six-foot-tall concrete statue—donated to the city by the great artist himself in 1965—looked like a large bird about to land on the same grass she was now sitting on.

The ground around them was littered with winged samara nuts that twirled to the earth like whirligigs when a strong wind blew through a small grove of maple trees growing a few feet behind them. From their position, Friedrich had thirty feet of open airspace to fly around in. All he had to do was watch out for the picnics and barbecues spread out on the grass below.

She smiled as she watched tourists and locals throwing Frisbees, kicking balls, and roasting meat while basking in the sunshine. Plumes of gray smoke and the smell of marinade filled the air. On sunny days like today, she could easily believe Vondelpark received ten million visitors a year, as Amsterdam's tourist office asserted. The hundred-and-twenty-acre park was always busy. Another reason why Friedrich preferred the relative quiet of Museumplein to fly his remote-controlled planes—less chance of hitting someone.

"How are you doing today?" he cautiously probed.

"I don't know, to be honest. I'm glad Karen's going to have to go through the whole claims process. But I don't think either Bernice or Huub are going to give Rita's claim a second glance, especially with Gerard in the picture." Zelda knew she should be satisfied knowing she'd thwarted Karen's hopes of quickly claiming *Irises*, but she still couldn't get Rita Brouwer out of her mind. She was the one who truly cared about the painting, not Karen O'Neil or Gerard van Heemsvliet. But even if Arjan's letters proved the New Yorker was a fraud—and Zelda had to admit it was a long shot—Rita would be no closer to claiming her painting than she was a week ago; Arjan's brother would inherit the lot.

"She emailed me again last night."

"Who?"

"Rita Brouwer. Her nephew scanned in five of the letters her dad sent her mother when they were in Venlo. They were heartbreaking to read; Philip Verbeet obviously loved his family. I can't believe he would have taken the money and started a new life somewhere else, like Huub seems to think."

Zelda paused momentarily, almost tearing up as she remembered the tender words Philip had written to his wife and children.

She cleared her throat and changed the subject to keep her emotions in check. "I don't think they're going to help her claim, though. In one he does write that he's found the perfect place to store them, just as Rita said. But he doesn't mention any names, and he never explains where he got the ten thousand guldens from. However, she did stumble upon another letter that might prove her father knew Arjan van Heemsvliet, at least casually."

"What do you mean?"

"Her mother had written to several friends and acquaintances after the war, asking if her father had stayed with them during the summer of 1942 or stored any art or supplies with them. Rita found the letter her mom mailed to Arjan van Heemsvliet, only because it had been returned as undeliverable. It's not much, but it does indicate the two families knew each other."

A whoosh of wings and screeching calls drowned out Friedrich's answer as a flock of ring-necked parakeets passed low over the picnicking public. Amsterdam was home to more than two thousand of these small green parakeets, presumably the result of captive birds being released into this very park in the 1970s. To Zelda, their presence was just one of the many unexpected delights of living here. She shielded her eyes with one hand to get a better look, admiring their fluorescent green color offset by orange beaks and the light rings of blue and pink circling their throats like necklaces.

"That letter's existence, the one Rita's mom sent to Van Heemsvliet after the war, means there's still a chance her father asked Arjan to store his artwork for him, as a favor for a friend," Zelda persisted, as soon as the birds had flown off and they could hear each other again. "It was addressed to his home so they must have known each other."

Friedrich shook his head, "Not necessarily. Rita's father probably worked with gallery owners all over the city at one time or another. If I was Karen's lawyer, I'd argue that Rita's mom took a shot in the dark and mailed every art dealer in Amsterdam."

Zelda pursed her lips, frustrated that he refused to agree with her. "There is one upside to her email. Rita still wants to pay me to find the rest of her father's art, or at least do my best."

"That's generous of her, especially considering the chance of you finding anything is virtually nil. And even if you do, it all belongs to Karen O'Neil anyway."

"*Irises* surfaced, didn't it?" she snapped, becoming as irritated with Friedrich as she was with the whole situation. "It's not fair to Rita or her sisters; they deserve those paintings so much more than Karen. I wish I could find out what her real motive is. It can't just be precedent; her lawyer's pushing way too hard for it to be that."

"That's what he's paid to do, isn't it?"

Her shoulders slumped. "Yeah, I guess. I just don't get why Karen's so hell bent on getting her hands on Iris's portrait right away. It doesn't make sense. Why can't she wait for the state secretary to award her the title? Her lawyer doesn't seem to think Gerard can hinder their claim. It's not like she's going to hang *Irises* in one of her many residences; it's not important enough."

"We've been through all of this before: power, control, precedent, boredom; who knows why Karen wants *Irises* so badly? And more importantly, why do you care? As far as you're concerned, the case is closed. The professional researchers have taken over, or will soon at any rate."

She knew Friedrich thought she should leave the claims on *Irises* alone and focus on her own future. In three weeks she had her appointment with the selection committee; that was where her head should be. But she couldn't seem to let Rita's claim go. And because the old lady was offering to pay her to help find the rest of her father's collection, she felt obligated to defend her to the bitter end.

"They won't take Rita's claim seriously either, I know it," she said sullenly. "Since Karen O'Neil walked into the museum last week, Huub has rolled over and agreed with everything she's said." She felt her cheeks flushing just thinking about yesterday's meeting. Karen had done her best to humiliate and belittle her, and Huub had finished off the job. Despite the overwhelming evidence she'd presented of Karen's treachery, she and her high-priced lawyer had found an answer for everything. They were probably at the Amstel Hotel laughing at her right now. If only she could be a fly on the wall of Karen's room; that was probably the only way to find out what she was really up to.

"You know, there was something odd about the way Karen was acting at the meeting yesterday. She was so incredibly angry I'd gone poking around in her family's records, almost like she was scared I'd find out something she didn't want the museum to know about. I wish I knew what she's hiding. Maybe then I could prove once and for all that *Irises* really is Rita's painting."

"Whoa, you're not going to prove anything. Bernice and Huub made it clear they don't need or want your help. And thanks to Bernice's recommendation, you shouldn't have any trouble getting into the master's program next month. Why would you want to mess that up just because Karen hurt your feelings?"

"Because she's lying and I'm not the only one who thinks so. Bernice suspects something; I could see it in her eyes. But her hands are tied by bureaucracy. No, if I don't do anything, Rita's claim doesn't stand a chance."

"So? It's not your problem. You don't owe Rita Brouwer anything, even if she does pay you to search for the rest of her father's collection."

Zelda wanted nothing more than to get Huub and that rich bitch back, but Friedrich was right; revenge wasn't worth giving up the master's program for, and it wouldn't help Rita's claim either. She zoned out, thinking about her options as her eyes focused on Friedrich's quadrocopter resting on the grass between them, its little metal blades gleaming in the sunlight.

Suddenly an idea popped into her head. "Friedrich, could I borrow one of your planes tomorrow?"

He snorted loudly and shook his head resolutely. "No way—the Spitfire's landing gear still isn't working properly since you took it up."

She went red as she recalled her feeble attempts to fly one of Friedrich's easier-to-control model airplanes. After she'd crashed the Spitfire five times in a row, he'd refused to let her try again.

"Some people have it, and some people don't."

Zelda looked up at her friend, bewildered.

"Good eye-hand coordination. Yours is appalling."

"Fine, I'll buy one myself. Where do you get them anyway, a toy store?"

"Why do you suddenly need a model airplane?" Friedrich asked, keeping his voice even. She said, baiting him, knowing he never referred to his remote-controlled planes as "toys."

"Because it might be my only way of finding out what Karen O'Neil is hiding from the museum."

"Are you going to fly planes with her? Try kites, they're easier to get off the ground."

"No, to spy on her. I didn't hear that little drone thingy of yours until it practically ripped my cheek open. It's warm today; she'll probably have her windows open again. If we could hear what she says and see who she talks to, we might find out why she wants *Irises* so badly." Zelda realized too late that she'd said too much. She didn't want to admit to Friedrich that she'd biked by the Amstel Hotel every day this week to keep tabs on Karen. Zelda knew which rooms she and her lawyer occupied and that the New Yorker kept her windows open when she was there.

Friedrich went white, apparently too shocked by her proposal to have noticed her slip-up. "By 'she' you mean Karen O'Neil."

"Of course."

"You want to spy on Karen O'Neil, one of the richest women in America? At the Amstel Hotel, one of the most expensive hotels in Amsterdam? The one where all the rock stars and Hollywood actors stay? Which is probably surrounded by a gazillion security cameras and beefy personnel?"

"Not Karen's room. She's on the left side of the hotel, far from the entrance. Your quadrocopter can easily avoid the only security camera on that end of the building. There's even a park bench across the street from her room that's partially hidden by some trees; it's perfect," Zelda explained, remembering how she'd sat on that very bench last night trying to see what Karen was up to.

"Perfect? Try extremely illegal. What if she sees you? Or my drone?"

"If you're steering it, you could maneuver it up across from her window, and nobody would be the wiser. You've got a few toy planes with cameras in them, right?"

"Try expensive model aircraft I built from scratch," Friedrich raged. "And

154

don't you dare try to drag me into this. Driving you to Urk was one thing, but spying on Karen O'Neil is out of the question!"

"Fine, I'll do it myself," she pouted. "If I can't use a model plane, I'll pretend to be room service and hide my Dictaphone in her room. She'll probably be leaving Amsterdam soon; I'll have to move quickly." She stood up and brushed the grass off her jeans. "With or without your help, I am going to do this."

"Good luck to you," he stoically replied.

"Fine." Zelda spit the word at him as she stormed off.

"Oh, damn," Friedrich grumbled, as he grabbed his drone and ran after her.

27

Drone Flyby

"If anything happens, you forced me to do this," Friedrich groused.

"At gunpoint," Zelda said, smiling as she patted him reassuringly on the shoulder. They were sitting on a park bench across from Karen O'Neil's room in the exclusive Amstel Hotel. The massive nineteenth-century building stretched an entire city block along the edge of the river from which it took its name. From their perch on the far left side of the hotel, Zelda could see the red-carpeted staircase in the center of the building, which led up to the elegant lobby.

A small bike path and sidewalk were the only things separating them from the imposing steel fence that shielded the hotel's lawn from unwanted visitors. Though bikers whirred by every few seconds, none gave either of them a second glance. The few tourists wandering along the river's edge were only interested in the fantastic views of the historic canal houses across the water, not Zelda or Friedrich.

The maple trees lining the fence shaded them from the sun and Karen O'Neil's gaze, should she look outside. From their vantage point, they could almost see inside the windows of her second-floor suite.

"I told you no one would even notice us, didn't I?" she gloated.

"Do you really think no one is going to notice a quadrocopter hovering above their heads?" he asked, keeping his drone's hard-shell case resolutely closed.

"I've been sitting here for over an hour now, and not one person has even glanced at me. Besides, it's not like you're going to have a clunky joystick in your hands. You use your tablet to steer it; people will think you're just surfing the net or playing a game."

"What about security guards and cameras?"

She pointed to a large camera bolted to the front of the hotel, positioned under the roof's eaves. "That's the only one on this side of the building, and it's aimed towards the entrance. Karen's window is behind it, outside of its range of vision." Sensing Friedrich's hesitation, she rushed on, "The hotel entrance is almost a block away. And the way it's been built, tucked up under the portico like that, we can't even see the front doors from here. Which means the hotel staff won't be able to see us either," Zelda concluded, pleased with herself.

"Show me where her room is again."

"It's the one closest to the corner, on the second floor. See, her windows are already open," she repeated patiently. "That tree next to the fence is taller than her room, and the branches almost touch the first window. If you can maneuver your plane up there, you should have a clear shot inside." She pointed to a series of branches close to Karen's suite. The maple tree was obviously old and well cared for, its numerous branches heavy with broad green leaves and samara nuts. "Do you think the tree will be a problem for your plane?"

"Quadrocopter," Friedrich sighed.

"Quadrocopter," she restated.

"No, it shouldn't be. But I'll have to stand under it to get her into position." He finally snapped his drone's case open, adding, "I hope you know what you're doing."

"Of course I don't," Zelda answered affectionately. She really didn't know what she was doing or whether this little stunt would actually produce any results. But she was smart enough to know she wouldn't be sitting here getting ready to spy on the New Yorker if it weren't for Friedrich. Without his help, she wouldn't have dared to try, despite all her bravado yesterday.

If she was honest with herself, he was probably the only real friend she had made since arriving in Amsterdam. Her fellow students were interesting people, but she hadn't truly clicked with any of them. Besides, the rest of her classmates were already focused on going home, returning to their jobs, houses, and loved ones—exactly what she was determined to leave behind. And Pietro had been gone all summer; he wouldn't be back until September, only a few days before classes began. Sure, they texted every few days, but it wasn't the same. Without Friedrich, Amsterdam would have been pretty lonely this summer.

Zelda checked her watch then wiped the sweat from her brow with the back of her hand. "Karen and her lawyer got back about a half-hour ago. She opened her windows almost immediately. That's when I called you."

Her friend started up the flight steering app on his tablet, double-checking that both the aircraft and its built-in audio and video feeds were working properly. His concentrated frown lessened only after he finished his preflight checklist. "Okay, she's ready to go. Don't forget, I can record fifteen minutes of video before the battery runs out. Are you absolutely sure you want to do this? We don't have to, you know."

"And not even try to find out what Karen's hiding from Rita and Bernice?"

"If she's hiding anything."

"She is. Let's do this before you talk me out of it." She jerked her head towards the hotel, signaling for him to get on with it.

Friedrich sprinted over to the old maple's wide trunk and laid his drone gently onto the sidewalk. As the quadrocopter rose silently into the air, he guided it towards the tree branches closest to Karen O'Neil's room. Its four tiny rotors hummed slightly as it wafted into position. Watching his monitor carefully, he maneuvered it within earshot of anyone who might be talking inside. Satisfied with its placement, he locked the aircraft into the hover position and sprinted back to Zelda.

"There they are," Friedrich grinned as he showed her his video monitor. Karen O'Neil was pacing back and forth in front of her lawyer, who was seated in a large wingback chair facing the window, smoking a cigar.

Zelda hugged him briefly, ecstatic they could see anything at all. Friedrich turned a bit crimson as he pulled away. He put one earbud in his right ear

158

before handing her the other.

"I want this claim wrapped up, as soon as possible!" Karen's voice was high and whiny, but otherwise clear as day.

"As do I," Konrad Heider soothed.

"If that stupid intern hadn't gone poking her nose around where it didn't belong, this whole nightmare would have been over by now. I'm sure the director was about to cave in and give me *Irises*, after my last surprise visit interrupted his meeting with potential sponsors." Karen stepped in and out of the frame as she circled the large room. Zelda smiled in delight upon hearing that she'd gotten under Ms. O'Neil's skin.

"All she did is give us a path to proving you are the rightful owner, not Rita Brouwer. Nothing she found can derail your claim. Your mother's birth certificate will ensure that," her lawyer said.

"And what about the brother—Gerard? What are you going to do about him?"

"He's nothing to worry about. Once we prove your mother was Arjan van Heemsvliet's daughter, he will have no claim on the paintings."

"And how exactly are we going to do that?" Karen replied angrily.

"I have people working on the documents. With enough money you can buy—" The lawyer's sentence was interrupted by the shrill calls of ring-necked parakeets landing on the maple tree's thickly laden branches. Their piercing whistles and screeches sent a jolt through Zelda's body. She jerked the earbud out, sure she'd gone deaf.

"What did he just say?" she demanded.

"The birds, I don't know what he—oh, damn," Friedrich babbled, staring up at the hotel. Karen stood by the window, wistfully gazing out at the Amstel River, filled with large vessels plowing up the strong current towards the city center. He and Zelda exchanged worried glances. If Karen looked over at the maple tree filled with feeding birds, she'd undoubtedly notice the tiny quadrocopter hovering a few feet away.

"On the plus side, she apparently can't hear its motor over the birds squawking; otherwise she would have spotted us already. That's good news," she whispered, still surprised by how silent remote-controlled drones could be.

In the video monitor, they could see the lawyer rising, joining Karen at the window, wrapping his arms around her and kissing her softly on the neck and cheek. She relaxed into his chest, nuzzling his chin.

Zelda nudged Friedrich in the ribs. "Would you look at that!"

"I'm so tired of Amsterdam. I want to leave this place and fly to Saint-Tropez, like you promised," Karen murmured into her lawyer's ear.

"I know, my darling. We're almost finished here. Just a few more days, that's all I ask."

"Why don't we let the Restitutions Committee decide the fate of *Irises*? Neither Rita Brouwer nor Gerard van Heemsvliet will have a leg to stand on; you and your firm's team of lawyers can make sure of that."

Konrad Heider stiffened visibly, an angry expression crossing his face. "You know that's not possible." He turned her around, kissing her roughly on the mouth before hugging her close. "This search has dominated my life for far, far too long. *Irises* is the key to the rest, I'm sure of it. We can't let it out of our sight, not now, not when we are so close. A treasure trove of priceless artwork is worth waiting a few more days for, isn't it, *mein Liebling?*"

"*Irises* is the key to finding a treasure trove of art?" Zelda repeated incredulously. "He must be talking about Arjan's collection; it's supposed to be worth a fortune. See, I told you there's something fishy going on!" She looked over at her friend triumphantly, but his attention wasn't focused on the video monitor.

"Look," he whimpered, pointing at the tree. The wild parakeets were feasting, tearing the samara nuts out of their spiky shells before letting the husks fall to the ground. Friedrich pointed to a bird feeding on the branch directly above his quadrocopter.

"I've got to get her out of there," he cried as he unlocked the aircraft controls, two seconds too late. Zelda could see a flicker of movement as the nutshell fell, milliseconds before it was vaporized by one of the drone's rotors. The little quadrocopter couldn't handle the unexpected intrusion; the assaulted motor stopped turning, throwing the drone off balance and into a tailspin. It crashed into the steel fence with a loud bang before exploding into a shower of tiny parts.

"No!" Friedrich screamed, dropping the tablet as he ran to his drone. He ripped off his T-shirt, using it to gather up the bits of metal and plastic scattered across the sidewalk.

Zelda looked up to see both the New Yorker and her lawyer leaning out of the hotel room window, trying to see what was happening. She held her backpack over her head and raced over to her friend, sure the hotel's security guards were only seconds away.

"Come on, Friedrich, leave the rest. We've got to get out of here!" She tore the bundle of parts out of his hands and sprinted up the sidewalk. Friedrich grabbed two more pieces before running after her, tears streaming down his cheeks.

28

Occupied Amsterdam

May 6, 1942

Arjan gently brushed his feather duster along the elaborately carved and gilded frame encasing Jan van Goyen's *Boy with Harp*, careful not to touch the painted canvas. A real-life boy rode slowly by his gallery window, his bicycle's tiny front wheel forcing him to bend over the steering wheel at an awkward angle as he worked the pedals. The few bikes still riding around the city were all silly-looking contraptions, with one or both wheels having been replaced by that of a wheelbarrow or child's buggy to prevent it from being confiscated by the Gestapo.

Only a handful of pedestrians dressed in ill-fitting suits and poorly cobbled shoes meandered down the once lively Spiegelgracht, gawking at anything and everything still on display. The cosmetics, stockings, and luxurious fabrics once worn by the patrons of the exclusive galleries lining his street were as scarce as his clientele these days. The gray and green uniforms of the German army passed by far more often, going to or coming from the nearby Museumplein, around which the occupying forces had set up their headquarters.

Arjan wasn't sure how much longer he could take it here. The silence was oppressive. As trams were forbidden to ride and most churches' bells had been melted down and molded into cannons, the occasional clomping of hooves from horse-drawn carriages and taps from walking canes were often the only sounds penetrating his window. Before the war, those more subtle noises had been drowned out by the many cars, bicycles, and pedestrians jostling for position on the narrow street. It had been months since he'd seen a private car driving by; the only engines he heard on the streets of Amsterdam anymore were those of German tanks, jeeps and transport trucks.

Lost in his thoughts, it took his mind a moment to register that his gallery's door had opened, jingling the chimes attached to its back. Arjan's standard polite yet inquisitive smile disappeared as soon as he stepped away from the window and saw the familiar black SS uniform of his blackmailer already standing inside.

Oswald Drechsler was quickly becoming his most frequent customer, he ruminated, realizing this was his second visit this week. The Nazi's mere presence set him on edge. *First my father disowns me, and now this monster wants to take away everything I worked so hard to build up, simply because I am attracted to men,* Arjan thought, a helpless rage building up inside of him. When would it end? Was he to be persecuted because of his sexual preference for the rest of his life?

He rushed past Drechsler and twisted the lock shut. While he didn't expect much business today, he wanted to make certain no one could unexpectedly enter and overhear their conversation. The repercussions were too horrible to consider.

Drechsler stuck out his hand in greeting. Arjan ignored it, choosing to walk around him and sit behind his desk. His blackmailer laughed before joining him, the many medallions lining his chest jangling softly as he crossed the room.

"What do you want today?" Arjan asked as gruffly as he could, his voice still sounding shrill despite his best efforts.

"Now, now. Is that the correct tone to use with me?" The colonel smiled easily, showing no sign of being perturbed.

"This is your tenth visit since our unfortunate acquaintance. Won't your superiors be surprised to see so many modern paintings hanging in your quarters?" Arjan knew Hitler had forbidden his troops from profiting off their Dutch "brothers," because he saw them as sharing a cultural and linguistic bond. Yet most of the SS's higher ranks viewed the war as an easy way to expand their personal collections at substantial discounts.

"Don't worry about what my superiors think. Most have no idea what is acceptable and what is degenerate. And those who do will never see the paintings you've so graciously given me."

"Given you? Surely you mean the paintings you've blackmailed me into parting with."

Drechsler's expression grew grim. "My silence guarantees your freedom. If the Gestapo learns you escaped their raid of Grote Geerts in February, they will certainly arrest you, then confiscate your home, gallery, and everything inside before sending you to a re-education camp. My price is quite small in comparison. If you are not satisfied with our arrangement, you can always volunteer for castration. I hear they are sometimes more lenient."

Oswald's wide grin turned Arjan's stomach. He knew too many homosexual acquaintances who'd been detained, beaten, raped, and even forcibly castrated before being sent to work camps in Germany, never to return. "What will you be taking with you today?" he asked through gritted teeth, doing his utmost to keep the sarcasm out of his voice.

"The five paintings in the window will suffice." Drechsler gazed evenly over at the art dealer, obviously expecting some opposition.

Arjan's face drained of color. Those were the five most expensive paintings left in his gallery. His stock had dwindled to a mere thirty pieces. At this rate, his gallery would be empty within a few weeks. It had been months since a Dutch citizen had brought him a painting to sell. His clientele consisted almost entirely of Germans and others sympathetic to the National Socialist ideals, only on the lookout for sales.

Once Drechsler cleaned out his gallery, how long would it be before the Nazi turned up on his doorstep and demanded the plethora of masterpieces filling his regal residence? The mere thought consumed Arjan with panic. It wasn't his own paintings or furnishings he was concerned about. Once Drechsler was inside his home, how long would it take him to find Arjan's private storeroom and discover his friends' artwork inside? He'd had the door reworked to look as if it was part of a bookcase, but nothing was foolproof. Arjan knew he had no choice but to give the colonel what he wanted, if only to get him out of the gallery so he could start looking for a new location to hide everything. But where?

In the back of his mind, Arjan had long known that he might have to flee Amsterdam one day and leave his artwork and that of his friends behind, yet it was a course of action he had never realistically prepared for. His summer home in Marseilles was located in one of the few areas in Europe yet to be occupied by Hitler's troops. But to get there, he would have to pass through occupied Belgium and northern France. That would be almost impossible considering the number of checkpoints he'd have to cross. As soon as Drechsler discovered he'd fled, the colonel would certainly send word to his commanders to have him detained and brought back to Amsterdam.

He would have to buy a falsified passport before he could even attempt to leave the Netherlands; Drechsler would never let him obtain a visa to travel abroad legally. He'd heard rumors of a resistance group on the Prinsengracht that had set up an escape route to Switzerland. If the rumors were true, they could surely help him obtain the documents needed to travel through the occupied zone safely.

Yet even if he managed to slip out of the country without Drechsler noticing, what of the paintings? He might be able to fit a few pieces into his suitcases, but not enough. And a transport truck full of priceless artwork would never make it all the way to Marseilles without someone confiscating them along the way.

He had no choice but to find a suitable hiding space somewhere in the vicinity of Amsterdam. But where could he possibly hide the two hundred and fifty or so paintings he was storing for his friends, not to mention his own collection of seventy canvases?

Arjan could feel tears forming as the hopelessness of his situation sunk in. "Fine, I'll pack them up for you now." He rose and walked absently to the front window. Oswald Drechsler's surprise was evident, yet he said nothing, choosing to let the art dealer crate up his latest acquisitions in silence.

29

An Exhibition In The Van Gogh Museum

"Aren't they beautiful?" Zelda gushed as she and Friedrich maneuvered through the throngs of visitors slowly moving from one vibrant painting to the next. Thanks to the strange color combinations, thick streaks of paint, and funky perspectives that Vincent van Gogh favored, he was one of her favorite artists. It was sheer luck that she now lived within walking distance of the world's most comprehensive collection of his work. For the millionth time since she'd moved to Amsterdam, she had to pinch herself, sure she was dreaming that she lived in such a wonderful city.

Friedrich frowned. "Looks like he needed lessons in painting perspective." He turned his head this way and that, trying to understand the canvas hanging before him.

"He was self-taught, but only because no academies would have him. He didn't paint traditionally enough."

"There you have it."

"He was ahead of his time, that's all," she sniffed, reminding herself not to get riled up by his remarks. Friedrich had kept their date, even after everything that happened at the Amstel Hotel yesterday; she had to give him kudos for that.

"So, where's this mysterious exhibition, the one you say explains why Karen O'Neil wants *Irises* so badly?" he asked, sarcasm dripping from his voice.

"I am sorry—so very, very sorry—about your quadrocopter. How many more times do I have to say it before you believe me?"

Friedrich gazed at her sternly for a moment before holding up his hands in mock surrender. "Okay, okay. I believe you."

"Are you sure I can't buy you a new one?"

"I told you before, a new one costs around five hundred euros. I'll let you know how much the replacement parts are once I've sorted through all the pieces I managed to salvage. At least the camera still works; that would have really cost you. The video we shot looks good. Oh yeah," he said, fumbling through his shoulder bag, "here's your copy."

"Thanks. It went better than I expected—well, except for crashing your drone at the end," she said, flushing slightly as she clutched the DVD tight. "I can't wait to show this to Bernice Dijkstra. Let's see Karen and her lawyer try to wriggle their way out of this mess."

"Okay, so which way do we go?"

Zelda had purposely taken him through the museum's permanent collection on their way to the temporary exhibition she actually wanted him to see. As this was his first time inside the Van Gogh Museum, she figured he should see it all. She opened her mouth to tell him that but quickly bit her tongue. He was doing her a big favor by even coming here today; the least she could do was accept he might not love Vincent van Gogh's artwork as much as she did.

"This way." She guided him through the many visitors jostling for the best viewing positions, towards the nearest stairwell. As they trudged upwards, she said, "We're headed to the Print Room. Usually a selection of the Japanese prints Vincent van Gogh collected are displayed there, hence the name."

"Oh yeah?" Friedrich perked up for the first time since they'd set foot inside the museum. "I like Japanese prints a lot better than the paintings we just saw," he said, referring to the many priceless masterpieces they had walked past.

"They also organize smaller, temporary exhibitions up there, like the one we're going to today," she quickly added.

"Oh," he said, his pace slowing.

At the top of the staircase was a small windowless room, softly lit by carefully placed spotlights. Large metal workbenches were set up in three corners, each covered with a variety of microscopes, test tubes, petri dishes, and small metal tools that belonged more in a medical laboratory than a museum's restoration department. Spread about the room were several reproductions of Van Gogh paintings displayed on large wooden easels.

Friedrich stopped inside the entrance. He turned to Zelda without even bothering to look around first. "Well?"

"Remember how Karen's lawyer said *Irises* was the key to finding the rest? This exhibition shows how several Van Goghs have been painted over in an effort to temporarily disguise them as another painting." She gestured towards the easels. "Those are reproductions of all of the Van Gogh paintings the museum is certain were once covered up for one reason or another. Some were painted over by smugglers, thieves, and tax evaders for the more obvious reasons. But others were saved from being destroyed by the Nazis because their owners hid them under a type of painting more suited to Hitler's tastes."

Zelda stepped over to a wall of text and small photographs, which explained the purpose of the exhibition in more detail. When Friedrich sidled up alongside her, she pointed to a paragraph in the middle. "See those photos? At least three Van Goghs were saved during the Second World War because they had been painted over."

"Interesting, but why exactly am I here?"

"This exhibition illustrates some of the techniques conservators and art restorers use to examine paintings. With the right tools and machinery, they can find traces of paint that have faded or even come loose from the canvas, as well as drawings or other paintings hidden underneath the visible composition."

"And your point is?" Friedrich asked, eyebrows raised.

"We haven't been able to figure out why Karen O'Neil wanted *Irises* so badly, right? What if it's not *Irises* by Lex Wederstein she wants, but a map hidden somewhere on the canvas or frame? Someone could have added a diagram or text to the back, but now it's too faint to see or the paint has rubbed off since. Whatever clue is hidden on *Irises*, it must not be visible to the naked eye, at least not anymore. Otherwise Karen O'Neil would have already seen it when she manhandled the painting during her first meeting with the exhibition's project team. And she's been pushing hard to have her own conservator examine it under the guise of wanting to have it taxed."

Friedrich stared at her as if she was crazy. Her cheeks began to burn. "It's the key to finding a treasure trove of artwork," she reminded him.

"This is your big revelation, the reason I *had* to come to the Van Gogh Museum with you?"

"Well, yeah. I figured if you saw for yourself how easy it would be for a conservator to find any text or diagrams hidden on *Irises* or the frame, then you might take me seriously."

Zelda tensed up, waiting for Friedrich to say something nasty, but instead he calmly replied, "Okay, show me."

Zelda led him towards the first display describing four different methods art restorers and researchers employed to see "underneath" a painting, enabling them to identify any changes the artist made to either the scene depicted or the color used while he or she was working on it. A video camera was suspended over the large workbench before them, aimed down towards a rectangular painting of a man and a woman walking through a cornfield. Fluorescent neon tubes were positioned around the edges of the canvas, casting a purplish glow over its surface. Via a monitor positioned to their left, they could see that the lens was zoomed in on the center of the painting. Thanks to the shimmering ultraviolet light, she could make out another design underneath the cornfield, one not normally visible to the naked eye. Traces of a man's portrait seemed to hover just below the painting's surface.

Hanging on the wall behind the worktable were three poster-sized prints. Blocks of text explained that these images were the results of using different types of X-ray scans to examine the same painting.

The first of the three posters was the result of a standard X-ray, the same sort of imaging technique hospitals used to identify breaks in bones. The image was a confusing muddle of gray; the man's portrait was visible if she squinted her eyes just right, but almost indiscernible from the cornfield above.

The second print showed the results of infrared reflection, a technique used by art restorers since the 1970s. The man's portrait was somewhat sharper and more distinguishable than in the X-ray, but she still had to use her imagination to fill in the details.

The third print, created by an X-ray fluorescence analyzer, was a revelation. The machine could detect and analyze even the most minuscule remnant of pigment used to create every line and stroke still present on the canvas. In the poster hanging behind the workbench, the lines forming the man's head and upper body were bright and crisp; even the coloring and shading of the hidden portrait were clearly visible. Thanks to the scanner's ability to distinguish between the composition's many layers, the image of the cornfield had been completely removed from the results. Looking at this digital printout, one would never suspect this portrait had been painted over. Zelda studied the third poster, then the painting on the workbench, amazed at how much information could be gained when using the right technology and without damaging the visible painting above.

She tried to gauge Friedrich's thoughts as he gazed up at the three poster prints.

"Do you really think there's a map hidden under Iris's portrait?" Friedrich finally asked.

"Not underneath. It was painted before the war started. But Arjan van Heemsvliet could have easily added a drawing or text pointing to the location of the rest of his collection somewhere on the back of the painting or frame. It must have faded over the years, which is why it can't be seen with the naked eye anymore. If *Irises* is a sort of treasure map, then we have to assume Arjan would have wanted someone to be able to find the rest of his artwork."

"I don't know, Zelda. You don't really have any proof, do you?"

"It makes perfect sense. Why else would Karen O'Neil push so hard to get her hands on *Irises* and not want to wait for the claims process to run its course? She can't risk having the experts running tests and possibly finding the hidden map before she does." Zelda knew she shouldn't shout in a museum, but they were alone in a gallery full of replicas. Any security guards eyeing them through the electronic surveillance probably wouldn't intervene unless she knocked one of the fake Van Goghs off its easel.

"Wouldn't someone working at the Amsterdam Museum have already noticed that something was amiss? *Irises* has been sitting in their depots for more than sixty years now; who knows how many times it's been cleaned or studied since then. If there is a description or diagram on the back, wouldn't somebody have spotted it by now?"

"Why would they have? Why would the museum waste their precious man-hours and research dollars running expensive tests on it? *Irises* is an insignificant painting created by an unknown artist. It's not the sort of piece that would get lent out for exhibitions or be studied by art history students. Think about it, Friedrich, it would have been the perfect painting to hide a clue to the whereabouts of Arjan's collection." She began pacing back and forth in front of the display, excited to share her theory.

"Van Heemsvliet must have left a letter or other document behind in his study that explained what he'd done. Karen O'Neil's grandmother took all of his business records with her to America, the same documents Karen O'Neil eventually inherited. That's why she's been so unbelievably keen to get her hands on *Irises*," Zelda finished smugly, sure she was right.

"I suppose if Karen knew it would lead her to the rest of Arjan's collection, it could explain her persistence. But if that were true, wouldn't that explain why Rita was so interested in it, too?"

"No," she replied doggedly, "think about it. Rita and her sisters want *Irises* back so badly because of its sentimental value. It's a portrait of Iris painted by the girl's first love. Besides, their father gave or sold his entire collection to Arjan after they'd all left for Venlo. How could Rita or her sisters have known what he'd done?"

"Arjan must have decided to make that painting the key to finding the rest because it was the least valuable piece in his collection of masterpieces," Zelda continued, convinced she'd figured out the secret that Karen O'Neil was trying so hard to keep from the exhibition's project team. "If he was being blackmailed, you'd think he would have tried to hide his more valuable paintings from that Nazi. Maybe the clue added to *Irises* was meant for his brother Gerard, so he could find the rest, even if Arjan was arrested or killed."

Friedrich folded his skinny arms across his chest and rocked on his heels, mulling over her theory.

A few moments later he patted her roughly on the back, smiling as he said, "Zelda Richardson, you might be on to something."

To her great delight, his smile and tone were genuine.

"But how are you going to prove it?"

30

A Cache Of Missing Masterpieces

"When did you get so smart, Zelda?" Jasper de Vries teased.

They were in one of the restoration department's laboratories, tucked away in a canal house across the street from the Amsterdam Museum. The senior conservator's workplace was the largest, but even so, the windowless lab was jam-packed with chemicals, powders, paints, and tools. The only space relatively free from clutter was the long white table in the center of the square room. *Irises* rested in the middle of it; a soft spotlight shining down onto its surface made the paint glisten. Small metal picks and tiny brushes were lined up on one side as if someone was preparing for surgery. Jasper and Zelda sat on bar stools, their drinks resting on the edge of the hip-high table. Despite the audible hum coming from the ventilation system, the room still reeked of linseed oil and turpentine. She tried to breathe through her mouth and not think about how nasty her clothes would smell after even a short visit to the art restorer's workshop.

"Conservation and restoration weren't part of your study. I'm surprised you've seen an ultraviolet light, let alone know how it works. Have you been studying books on art restoration behind my back? Or did you visit the Van Gogh Museum recently?" Jasper smiled easily before taking a swig of the *koffie verkeerd* she had brought him, taking care not to spill any on the table.

She still had to laugh every time she ordered the Dutch equivalent of a latte, translated into English as "coffee wrong," but knew it was his favorite drink. Not that a bribe was necessary. During her brief internship at the Amsterdam Museum, Jasper had been her favorite lunch companion, thanks mostly to his witty sense of humor. He was always hanging around the staff lunch room, cracking jokes and spreading gossip. Old enough to be her father, he'd taken a shine to her right away—to her utter delight. She reminded him of his oldest daughter, he liked to say, the same one who'd immigrated to San Francisco years ago. Zelda didn't really care why; she owed him a debt of gratitude for making her feel so welcome.

"The exhibition in the Print Room is pretty interesting, isn't it?" she said neutrally, unsure of how to explain her theory to Jasper. She knew he was one of the few people in the museum she could ask anything of, but she was still worried he might laugh her out of his workplace if she told him what she suspected.

She didn't need to fret; he saw right through her. "Very interesting. However, I've already run several tests on *Irises* and am certain there is no painting, sketch, or other message hidden anywhere on the canvas or frame."

Zelda frowned at the portrait, sure he must have missed something. "And there were no documents or papers stuck between the canvas and frame?"

"No. The original owner, Philip Verbeet, wrote his address onto one of the stretcher bars with a fountain pen, but you already knew that. The only strange thing about *Irises*—if you can even call it that—is that Arjan van Heemsvliet hadn't attached his gallery sticker to the painting. I didn't find any traces of glue either. It was standard practice for galleries to attach a label to their stock with a specific kind of rubber cement, so that even after it was sold, people would know where it was purchased from. Back then gallery owners did it as a marketing ploy. Now we use these stickers to re-create a painting's provenance. I couldn't find any trace of adhesives on the back of *Irises*, leading me to believe that a sticker had never been attached to it. Even after seventy years, I should have been able to find some residue."

She nodded in understanding, thankful Jasper was taking her seriously.

"But then," he added lightly, "Huub Konijn did say *Irises* was only in Arjan van Heemsvliet's possession for a few days before he went missing. That could explain why his gallery's label had not yet been glued to this piece."

Jasper's answer threw her for a loop. "Huub Konijn, the curator? Did *he* request these tests?"

"Yes, and he was here when I ran them this morning."

"But why?" Huub was the last person she thought would bother with *Irises*. He'd made it quite clear that he considered Karen O'Neil the rightful owner and that any further research into the painting's provenance was a waste of time. Besides, she could hardly believe he'd have risked sullying his pristine suit or shoes with chemical smells and paint by actually coming down to Jasper's workshop.

"Perhaps he was curious to learn more about the portrait, as you are. It's turning out to be quite a controversial piece. But when Huub left this morning, I don't think he was any wiser," he said.

Zelda was silent for a moment, trying to understand this strange turn of events, before finally asking, "Is it normal for a curator to be present when you run tests on a painting?"

The conservator rocked on his bar stool, considering her question. "No, I guess it's not. But it was good he was here when I removed the painting from its frame. It saved me from having to clamp it down to the table first."

"What do you mean?"

"The amount of dust and grime on the canvas and frame suggests that it hasn't been properly cleaned for several decades. Over the years, that type of built-up filth can turn into a sort of glue and stick the two together. Most of the paintings I handle are much better cared for. If I'd been alone, it would have taken longer to get everything set up. Because Huub was here to hold the frame down, I was able to remove the canvas quite easily and had time to run all of the tests he requested this morning. I even had time to update the condition report."

"You mean you'd already written one up for *Irises*?" she asked.

"During the past ten years, I've made condition reports for all of the paintings in the *Stolen Objects* collection, in preparation for this exhibition. But I didn't have time to take them all apart and clean them, only document their current state and suggest restoration work. Since then, most of the paintings haven't been touched. Only the pieces hanging in the exhibition were cleaned, but we didn't have the time or money to restore any of them," the conservator explained.

"Once I realized the extent of testing he wanted done, I ran back up to my office and printed off the original report so I could update it as we went along," Jasper said, chuckling and shaking his head as he recalled what had happened only a few hours ago. "When I got back, Huub had already removed all of the nails from the back of the frame. I was a little perturbed that he hadn't waited for me to return, in case the frame cracked. I am responsible for the canvas after all, as long as it's in my lab."

"Wait a second. So Huub was alone with the painting? For how long? Why couldn't he wait to remove the nails until after you'd gotten back?"

"He had a meeting this afternoon and didn't want to be late. He was just trying to help," Jasper said.

"Huh," was all she could muster. Her mind was swirling with possibilities. Was it easy to remove the canvas from the frame because Huub had already done so, while Jasper was upstairs in his office? Is that why the curator removed the nails, so he could examine the painting undisturbed?

What if the location of Arjan van Heemsvliet's artwork wasn't written on the painting, but hidden inside of it? The narrow space between the canvas and frame was large enough to hold a slip of paper or even a key, Zelda suddenly realized. But how would Huub have known to look for something there in the first place? Had Karen O'Neil told him *Irises* held the key to finding the rest of Van Heemsvliet's collection and asked him to look for it? Or had her repeated requests to have her own conservator examine *Irises* sparked his interest?

"What do you think of Huub?" she asked cautiously. She would never have dared ask anyone but Jasper such a question. She knew she could trust him to keep their conversation—and hopefully her visit—between them.

The conservator looked at her thoughtfully before responding. "I know you've had your differences. Huub can be demanding, intense, and sometimes irritating, but he is a consummate professional and one of the best researchers in the Netherlands. Considering his upbringing, I can't fault him for being socially inadequate." He sniggered before quickly straightening out his face, realizing too late that he'd said too much.

"What do you mean, 'his upbringing'?"

Jasper seemed nervous. "I don't know if I should be the one to tell you; it's really Huub's business."

"Oh, come on, you know he doesn't like me. He'd never tell me himself. And now you've got my curiosity piqued."

Jasper hesitated for a moment before confiding, "Most of his family was killed during the war, shipped off to concentration camps because they were Jewish. Only he and his oldest sister, Margo, survived. Huub was an infant when the war started. His parents knew they couldn't keep him quiet, so they couldn't take him into hiding with them. He and Margo were sent to live with a distant relative in Oosterbeek, a small village far from Amsterdam. His parents, three brothers, and two sisters all hid in their Catholic neighbors' attic. During a raid in 1944, they were discovered and arrested. None of them came back from Auschwitz. Most of our Jewish population didn't make it through the war; did you know that?"

Zelda nodded somberly. She'd recently been to the Jewish Historical Museum and was shocked to learn that of the one hundred seven thousand Jews deported from the Netherlands, only three thousand survived the concentration camps.

"When Huub and Margo returned to Amsterdam, strangers were living in their house, claiming they'd never heard of Huub's family. Margo didn't know the bank had seized it and resold it a few months after Huub's family went into hiding. Margo recognized their family's furnishings and other possessions still filling the rooms, but she couldn't do anything about it. No lawyer would talk to her, not without official documents that would stand up in court. They lost everything. She was only fifteen years old, yet she had to take a job washing sheets and cleaning rooms in a dingy hotel in the Red Light District to support them. Huub grew up in the hotel's attic. Margo died a few years later from tuberculosis. Huub had just turned ten; they put him in an orphanage, where he ended up growing up. So no, he did not have an easy childhood, but he is a survivor, I will give him that," he said.

"The paintings!" Zelda exclaimed suddenly, making Jasper jolt. In a calmer voice, she continued, "A few days ago, Huub mentioned he'd done extensive research tracing the provenance of his family's artwork for a claim."

"That's what got him noticed. He'd just started high school when he began to look for his family's collection, yet he doggedly followed a jumbled paper trail to find proof of his family's ownership of several paintings, etchings, and sculptures. It took him years, but he ended up submitting one of the most comprehensively documented claims ever sent to the secretary of state for culture. The head of the Jewish Historical Museum asked to meet with him. At the end of their talk, he encouraged Huub to make his obsession his profession, even offering to personally mentor him if he chose to study art history. Huub graduated at the top of his class and began as an assistant curator the next day."

Zelda nodded distractedly. She knew the curator's earliest years must have been a sort of living hell and she should have the utmost sympathy for him. But deep down she wondered whether Huub's past hadn't given him a selfish reason to disbelief Rita Brouwer's claims.

What if he had discovered that several of Carel Willink's paintings were missing during his research into the artist's body of work last year, despite telling Rita he'd found no references to them? If he had learned those pieces went missing during the war, he may have found out about other canvases that had disappeared in the 1940s. And as a senior curator at the Jewish Historical Museum, he'd had unlimited access to the entire *Stolen Objects* collection—and the documentation associated with it—for the past ten years.

What if he'd already found paperwork indicating the missing Willinks were part of Arjan van Heemsvliet's missing collection? He'd already proven himself adept at this kind of research. For someone like him—with the right motivation, knowledge, and access—figuring out that Van Heemsvliet's entire collection was missing and presumably still hidden somewhere in Amsterdam would have been a piece of cake.

Was Karen's arrival on the scene a godsend for him, providing him with the last few clues to the artworks' whereabouts? Or was her claim a fake? Were they working together to steal the whole lot from the rightful owners? Whatever the truth may be, if *Irises* did hold the key to finding a cache of missing masterpieces, Zelda realized grimly, Huub would have found it this morning.

31

Invasion Of Privacy

"What are they doing here?" Zelda demanded, as she took a seat at the head of the Amsterdam Museum's conference table. Bernice Dijkstra and Huub Konijn were seated on her left, Karen O'Neil and her legal counsel on her right.

"When you called up and said you had new information that affected Karen O'Neil's claim, I thought it prudent to invite them in to see the evidence," Bernice replied evenly, glancing at the New Yorker and her lawyer as she spoke.

As always, a recording device was set up in the middle of the conference table, the microphone picking up all that was said. No one was here to transcribe the meeting, she noted, but both Bernice and Huub did have their notepads open. Per request, a push trolley containing a small television and DVD player had also been placed next to the table close to her chair.

Zelda drew in a deep breath and told herself to relax. When she'd called Bernice this morning and demanded a meeting, she'd wanted to blurt out everything she'd learned right then and there on the telephone. But she'd held her tongue, knowing the video she and Friedrich shot would be far more convincing than anything she could say. She'd told the project manager she had proof Karen O'Neil was lying about her family history, but she hadn't mentioned the New Yorker's possible connection to the curator. She definitely didn't know how she was going to broach that subject.

After taking the DVD out of her bag, Zelda briefly made eye contact with the project manager and curator. Bernice appeared tired and irritated; Huub just scowled in her direction, as usual. It was now or never. Karen or not, she had to present her case in full and unmask this imposter. Rita deserved it, and Zelda's pride demanded it.

Apparently annoyed by her stalling, Bernice snapped, "What exactly have you found out that is so important to warrant this 'emergency meeting,' as you called it? Huub and I have other, more significant problems to attend to this morning, so be brief."

More serious than a false claim and lying claimant? Zelda wanted to ask. She was astounded by Bernice's attitude, expecting her to be the most receptive. Pushing her confusion aside, she focused on stifling the excitement growing inside of her. *Now is the time to be calm and collected,* she told herself, *not overly dramatic.*

"I have discovered something you need to be aware of before proceeding with Karen O'Neil's claim." She tried to choose her words carefully and keep her voice neutral. Gloating was not yet in order.

"Yes, yes. We know that, otherwise we would not be here," Bernice replied.

"I have definitive proof that Ms. O'Neil is not the granddaughter of Arjan van Heemsvliet," she blurted out. *And Huub knew it all along,* she wanted to add but didn't dare. Zelda stared at the rich widow across from her, waiting for her to deny it.

Karen laughed heartily. "Well, I never! What will she think of next? My lawyer and his team are working to obtain an *official* copy of my mother's birth certificate, as we speak. Once it has been located, a notarized copy will be mailed directly to Leo de Boer, who is currently reviewing my claim," she said, her tone triumphant.

Bernice's eyebrows shot up, evidently unaware that the museum's director was still considering recommending her claim be approved, instead of letting the standard process run its course.

Karen smiled in satisfaction before turning back to Zelda. "What, pray tell, is your evidence to the contrary?"

"Bernice, you have to tell Leo, I mean the director, that the birth certificate will be fake," she stated matter-of-factly, ignoring the New Yorker as she spoke. "You can't assume that any documents Ms. O'Neil or her lawyer provides the museum with are genuine."

"How dare you!" Karen was on her feet, screaming at Zelda. "Do you even know who I am? I have put up with your impertinent—"

"Stop!" Bernice held her hands up, shaking her head in disbelief. "Zelda, what are you talking about? These are enormous accusations that you are making. I hope you have strong evidence to back them up."

She nodded gravely. "I do," she said, patting the DVD before her.

"Then you'd better show it to us."

Her hands were shaking so badly she had trouble getting the disc into the player. At first, a blur of green filled the television screen, and only a soft whirling noise was audible. As the quadrocopter slowly rose into position, the camera began focusing automatically on a brick façade broken up by several large windows. The image stopped before an open window. As the focus fine-tuned itself, a seated man and standing woman became visible inside the room.

Here it comes, Zelda thought, smiling as she turned the volume up a bit more. Karen's whiny voice boomed through the speakers. "I just want this claim wrapped up, as soon as possible!"

The New Yorker's smug grin disappeared as she watched herself pacing around the television screen. "How did you—wait a second—that's my hotel room! That idiot with the helicopter, he was working with you? You were filming me?"

"Invasion of privacy!" her lawyer yelled, his eyes glued to the screen. "How dare you film a private conversation, one taking place inside Ms. O'Neil's hotel room nonetheless? Nothing you filmed is admissible in court, and this recording—" Konrad leapt out of his chair, strode over to the DVD player and popped the disc out, "—is your ticket to jail, Zelda Richardson. Bernice, I demand you call the police at once. I want this intern arrested immediately."

Zelda couldn't believe how badly this was going. Why couldn't the project manager have met with her one on one before getting Karen and her lawyer involved? Thanks to that German prick and his legalese, neither Bernice nor Huub had gotten a chance to hear the damning parts of the video. All of her work was for nothing.

Bernice waved Konrad Heider back into his chair. "We don't need to call the police, they are next door," she said, shaking her head instead of elaborating. "Zelda, what have you done? What were you thinking, filming them like that?"

"Bernice, don't listen to this man. They are hiding something from you, from all of us. You need to see the whole recording; I have another copy here in my backpack..."

"No, I don't want to see it. You shouldn't have made it in the first place."

"Bernice, Karen all but admits that she's not Arjan's granddaughter!" Zelda whipped around to face the New Yorker. "With lots of money, you can buy anything—including fake documents. Right, Karen? Isn't that what your lawyer told you?"

"That is Ms. O'Neil to you," Konrad Heider snarled. "You are taking a private conversation out of context. You have absolutely no right to—"

"Why isn't Gerard going to be a problem for much longer?" Zelda talked over him.

"This is ridiculous!" he shouted.

"Then tell us why." She leaned back, crossing her arms across her chest.

Karen's lawyer spit his words out. "Because we expect to locate Karen's mother's birth certificate quickly, thereby rendering any potential claim he might submit moot." He stared defiantly at Zelda before turning to the project manager and curator. "Neither I nor Ms. O'Neil has to explain a private conversation to you or your intern, one she should never have been privy to in the first place. Is this how your museum normally conducts its research, by harassing claimants and spying on them?"

"Of course not," Huub replied angrily. "Zelda's deplorable actions were in no way sanctioned by me, Bernice, or anyone else associated with our museums."

"Bernice, they are a couple! I caught them kissing on camera! If only you would watch the DVD," Zelda pleaded.

The project manager opened her mouth to speak, but it was the curator who responded first. "They are consenting adults; there is no law against clients and their legal representatives having a personal relationship. Your stunt with the plane seems to have proved nothing, though it has gotten you into quite a bit of legal trouble." Huub smiled as he spoke.

His haughty attitude was too much for Zelda to take. "And you've been kissing Ms. O'Neil's ass since she walked in the door," she fired back.

"Excuse me?" Karen raised her eyebrows and voice in protest, but Zelda plowed on.

"You never had a moment's doubt she was the rightful owner. How did she find out about Rita's claim on *Irises* so quickly, anyway? You told Ms. O'Neil about it, didn't you? You've been working together the whole time, haven't you?"

"I told you already that my private investigators—"

"Are you actually accusing me of helping Ms. O'Neil falsify her claim? Why would I do that?" Huub talked over Karen, staring at Zelda like she was insane. "I met her for the first time one week ago, at the same meeting you were present at, right here in this conference room. I believe Ms. O'Neil because her version of events makes more sense and because it has been consistently confirmed by legal documentation, whereas Rita Brouwer's claim relies heavily on photographs and secondhand information. She was a young girl when her father died, far too young to truly be aware of what was happening around her. I want the painting to be returned to the rightful owner, no matter what I think of them personally. This is about justice, not righting moral wrongs."

Bernice shook her head sadly. "Zelda, you really went too far."

Somehow the project manager's deep disappointment hurt more than Huub's heated accusations. A wave of shame rolled over her. In her rush to try to find out what Karen was hiding, she had crossed a line; of that, she was now sure. "Bernice, I'm sorry. I shouldn't have spied on Karen O'Neil. But I just had to try to find out what was really going on, before it was too late, for Rita's sake."

"Rita Brouwer again!" Huub roared. "Why are you so obsessed with her claim?"

"Because *Irises* was, and is, hers. And I can't believe that you, of all people, would give a painting to someone who doesn't deserve it."

"Me, of all people?" he repeated.

"Because of your family and…" Zelda's voice trailed off.

Huub's face went white. "What happened to my family has made me realize how important it is to give stolen goods back to their legitimate owner, not the first person who claims them," he said quietly.

"But Mr. Konijn—"

He held up his hand to silence her. "No. Listen, really listen, to what I have to say, Zelda. The fact is, Rita's father sold his collection to a respectable art dealer for a large sum of money. Why he chose to do so, we may never know. As painful as that is for Mrs. Brouwer—and you, for some reason—to come to terms with, that is what the paperwork submitted by Karen O'Neil is telling us."

The curator continued before she could interrupt. "Why did Mrs. Brouwer wait so long to claim the painting? Perhaps you should ask yourself that. What if she did know her father had sold it? If that is the case, then she and her sisters must have hoped that after all this time, Arjan van Heemsvliet's heirs wouldn't care about *Irises* anymore. They probably thought they could waltz off with it and no one would be the wiser. Had you even considered that possibility?" he asked.

Zelda could only slither down in her chair.

"This is exactly why I did not want you meddling with these claims. In order to be a professional researcher, you need to gather as much information as possible, then take an objective look at all the facts before determining who the rightful owner is. It is quite obvious you bonded with Rita Brouwer immediately and have been relentless in your defense of her claim, in spite of the documents presented to this museum. In my opinion, your subjectivity has only muddled this investigation and caused unnecessary setbacks. You never should have been allowed to do any research for us, even if you are Marianne Smit's prize pupil." He shot Bernice an evil look.

Zelda wished she could just disappear under the table, but Huub pressed on. "Unlike you, I refuse to be swayed by my emotions. The official documents provided with these claims will be used to decide who the rightful owner is, and not an illegally obtained video or whatever other evidence you say you have," he said decisively. "And Leo de Boer agrees with me. Once Ms. O'Neil's lawyers have located her mother's birth certificate, her claim will be strong enough that Leo sees no need for our researchers to waste their time on it."

Bernice's whole body caved in. Zelda couldn't believe Huub hadn't told her he was still pushing the museum's director to approve Karen's claim.

"Tell me, Zelda, are your actions really only driven by your emotions? Or perhaps by a misguided loyalty to your employer?" he asked.

Zelda felt her cheeks flame up. "How did you know?" she whispered.

The curator chuckled. "She is paying you to search for the rest of her father's paintings, is she not? She emailed Bernice and me this weekend, asking us to grant you full access to the museum's archives on her behalf. And you accepted the job, knowing her father had sold his collection to Arjan van Heemsvliet days before he died?"

She tried to turn her face to stone for fear she'd otherwise burst into tears. This couldn't be happening! Huub was doing his best to turn *her* into the bad guy.

"Who's lying to whom, Zelda?" he pushed.

His smug expression made her blood boil. She wouldn't go down without a fight; she couldn't just let him win. "Until the claim is settled, it's unclear who owns Philip Verbeet's collection," she rebutted.

"You refuse to try to be objective." Huub glared again at Bernice, as if to say "I told you so." "What were you doing in the restoration department yesterday, anyway? Jasper de Vries said you were very interested in the tests he'd run on *Irises*. Were you there on Rita Brouwer's behalf?"

Zelda's brow creased. What did her visit to the restoration department have to do with anything? "I was just curious if Jasper—I mean, Mr. De Vries—had ever examined the painting."

Karen's lawyer, having let the curator denigrate Zelda for the past few minutes, now pushed his way back into the conversation. "Pardon, what tests are you talking about? No one told us you were running tests on *Irises*. We should have been informed immediately so we could have been present."

Huub ignored the man, keeping his eyes locked on Zelda's. "And where were you last night?"

"Home, alone."

"Convenient."

"Sorry?"

"Someone attempted to break into the restoration department last night. Two guards are in critical condition. That is why there are police in the building across the street. Who is this friend of yours, the man who filmed Ms. O'Neil in her hotel room? Did Rita Brouwer hire you two to steal *Irises*? Is that what she is really paying you to do? She must know by now that her claim doesn't stand a chance."

"What? No, Friedrich wouldn't hurt a fly! Rita would never pay someone to steal her painting, I'm sure of it. None of us had anything to do with any break-in."

"Was anything stolen?" the lawyer asked anxiously.

"No, the thieves set off the silent alarm as soon as they entered the building. If a patrol car hadn't been parked a block away, I don't know what would have happened. They fled when they heard the police sirens approaching, but shot two guards while escaping. They tried to force open the door to the restoration department's workshops with crowbars and a welding torch," Huub explained calmly, watching Zelda's reaction like a hawk. "Because of the summer vacation, *Irises* is the only painting being stored there at the moment."

32

I Told You So

"Damn it, Pietro, answer your phone!" Zelda yelled into her own mobile, tears streaming down her face. An approaching group of Asian tourists eyed her warily as they stepped off the sidewalk and out into the bicycle path, giving her a wide berth.

Zelda had never felt like such a failure in her whole life. Her dreams of studying in Amsterdam and ever working for a museum were as good as over. And her supposed boyfriend wasn't answering his phone. She hung her head over the bridge's railing, gazing down into the brown-green water of the Prinsengracht, briefly wondering whether she shouldn't just leap over the side and end it all. Moments later, a party boat passed under her feet, one of the many vessels attracted to Amsterdam's picturesque waterways on this warm August afternoon. A bunch of twenty-somethings wearing orange boas and white fedoras cheered as their boat cruised back into the sunlight. If she jumped, she'd probably only end up breaking her leg on a boat's deck or contracting some weird disease from the junk-filled canals, but surely nothing fatal. What was the point in that?

She plodded on, meandering aimlessly along the narrow streets and bridges spanning the inner city, wondering how today could have gone so very wrong. Her intentions were good and noble. She knew she should call Marianne and explain her actions before Huub did. But she'd been so emotionally wrung out by his dressing down that she began to wonder whether he was right. Maybe she should be banned from ever working in a Dutch museum. She was incapable of working in a team, had needlessly insulted a rich and influential claimant, and had made wild accusations about a senior member of staff without having any real evidence of his wrongdoing.

She stared at her phone, trying to remember what her mentor's office hours were and wondering whether it wouldn't be better to email her. Though it hardly mattered now what she did. Huub had surely spoken with her already and explained why Zelda should be refused entry into the museum studies program. And even if he didn't go through with his threat to call her straightaway, Bernice would eventually tell Marianne everything that had happened; they were good friends after all.

Now Karen would certainly get *Irises*, without so much as a fight from Bernice. Her actions had made a bad situation so much worse that even the project manager would do just about anything to get the New Yorker out of her hair.

Thanks to her, Rita Brouwer would never see *Irises* again. Worst of all, she'd blown her chance to stay in Amsterdam for nothing. There was no way Marianne would still support her application to the master's program after she'd learned what she'd done.

Zelda smashed her fists against her thighs. *Where was Pietro?* All she wanted to do was cry on his shoulder and hear him say it was all going to work out. But for the past two hours, he'd refused to answer his phone. *If only his grandmother would die, then he would have time to talk to me*, she thought bitterly. Instantly guilt washed over her. She didn't really wish an old woman harm, but Pietro should have made time to be there for her, today of all days.

When her phone did begin to beep seconds later, she snatched it out of her pocket, sure her boyfriend had finally seen her many voicemails and text messages. Her face fell when she saw that it was Friedrich texting for the sixth time. He was here for her, whether she liked it or not. Though she was not looking forward to rehashing her terrible morning and having to hear him say "I told you so," she knew he wouldn't give up until she phoned him back.

She dialed his number as she turned towards home.

"Hey, Zelda, how did your meeting with Bernice go?"

"Badly, very badly."

"No, seriously; how did your bosses react when you showed them our video?"

"Karen O'Neil wants to have me arrested for invasion of privacy, Huub Konijn thinks we tried to steal *Irises* for Rita Brouwer, and Bernice Dijkstra refused to watch even a few seconds of our DVD."

"That is bad."

"And to top it off, both Bernice and Huub said they will be getting in touch with my mentor and letting her know what a total idiot I am. Bye-bye, master's program, and hello, Seattle."

"Come on, give yourself some time to process everything that's happened. I'm sure you will find a solution to your problems—"

"I'm sorry, I can't do this right now," she sniffled, her voice breaking. "I need some time alone." *And to call Pietro again*, she thought, wondering whether her Italian lover was trying to reach her right now.

"I'll call you later, okay?" She ended the call before he could respond and quickly checked for missed calls or messages. There were none.

A few blocks later, Zelda opened the front door to her building. As she climbed the four flights to her studio apartment, her anger at Pietro turned to concern. Maybe something terrible had happened to him. Pietro knew today's meeting was important to her and that she'd want to talk about it. Maybe he wasn't answering because he couldn't.

Zelda ran up the last few steps to her studio. Once inside, she rushed over to her desk and rifled through its drawers, searching for Pietro's parents' home phone number. She knew his grandmother was bedridden and his parents couldn't speak a word of English; it was just nice to know she had another way of reaching him. When she'd first asked, he had refused, whining that he didn't trust her to show some discretion. Confronted by her crocodile tears, Pietro finally relented, writing it down on a piece of stationery after repeatedly warning her to only use it if there was a *real* emergency. Her entire world was collapsing around her, and she needed her boyfriend. If this wasn't an emergency, she didn't know what was. She'd picked up a few Italian words in their three months together; she only hoped that would be enough to get him on the line.

She carefully punched in the eleven-digit number, wanting to get it right the first time. After a few rings, a young woman answered, "*Casa Moretti. Pronto?*"

Relief washed over her. This must be Pietro's younger sister. "*Buongiorno.* Is this Rosa? This is Zelda Richardson. I am calling for Pietro. Is he home right now?" She spoke slowly and distinctly. Pietro said his sister spoke English quite well, but the phone's connection crackled with static. She hoped the younger woman could hear her well enough to understand what she was asking.

"Who is this? How do you know my name?" the young woman asked in halting English spoken with a thick, melodious accent.

"Pietro's told me all about you. I feel like I know you already," Zelda smiled to herself at this unexpected surprise. Pietro always talked about how great his little sister was and what a pleasure it was to be around her.

"Pietro?" Rosa repeated, before launching into a string of Italian expletives. It reminded her of Pietro's outburst after he'd slammed his thumb hammering a nail into the wall. "That lazy bastard should be here helping me with the harvest, not out with his girlfriend again. I don't know when he will be back," she spat into the phone.

Zelda was sure she'd misheard the girl through the static on the line. Or maybe her English wasn't as good as Pietro said it was. "You must be mistaken," she chuckled, "this is his girlfriend calling. Zelda, Zelda Richardson. That's me."

Rosa started giggling. Zelda relaxed; it was just a silly cultural misunderstanding after all.

"Oh, so you are that *fessa* American my brother's been living with?"

Zelda's heart froze. "What?" was all she could muster.

"Pietro's with his girlfriend right now, the same one he's had since high school." Her words were daggers in Zelda's heart. "You are just the *stupida* who's been paying his bills."

"No, there must be some mistake. He's taking care of his grandmother, your grandmother. She's sick," Zelda whispered, sinking onto the edge of her couch.

"He told you that? That he's taking care of our grandmother?" Rosa roared with laughter. "She died five years ago."

Zelda couldn't get a sound out. This must be a cruel joke or the Italian sense of humor. Pietro hadn't been using her this whole time; he couldn't have been. He loved her!

"I will be sure to tell my lazy brother that his American girlfriend called," Rosa cackled before hanging up.

Zelda's heart shattered into a thousand pieces. Her phone dropped to the floor as she covered her eyes with her hands and let the tears flow. *Stupida* was right.

"How could I have been such an idiot?" she seethed. She should have known Pietro was too good to be true. He didn't even ask her out on a date until he was about to get kicked out of his apartment. He must have known it would be easy to get her into bed. From the first day of class, it was obvious to everyone that she lusted after him. He was an Italian god with perfect wavy black hair and pearly white teeth; how could she *not* fall head over heels in love with him? Wasn't she the one who'd suggested he move in, at least until he found another place? Wasn't she the one who'd said he didn't need to ask his father for money again, that she had enough saved to pay for everything? Stupid, stupid, *stupida!*

All those months living together, sleeping together, laughing together, and she had never suspected it was a big lie. Such a fool, such a blind, lust-struck fool!

As the reality sunk in, a wail of agony rose from her throat, filling the room. Friedrich had been right about Pietro all along. This realization, on top of everything else that had happened today, was simply too much to bear. Zelda curled up into a ball on the couch and bawled her eyes out.

33

Taking Stock

June 16, 1942

Arjan van Heemsvliet flipped slowly through the pages of his inventory ledger, marking the paintings he needed to find a new hiding place for as he went. He'd never assembled a separate list, instead choosing to include his friends' canvases in his business records so that, to the casual observer, the entries would appear to be part of his unsold stock. Because he'd never intended to leave Amsterdam, he hadn't kept track of the exact count. Now as he numbered the paintings in his ledger, currently totaling two hundred fifteen with more than twenty pages left, he could feel his sense of hopelessness growing.

A long shadow darkened his gallery window, startling him. Certain it was Drechsler returning for more paintings, he rushed to hide the inventory ledger inside the top drawer of his mahogany desk, quickly shoving it under an unfinished letter to his family before the door's chimes began to ring. When they did, Arjan was already standing a foot away from his desk, casually examining his only remaining portrait by Gérard Dou.

A stranger in a bowler hat with a handlebar mustache entered Galerie Van Heemsvliet. The older man was unfamiliar to him, yet Arjan felt as though they had met before. His guard went up instantly.

The stranger removed his hat and began fidgeting with its brim. His eyes remained downcast.

Arjan asked warily, "How can I be of assistance?"

"Are you Arjan van Heemsvliet?" the stranger asked, his expression serious.

"Yes, this is my gallery. Are you interested in purchasing a painting or sculpture?" he asked rather brusquely, certain this man was not here to buy anything.

"No, not exactly." The stranger glanced around as if to ensure they were truly alone.

Arjan felt a bit dizzy. He leaned against his desk, worried about what might come next. Had Drechsler told others about their arrangement? This man wasn't from the Gestapo, otherwise he would have burst inside with twenty armed officers on his heels.

Or was this a trap? Was this man tasked with first confirming what Drechsler had told his superiors about Arjan's sexual preference, before signaling a platoon of officers from around the corner to seize him?

"A friend told me about you," the stranger began.

Arjan felt his knees give way; then, as he fell to the ground, his head cracked against something sharp, and he slipped into unconsciousness.

Arjan gasped slightly as his eyes shot open. Certain he was in a jail cell, he glanced around in confusion, calming only slightly when he grasped that he was stretched out on a chaise sedan in the back of his own gallery.

"Oh good, you've come around. You hit your head on your desk when you fainted. You're going to have quite a large bump on your forehead, I'm afraid." The stranger was sitting on a chair beside him, sipping tea from one of his cups. The porcelain beaker seemed positively dainty in the man's large hands. The dim light emitting from an oil lamp placed on the floor between them created menacing shadows on his gallery's walls. Through the front window, he could see it was already dark outside.

"What do you want?" Arjan asked, his voice hoarse from fear.

"Siegfried and Jiske once told me that I should turn to you if I ever needed help."

"Siegfried and Jiske?" Arjan tried sitting up, but his head throbbed so painfully he lay back down, silently trying to work out how this man knew his good friends and longtime clients.

"We were introduced at Max's bar mitzvah."

Arjan studied the stranger's face intently in the weak light, trying to remember. Siegfried had invited hundreds of people to his only son's thirteenth birthday party. He'd shaken hands with so many that night, what was it now, four years ago? He hadn't seen his friends since December 3, 1940, when Siegfried brought his exquisite collection of paintings to his home. Those canvases were now his responsibility.

"You ordered two frames from my shop on the Stadhouderskade the following week. I always appreciated you doing that," the stranger added, genuine warmth in his voice.

Of course! Now he remembered the frame maker. "Philip Verbeet," he said aloud.

"Yes, Philip Verbeet." The man appeared relieved the art dealer had finally recalled his name.

"But why are you here?"

"Siegfried told me what you did for him before he and his family went into hiding. His daughter Rachel and my Fleur were best friends at grade school. They're still safe—at least they were the last time I brought them supplies, about a month ago," Philip said, uncertainty creeping into his voice.

"What I'd done?" Arjan felt the darkness returning, dreading what the older man would say next. When Siegfried had come to his house that stormy night and told him he'd decided to take his family into hiding, Arjan had immediately offered to store his art collection for him until the war was over. He'd never intended to help anyone else. Yet being on the boards of so many charities, museums, and cultural institutions meant that he knew too many influential people who'd been forced to disappear because of their ethnicity, religion, or sexual preference. One had snowballed into thirty-seven. Thirty-seven desperate friends who had to flee Amsterdam or go into hiding, taking nothing more than the clothes on their backs and whatever they could fit into a small travel case.

"A German general arrested my oldest daughter's boyfriend last week and has been asking questions about her. I don't know exactly what he wants with Iris, but I put my family on a train to Venlo two days ago, for their own safety. I have thirty-six paintings, sketches, and watercolors I don't want the Nazis getting ahold of. I've already been to every acquaintance and friend I trust, but no one who can help me, not like you can."

"Please, no," Arjan whispered. He'd cautioned those he'd aided to never mention his name to another living soul; their silence was his only condition for taking such an enormous risk.

"Could you possibly hold onto them for me, at least for a few months?"

If Siegfried told Philip what I'd done for him, how many others knew? Arjan wondered. Siegfried had built up one of the most important collections of French impressionists in the Benelux. If the wrong person discovered Arjan had his masterpieces in his possession, he would be robbed and killed the very same day, he was certain of it. And his other friends' collections were just as valuable. With Drechsler in the picture, even a rumor he had them would be reason enough for the SS officer to break down his door and tear his house apart. Then it would be a matter of hours before he found the hundreds of masterpieces stashed in his storeroom.

As reality sunk in, Arjan's mind shut down from fear and willingly slipped back into the darkness.

34

Lover's Deceit

"Hey, Zelda, you left these in the front door."

She slowly lifted her head off the couch and blinked the moisture out of her eyes. Friedrich was standing in the doorframe, her keys dangling from his right hand.

"What are you doing here?" she managed.

"It sounded like you could use a friend," Friedrich sat down next to her and lightly stroked her shoulder. "Are you okay?"

Zelda wrapped her arms around his neck and whimpered, "No, I am absolutely not alright," before breaking down again.

He held her close, rocking her gently. After she'd soaked his T-shirt, she pulled back from him, her flow of tears reduced to sniffles. "It's Pietro. You were right; he's a bastard."

"What happened?"

"He's got another girlfriend," she wailed.

Friedrich looked away, embarrassed. "Oh."

She wiped her nose on her sleeve before continuing. "They've been going out for years! So I guess that makes me the other woman, doesn't it?" She looked to Friedrich for an answer, but to no avail. He kept his gaze diverted.

Anger coursed through her veins just thinking about the lies Pietro must have told her during their three months together. She jumped off the couch and began pacing back and forth, unable to sit still any longer. "Pietro always spoke in Italian when he called his family, or at least he said it was his family. He was probably talking to her the whole time, telling her how much he loved her, right under my nose."

Zelda threw her hands up in the air. "What kind of girl is she? She must have known Pietro was living with me in this broom closet!"

"Maybe she thought you were his housemate."

"Then she must be an idiot or doesn't mind sleeping with a man-whore." She laughed manically at the idea of Pietro working as a gigolo.

"He must have known you had a crush on him and took advantage of the situation. You told me he was getting kicked out of his apartment, right? That's why you let him move in so quickly." Friedrich shook his head. "He used you, Zelda; there's no getting around it."

She blew her nose loudly into a paper towel. "Please don't say 'I told you so,' Friedrich. I can't bear it right now."

She couldn't believe how stupid she'd been. Though she would never admit it to Friedrich, she was deeply in love with Pietro. Granted, they barely knew each other, and since the beginning of summer, she had rarely heard from him. But Pietro's virtual love notes and their sporadic Skype sessions were enough to make her feel important and loved. And there was always a mention of September, when he would return to Amsterdam and share her bed once again. She'd thought he really cared about her, but in reality he had been using her the whole time.

Zelda slammed her knuckles against her forehead, trying to block out the memories of their nights together. "I am such a fool."

"He's the fool," Friedrich murmured, kissing her full on the lips.

She pushed him away, smacking him on the cheek as she did. "What are you doing?"

He looked down at the floor as he spoke. "I don't know, I just—"

She held one hand up, shaking her head vehemently. "Stop right there. I can't deal with you and Pietro at the same time."

Her phone began to ring, startling them both. Zelda picked it up off the floor and checked the screen. "Now he has time for me? Unbelievable. Don't you say a word."

She turned away from him as she answered. *I wonder what the bastard's excuse will be*, she thought. "What?"

"Zelda, *mi amore*, my love."

Hearing him whisper those words used to melt her heart. No longer. "After three months of living with you, I know what *mi amore* means. The question is, do you?"

"Do not believe a word my sister said to you. Rosa was playing a cruel joke on you. She was angry I was not there to help her with the harvest."

"Bull."

"Zelda, I do not know what I can do to—"

"How's your grandmother feeling today?" The line was silent. "Don't bother lying, Pietro; Rosa told me she died five years ago."

"You are my true love, Zelda."

"But am I your *only* love?"

Pietro's split second of hesitation was long enough to confirm what she knew to be true.

"Can't a heart love more than one person?" His voice sounded so sweet.

"No, it can't, at least not when I'm involved. Don't you ever call me again. You don't deserve me. You never did." Zelda punched the end-call button and threw the phone across the room.

"Man, I'm batting a thousand today; I screwed up my internship, master's degree, and relationship in just five hours. That must be some sort of record for destroying your life," she moaned, dropping onto the couch and letting her head fall into her hands.

As Friedrich moved in to comfort her, she jumped up and began throwing open her drawers and cabinets, surveying their contents. "I might as well start packing. What do I have to stay here for now? I'm going to get kicked out of the country in a few weeks anyway. If I get in touch with some headhunters back home, they might be able to line up a computer gig for me."

Her practicality was belied by the shrill tone in her voice. She couldn't believe she was uttering these words of defeat, but she had no idea what else she could do. Her whole world had collapsed in the span of a few hours.

Surely the combination of events was some sort of sign from the universe telling her to give up and go home. What other options did she realistically have? None.

"Do you really want to go back to Seattle?" Friedrich quietly asked. "Back to computer programming, endless project meetings, nightmare traffic—all the things you've repeatedly said you hate about big American cities and corporate jobs?"

"Of course I don't want to go back, not like this, with my tail between my legs." She felt another surge of anger welling up. "I've never been as happy as I have been these past nine months. I've found a career I'm passionate about, and Amsterdam feels like home."

"Come on, show some backbone. So what if Huub thinks you're tenacious and stubborn? You're an American—the selection committee would expect nothing less. Marianne Smit knows what you're like, yet she still recommended you. And Pietro—well, he's just a fool. You didn't come to Amsterdam because of him, and you weren't planning on staying here for him, so why should you go home and give up on your dreams just because he's an idiot?"

"You might have a point," she mumbled.

"You are only going to get kicked out of the country if you don't get into the master's program. You still have time to talk to Marianne and explain your version of events before your interview with the selection committee. Sure, she'll probably be angry at first, but you have to try. She's been your biggest advocate since you arrived in Amsterdam. And even if she doesn't agree with your actions, she can't stop you from showing up and doing your best."

"Without Marianne's blessing, I don't stand a chance. I might as well *not* show up."

"You don't know what Bernice or Huub told Marianne about this morning's meeting. And you did show a lot of initiative; she might be impressed by what you managed to accomplish in such a short amount of time," he teased, doing his best to get a smile out of her.

It worked. Maybe everything wasn't as hopeless as it seemed. She still had a shot at impressing the selection committee. And Zelda couldn't forget how her mentor had stood by her all these months, encouraging her to follow her passion, even when she felt like ever working in a museum was a pipe dream. Why should Marianne accept Huub's version of events as the truth? Zelda had already mentioned they didn't get along very well. Her mentor would at least want to talk to her about his accusations before writing her off as a troublemaker, wouldn't she?

She rubbed at her red-rimmed eyes and sat up a little straighter. "It is too soon to give up and run away, isn't it?"

He smiled encouragingly. "Yes, it is."

"I'd better call Marianne and see what the damage is. Hopefully Huub and Bernice were too busy with the police inquiries to have called her already." Zelda looked around the room, searching for her agenda when she spied a pile of documents lying on top of her desk.

"Oh no, Arjan van Heemsvliet's letters!" she yelped. "If I don't get them back to Gerard before someone from the museum contacts him, I really am screwed. I told Bernice I only looked at them, not that I'd taken them with me." Zelda felt her stress levels rising again. Yet another lie to cover up. She ordered herself to breathe normally and remain calm. As long as Bernice or Huub hadn't already contacted Gerard, it would be easy enough to rectify this situation.

She turned to her friend. "Can you do me one more favor?"

"Sure," he grinned, "a ride to Urk, perhaps?"

35

Return To Urk

"Have you read any of the letters yet?" Friedrich asked, gesturing towards the pack on Zelda's back. They were slowly making their way to Gerard's house, their bellies full after a three-course lunch in a café overlooking Urk's marina. On their left, the large fishing boats and small pleasure craft filling the harbor bobbed softly in the lapping water of Lake IJssel. Small shops lined the right side of the wide boulevard, occasionally interrupted by narrow cobblestone streets snaking up the small hill upon which most of Urk's homes were built. The perpetual sound of waves splashing against the high brick walls of the haven muffled most other noises, making her feel like they were walking along the seashore, not through the heart of a busy village. This sensation was only strengthened by the stench of sea salt and rotting fish permeating the air.

"I've read about half of the twenty-two letters," she said with a sigh, thinking back to the three late nights she'd spent hunched over her desk, painstakingly translating his long, gossipy letters to his family. "It took forever to translate them. So far they're almost exclusively questions about their mother's various illnesses and Gerard's religious training; Arjan rarely mentions his gallery or life in Amsterdam. Gerard did say his brother knew no one in his family was really interested in art. He's made several references to charity events and parties he'd attended and mentions the names of people he'd talked with. But it's not clear to me if they were family friends or important people back then and Arjan was bragging. I was hoping to ask Gerard about that today."

"But what about Arjan's boyfriend or being blackmailed?" Friedrich asked. "I thought that's what makes them so significant."

Zelda nodded, troubled she'd not found a single mention of the Nazi blackmailer or live-in lover thus far. "I took Gerard at his word," she replied. "The information he shared with us must be in Arjan's later letters, that's all. He started saving their correspondence in 1939, before the war even started, and I've only read through the spring of 1941. Arjan does mention a man named Gijs Mansveld a few times, but there's nothing sexual about his remarks. He sounds more like a personal assistant or butler."

"I hope for your sake you were right to believe Gerard. Karen's lawyer sounds pretty aggressive; without definitive proof of Arjan's lover or blackmailer, he'll have Gerard's assertions dismissed immediately."

"I know that," she responded irritably. "But why would he lie to us? He gave me the letters to give to Bernice Dijkstra. He knew they would be read by professional researchers."

"You should ask him to be more specific, to tell you which year you should be looking at and save yourself some time."

"Or we should return the letters and let the professionals deal with it. There's nothing I can do for Rita anyway, not anymore. I just want to get these back to Gerard before Bernice or Huub found out I took them in the first place," she grumbled, suddenly darting to the right and up the street that led to Gerard's house. All she wanted was to be done with this errand and forget about the Wederstein painting. She'd given up all hope of Rita Brouwer ever seeing *Irises* again. Huub Konijn had made it abundantly clear that, as far as both he and the museum's director were concerned, Karen O'Neil was the rightful owner. End of story.

Zelda touched the cell phone in her pocket, willing it to ring. Until Marianne Smit called her back, she had to stay positive and hope for the best. After she returned these documents to Gerard, she needed to focus her energy on getting her mentor back on her side and impressing the selection committee. The master's in museum studies was her reason for wanting to stay in Amsterdam, not Pietro Moretti, the internship at the Amsterdam Museum, or Rita Brouwer's search for her father's treasures.

She automatically slowed when she reached the next block, confused by the flashing red and blue lights reflecting off the windows of the houses and parked cars lining both sides of the road. For a moment, she thought there was a party going on, until she looked farther down the street.

Friedrich jogged up to her side. "Are those police cars?" he asked, slightly out of breath.

Two police cars were indeed parked along the curb up ahead, their lights still on. White and red tape was strewn around a whitewashed house on the left side of the street, its number partially hidden by the thick carpet of ivy covering the façade.

"Hey, that's Gerard's house!" she exclaimed, stopping suddenly. Friedrich plowed into her, almost knocking her over.

An officer was posted next to the front door. Through the windows, she could see other uniformed officers swarming around Gerard's living room. Or what was left of it. It looked like someone had taken an ax to his furniture. Shards of wood and bits of textile were strewn across the floor. Books, LP records, and framed photographs had been tossed into wobbly heaps and piles. Feathers and bits of foam floated around the room, sent airborne by the police shuffling around the ruins. Zelda and Friedrich stood gaping at the sight before them, unsure of what to do.

"What happened here?" he wondered aloud.

Zelda shook her head. "I don't know, but I'm guessing Gerard didn't make that mess himself; he could barely walk up the stairs, let alone break the legs off his couch."

"We could ask that officer."

"It's a real tragedy, isn't it?" An elderly woman's voice called out to them in Dutch. They turned to see Gerard's next-door neighbor hanging out of her kitchen window, a large mug in her hand.

"Do you know what happened to Mr. Van Heemsvliet?" Zelda spoke carefully, hoping the woman would understand her Dutch.

"He's been murdered!"

"Murdered?" She suddenly felt light-headed and swayed a little. Friedrich grabbed her elbow to steady her.

"Oh my dear, I'm sorry to be so callous. Please come inside." The neighbor rushed to open her front door, waving them inside.

"Did you know Gerard?" she asked as Friedrich and Zelda followed her into the kitchen.

"No. Yes. Not very well," Zelda sputtered, as they settled around a large oak table. The woman grabbed two more cups and poured them tea. Zelda wrapped her hands around the warm mug and slowly asked, "What happened?" She was having a hard time processing Gerard's death and speaking in a second language at the same time.

"There was a robbery," the woman whispered conspiratorially, her eyes gleaming. She was obviously enjoying being the bearer of bad news, Zelda thought. "They tied him to a chair, then tore his house apart. Maybe they didn't mean to kill him, but still, he died of a heart attack while he was bound and gagged. It must have been the stress. Can you imagine someone breaking into your own home and mishandling you like that? How scary that must have been for him." She shook her head in bewilderment.

Zelda nodded, amazed Gerard's neighbor had learned so much so quickly. But then, she could follow the police's investigation from her kitchen window.

"No one here can remember the last time there was a robbery in Urk, let alone a murder."

"Technically it wasn't murder but accidental death, if he died of a heart attack," Friedrich mused.

Gerard's neighbor glared at him for nitpicking her story.

"When was he, I mean, when did the police arrive?" Zelda asked softly. If they were still in his house, it couldn't have happened long before she and Friedrich got to Urk, she realized. They'd arrived an hour and a half ago, but she had treated them to a late lunch, figuring Gerard wasn't going to be going anywhere. And thanks to her disastrous morning at the museum, she hadn't eaten anything all day and was faint from hunger. Were the robbers still in his house when they'd arrived in the village? Or was Gerard already dead?

"I heard the police sirens about an hour ago, a few minutes after I got back from the shops. I'd popped down to the butcher's for some sausages. Johan, our mailman, noticed Gerard's front door was ajar, but no one answered his calls. When he went inside and saw the state of the living room, he called the police. Johan said there wasn't a piece of furniture or knickknack that hadn't been smashed or bashed in. He always comes down our street around three thirty in the afternoon. It couldn't have happened much earlier because little Marijke brought Gerard his groceries around noon. Gerard opened the door himself. Nothing was amiss, or she wouldn't have gone inside."

The woman sipped her tea, a sad look in her eye. "He waved at me. If I had known…" She glanced wistfully out the kitchen window.

"But why Gerard?" Zelda asked. "I didn't get the impression there was much to steal."

"Gerard van Heemsvliet was a good, honest, God-fearing man. He was not financially wealthy, but spiritually and morally he was richer than most. Heaven knows why someone would want to hurt him, let alone steal from him." The woman was obviously troubled by similar thoughts. "But the police don't think this was random. And they certainly were professionals. I mean, I never saw them come or go, and I was probably home when poor Gerard…" Her voice trailed off as she looked again towards her neighbor's home, now encircled by police tape.

Zelda imagined if anyone in Urk had seen the burglars enter Gerard's house, it would have been this woman. She sipped her tea, trying to wrap her head around everything that had happened this afternoon, but especially the timing of Gerard's death.

When Zelda and Friedrich had left for Urk, Arjan's brother was probably still alive. But when they reached the tiny fishing village less than an hour later, there were thieves in his house, tying him to a chair, literally scaring him to death. What if she and Friedrich had gone directly to Gerard's home instead of having a late lunch? Would the police be investigating a triple homicide right now? The thought sent shivers up her spine.

36

Burglary In Amsterdam

Friedrich and Zelda drove back to Amsterdam in silence, he fixated on the road ahead and she on Gerard's untimely passing. Why him? Why now? His neighbor couldn't think of why anyone would want to steal from him, let alone kill him. The extreme and seemingly random violence that ended Gerard's life really spooked her. She'd never known anyone who'd been murdered before. Last week she and Friedrich were having coffee and cookies with him, and now he was gone, his life taken from him by persons yet unknown, for reasons only to be guessed at.

And here she was, stuck with his letters. The museum researchers had to have them, Zelda decided as she gazed unseeingly out the car's window, even if no one bothered to actually read them. That was the least she could do to honor the memory of both Gerard and his brother Arjan, and the only thing she could still do that might help Rita Brouwer's claim on *Irises*. If she mailed them to the Amsterdam Museum's director tomorrow morning, there was a chance Leo de Boer would think Gerard had posted them before he died. There was no need for Bernice Dijkstra or Huub Konijn to know she'd taken the letters with her. It didn't really matter how they were sent, she reckoned, so long as they ended up at the right place.

After she put the letters in the mail, she needed to concentrate on her own imminent future. Her mentor still hadn't called back, but she was so unbelievably busy teaching classes, researching new book ideas, and giving lectures that it usually took her a few days to return anyone's call. Still, her nerves were about to crack. She reminded herself to stay positive. She'd already made it through the first selection of two hundred students, albeit with Marianne's help, and until she learned otherwise, she still had a shot at being accepted into the museum studies program.

Zelda frowned at her reflection in the window, realizing if she did get in, she'd see Pietro regularly. Several of the classes required for her program were also compulsory for the art history students. A week ago, that thought had filled her with joy; now it brought a sick feeling to her stomach. All she wanted to do right now was forget her Italian boyfriend ever existed. But damn it, Friedrich was right. Pietro was simply icing on the cake and certainly not the only reason she'd wanted to get into the master's program or stay in Amsterdam. As long as they didn't end up in too many of the same classes together, she would be able to keep her emotions in check.

The sounds of beeping car horns interrupted her thoughts. She looked out the window and saw that Friedrich was turning onto the Stadhouderskade. "Do you want to come up for a glass of wine?" Zelda asked. "I know I could sure use one. You can always borrow my bike if you get too tipsy."

He nodded slightly as he ignored the honking behind him and carefully backed into a tight parking space on her busy street. After killing the engine, he said, "That sounds fantastic. It's been a pretty strange day, hasn't it?"

Zelda opened her building's front door, expecting to be greeted by a cabal of noise coming from the kitchen. Instead, there was only silence. It was Friday night, she realized, so her housemates—all students—would be out celebrating the end of the study week. Though Zelda usually liked to stay in on Fridays and have the house to herself, she was glad Friedrich was with her tonight. She was in no mood to be alone.

As they ascended the fourth flight of stairs, Zelda was surprised to see her studio's door cracked open. She slowed a little, causing Friedrich to stumble against her legs.

"What the—" he exclaimed, grabbing the railing in time to stop himself from tumbling backwards down the steep stairwell.

"Look," she whispered, pointing at a narrow shaft of light spilling into the hallway. She tried to tell herself there was nothing amiss; one of her housemates must have borrowed a shirt and forgotten to turn off the light. But Zelda was sure she had locked her door when she and Friedrich went to Urk. And none of her housemates would have been so desperate to get at her cheap clothes that they'd have jimmied it open.

Friedrich pushed her gruffly aside, maneuvering himself in front.

"Be careful," she softly squealed, unsure whether to call the police or let her friend look inside first. Before she could decide, he kicked the door open and jumped through the entryway in a karate pose straight out of a B movie.

"Oh, shit," Friedrich exclaimed from inside her apartment. He poked his head back through the doorway. "You'd better call the police."

37

A Safe Place

"No, that closet is much too small, especially after we crate them up. That's the best way to protect them from insects and light. It may be months, even years, before it will be safe to move any of these paintings again," Arjan explained. He'd had the foresight to begin collecting suitable wooden boxes as soon as the war started, figuring he may one day need them to store his most delicate pieces. Because of the current fuel shortage, they were impossible to come by nowadays. He had one hundred and fifty-two crates stacked up in his formal dining room, the space he and Philip Verbeet were now standing in, unused since Gijs's death. He'd hoped they could squeeze all three hundred and twenty-seven framed canvases into them.

But even if they did fit, neither he nor Philip knew of a space large enough to hold them all. When the bombing raids and skirmishes within the city limits had intensified a few months before, Arjan had sketched up plans for a storage room disguised as an emergency shelter to be constructed in his backyard. But once Gijs fell ill, he'd stopped searching for discreet workmen suitable for the job. And now with Drechsler looking over his shoulder, he would never be able to build something like that on the sly.

"And the bomb shelter on Stadhouderskade?" Philip offered, scouring the map of Amsterdam he'd spread out on Arjan's dining room table. "Or the shelter in the Leidsebosje? We might be able to store them there amongst the rations."

"As soon as there's a bombing raid or fire anywhere in the vicinity, the shelter will fill up. Someone's bound to notice those crates don't belong. If the locals don't look inside and take the paintings, the Nazis will," Arjan said dismissively. They'd been at this for hours, and neither of them could think of a single worthy location. He pushed back his chair and rose. "I could use a drink. Is red wine alright? Or do you prefer something stronger?"

"Red is fine," Philip said, perking up. "The only liquor I drink is the schnapps I brew myself. Raspberry is my specialty."

Arjan looked at the older man with interest. "I've never heard of a raspberry variation before. Can you still taste the fruit after it's been fermented?"

"It's quite subtle. I'm going back to check on our house tomorrow morning. I'll get a bottle of schnapps out of our root cellar while I'm there," Philip said.

"Root cellar?"

Philip smiled. "That's what the Americans call it. My brother-in-law lives in Boston and has an unfinished cellar under his house. The earthen walls keep the room damp and cool, no matter what season it is. I dug one out under our garden shed so we can store my wife's preserves and my liquors down there without having to worry about them spoiling. It's not large, but big enough to stand up in," he said.

"How large is it exactly?" Arjan asked, urgency in his voice.

"Ten by twenty meters square?"

"How many crates do you think we could we fit inside?"

Philip began to scoff, but Arjan's serious expression stopped him cold. He studied the oak boxes stacked up around the room. "Seventy, if we're lucky."

"If we enlarged it, could we fit them all in?"

"It would take a few days of hard labor, but it is possible. I dug out the current cellar myself in less than a week," Philip said with pride. "The entrance is in the floor of the shed, so the neighbors won't notice us working as long as the door is shut tight. We can dump the dirt we dig up in the flower beds along the fence after nightfall."

"If the entrance is inside the shed, then anyone could find the paintings, couldn't they?" Arjan said, his enthusiasm waning.

"Not if we cover the door up with cement tiles. No one would think to look for a room hidden underneath a floor," Philip countered, clearly becoming more convinced of the plan's feasibility.

Arjan's mind swirled with possibilities. He'd been searching for a suitable location for weeks, without success. What other choice did they have? Philip's root cellar wasn't the best option, but it was probably their only option. "We'll need to buy a pickax and wheelbarrow," he said.

"I already have both in the shed. Working together, we should be able to expand the cellar in three or four days. I would rather not get anyone else involved."

"I agree; we need to keep this between us," Arjan said. If the space was suitable, he would write to his brother Gerard and tell him to contact Philip if anything happened to him. But he couldn't tell Gerard where the artwork was hidden; simply knowing the location would mean risking his life.

Is a week enough to get everything done? Arjan wondered. He would have to close up shop, write a note on his gallery door claiming he was ill, and pray Colonel Drechsler didn't come to his home to check up on him in the meantime.

"Wait a moment; you said a Nazi was looking for your daughter. Won't he have someone watching your house?" Arjan knew he should not have gotten excited quite yet; there was still a snake in the grass.

"If he was desperate enough to lie in wait for Iris, he would be staking out my frame shop. That's where she worked and where she socialized with most of the art students who knew she and Lex were in a relationship," Philip responded calmly. Arjan's nervous expression didn't change, and he continued, "Honestly, I'm not even certain he's still looking for her or how badly he wanted to find her in the first place. I couldn't have lived with myself if my family had stayed and he did come knocking; that's why I sent them all to Venlo straightaway. However, I haven't seen anyone show the slightest interest in our house or my shop in the four days since my girls left Amsterdam. The only way to get to the shed is through our apartment. Once we're inside, no one will be able to tell that we're there."

"Alright, why don't we go take a look at your root cellar together?" Arjan said, mustering up his enthusiasm, knowing there were no other realistic options to consider.

38

Somewhere To Stay

"Are you sure nothing's missing?"

Zelda massaged her temples as she took a mental survey of her few belongings, now strewn around the room like worthless trash. Her clothes, CDs, photo albums, travel souvenirs, and books had been ripped out of their drawers and shelves. Her desk, futon, and bed had all been tipped upside down and the legs busted off. Shards of her television and stereo peeked out from under the broken furniture. She could hardly believe this was her studio apartment, the same one she'd left so neat and tidy a few hours earlier. How could she tell at a glance if something was missing? Not a single thing was in its rightful place.

"I don't think so," she mustered, finally answering Officer Eenhuizen of the Amsterdam police department, a tall blond man who couldn't have been older than thirty. He had already taken her statement, listening intently to her account of the evening before asking questions. Two cars full of cops had arrived minutes after she'd called 112. Though Zelda was extremely grateful to have so many agents working on the case, right now all she wanted to do was drop onto her couch and cry. But she couldn't even do that because there was nothing left to sit on.

"Did you have any expensive jewelry or other valuables stored here?" the young officer asked.

She shook her head. "The most valuable thing in here was my television," she said, pointing under her futon mattress at the small set with a smashed-in screen. "Everything else was secondhand, even the stereo. I'm a student; I don't have any real valuables and certainly no expensive jewelry," she replied, clearly at a loss.

"We've already checked your housemates' apartments. None of their rooms were disturbed, so we don't think this was a random break-in," Officer Eenhuizen said.

As the weight of the violation she'd experienced began to sink in, Zelda dropped to her knees and covered her face with her hands. Her backpack's straps cut sharply into her shoulders, manifesting the pain she was feeling inside. This wasn't random; she was the target of some nut job. "I really don't know why anyone would want to rob me," she replied, her voice trembling. "Even if someone thought I had something worth stealing, why would they tear up my apartment like this?"

The young policeman grew somber. "Intruders usually don't take time to destroy property, at least not to this extent. You're very lucky you weren't home." He paused for a moment, then cleared his throat, obviously embarrassed by what he had to ask. "Are you sure you can't think of anyone who has a grudge against you? An angry ex-boyfriend or a stalker?" He gestured to the chaos around them. "This seems personal, all this damage. Especially considering nothing obvious was taken."

Zelda's face went white: *Pietro!* Was the thought of spending a few classes together so horrible that he'd ransacked her apartment to try to scare her into leaving Amsterdam? He'd have to have called someone moments after she'd hung up on him. And frankly he didn't sound that upset about losing her—more like irritated that he'd been caught cheating. She couldn't believe he would be so desperate to get rid of her that he'd go this far. But then she'd never suspected he had a girlfriend back home either. She evidently didn't know him as well as she'd thought.

"Well, I did split up with my boyfriend about four hours ago," she said reluctantly.

Officer Eenhuizen perked up. "What is his name? Do you know where he is?"

"His name is Pietro Moretti, and he's probably still at his parents' home. They live in a small village near Florence, Italy. We broke up over the phone."

The young officer frowned as he flipped open his notepad. "Still, he has lived in Amsterdam and presumably knows people here he can call on, perhaps someone with a key to your apartment. None of the locks were forced. I'll still need his full name and contact information."

Zelda read off his phone numbers and address, spelling Pietro's name letter for letter. As she spoke, she took off her backpack and rolled her shoulders, trying to relieve the tension in her neck. Nothing made sense anymore. First Gerard's house was broken into and torn apart. Only hours later, her own apartment was pillaged. And neither of them owned anything worth stealing.

Was it just some weird coincidence that she and Gerard were both burgled on the same day, or were they both targeted by the same person? But for what reason?

Zelda rested her knees on her backpack, feeling the thick pile of paper inside. The letters Arjan van Heemsvliet had sent to his brother! That was the only connection between them. If someone was looking for the letters, that would explain the damage to both of their homes. But why would someone go to all this trouble—to steal and even kill—just to get their hands on letters written by a dead man more than seventy years ago?

"Why is this happening?" The words escaped her lips as a whisper.

"Do you have somewhere to stay?" the young policeman asked sympathetically.

"She can stay with me," Friedrich piped up. He'd been standing in the doorway listening the whole time. There was no room for him inside, considering the number of detectives and uniformed policemen wandering around her tiny apartment. She smiled at her friend gratefully, mouthing "thank you" as she stood up and slipped her bag onto her back.

"We'll be busy here for a while longer," the policeman explained. "If we are lucky, we'll find fingerprints we can trace. We will have to fingerprint all of your housemates and any friends who've been by recently so we can eliminate them from our search."

216

"My housemates are all out drinking and won't be home until late tonight. I'll leave them a note letting them know what happened, and that you'll be back in the morning and why. I'm sure they'll cooperate; none of us will feel safe until we know who did this."

Officer Eenhuizen closed his notebook and held out his hand. "You are free to go. We'll see you back here tomorrow morning, around nine o'clock."

She nodded distractedly as she shook his hand. Were the letters really important enough to kill for? Zelda despised Karen O'Neil, but she couldn't believe the New Yorker would murder to get ahold of *Irises*, the letters, or even Van Heemsvliet's entire collection. Her unsullied reputation was worth so much more. Besides, as soon as her lawyer supplied the museum's director with her mother's birth certificate, the Wederstein was hers anyway. But who else would be so anxious to read these letters they would scare an old man to death in order to do so?

Friedrich hurried Zelda down the stairs. Once they were out on the street and well out of earshot, he whispered, "You know what they're after, don't you? I can see it on your face."

She patted her bag. "It must be Gerard's letters. It can't be a coincidence both of our homes were broken into today. But Friedrich, it doesn't make any sense. I've read half of them, yet so far Arjan hasn't said a thing about having a gay lover or being blackmailed by a Nazi."

"I think you are right. Someone seems to want those letters badly enough to kill for them. There must be something important in them, or at least the killer thinks there is."

Zelda stopped in her tracks. "Friedrich, do you realize what this means?" She could feel the blood draining from her face as her mind put the pieces together. "Either Bernice Dijkstra, Huub Konijn, or Karen O'Neil must be behind these break-ins. Nobody knew Gerard had Arjan's letters until I told everyone about them at the meeting yesterday."

Zelda grabbed her friend's shoulders, turning him towards her. "If it is one of them, then I killed Gerard by lying about where the letters were. If I had told the truth, the robbers would have never gone to his house." Tears poured down her cheeks as she moaned, "Oh, Friedrich, what have I done?"

39

Hopes And Fears During World War II

Zelda's head was spinning. She wasn't sure whether it was the caffeine rush from her ninth cup of coffee, the lack of sleep finally catching up with her, or the pure monotony of translating Arjan van Heemsvliet's letters into English that was doing her head in. His handwriting was, thankfully, neat and easy to read despite the multitude of swirls he used in his cursive text. However, the ink had faded, and the paper had yellowed to the point where many paragraphs seemed to disappear off the page and were only visible if she held the thin paper up to the kitchen light. To make matters worse, Arjan's style of writing and word choice was quite formal. She was constantly flipping through Friedrich's Dutch-English dictionary, slowing her progress even further. Luckily, Friedrich seemed to be faring much better. In the time it took her to translate one page, he'd cruised through three.

"Oh man, I need a break," she said, pushing her chair back from his kitchen table.

Her friend looked up from the pile of letters in front of him, weariness evident in his bloodshot eyes and slumped shoulders. "Yeah? Me too," he replied, relieved.

"Do you have any juice?" Zelda asked, already walking towards his refrigerator. "If I have any more coffee, my heart might explode."

"The orange juice is Sam's. I guess he won't mind. Pour me a glass, will you?" Sam was the friendliest of Friedrich's five housemates. As was the case in her building, they each had their own room but shared the toilet, shower, and kitchen on the second floor. But unlike her canal house, theirs was owned by an absentee landlord who refused to repair anything, with the small exception of leaking water pipes.

Zelda tried to avoid Friedrich's place at all costs; a house badly in need of renovation and shared by six bachelors was never especially tidy. Considering her own apartment had been torn apart by unknown assailants, she really didn't have a choice. In fact, she was glad Friedrich had offered to let her sleep on his floor; even a few nights in a hotel would have certainly blown her monthly budget. Amsterdam was one of the most expensive cities in the world, and hotel prices definitely reflected that exclusive status.

"Have you found anything else in the last batch?" he asked, while Zelda hunted around the kitchen for clean glasses.

As soon as they had arrived at Friedrich's place, they'd started translating the twelve letters she hadn't read yet—first in his private abode on the third floor, then in the roomier kitchen after his housemates had gone out for the night—pausing occasionally to fill each other in on any interesting tidbits they'd come across. Zelda had been tempted to start at the end and work backwards, in the hope of finding out faster about this supposed blackmailer, but Friedrich managed to convince her it would be better to read them in the order written, so they didn't misinterpret something Arjan referred to later on.

The ten letters that Zelda had already translated went from November 1939 to March 1941, and luckily, she'd had the foresight to keep her translations in her backpack with the originals. But after hours of reading these later letters, they hadn't found much that differed from those earlier ones; the art dealer barely mentioned his gallery or the war in any of them. If Arjan hadn't dated his letters, Zelda would have never guessed they had been written during the German occupation of Amsterdam.

To make matters worse, neither she nor Friedrich had found even a subtle reference to Arjan's sexual preference. Although he referred to his manservant and personal assistant Gijs Mansveld in several of them, he never gave the slightest hint that the man was more than an employee. The more Zelda read, the more frustrated she became. At this rate, they wouldn't be able to prove Arjan was gay or being blackmailed without Gerard's sworn testimony, meaning Karen's lawyer would make mincemeat of them all.

"I haven't found out anything worth reporting, unfortunately," she said, as she handed Friedrich a glass of juice, then took a sip of her own. "I don't think he was being blackmailed at this point. And you? Has he mentioned his gallery or lover in that letter?" she asked, nodding at the aged paper in front of him as she sat back down at the kitchen table.

"No, as of December 1941 still no references to either." Friedrich stared at the letter before him, a puzzled look on his face. "What I really find strange is that he's barely mentioned the war in his letters."

"That's been bothering me, too. What if Arjan wasn't being blackmailed by the Germans, but working with them? That would explain why he didn't seem to worry about the Nazis," she wondered aloud. "Yet Gerard was so certain about the blackmail and his brother's homosexuality that he gave me the letters so they could be used as evidence against Karen's claim."

Zelda prayed that they would find something soon, anything that substantiated what Gerard had told them about his brother. *If only I'd recorded our conversation, as the museum's professional researchers would have done,* she chided herself again. Now that he was dead, it was her word against Karen's. Huub was right; she had screwed up the investigation—and, ultimately, Rita's claim—by interviewing Gerard herself.

"None of this makes sense," Friedrich said, clearly exasperated. "But we haven't read them all yet."

"Maybe the friends he writes about are a clue. If they are German officers or prominent members of the Nazi Party, that might explain why he mentioned them." Glancing back through her translations, Zelda recognized some of the names Arjan mentioned in his letters, but she couldn't figure out why. Perhaps when they finished translating everything, she could compile a list of people he'd written about. That might help jog her memory. But for now, they had to push on.

"We shouldn't jump to conclusions before we've finished translating everything," he reminded her.

"You're right; we don't have a whole lot of choice but to keep reading," she said, without a whole lot of conviction. It was two o'clock in the morning; all she really wanted to do was crawl back upstairs and crash on Friedrich's floor. Her eyes drooped shut just thinking about sleep, but the thought of Gerard, literally frightened to death, jolted her back awake quicker than a shot of espresso ever could. She couldn't go home, let alone sleep soundly, until they knew what piece of information his killer was really after.

She glared determinedly at the pile of unread letters in the center of the table. Only five more to go. Zelda grabbed the topmost letter and picked up her pen.

40

Friedrich Makes A Discovery

"*Scheisse*, that's it!" Friedrich cried out as he slapped the tabletop, jolting Zelda out of her daze. She had fallen into a trance while translating one of the longer letters word for word, virtually unaware of what she was writing down. "What is it?"

Her friend's face shone, lit up with excitement. "Listen to this," he said. "'May 7, 1942. My dearest Gerard, blah, blah, blah. Something horrible happened in March that I thought I could deal with on my own. But it's all gone wrong, and now that Gijs is dead, I have no one left to turn to for guidance.'" Friedrich noticed her eyebrows furrowing. "Arjan also writes that Gijs Mansveld had died from a bronchial infection in February," he explained.

Zelda nodded in understanding, waiting for the bombshell.

"So, anyway, Arjan says he needs some advice." Friedrich scanned his translation, looking for where he'd left off. "Oh yeah...'a Nazi colonel has been blackmailing me for weeks.'"

"So Gerard wasn't lying!" she shouted triumphantly, relieved the old man hadn't unintentionally set them on the wrong track. In the past few hours, she'd almost convinced herself he'd mingled family gossip with what Arjan had actually written.

Friedrich's head bobbed vigorously up and down. "Arjan writes that a German officer caught him sneaking out of Grote Geerts during a raid." He looked up from his translation. "Grote Geerts was a gay bar in Amsterdam on the Zeedijk, close to Central Station. It opened in 1927 and closed in 1984. I googled it." Friedrich nodded towards his laptop, open on the kitchen table. She'd been in such a stupor she hadn't even noticed he'd gone up to his room to get it.

"That's incredible!" she yelled.

"Shh, my housemates are asleep." Friedrich cringed, well aware it was four in the morning. The other five residents had stumbled up the stairs shortly after the bars closed a few hours earlier.

"Sorry, it's just, now that we can prove Arjan was gay and being blackmailed..." Her voice trailed off. "Wait a second, a gay bar? I though the Nazis made homosexuality a crime. How could gay bars have operated here during the war?"

"According to this letter, Arjan was in Grote Geerts when it was raided on March 21, 1942. Maybe it was an underground bar, like a speakeasy during America's Prohibition?"

She nodded slowly. "I guess that makes sense."

"Let me finish reading you this letter. It gets even better."

"Oh, of course." Zelda, slap-happy from the lack of sleep, rested her chin on her knuckles and smiled serenely up at her friend.

"When Arjan ran outside, he passed a man on the street walking his dog. He wrote: 'For only a split second did our eyes meet, yet I recognized him instantly: Colonel Oswald Drechsler of the Reichskammer der bildenden Künste,'" Friedrich read aloud before clarifying, "Or, as it was more commonly known in the Netherlands, the Kultuurkamer. It was the Nazis' Chamber of Culture—they were in charge of making sure any artwork exhibited in public places upheld the National Socialist ideals regarding art and culture. I googled that, too."

"Jeez, that is bad luck," she murmured.

"This next paragraph is intriguing," Friedrich continued, "'With much trepidation, I opened my gallery the next day, unsure if it was better to flee the city or act normally. I couldn't just leave my artwork behind; too many people were relying on me to be cautious and survive the war. And I risked everything for one night of companionship. The fates are punishing me and all who trusted me!'"

"'Too many people?' Who could he be referring to?"

Friedrich shrugged. "Then he tells his brother that Drechsler came to his shop the next day and demanded artwork in exchange for his silence. If Arjan didn't comply, Drechsler promised to report Arjan to the Gestapo as a 'repeat offender' homosexual. His home and gallery would have been seized, and he would have been sent to a work camp in Germany. That first night, Drechsler took several pieces from Galerie Van Heemsvliet, calling it his 'initial fee.' Since then he'd returned weekly, demanding more and more paintings each time as payment for his continued silence. And Arjan's supply of artwork was rapidly dwindling. He knew he wouldn't be able to keep the Nazi happy for much longer."

"Drechsler really sounds like one sick puppy," she said, disturbed by what the German officer was threatening to do to the art dealer, "but Friedrich, this means we know why our thief wants these letters so badly. They must have known someone else had taken possession of Arjan's art collection during the war and hidden it somewhere in the city, but not who or where. If Galerie Van Heemsvliet's inventory really is worth millions, then finding Drechsler's name would definitely be worth killing for." She sprung out of her chair and began pacing back and forth, re-energized by their findings or, rather, Friedrich's.

"But what about *Irises*? Why wasn't it hidden away with the rest of the paintings? And how does Rita's father fit into all of this? He wasn't the blackmailer," Friedrich pondered.

"Arjan said too many people were relying on him to survive the war. Maybe he was hiding art for Jewish friends?"

"Rita's father wasn't Jewish. Or gay, or a gypsy, or a Jehovah's Witness, or a communist, or even a political dissident," Friedrich countered.

"He did have to leave Amsterdam in a hurry and was looking for someone to store his collection with." She yawned again, not bothering to hide her gaping mouth behind her hand. She turned towards the window behind her. Through a tear in the curtains, she could see the sun was starting to color the morning clouds in pinkish-gray hues. They'd now officially been up all night reading and translating.

She spun around suddenly, as a new realization popped into her head. "Friedrich, do you know what else this means? Karen can't be Arjan's granddaughter. If he did have a wife and child on the way, the colonel wouldn't have had a reason to blackmail him anymore."

"Or that is exactly what happened and we are about to read about it."

Both looked to the two remaining letters on the table.

"I can translate those faster than you," he said. "Why don't I do that while you reread our translations? Perhaps we missed something."

Zelda smiled and nodded wearily, frankly relieved by his offer. Friedrich was three times as fast as she was under normal circumstances, but thanks to the sleep deprivation, her productivity level had dipped to an all-time low.

Over the course of the next hour, she read and reread all twenty of the translated letters until her eyes crossed, yet found nothing new. The shock of the robberies and Gerard's death was catching up fast, making it extremely difficult to concentrate on the text before her.

She glanced at her friend, bent over the kitchen table as he read, his forehead furrowed in concentration. Simply knowing Arjan was really being blackmailed, and by whom, lifted a huge weight off her shoulders, but they still didn't have any idea as to who was behind the robberies and Gerard's death.

Zelda felt her mind drifting away from the letters as she considered the possible suspects. She could cross Bernice Dijkstra off the list immediately. As project manager, she had never been involved in researching any of the pieces in the *Stolen Objects* collection, only organizing the physical exhibition and publicizing it. More importantly, she'd never openly favored Karen O'Neil or Rita Brouwer during any of their meetings together, but had repeatedly demanded that the researchers assigned by the Restitutions Committee be allowed to fully investigate both claims before awarding *Irises* to either party.

On the other hand, as senior curator for the Jewish Historical Museum,

Huub Konijn had enjoyed unlimited access to all of the unclaimed artwork since it had been moved to his museum's depots ten years earlier. Despite his earlier outrage, it was entirely possible that, while investigating *Irises'* provenance or even during his preparations for the Carel Willink exhibition he'd mentioned, he'd stumbled upon the existence of Arjan van Heemsvliet's collection and figured out it was still hidden somewhere in Amsterdam. What if the documents Karen O'Neil presented with her claim had provided the final clue to its whereabouts?

The curator's tragic personal history was another reason for him to remain under suspicion, as far as she was concerned. Not only had most of his family been murdered by the Nazis, but also, the Dutch government had done nothing to help him or his sister when they'd returned to Amsterdam and discovered that their possessions had been seized and sold off, ultimately leaving them penniless and homeless. He had every reason to feel betrayed and perhaps even seek revenge. How far would Huub go to rewrite history? Would finding Arjan's collection somehow make up for his suffering?

Then there was Karen O'Neil, Arjan's supposed granddaughter and sole heir. Was she truly a blood relative, or was she pretending to be? There was no indication in Arjan's letters that he'd had any relationships with women or fathered a child. How did her relatives get ahold of Arjan's inventory books and those bills of sale? They didn't appear to be fake. In fact, the list of paintings compiled by Rita's mother was almost identical to the Verbeet collection listed in Arjan's ledgers. To her chagrin, Zelda recognized that Rita's documents helped to confirm that Arjan's ledgers hadn't been fabricated.

But if Oswald Drechsler had blackmailed Arjan into turning over his extensive collection, what had the Nazi done with all of the art? Had he hidden it away somewhere in Amsterdam, in the hopes of recovering it after the war? It was as if all three hundred and twenty-seven canvases had disappeared from the face of the earth. Well, three hundred and twenty-six; *Irises* had resurfaced, though she still couldn't figure out why. She rubbed the bridge of her nose, automatically closing her eyes. She was vaguely aware of her head sliding down towards the pile of translations on the kitchen table before she fell into a deep sleep.

41

Preparing The Space

Arjan held down the stencil with one hand as he sloshed black paint over the side of the oak crate with the other, choking as the harsh fumes burned his nostrils and throat.

For the past four days and nights, he and Philip Verbeet had taken turns packing up the paintings and digging out the root cellar. His wrists ached from tightening the screws onto the lids and his back from shoveling. Yet it was the overpowering stench emitting from the cheap house paint they were using to stencil numbers onto each crate that was the hardest to take. They didn't dare open a window lest the smell drew someone's attention, and the fumes were suffocating him.

He covered his mouth with a handkerchief to dampen the noise as another cough racked his body. After his choking fit subsided, he turned to his inventory ledger and placed a small check mark next to the Monet, Renoir, and Redon belonging to his old friend Frans Keizer.

Holding the handkerchief to his nose, he glanced around the room, frowning as he counted the paintings still stacked up on the left wall of the shed. Sixty-five paintings to fit into forty-five crates. And there were still the ten paintings hanging in his gallery to consider. It would be a tight squeeze.

Despite their hard work, there was so much more to do. Yet his body was shutting down from pure exhaustion. He had no choice but to go home soon and get a few hours' sleep.

Arjan swatted at his pants leg, trying in vain to get the powdered lime out of its dark fabric before going back outside. He didn't want to give the police any reason to stop and question him. He'd spilled some onto his legs while carrying three heavy buckets of the chalk-like substance down into the root cellar, placed there to help absorb extra moisture while the paintings were hidden away.

Once he was satisfied his pants wouldn't be a source of concern, he pulled on his waistcoat and jacket before opening his pocket watch, the same one his father had given to him for his eighteenth birthday. He sighed in dismay when he saw it was after midnight.

"I'm ready to leave," he called down to his cohort, currently spreading the last layer of plaster onto the walls of the newly enlarged cellar. In two days, the plaster would be dry enough that they could begin shifting the filled crates, now stacked up in towers to his right, down below. If they picked up the paintings from his gallery tomorrow evening, they'd have a full day to crate up the rest.

But now, he had to go home, wash the filth and grime out of his clothes and body, then get some rest. After he started packing, that is. Philip had brought his suitcases around this morning, the portrait of his oldest daughter the only painting tucked inside. Once they'd finished up in the shed, they would take the train down south together, before parting ways in Venlo. His contact at the resistance group had warned him not to bring more than his two smallest suitcases. But that would be enough—it would have to be.

42

Answered Prayers

"Yoo-hoo, Zelda. Wake up already. I've got something interesting to show you." Friedrich's voice rang through her head as a hand shook her shoulder. "Trust me, you're going to want to hear this." He spoke in a sing-song rhythm, his tone cheery and bright. Friedrich always talked like that when he was pleased with himself.

"Ten more minutes," she mumbled, eyes still closed.

"You've been asleep for two hours."

"Oh, man!" Zelda snapped to attention, wiping the drool off her hand and chin. She hadn't meant to fall asleep, and certainly not for so long. After running her tongue over her lips, she smirked in disgust. Her mouth felt like it was covered in a thick layer of sugar and cream. *No more coffee today,* she promised herself.

"What if Arjan managed to hide all of his friends' artwork from his blackmailer?" Friedrich asked.

"What do you mean?" she said, struggling to sit up straight. The catnap had definitely taken the edge off her sleep deprivation and coffee overindulgence, but she still felt like crap.

"What I mean is, I translated the rest of the letters. I don't think the thieves are looking for a name, but a place."

"Wait, I'm not awake enough yet to follow you. Can you start where we left off, with finding out Drechsler was blackmailing Arjan for artwork?"

she asked, stretching her arms out above her head.

"Arjan wrote to Gerard that he wants to leave Amsterdam but has to find a hiding place for his artwork first."

"You can't stash three hundred and twenty-six framed canvases up in your attic and expect them to be safe, especially if you're not going to be around to check on them," she chimed in, sure she was following the story now.

"It's not what you think. Let me explain everything first. He's afraid to leave Amsterdam because of a moral dilemma. He confesses to Gerard that he had several collections in his possession, artwork he promised to hold onto for friends who'd fled the country or gone into hiding."

"That's where I've seen those names before," she said, her sleepy brain slowly connecting some of the dots. "The friends he mentions in his letters—I made a list of their names before I fell asleep. Several of them are the owners of paintings listed in Arjan's inventory book. That's why he had so many unsold, high quality pieces listed in it—they were never meant to be sold. That inventory book must have been Arjan's way of remembering which paintings he'd stored and for whom—including Rita Brouwer's father!" she exclaimed. "But if Arjan did leave Amsterdam, what did he do with it all?"

"Let me finish telling you what he wrote," Friedrich responded gruffly, clearly fed up with her interruptions.

Zelda folded her arms behind her head and leaned back in her chair. "Please continue."

"After Arjan was seen running out of Grote Geerts, he felt incredibly guilty about letting his friends down. Up until then, no one had suspected he was gay, not even his closest acquaintances. His boyfriend, Gijs Mansveld, was just as concerned that no one find out about their relationship. Yes, boyfriend," Friedrich repeated, as he looked her in the eye, bringing an instant smile to her face. "He'd never had to fear being exposed. But Drechsler changed all that. Arjan wrote to Gerard that he knew the colonel would never be satisfied, he would demand more and more artwork until Arjan had nothing left to give him. And as soon as that happened, Drechsler would gladly turn him over to the Gestapo. He has no choice but to flee."

"On May 27th, Arjan writes that his friends' pieces were currently stored in his house and gallery, but he was trying to secure a better hiding place for them; he owes his friends that much. So far he's not found any one location where he can store them all without raising suspicion. Based on his word choice and the tone of the letter, Arjan is obviously frantic. Several times he asks Gerard if it is morally wrong to leave Amsterdam without hiding the artwork first, or if his own personal safety outweighs his pledge to his friends. Arjan clearly doesn't see a way out of his dilemma and is hoping his brother will tell him it's okay to up and leave."

"Then two weeks later, Arjan sends Gerard his last letter," he said, holding up two sheets of yellowed paper, "writing that his prayers have been answered. He's met someone who can provide him access to a space large enough to hold all the artwork for the duration of the war."

"When did Arjan send it?"

"June 18, 1942."

"That's only four days after Rita and her family went to Venlo," Zelda stated somberly. "Does he mention his friend's name?"

"Yes, he does. It's Philip Verbeet."

"My God, Rita's father really did know Arjan van Heemsvliet." She was silent a moment as she absorbed this shocking, yet wonderful news. "What else does the letter say?"

"Verbeet came to his gallery on June 16th. He knew Arjan was holding artwork for some mutual friends of theirs and hoped he could help him out too. Philip's family had already left for Venlo, and he wanted to join them as soon as possible, but he couldn't bear to leave his collection behind for the Nazis to take. The fact that Verbeet, a mere acquaintance, knew what Arjan was doing sent him into a panic. In his mind, it was only a matter of time before Drechsler found out about the artwork he was storing. He broke down and told Philip everything."

"That means Philip Verbeet didn't sell it to Arjan after all. Rita is going to get *Irises* back! We've got to get these letters to the Restitutions Committee straightaway," Zelda said, momentarily rejoicing before her friend cut her off again.

"There's more. Philip knew of a place they could hide the artwork, but he needed Arjan's help readying the space for long-term storage. They visited it the morning Arjan sent the letter. He writes that it's almost perfect; his only complaint is that it will cost him a large sum of money to secure the space for five years. But he'll pay it gladly, if it means the artwork will be safe."

"And? Where's this place Rita's father told Arjan about?"

"I don't know; he never states specifically where it is. Only that it was solid enough and secret enough to remain hidden throughout the war. Arjan finishes by writing that Gerard should find Rita's father if anything happens to him. 'Philip Verbeet will know who you are and what to do.'"

Zelda wondered whether Gerard ever tried.

43

Family Trees And Chocolate Croissants

"But that's the last letter Arjan sent to Gerard. What happened next?" Zelda demanded, perturbed the gallery owner hadn't been more specific in describing the location of his costly stash.

Friedrich simply shrugged his shoulders.

Her head rapidly filled with unanswered questions. She grabbed their empty cups and made her way over to the refrigerator, pondering all they had learned. As she poured the last of the orange juice into their glasses, she said, "Okay, let's assume for a moment that Arjan van Heemsvliet and Philip Verbeet did manage to move all the artwork into the secret storage space before the Nazi could get ahold of it. Why didn't Rita's dad go to Venlo after they were finished?" She threw away the empty carton and returned to the table, choosing to stand as she drank.

"Arjan and Philip must have stashed the art away but were killed soon after, or at least before they could tell anyone where it was hidden. It stands to reason that if either one of them had lived, Rita would know what had happened to both her father and his collection." Friedrich spoke unhurriedly, as if he was thinking aloud.

Rita Brouwer. Just hearing her name conjured up a mixture of emotions. On the one hand, Zelda couldn't wait to tell her about the letters. Not only did they prove her father knew Arjan van Heemsvliet, but they also made clear that he had only asked the art dealer to hold onto his collection for the duration of the war, rather than having sold it to him. Zelda only wished she could also tell the old lady where the rest of her father's artwork was hidden.

Wait a second, she thought, *if I told Rita about the clues in the letters, she might know where Arjan was referring to.* After all, it was her father who had suggested the space they ended up using. Zelda glanced at the clock on the kitchen wall and frowned. It was well past midnight in Missouri. It would be better to wait until Rita was rested and awake before she tried to explain everything over the phone, at least if she expected to get a coherent answer.

"Wherever this secret hiding place is, it can't be in a public space if they had to pay rent on it." She put her glass down and raised her hands high up over her head, stretching out her back until she felt it crack.

"I still don't understand how *Irises* fits into all of this," Friedrich admitted.

"It's the only piece in Arjan's inventory ledger that has surfaced since the war. If someone is still searching for his paintings, *Irises* would be the logical place to start," she said, before pausing to contemplate another aspect. "But that means whoever is trying to steal these letters must think the exact location would be revealed in them, just like we did."

They both stared at the letters and translations piled up on the kitchen table between them. If only Arjan or Philip had dared to tell their families where they'd hidden the artwork, then this whole nightmare would be over, Zelda thought bitterly.

"What if Oswald Drechsler had children?" Friedrich said. "If he knew Arjan had hidden his artwork away but wasn't able to find it during the war, it could very well be that one of his relatives is still looking for it. It probably won't help us find the hiding place," he conceded, "but it might tell us who's after these letters and behind the robberies."

"That would be great," she replied wearily. "But how would we do that? Drechsler was a Nazi officer who presumably went back to Germany after the war, if he even survived that long. We can't make a road trip to Berlin or wherever those kinds of archival documents are stored, can we?"

"We shouldn't have to," Friedrich said with a grin as he pulled his laptop close and typed in a search query. "The German national archives are online." He clicked on the frequently asked questions link and scrolled quickly through the German text. "Okay, provided Drechsler is already deceased, we should be able to access his biographical information in their database."

"Really?" Zelda perked up again. If Drechsler had been blackmailing Arjan for artwork, he could have taken his gallery's inventory ledgers. She wouldn't be surprised if Karen O'Neil was related to the Nazi colonel somehow. That would explain how Karen knew about Arjan's vast collection of unsold canvases. Zelda moved her chair next to Friedrich's and silently watched as he went to work.

A few moments later, he nudged her shoulder with his own. "Check it out. This record contains his family history." He skimmed the official-looking document before translating the German text for her. "Oswald Drechsler was born in Düsseldorf in 1910, the third of seven children. This was his parents' address, and these are the names of his siblings. It looks like three of them died young; Oswald was the only boy to reach manhood."

Friedrich clicked on another link, and a different document filled the screen. "This record shows us where he lived in Germany. In June of 1945, Drechsler moved back to his parents' house in Düsseldorf and stayed there until his death in 1987. On November 5, 1947, his older sister, Frieda Drechsler, and her son were officially registered as living there, as well. But I don't see any indication that Oswald Drechsler ever married or fathered any children."

"What? But he has to have!" Zelda was just warming up to the idea that Karen O'Neil was his daughter or granddaughter. What else could justify her aggressive behavior or explain how she had gotten ahold of Galerie Van Heemsvliet's paperwork? "What about his sister or her boy; can we find out more about them?"

"Let's take a look." Friedrich typed the sister's name into the archive's search engine. "Frieda Drechsler married Gotthard Heider in 1935, but was widowed in 1947. Gotthard died in an auto accident in Cologne. Three months later, she moved back to Düsseldorf. They had one son, Konrad, born in 1938. The boy would have turned nine years old the year his father died and he moved in with his uncle. Frieda remained at the house until her death in June of 2002. There's no indication on this record that her son ever moved out."

Zelda sat back, thinking. "Nine years old is an impressionable age. So this Konrad could have easily been influenced by his uncle. And he kept his father's last name—what is it again?"

"Konrad Oswald Gotthard Heider is his name," he said, adding, "Heider is a fairly common German surname. At least in the region of Switzerland where I'm from."

"Konrad Heider!" she screeched. "That's Karen O'Neil's lawyer!" Zelda dug a notebook out of her backpack and shook it violently until a business card fell onto the floor. She grabbed it and shoved it under Friedrich's nose. "See?"

"'Konrad Heider, Founding Partner of Heider, Schmidt & Weber Law Firm,'" he read aloud.

"That can't be a coincidence, can it?" Zelda sputtered.

"Unlikely."

"But why this charade? Why involve Karen? Is he even a lawyer, or is that a lie, too?"

"I don't understand either." Friedrich turned to his computer and typed the lawyer's name into his browser's search engine. "He appears to be legit. He's worked on some pretty high-profile cases," he said, as he scanned the list of German and English language newspaper articles associated with Konrad Heider. A few moments later, he whistled softly. "You're going to love this. Here's an article about large donations he's made to American museums: the Museum of Modern Art in New York, the Smithsonian Institute in Washington, D.C., the Chicago Art Institute, the Getty Museum in Los Angeles... the list goes on and on."

He began clicking on random links, skimming the newspaper articles for interesting information while Zelda studied the photographs. "No references to his Nazi uncle," Friedrich noted, "but that's not strange considering he had a different last name and was a toddler when the war started."

"That's not exactly the type of information a prominent lawyer would want to get around," she agreed.

Her friend switched back to the German national archives' home page and typed Heider's name into the site's search engine. "Damn, of course. He's still alive, so none of his personal information is available to the public. The only link is to a record in his mother's file, but it's the same one we just looked at." He looked over at Zelda, clearly troubled and confused. "What does this all mean? The lawyer is Drechsler's nephew? Then why is Karen O'Neil pretending to be Van Heemsvliet's granddaughter?"

She leaned back in her chair, mulling over the possibilities. "Let's assume that Konrad Heider is still trying to find Arjan's artwork. He couldn't very well claim *Irises* himself, could he? Yet by acting as Karen's lawyer, he was privy to every meeting she was and had unlimited access to any documentation the museum might have already gathered regarding *Irises* or any of the other paintings in Arjan van Heemsvliet's collection. And he and Karen are obviously in a relationship; we both saw them kissing at the Amstel Hotel. She must be in on it, too."

"I suppose," Friedrich conceded, adding, "But why, when she has so much to lose?"

"That must be why they never went to the press—Karen didn't want to make her role in this fake claim public knowledge," she said. She chewed on her thumbnail, momentarily lost in thought. "Or Heider thought that the Wederstein painting held a clue to the location of Arjan's secret hiding place. Huub Konijn certainly did; he ran every test conceivable, according to the museum's art conservator. That would explain why Heider tried to steal *Irises* when it became clear Karen's documents would be examined by the museum's experts," she ventured.

"But it doesn't," Friedrich countered. "You said the tests the museum's art restorer ran showed there were no mysterious texts or drawings scrawled onto the painting or frame. And from what happened at your last meeting with Huub Konijn, it doesn't sound like he found anything hidden inside the frame either."

Zelda thought back to the meeting, remembering excitedly, "But Heider didn't know that Jasper de Vries had run any tests on *Irises*, at least not until after the botched robbery. It was during the meeting Huub accused me of trying to steal *Irises* that he mentioned the restoration lab's tests for the first time. Konrad Heider must have been behind the break-in."

Zelda was quiet a moment. "That must be why he was so interested in Gerard's letters when I mentioned them during our last meeting. Heider didn't know they existed. I mean, how could he have known Arjan wrote to his brother about being blackmailed, and that Gerard had held onto those letters all of these years? Heider must have assumed Arjan told his brother where the art was hidden in one of them. It must have been Heider who broke into my apartment and into Gerard's house."

Her skin turned to goosebumps as she realized what that meant. "Konrad Heider murdered Gerard," she cried out. How many times had she been in the same room with a thief and killer?

"But we've read through all the letters, and no exact location is ever mentioned," Friedrich said dismissively.

"We know that, but Heider doesn't." Zelda glanced at the pile of aged correspondence stacked up on the dining table, forcing her mind to forget about the Nazi's nephew and concentrate on locating the storage space. "We know Philip Verbeet told Arjan van Heemsvliet about a space that ended up being the solution to his storage problem. And they paid five years' rent to secure it."

Her face went white as a recent memory popped into her foggy brain. "Of course, why didn't I think of that earlier? After Rita and her family left for Venlo, her dad paid five years' rent on their apartment, even though her mother swore they were not planning on going back to Amsterdam after the war."

"Do you really think they could have hidden hundreds of painting in Rita's old house?" Friedrich asked. "It must be a really good hiding place, if the artwork still hasn't been found after all these years."

Zelda crinkled her nose, considering where they could have hidden it away. "When Rita and I were there, the new owners said they'd moved walls and torn out all the closets when they renovated it last year. If hundreds of paintings had been hidden inside that house, they would have found them by now."

"But where else could the art be?" Zelda pounded her fists on the kitchen table again, venting her frustrations and causing Friedrich to jump out his chair. "We are so close to figuring this all out, I know we are. But what are we missing?"

Friedrich shook his head. "We can go back to Rita's house later today and look around. Right now I'm too tired and hungry to think about this anymore."

"Oh yeah, great idea. Let's knock on the door and ask Eva if we can tear up her floorboards, in case a Picasso or Monet is hidden underneath," Zelda retorted.

"Do you think Konrad Heider is just going to ask for the art back?"

"Even if he gets his hands on the letters and figures out the artwork is hidden in Rita's old house, he won't know where to look either." Zelda closed her eyes and tried to recall all she had seen in the old lady's family home during their impromptu tour. Something was bothering her, tickling at her memory, but wouldn't come to the surface. She stood and pulled back the kitchen's curtains, groaning as daylight filled the room. She looked over at the wall clock, staring in disbelief. "It's already eight in the morning; we've been at this all night. We really should take a break, shouldn't we?"

"I could use some fresh air. Maybe my brain will function better after a walk and a croissant." Friedrich joined her at the window, watching as the sun broke through the cloud cover and briefly lit up the gardens behind his house. "The bakery should be open by now. Are you up for a walk?"

Zelda stared out the window, preoccupied as that niggling in the back of her brain grew stronger. Perhaps if she meditated on it alone for a few minutes, she would remember whatever it was. "No thanks, though I'd love a chocolate croissant."

"Coming up." He smiled as he patted her brusquely on the shoulder. "We've done everything we could. At least we know Heider and O'Neil are behind the robberies and why they're after the letters. The police will be able to handle the rest."

She nodded distractedly. "You're right. When you get back, we can head over to my apartment. Two officers should be arriving there in about an hour to fingerprint my housemates. We can give them the information we found online about Drechsler and Heider, as well as Arjan's letters."

"Sounds good. See you in a few minutes," Friedrich said, whistling as he skipped down the stairs.

Zelda wished she shared his optimism. She turned her chair towards the window and leaned forward, staring out at the tree-filled gardens below, letting her mind mull over all they had learned. They were looking for a large space that Philip Verbeet had access to, one he was certain would survive the war unscathed and undetected. And it would have to be pretty big if Arjan really did hide all three hundred and twenty-six pieces in it. Was there a neighborhood bomb shelter nearby? No, too public. And that wouldn't explain the five years' rent paid on the Verbeets' apartment. That couldn't be a coincidence, she told herself, convinced the artwork must be hidden there. But where?

She let her eyelids close and her thoughts wander. The sun's rays warmed her face as she relived her visit with Rita: walking through the living room and kitchen, climbing the steep stairs, seeing the girls' bedroom, and, finally, watching Rita's surprisingly strong reaction at seeing that run-down garden shed. Her dollhouse, that was what had made her so upset, her precious dollhouse, long gone, probably used as fodder for fire during the war.

Outside Friedrich's house, a strong gust of wind blew puffy white clouds across the sky. The full sun momentarily bounced off the corrugated metal rooftop of a neighboring shed and right into her eyes. The burst of light brought with it a burst of insight. The garden shed! Rita's dollhouse had been built in an L shape so her parents could access the root cellar below!

Zelda forced herself to exhale as a smile spread over her lips. Could it really be that simple?

44

An Unexpected Visitor

Zelda sashayed her way around Friedrich's dining table, whooping softly in delight. The art had to be in the root cellar, safely tucked away under the shed in Rita's old garden, well-protected from bombing raids and prying eyes. Where else could Arjan van Heemsvliet and Philip Verbeet have stored all that artwork and expected it to have remained hidden and safe until the war was over? And according to the current owners, the concrete shed was the only space on the property that had remained untouched all these years.

Friedrich's doorbell began ringing, putting a temporary halt to her jubilant dance. As it wasn't her house, she didn't feel comfortable answering the door. On the other hand, she knew that, after a long night out drinking, Friedrich's housemates would be comatose until noon or later and probably couldn't even hear the bell ring. When it began to chime again, Zelda listened intently for movement from one of the rooms above but didn't hear a single peep or creak. Eight o'clock on a Saturday morning was too early for door-to-door salesmen or even package deliveries. In his sleep-deprived state, Friedrich must have forgotten his keys, she reckoned, unless the Jehovah's Witnesses were getting an early start to their day.

Humming a jaunty tune, she began jogging down the two flights of stairs. The bell rang a third time, convincing her it was her friend trying to get back inside. "Keep your pants on, I'm coming," she called down, increasing her pace.

As she opened the door, slightly out of breath, her smile froze in place.

"Back up slowly."

Zelda looked from the barrel of a gun to the steely eyes of Karen O'Neil's lawyer and did as she was told.

"How did you find me?" she asked, her voice trembling as much as her body. She'd never had a gun pointed at her before. The fear was overwhelming; he only had to flinch, and her life would be over. Zelda willed her muscles to stop twitching as Konrad Oswald Gotthard Heider stepped inside and closed the door.

"I followed you two from your flat last night and saw you turn onto this street. If you hadn't run that last red light, I would have seen which apartment you went into. Instead, I had to wait in my Audi until one of you finally emerged," he said, rolling his shoulders. He spoke so casually and conversationally that Zelda had trouble remembering he had a weapon trained on her.

"Where are the letters?"

"Upstairs," she replied promptly, knowing she was in no position to argue.

He waved his pistol towards the stairs, and she began climbing back up to the kitchen. She hoped none of Friedrich's housemates, having heard them talking, would poke their heads out to see what was going on. She was sure Heider wouldn't just let them go back to bed.

As they entered Friedrich's kitchen, the lawyer stopped in the doorway to take in the scratched-up furnishings, peeling paint, and sink full of dirty dishes, disgust etched on his face.

Her eyes darted reflexively towards the dining table where Arjan van Heemsvliet's letters and their translations were piled up.

"Gather them up and put them in here." He set his shoulder bag down on one corner of the table and fished two manila envelopes out of it with his free hand.

Zelda did as she was told, careful not to tear the fragile documents. When she was done, the lawyer stuffed the envelopes back into his bag, the gun never leaving his right hand.

"Why did you have to hurt Gerard?" she asked.

Konrad smirked. "Just before his heart gave out, Gerard told me you had the letters all along. It's too bad about the old man, but you have no one to blame but yourself. If you hadn't lied to Bernice Dijkstra and Huub Konijn, Gerard would still be alive today."

His words were like a knife in her heart. If she had done what Gerard had asked of her—given the letters to the museum professionals straight-away—instead of trying to help Rita, Konrad wouldn't have gone to his house. Her deep-seated need to be right had in fact gotten him killed. Her legs were like jelly; she sank into a chair and hid her face in her hands, trying to come to terms with her actions.

"You're bad luck, aren't you?" the lawyer grinned, obviously enjoying himself. "Now Friedrich has to die, too. After I take care of you."

"We read all of Arjan's letters last night; I know where the artwork is," she blurted out.

"Even more reason to get rid of your friend."

"No!" Zelda yelped. Gerard's senseless death was more than enough pain to deal with; she couldn't bear it if anything happened to her friend as well. She had to get Konrad Heider out of this house before Friedrich came home, even if that meant revealing the truth straightaway.

"Why would you kill Friedrich? He doesn't know where Arjan's collection is hidden; only I do," she said in a defiant tone, trying to muster her courage.

Heider's gun sagged slightly. "You mean to tell me you've been in his house studying these letters all night long, yet only you know where the art is? Impossible."

"Yes, that's exactly what I mean. Arjan never mentioned the exact location of his hiding place in any of his letters." Heider cocked his gun, causing Zelda to speak even faster. "But he did leave his brother Gerard some clues as to its whereabouts. It was only after Friedrich went out a few minutes ago that I remembered something Rita Brouwer said when we were at her childhood home. Suddenly everything fell into place. Friedrich's never met Rita or been to her house; he wouldn't know where to look—only I do. But if you hurt Friedrich, I won't tell you a thing!" she exclaimed shrilly, resolutely crossing her arms over her torso. Every second they remained in this house was a second too long.

The lawyer frowned. "You think Arjan's art collection is hidden in Philip Verbeet's old house? I don't believe you. They didn't even know each other."

"Arjan wrote to his brother that it was Philip Verbeet who had access to a space large enough to hold all three hundred and twenty-six pieces. When Rita and I were at her family home, she told me about the root cellar her father dug out under the garden shed. The current residents didn't even know it existed, so the entrance must be hidden. Rita said it was as solid as a bomb shelter and as big as their living room. It's the only place Arjan's art collection could be. The rest of the house has been remodeled too many times since then for all those paintings to have been hidden inside their apartment."

A glimmer of hope crossed the lawyer's face, quickly replaced by disbelief. "My uncle spent his life studying Arjan's business records. Verbeet was not one of the frame makers he worked closely with. Why should I believe you?"

"Your uncle didn't have these letters. Read them yourself if you don't believe me."

The lawyer fell silent, obviously contemplating his options.

Zelda pushed on, willing him to move towards the front door. "If I'm right, all the paintings listed in Arjan's inventory book will be there."

Heider stared at her through the gun's sights; Zelda forced herself to breathe deeply and try to stay calm as she waited for him to decide what to do.

"Okay, walk slowly down the stairs to the front door. You try to run, I shoot you and wait for Friedrich."

Zelda didn't doubt him. The look in his eyes told her that he would happily pull the trigger if she disobeyed him. She followed his orders, waiting until he was beside her before opening the front door.

He grabbed her arm and pulled her outside, onto the sidewalk. "Remember what I said."

She nodded gravely. He tugged her arm towards the right. His silver sports car was parked two doors down. Even though the street was already abuzz with early morning shoppers and bicyclists, no one seemed to notice them. Zelda walked along silently, resisting any temptation to try to make a run for it, only hoping the lawyer would be true to his word and leave Friedrich alone if she did as he asked. She wished there was some way to warn her friend, to let him know what was happening and where they were going.

After they settled into his Audi R8, Konrad asked, "Where to?"

"Frans Halsstraat 14. Take a left onto Stadhouderskade and then the fifth left. Her house is in the middle of the block," Zelda answered, praying Eva and baby Cor weren't home.

45

Breaking And Entering

June 27, 1942

The streets were dark and empty thanks to the evening curfew, already in force when Philip Verbeet pulled the door to his apartment shut.

Arjan van Heemsvliet rejoiced internally, gratefully the arduous task of hiding the artwork was complete. They had done all they could to protect the artwork from insects and mold. The layers of sand and tiles covering the entrance to the root cellar would ensure no one would accidentally stumble upon the space underneath the shed. Until the war was over, it would have to do. After he left Amsterdam, he wouldn't have the means or opportunity to move it again.

The two men set off on their short walk over the cobblestone streets and metal footbridges connecting Philip's home in the Pijp District to Arjan's mansion situated close to the Museumplein. There were no streetlights to guide them. No lamp light spilled out of the many homes and offices they passed; the blackout regulations in effect required windows to be covered with thick paper or curtains after sunset, so as to deny the Allies' bombs any visible targets from the air. White chalk lines marking the sides of the canals, glowing in the moonlight, assisted them along the blackened waterways connecting the two neighborhoods.

Arjan unlocked his front door and waved Philip inside, automatically glancing around to see whether any of his neighbors were watching him return so late at night with a disheveled stranger. No matter, he thought, they wouldn't be here for long.

After following the older man inside, he stepped around their packed suitcases and switched on the hallway lamp. He looked into his sitting room, comforted that nothing seemed out of place. Because his gallery had been closed all week, Arjan half-expected to see his house torn to shreds after this thirty-hour stint in the shed.

"I'll show you to the guest room," he said, relief in his voice as he began climbing the wide marble staircase leading to the bedrooms on the third floor. How he wished he could take a long hot bath and soak the grime and weariness out of his bones. There was no time to heat the water, he realized; their train to Venlo left in two hours. Not that he'd be able to relax anyway. Now that the artwork was safely hidden away, all he wanted to do was get as far away from Amsterdam and Drechsler as he could. There would be plenty of time for rejuvenating dips in the sea once he'd reached his summer home in Marseilles.

When Arjan reached the third-floor landing, he reached out his hand and felt along the wall for the light switch. A jovial voice called out from the darkness, "There you are."

Arjan froze in his tracks. He could sense Philip Verbeet, a few steps behind him, doing the same.

Oswald Drechsler switched on the lamp, illuminating his wide grin and the Luger in his right hand. "I stopped by your gallery twice this week; a sign on the door said you are ill. I must say, you don't appear sick to me. But then, I am not a medical doctor. What is ailing you?"

Arjan's eyes blinked in protest, unwilling to accept what they saw. He opened his mouth to speak, but no sound came out.

His blackmailer plowed on. "When I went by your gallery this morning and saw all of the walls were empty, I thought it prudent to see if you were still ill. Lo and behold, you seem to have recovered nicely."

I should have known better than to close the gallery for so long, Arjan thought. But what other choice did I have?

The SS officer stepped towards him, glaring down at him over his long nose. "Where are my paintings?"

Arjan gulped audibly. The ten pieces his blackmailer sought were crated up with those of his friends. He'd packed them up last, figuring they would serve as the foundation for a new gallery in Marseilles. How stupid of him! He should have known his blackmailer would notice their absence immediately.

Drechsler sensed his hesitation. He waved for Philip Verbeet—motionless since the Nazi made his presence known—to climb the last three steps up to the small landing. Arjan's acquaintance did so reluctantly, moving as if he knew he was walking towards a death squad. When he was close enough, Drechsler grabbed Philip's arm and shoved the Luger's barrel against his temple. "Where are my paintings?" he asked again, his voice calm and unwavering.

Arjan remained speechless as he rapidly considered his options, unsure of what to do.

Drechsler cocked his pistol.

"I can get them for you!" Arjan screamed.

"You will take me to them."

"No." The words escaped his lips as a whisper. How could he? If he did, Drechsler would find the rest, and then all of their work would have been for naught.

Drechsler pulled the trigger. A cloud of red mist exploded out of Philip Verbeet's forehead seconds before his body crumpled to the floor.

"Yes, you will." The colonel whipped his pistol across Arjan's face.

The art dealer dropped to his knees, blood streaming out of a gash in his cheek. Drechsler kicked his boot into his victim's stomach, lifting him off the ground. When he landed, Arjan coughed up dark red mucus and instinctively tried to rise again.

"Where are my paintings?" Drechsler kicked out the backs of Arjan's knees, dropping him onto Philip Verbeet's torso. He squealed instinctively; the warmth of the man's lifeless body rattled him completely. As he thrashed around, struggling to stand, Drechsler kicked him in the back, throwing him off balance. He could feel himself teetering towards the staircase and began flailing his arms, searching helplessly for a holdfast.

His blackmailer screamed, "My paintings!"   and grabbed his shirt, momentarily halting his fall until Arjan's body weight pulled him forward, tumbling down the darkened stairwell.

What have I done? went through Arjan's mind as his ankle cracked on a marble tread and his shoulder popped out of its socket, only moments before he fell further, his neck snapping on the first-floor landing, killing him instantly.

46

Ladies First

Konrad Heider eased his Audi into a cramped parking space on the Frans Halsstraat, directly across from the empty lots in the middle of the block. Through the sections of wire-mesh fence, Zelda could see a broken wheelbarrow and a few forlorn buckets lying about, but no workers. She breathed a sigh of relief, glad to see that they wouldn't have to disturb Eva or her family to get to the shed. *No more innocent victims*, she chanted in her head.

The lawyer switched off the ignition and turned to study his passenger, clearly still debating as to whether he could trust her.

"That construction site butts right up against Rita's old house and backyard. We can easily climb through that first fence there," Zelda explained, keeping her voice neutral as she pointed at a large gap between two sections of fencing running along the sidewalk. "Two strings of barbed wire are all that's separating their garden from the open lots. We can slip through both fences and get into the shed without the current residents even knowing we're there."

"If this is some sort of trick, if you try to deceive me, I won't hesitate to kill you. And Friedrich, too." The lawyer tried to look her in the eye as he spoke, but Zelda was only aware of the gun pointed at her abdomen.

She nodded solemnly, knowing he would keep his word.

Heider reached across her, opened the glove compartment, and pulled out a small leather bag. Its contents rattled and clinked as he slipped it into his tweed blazer's inner pocket. "Lead the way."

Zelda stepped out of the car and took in her surroundings. The small residential street was dead quiet this Saturday morning; she didn't see anyone walking or biking by. After a quick scan of the apartment windows all around them, she didn't spot any busybodies watching them from above either. The lawyer watched while she squeezed through two sections of the metal mesh barrier, then mimicked her moves, looking over at her expectantly when he'd made it to the other side.

"There it is," she said, gesturing towards the shed a few feet away in the garden on their right.

The lawyer paused to stare at the crumbling concrete structure. "My uncle's artwork is under there?" He sounded incredulous, yet Zelda swore she saw him blink away a tear before motioning for her to get a move on.

Fifteen steps later and she was standing inside Rita's childhood garden, holding the two strings of barbed wire open so Heider could climb through. As much as she didn't want to die in Rita's old shed today, she knew if she screamed or tried to run away, he would shoot her dead before killing any neighbors who tried to get in his way. Zelda had enough blood on her hands as it was. Besides, if she could get him to drop his guard before they found the artwork, she might be able to escape without getting a bullet in her back.

The lawyer strode over to the thick wooden door and unzipped the leather bag he'd taken out of his glove compartment, revealing a small set of metal tools. "A useful skill taught to me by one of my less savory clients," he said, picking the lock with little effort. As he pushed open the door, Heider winked at her. "Ladies first."

It was pitch-black inside, save for a thin shaft of light streaming in through a narrow window placed high up on the opposite wall. Zelda looked back at Rita's childhood home before she entered the concrete shed, relieved she didn't see movement through the windows. Heider pushed her farther inside before closing the door and switching on the light.

A single bulb hung in the middle of the room, its weak glow casting eerie shadows along the interior walls. Zelda studied the ceiling, letting her eyes adjust. Here and there, chunks of concrete had come loose, revealing the thick steel beams that held the structure together. It was larger than it looked from the outside, roughly fifteen feet wide and twenty feet long. The shed clearly served as both storage and a workspace. Dominating the right side was a sawdust-covered workbench with two large steel vises screwed onto one end. A plethora of well-worn tools—hand drills, screwdrivers, chisels, saws, hammers, and a hatchet—hung from pegs on the wall behind it. At either end of the room, boxes were stacked up shoulder high, "Christmas," "baby's room," "King's Day," "kitchen" scrawled onto the sides. Jumbled together in one corner were rakes, spades, hoes, shovels, and a hand mower.

If only I could whack him with a rake or smack him with a shovel, Zelda ruminated, that might give me enough time to get away and warn the police before he can hurt anyone else.

Her thoughts turned again to Friedrich. What would he think when he came home and saw she was gone, along with the letters and their translations? Where would he look for her first? Would he think she'd gone back home to wait for the police? Or was following up a lead at the university's library or the city's archives? Considering her strenuous objections to visiting Rita's old house again, would he even think to check for her here?

"Where is the door?" Heider demanded as he scoured the room for an entrance to the root cellar. Rough concrete tiles covered the entire floor; a mixture of sawdust and sand filled in the narrow seams between them. There was no sign of a door or other way into the space below. *If there ever was one*, Zelda thought, hoping she'd guessed correctly.

Heider began shoving boxes and tools aside in his desperation to locate the entrance, seemingly unaware of the hoes and rakes clanging and banging to the floor. Despite his agitated state, he kept his weapon trained on Zelda the whole time.

She shook her head, scowling at him for making so much noise. "I don't think you'll find anything over there. Rita said the door was in the middle of the shed, built into the floor. The current owner didn't know there was a root cellar. The entrance must be buried under these tiles."

"Well, get digging then."

How? was on the tip of her tongue, but she knew there was no point in arguing. She looked around the room, taking inventory of the tools at her disposal.

"Get on with it," he barked.

She grabbed a flat-edged spade and whipped around to face him, the sharp blade scarcely missing his knee.

"Watch out," Heider growled.

"Oops, sorry," she replied innocently, wondering what would have happened if she'd swung the spade out a tad further. With difficulty she worked the thin blade between two tiles in the center of the room, managing to lift one slightly before it crashed back down, sending a plume of sand and dust into the air. Zelda coughed violently, choking on the grit in her lungs. When she finally caught her breath, she glared at the spade, wondering whether she had chosen the proper tool for the job. She looked up at Konrad expectantly, but he just waved his gun at her, clearly not planning on helping.

She shoved the spade back into the narrow, sand-filled gap. Pressing down and forward with all of her might, she tilted the tile up and got the blade under it, enough so it didn't fall back into place immediately. She curled the tips of her fingers around the rough surface, and lifted it out of the floor, relieved it wasn't more than ten pounds or so. She laid the tile in front of the stack of boxes on her left, briefly considering throwing it at the lawyer. But he'd apparently read her mind and already had his weapon aimed at her skull. Zelda let the tile be, choosing instead to scrape the thick layer of sand away, ultimately revealing another concrete tile.

"Darn," she muttered half-heartedly, secretly glad she hadn't found the door right away. She needed more time to think of a way out of this predicament.

Slowly but surely, she cleared a wide circle of twenty tiles from the middle of the floor, stacking them in neat towers to her left. She tried to make as little noise as possible so the homeowners had no reason to come investigate.

When she paused to wipe the sweat off her forehead, the lawyer handed her a broom. She smirked at him. "Thanks." *You jerk,* she added in her mind, dutifully sweeping the sand aside. When she'd finished up, they both studied the floor intently. There was still no sign of a door or any other opening, only another layer of concrete tiles.

"Looks like you have more work to do," the lawyer grumbled, nodding towards the spade. He remained by the door, the shed's only exit, blocking any hope of escape. Zelda bit her tongue and picked up the tool, wishing for the hundredth time she had the guts to smack him across the face with it, consequences be damned.

As she tugged and pulled at the second layer of tiles under her feet, a fit of anger welled up inside her. Once they'd found the entrance, there was no way Heider would let her walk away unscathed; she knew far too much. He was just using her to do his dirty work before killing her. She slammed the blade into the floor, glaring at him while she ground the edge deeper into the sand-filled crack. His smug expression made her blood boil. Despite all of the information she'd uncovered and pieced together, he still regarded her as nothing more than a nuisance, even though she was the one who'd figured out where Arjan's art was, not him or his sadistic uncle. Indignation seethed through her veins, briefly overruling her fear of getting shot.

"So Arjan outsmarted Oswald Drechsler, eh? Hid all of his artwork right under his nose, and your uncle never even came close to finding it," Zelda taunted, letting her anger bubble to the surface. If she couldn't fight her way out, she could at least try goading him into making a mistake.

Heider chuckled. "You have done your homework. Oswald Drechsler was indeed my uncle. His only mistake was trusting a double-crossing faggot."

"Trusting him? Your uncle was blackmailing Arjan van Heemsvliet!"

"Is that how Arjan described their arrangement in his letters? That pervert owed his life—and his manhood—to my uncle. If he hadn't tried to be a hero, we wouldn't be here today, would we?"

Zelda stopped digging, genuinely curious. "What are you talking about?"

"My uncle only wanted what was rightfully his, the contents of Galerie Van Heemsvliet, as they'd agreed. When he noticed Arjan had removed all the paintings from his gallery's walls, Oswald went to his home and found several packed suitcases by the front door. Van Heemsvliet was obviously preparing to flee Amsterdam, with the help of that Philip Verbeet fellow. If Arjan had only told my uncle where the artwork was hidden, instead of trying to be coy about it, Oswald wouldn't have had to kill Verbeet. How could he have known that Arjan would try to wrestle the gun away from him?" The lawyer grinned as he registered her shocked expression.

"Drechsler killed Rita's father and Arjan van Heemsvliet because of the artwork in Arjan's gallery?" she whispered. Arjan couldn't tell Drechsler where he'd stashed his gallery's inventory without revealing the location of all of the pieces he had hidden for his friends, she realized. It was clear from his letters to Gerard that Arjan felt as if he had betrayed their trust by getting caught running away from that gay club. The art dealer would probably rather have died than tell Drechsler where all the pieces were stored—meaning Rita's father was simply a victim of circumstance, nothing more. Zelda felt like weeping. She hoped she would survive this ordeal if only so she could tell Rita the truth—her father hadn't abandoned them but rather had died trying to help a friend. Finding out what had happened to her father was far more important to Rita than regaining possession of *Irises*, yet she would never know the whole story unless Zelda could find a way out of this shed.

"What did he do with the bodies?"

"He buried them in Arjan's backyard." Konrad smiled sweetly as he motioned with his gun for her to get digging again.

Zelda picked up her spade and lodged it under another tile. "How did you get ahold of Arjan's inventory ledgers and business papers? I take it you inherited them from your uncle?"

"Oswald Drechsler was more than my uncle. After my father died, he raised me as his own. His search for these paintings was always our search. When he passed on, I gladly continued where he left off." Heider stood a little straighter and squared his shoulders as he talked, clearly proud of the sadistic SS colonel Zelda had read about a few hours earlier, the same man Konrad saw as a father figure.

"It was pure happenstance that Oswald found those documents. After he'd shot them, my uncle discovered inventory ledgers in Arjan's suitcases that showed the art dealer's collection was far greater than he had indicated. Oswald had written down the titles of all the works hanging in Galerie Van Heemsvliet each time he visited, yet he recognized only a fraction of the unsold works listed in those books. That's why he stayed in Arjan's home for the remainder of the war, tearing up the walls and floors in his quest to locate the rest. He did find several secret compartments and concealed rooms, but all of them were empty."

That the Nazi was unsuccessful in finding a single piece of artwork was oddly comforting to Zelda. Arjan van Heemsvliet and Philip Verbeet must have finished hiding all of them under this shed mere hours before Drechsler shot them both. Which meant Rita's father's art collection must be safe too. She smiled to herself, pleased to know Arjan and Philip hadn't died completely in vain. That thought delivered a flash of satisfaction before confusion set in.

"But why was *Irises* found in Arjan's mansion on the Museumplein after the war and not buried here? It was listed in his gallery's inventory book along with the rest of Philip Verbeet's collection."

"Took you long enough," the lawyer said, his mouth twisted up in a perverse grin. "The bags by the door. My uncle never understood why Verbeet put *Irises* in his suitcase. The five Rembrandt etchings Arjan tucked into his bags made more sense." Heider chuckled. "Oswald would have liked to have known that Verbeet was taking *Irises* with him because of its sentimental value, not because it held a clue to the location of the rest of the paintings."

Philip Verbeet must have put Irises in his suitcase so he could take it to the farm with him, Zelda realized. He and Arjan were probably on the verge of leaving Amsterdam and making their way to Venlo when Oswald Drechsler caught up with them. "Wait a second; your uncle thought *Irises* was some sort of treasure map? Then why didn't he take it back to Germany with him?" she blurted out.

"*Irises* was the least valuable piece of art listed in Arjan's inventory book. My uncle could only take one suitcase with him when he left Amsterdam and didn't deem the Wederstein important enough to save. He took the

Rembrandts instead. Years later he became convinced the painting held some sort of clue to finding the rest. He could not understand why such an amateurish portrait would have otherwise been saved, when Arjan had works from Matisse and Van Gogh in his possession," Konrad Heider confided, shaking his head. "If only Oswald had known the truth. *Irises* may not be the treasure map my uncle thought it was, but it did get us this far," he laughed, tapping the ground underneath his feet.

"Is that why you tried to steal *Irises*? Because the museum wasn't going to hand it over to you before having Karen O'Neil's documentation verified by professionals? Her family's archival records, her grandmother's marriage license, and even her mother's Dutch birth certificate were all fakes, weren't they?"

The lawyer bristled. "If you hadn't been such a persistent advocate of Rita Brouwer, we would not be standing here. Karen did enjoy playing her role as scorned heiress immensely. A few more days of her ridiculous rants and the board of directors would have done anything to get her out of their hair. If they'd written that damned letter of recommendation to the secretary of state, her documents would have been sufficient," he snapped, clearly irritated by all that Zelda had done to hinder his plans. "Enough talk, get back to work."

Zelda shoved her spade between two tiles and froze. The sharp clang of metal on metal was unmistakable. Heider stared at the spade's blade, a sinister grin spreading rapidly across his face.

Her hands shook as she worked the blade into the narrow slit, slowly lifting the heavy concrete tile up. After adding it to the tower of tiles on her left, she used the spade to scrape away the sand. The glint of metal visible through the fine yellow grains could only be the entrance to the root cellar.

Zelda's legs began trembling uncontrollably as a whimper escaped her lips. Her time had run out.

47

Impatience Is A Virtue

Konrad Heider dropped to his knees before the small metal door, tears glistening on his cheeks. "I have dreamed about this moment for so many years. Oswald always knew I would find our family's treasures. It was indeed my destiny," he said, his voice a whisper, his eyes fixated on the entrance to the root cellar.

The lawyer seemed to have forgotten all about her. Was this her chance to make a break for it? Very slowly, she shuffled her left foot a few inches towards the shed's door, following it with her right a few seconds later. She'd just repeated the move when Heider snarled, "Against the wall." His weapon was once again aimed at her torso.

Zelda stepped back as ordered, trying not to snivel. If Arjan van Heemsvliet's art collection really was down in the root cellar, then she was a dead woman.

Using one hand, the lawyer tossed more tiles aside until the edges of the metal door were visible. He grabbed the broom and brushed the rest of the sand away, revealing a thick steel plate approximately three feet wide and four feet long with a large ring recessed into it.

Zelda pushed herself further against the wall, trying to disappear. The spade's handle cut into her back. Instinctively she wrapped her fingers around it. As soon as Heider opened that door and saw the paintings, he would shoot her, she was sure of it. Could the spade's blade deflect the bullet? Was she even fast enough to find out?

As Konrad worked his fingers around the rusty metal ring, she gulped reflexively and tightened her grip on the gardening tool's long wooden handle.

"Uncle, this is for you," he exclaimed as he yanked on the ring with his free hand. The door didn't budge. Muttering in German, he used his fingers to scrape sand out from around the edges of the metal entryway. He pulled again, heaving with all of his might, but nothing happened.

Scowling at Zelda, Heider barked, "You try it." He took a step back and waited for her to move forward and grab the handle. She didn't want to let go of the spade, yet staring down the barrel of Heider's gun, she didn't see any other options. Zelda reluctantly tugged on the ring. Nothing. She pulled again, really putting her back into it, curiosity trumping her fear of death. But the door remained sealed.

"It must be rusted shut," she wheezed, winded from the effort.

"Nonsense. Move back and turn around. Spread your arms out against the wall."

Zelda did as she was told, positioning her body over the spade. The lawyer lay his gun down by his feet and pulled on the ring with both hands, grunting and groaning from the tremendous effort.

All of a sudden the door sprung loose, jerking open unexpectedly. Heider toppled backwards in surprise, the thick metal door falling onto his left leg, momentarily trapping him. His cry of pain turned to one of joy as he gazed down into the dark space below. *"Mein Gott, es stimmt!* My God, it is true!" he cried out, transfixed by the sight.

As he stared into the root cellar, his leg still ensnared, Zelda instinctively knew this was it, her last chance to escape this shed alive. Grabbing the spade with one hand, she leapt over the opening and onto the metal door, crushing Heider's leg. They both screamed as she whacked the lawyer with the garden tool, hitting him as hard as she could across one cheek. His screaming stopped instantly, replaced by blood streaming out of his scalp and mouth.

Zelda stared down at the lawyer's disfigured face, trying to process what she'd just done, when another anguished cry arose from behind her, moments before the shed's door burst open. She swung her spade wide as she turned to face her attacker.

"Friedrich?" She blinked in surprise, sure she was hallucinating.

"Zelda? Here you are!" Friedrich cried out as he ran to her. "You're okay." He hugged her tight, rocking her back and forth. "I heard a scream and thought that if I didn't do something now, it would be too late."

Tears of relief welled up in her eyes as she relaxed into his embrace, one hand still wrapped around the spade's handle. "But how did you find me?"

"When I got back and saw you were gone, along with the letters and our translations, I woke up all my housemates to find out what had happened, but no one had heard a thing. I couldn't find a note, so I tried calling you, but your phone was in the kitchen. At first I thought you'd gone home, but neither the police nor your housemates had seen you. That's when I guessed you had figured something out about Arjan's hiding place and had rushed off to Rita's old house. I rang the bell, but no one was home. I was about to give up when I saw that construction site you'd mentioned. When I looked through the fence and saw a light on in their shed, I wondered if you were inside. I'd just snuck through the two fences into their backyard when I heard you scream. What happened? Why were you yelling just now?" Friedrich searched her face for an answer, following her nervous gaze to Konrad Heider, his head now encircled by a pool of blood.

"Is that the lawyer?" he said, gaping in horror.

Zelda pushed back from her friend and nodded.

"What happened to him?"

"I hit him with this," she replied sheepishly, holding up the blood-covered blade for him to see. "He was going to shoot me once we found the artwork! I don't think I killed him, but maybe we should call an ambulance." She still couldn't believe she had actually hit Heider hard enough to knock him out, let alone to mangle his face so badly. Zelda began to shake a little as the shock set in, hugging the spade close to her body.

"Wait, what were you two doing in here?" Friedrich asked, finally noticing the towers of concrete tiles stacked up around the room. "Why did you dig up the floor?" All at once, the opening to the root cellar registered. "Is Arjan's artwork down there?" her friend asked.

Zelda nodded. "I think so. I haven't looked yet."

She gazed across the shed, wondering what exactly was stored below. The entrance to the root cellar was now splattered with blood, Konrad Heider's blood. He was lying on his side facing them, his eyes closed and one leg still trapped under the metal door. She told herself she could see him breathing, that he was just unconscious, but knew the longer they waited to call the authorities, the smaller the chance that Heider would survive the day.

"We really should call the police, shouldn't we?" she asked again, leaning heavily on the spade. Neither moved. Zelda was torn. Heider did try to kill her and was in fact responsible for Gerard's death. He had caused so much confusion and pain, as his uncle had done before him. Zelda hated him for what he'd done, but she couldn't consciously allow another human being to die, even if he deserved to. Besides, all she really wanted to do was get out of here and let someone else deal with this mess. She couldn't have cared less about what was down in that hole.

"Do you have your phone with you? We should go outside and call them..." she finally mustered, too late.

Friedrich was already moving towards the root cellar. "It won't hurt to take a quick peek," he grinned, swiveling his head back to look at her.

A shot rang out. A red stain began spreading across Friedrich's shoulder as he sank to his knees. The lawyer was up on one elbow, unsteadily trying to cock his gun again.

"No!" Zelda yelled. In one fluid motion, she pushed Friedrich down to the ground and swiped the spade across Heider's neck and shoulder. As the lawyer's head snapped back, the gun dropped out of his hand. Primal screams filled the room as she hit him again and again, her rage fueling her strength.

She looked down at the lawyer, his head and torso now a mass of red. She released the bloody spade, letting it drop noisily to the ground. Her stomach clenched as she stared at her hands. How could she have done something so horrible?

Friedrich moaned as he tried to prop himself up. Zelda went to her friend and gently cradled him in her arms. "I'm so sorry."

He smiled slightly. "It's nothing. Just a flesh wound." His words were slurred. Zelda could hear sirens in the distance, rapidly approaching. Any neighbor who'd heard that shot would have called the police immediately.

The bloody spot on Friedrich's T-shirt was growing by the second. "Why did you have to be so damn impatient? That's my job," she whimpered while kissing his cheek, praying an ambulance was already on its way.

"It was worth it, to get you to kiss me." His eyelids began to drop.

"Oh, Friedrich." Zelda kissed him full up on the mouth.

"Ah, let the morphine commence," he mumbled as his body relaxed into hers.

The sirens were racing up the street. Zelda could see flashing blue lights through the shed's open entryway and hear car doors slamming shut. "Stay with me, Friedrich, help is right outside!"

She looked over at the lawyer—now a bleeding heap on the floor, his head bent back at a strange angle—wondering whether she'd just killed a man, and then at her friend, slipping slowly out of her embrace as the pool of blood around him grew.

Zelda gazed at the root cellar's opening, wondering whether any amount of artwork was worth all of this chaos and death. Was it even true? Was there really a cache of lost masterpieces only a few feet away? She resisted the urge to look inside, instead holding her friend tight. There would be time enough to find out what, if anything, was stored down below. Right now Friedrich needed her. And that was enough.

48

Justice Served

Zelda sipped tea in interrogation room number four, too tired to care how bitter her drink was or how cold it had gotten. Detectives Oosterbaan and Merks had been questioning her for hours, trying to get their heads around the information she had to share about Konrad Heider, Oswald Drechsler, Karen O'Neil, Philip Verbeet, and the Van Heemsvliet brothers.

Sighing wearily, she tilted her head back and stared up at the ceiling, wondering how much longer they'd keep her here. She'd meticulously recounted everything she could remember at least ten times now, starting from the moment her internship began and ending with her bashing the lawyer's head in with a spade. Though his nose and jaw were shattered, Konrad Heider would survive. He would never be handsome again, but that didn't really matter in prison where, according to the two detectives, Heider would be spending many years, once his wounds had healed.

Zelda was as relieved to hear she hadn't actually killed the lawyer as she was to know that he would pay for his crimes—all of them. The police had found evidence on his laptop that clearly linked him to both the break-in that had killed Gerard and the bungled robbery at the Amsterdam Museum. The police had even found proof he'd falsified several of the documents submitted with Karen O'Neil's claim on *Irises*. Not that more evidence of her wrongdoing was really necessary. Detective Oosterbaan chuckled when he told her that Karen had admitted to lying about being Arjan's granddaughter before the cops could even cuff her.

The police could add to their list of charges kidnapping and two counts of attempted murder, Zelda thought ruefully, another wave of guilt washing over her as she remembered how quickly Friedrich's jovial expression changed when Heider's bullet entered his shoulder.

She scratched at her neck, the collar of her white jumpsuit still stiff with starch. She wondered when she would be able to wear her own clothes again. Neither Oosterbaan nor Merks would tell her what the punishment was for bludgeoning someone in self-defense. She knew that Dutch jail terms tended to be light in comparison to American sentences; she prayed the judge would consider all of the mitigating circumstances.

The detectives had excused themselves ages ago, and Zelda was having trouble keeping her eyes open. Now that the interrogation was over, she was totally drained. Using her folded arms as a pillow, she laid her head on the table and let her eyelids droop closed. All she wanted to do right now was crawl into bed—any bed—even if it was attached to the wall of a prison cell.

Just as she was drifting into unconsciousness, loud rapping on the metal door snapped her back awake. The two detectives re-entered the interrogation room. Oosterbaan laid a printout on the table while Merks handed her a cup of fresh tea.

"This is a copy of your statement. Read it first, then sign at the bottom," Oosterbaan said, taking a seat across from her. Merks leaned back against the door, his arms folded across his chest.

As Zelda quickly skimmed the document, Merks asked again, "So, you never did see what was inside the root cellar?"

She gazed up at him, briefly wondering whether this was one last test to see if she was telling the truth. "No, like I said before, I didn't get the chance. I rode with Friedrich to the hospital in the ambulance. Two officers showed up a few minutes after the doctors rushed him into the emergency room and brought me here to this police station." She was thankful to hear the bullet hadn't done much permanent damage. After few days in the hospital, he would get to go home, where Zelda would hopefully be waiting to nurse him back to health. He'd be good as new soon enough.

"Our forensics team has finished their work, and representatives of the Amsterdam Museum will be on scene shortly. Bernice Dijkstra and Huub Konijn—I believe you know them?" Merks asked, a smile playing on his lips.

His seated partner leaned forward, joining the conversation. "We are quite impressed by how you figured out where Arjan van Heemsvliet had hidden his artwork, especially considering Drechsler and his nephew had been actively searching for it for so many years."

She blushed. "They didn't have his letters."

"Regardless, we think you deserve to see what Van Heemsvliet and Philip Verbeet stored in that root cellar, before the crates are removed. It is quite an extraordinary sight." Both detectives were grinning broadly.

"Are all of the paintings in Arjan's inventory book really down there?" She could hardly believe it to be true, regardless of all that had happened, but the expressions on the detectives' faces made it clear that this was indeed the case.

"We believe so, though until all the crates have been transported to the Amsterdam Museum's depot and opened, we won't be certain. However, our officers did open three crates when they first arrived on scene. They've reported that the boxes contain framed paintings and paperwork documenting their provenance. It should be quite simple to track down the current addresses of the owners or their heirs. Your discovery will make many families very happy."

Zelda felt a surge of pride. All she'd wanted to do was help Rita Brouwer get *Irises* back, yet thanks to her persistence, her naiveté, and a lot of luck, she had stumbled upon Arjan's entire cache of artwork. Now all of those families he had helped would be reunited with what was rightfully theirs, including Rita and her sisters.

"But what about hitting the lawyer with the spade? What crime are you going to charge me with?" Her voice trembled.

"Considering he had kidnapped you and repeatedly threatened to shoot both you and your friend Friedrich Rutz, we view your actions as a clear case of self-defense. You do not have to worry about him pressing charges against you."

Relief swept through her body as the detective's words sank in.

"So, would you like to see the root cellar?" Merks asked again.

Zelda nodded, giddy with excitement. Sleep could wait.

49

Returning To The Scene Of The Crime

Thirty minutes later, Zelda was stepping back into Rita's childhood garden, this time through the kitchen door. According to the neighbors, Eva and her family were on vacation in a faraway land, blissfully unaware of what was taking place in their backyard. With the sun shining, the birds chirping, and no one pointing a gun at her, the garden seemed a lot less sinister now than it had a few short hours ago. Her feeling of security was most certainly enhanced by the hordes of uniformed police officers spread around the small patch of grass, guarding the crime scene and its valuable contents.

Zelda hesitated slightly as she approached the shed's open door. Fresh memories of the gunshot ringing in her ears, blood seeping through Friedrich's shirt, and Konrad Heider's mashed-up face flashed through her brain. She shuddered, thinking about how easily it could have all gone wrong. Yet here she stood, exhausted but unscathed, about to see the treasure trove Arjan van Heemsvliet and Philip Verbeet had managed to hide from Oswald Drechsler seventy-three years ago.

Sucking up her courage, Zelda stepped around the piles of concrete tiles she'd stacked up earlier that morning and quickly crossed to the opening in the middle of the floor. As she climbed down the small metal ladder, she felt as if she was traveling back in time, her own steps mirroring those taken by Philip and Arjan all those years ago.

The ceiling was high enough she could stand upright. A wide path had

268

been left clear in the middle, allowing her to walk unhindered from one end of the room to the other. Portable floodlights placed along the pathway illuminated the space. It seemed even larger than the shed above and was completely filled with wooden crates stacked up on top of each other. Most of the towers touched the ceiling. A number had been stenciled onto the side of each crate with black paint.

Close to the ladder, three crates had been pulled down onto the floor and opened, their lids still ajar. Zelda knew that one of the first officers to arrive at the scene had pried their tops off. She didn't blame the police for not believing her when she'd told them the root cellar was filled with priceless artwork. Who would have expected to find any of this tucked away beneath Rita's old shed? Especially when a hysterical foreigner, screaming for an ambulance, was the one telling them about it.

Figuring it was alright to touch everything now that the police had released the scene, she lifted the lid off the crate closest to her and peered inside. A mustached man in a clown suit stared back at her, guitar in hand. She crouched down to get a better look at the canvas. As her eyes adjusted to the low light, her heart skipped a beat. "Oh my God," Zelda whispered aloud, instantly recognizing the artist's distinctively cubist style. How could she not? He was one of the world's most famous modern painters and prominently featured in every art history book known to man.

Sure her eyes were deceiving her, she pulled the yellowing sheet of paper sticking up from behind the painting, out of the box. Written at the top in Arjan's unmistakably neat handwriting was "Pablo Picasso, *Harlequin Study Number Three.*" She laughed aloud, lightly stroking the painting's surface while she absorbed every detail, figuring that in her lifetime, this would be her one and only chance to actually touch such an important and expensive piece of art.

After studying the painting awhile, she finally tore her eyes away and looked again at the paper included in the crate. All of its owners were listed, starting with the person who'd bought it directly from Picasso in 1904 and ending with the man who'd purchased it from a Dutch art gallery in 1927. She squinted a little to better read the final name listed: Frans Keizer. She recognized it from Arjan's inventory book; the Keizer collection filled five pages. Thanks to this slip of paper, it would be a cinch for the museum's staff to return the painting to its rightful owner. Zelda felt tears welling up as she realized that Frans Keizer's relatives and all of the other families Arjan van Heemsvliet had helped would soon be reunited with pieces of their past, objects intertwined with their own histories, as *Irises* was to the Verbeet family.

The clanking of dress shoes against the metal rungs of the root cellar's ladder interrupted her thoughts and sent her stomach spinning. She wiped the tears from her cheeks and tried to compose herself, unsure of how Bernice Dijkstra and Huub Konijn would react to her presence. She hadn't spoken to either of them since their last disastrous meeting two days ago, at the end of which she'd been kicked out of the Amsterdam Museum and told not to come back. Detectives Merks and Oosterbaan had assured her that both museum professionals knew what had taken place this morning in the shed above. Zelda hoped this major find would wipe away any residual hard feelings generated by her own bullheaded behavior.

She turned towards the ladder to see the project manager standing with her feet on the floor but her hands still clutching a metal rung. Bernice was mumbling to herself in Dutch as she took in the root cellar's contents, clearly mesmerized by what she saw. Just above her was Huub Konijn, tilting his head sideways to get a better look. Only after the curator cleared his throat for the third time did Bernice release the ladder and move aside. Huub acknowledged Zelda's presence with a nod before turning his attention to the crates filling the room.

"How did you figure out the artwork was hidden here under this shed, Zelda?" the project manager finally asked, still gazing reverently around the room.

Zelda chuckled. "I'll tell you all about it after I've had a good night's sleep. Right now my story would come out a jumble," she answered slowly in Dutch. She felt embarrassed to still be dressed in the white jumpsuit—a type usually worn by the police's forensics unit when on-site—that the detectives had given her after asking to keep her blood-stained clothes as evidence. Sure, she could have gone home and changed, but that would have meant passing up the detectives' offer to see what was down in the root cellar before the crates were transported to the Amsterdam Museum. There would be plenty of time for a shower and clean clothes later.

As Zelda began to apologize for her outfit, she noticed both Bernice and Huub were too busy studying the open crates and their contents to be curious about her clothing.

"If all three hundred and twenty-six pieces are here, Bernice, that would make this the single largest discovery of missing artwork in the Netherlands," Huub cried out, shaking his head in disbelief. "How wonderful to be able to see and study all of these works again."

"And how fantastic that so many will soon have their family's long-lost artwork returned to them," Bernice added, almost as if to remind the curator that the paintings wouldn't be staying in the museum's depot for long.

The project manager's words brought Rita Brouwer to the forefront of Zelda's mind. "Philip Verbeet's collection must be down here, too," she exclaimed. "Rita and her sisters will get their father's paintings back after all."

"Rita will be so pleased," Bernice replied sincerely.

Zelda wiped away a tear, happy the project manager agreed so whole-heartedly. There was no more doubt as to whom Philip Verbeet's artwork belonged to. Not only would Zelda get to tell Rita what happened to her father, but the Verbeet girls would also get his entire collection back. Iris would once again get to lay her eyes upon her own portrait, painted by her first love so long ago.

"It will take us months, possibly years, to reconstruct the provenance of all of these pieces," Huub muttered, irritation creeping into his voice.

"Not months, Huub, weeks at most," Bernice corrected him, holding up the Picasso's list of owners for the curator to see. "Arjan van Heemsvliet has done our work for us."

"We're going to have to assemble a new project team, one that will be responsible for locating and contacting the owners or their heirs," Huub said. He was silent a moment, obviously considering something, before he

50

The Healing Power Of Tea

September 1, 2015

"What a beautiful boat," Rita Brouwer gushed, pointing to an old but well-restored steamboat chugging up the Amstel River. Wisps of smoke puffing out of its tiny smokestack slowly propelled it forward through the choppy waters, its highly polished wooden hull bobbing up and down like a seesaw. Zelda had managed to get them a table on Café De Jaren's popular waterfront terrace, situated alongside a bend in the river before it narrowed and joined the Rokin canal, the main entrance to the city center's network of ring-shaped canals. In the waters before them, boats of all sizes and shapes glided by; their rocking motion and the sound of lapping water were slowly lulling her into a meditative trance.

"If I were rich, I would buy an old steamboat like that one and sail around on it all summer long." Rita smiled at the thought, sipping her tea contentedly.

"But, Rita," Zelda sputtered, "you are rich."

"Hush, child. Getting my daddy's art collection back doesn't automatically make me a wealthy woman," the older lady giggled.

Zelda knew she'd been courted by pretty much every art museum in the Netherlands and several others dotted across Europe, since she'd returned to Amsterdam a week ago. Many of the pieces in her father's collection were deemed to be crucial to the oeuvres of their famous Dutch creators as illustrations of their early development and progress as artists. Zelda was certain the numerous institutions salivating for Verbeet's artwork were mercilessly calling and contacting every sponsor and donor they could think of in a desperate attempt to outbid the competition. And the wining and dining would surely continue until Rita and her sisters decided which museum would get some, or even all, of their father's impressive collection.

"You mean you aren't going to sell?" Zelda asked hopefully. Rita had just told her about some of the extraordinary sums of money offered for a single painting. She could understand how tempting it would be to cash in, especially when none of the Verbeet girls had seen the pieces in so many years.

"Heavens, no. I have to talk everything over with my sisters first, but I can't imagine them wanting to sell any of them. None of us girls are rich, but we've all worked hard and saved up enough to live comfortably. We don't need the money. I'm going to suggest we donate most of the paintings to one Dutch museum, but only after we've all passed on. This kind of collection deserves to be seen as much as Daddy's story deserves to be told. All of those fancy dinner meetings with them museum directors have sure convinced me of that. But until we're gone, my sisters and I are going to hang our daddy's artwork in our homes and enjoy it for as long as we can."

"What about your children, and your nieces and nephews? Won't they expect to inherit your father's collection?"

"Why should they expect anything? For starters, neither Rose nor Fleur has got any children to leave them to. Viola hasn't heard from her daughter in going on ten years, since she went off and joined some silly commune. And Iris's son, Joe, has never been interested in art or our family history. Come to think of it, my boys aren't either. I might want to leave a piece or two to my daughter; she wants to work in a gallery someday and has a keen eye for art to boot. But I wouldn't want to leave all of it to her; it wouldn't be fair to the others. Besides, do you know how much inheritance taxes are these days? Keeping the whole collection would cost our kids a fortune!" Rita exclaimed.

"Have you told anyone you are thinking of donating the paintings to a museum instead of selling them?"

"No one's asked. To be honest, I don't think they want to wait until all of us Verbeet girls have passed on before they get their hands on the artwork," Rita guffawed loudly, attracting stares from other café patrons. "Besides, I've never had caviar or real champagne before. What's the harm in leading those museum professionals on a bit?" She grinned conspiratorially. "And the pricey meals have been a good way for me to learn more about the types of artwork all those different museums specialize in. Whichever one we end up choosing, they will have to display all of our daddy's collection—not just the pieces from artists who later became famous. Those promising young artists who didn't survive the war deserve our recognition and respect, too."

"Just like Lex Wederstein," Zelda said, nodding in understanding.

"Exactly," Rita agreed, her voice tinged with sadness. She fell silent for a moment, staring off into the boat-filled waters.

Zelda wondered whether she was thinking about Lex or her father, both taken too soon. She'd had the dubious honor of telling Rita in person all that Konrad Heider had said about Philip Verbeet's murder, as well as the information she'd gleaned from Arjan van Heemsvliet's letters about his last days. Rita had listened silently as Zelda relayed everything she could remember, the old lady's lips a drawn line, glimpses of sorrow and anger crossing her face like clouds on a stormy day. Zelda could only imagine how freeing, yet devastatingly painful, it was for Rita to finally know how her father had died and why. The senselessness of it all was what she had so much trouble explaining to the older lady.

Before Zelda could think of something appropriate to say, a large touring boat cruised too quickly around a plodding rent-a-boat trying to moor on the café's dock a few feet from their table. The larger vessel threw up waves and gray clouds of burnt diesel fuel in its wake, the stench momentarily overpowering that of their tea and eggs. The sickening smell seemed to bring Rita Brouwer back to the present day.

"Anyway, I've got what I really wanted, right here." The older lady patted the larger of two boxes resting on the chair next to her. "Thanks to you, I

275

got my daddy back."

Her sincerity overshadowed Zelda's discomfort at eating lunch with a cremated body. Philip Verbeet and Arjan van Heemsvliet were both buried in the art dealer's backyard, as Konrad Heider said they were. However, only Verbeet had been shot; Arjan's broken neck was the official cause of his death. Why Konrad's uncle told him a different version of events, or what really happened that night in Arjan's home, they would never know. This morning she'd gone with Rita to the police department and collected her father's remains. After letting the older woman cry on her shoulder a while, she'd suggested they come here for a late breakfast, hoping the fresh mint tea and breathtaking views would help calm her down before her long flight home.

Zelda leaned over and squeezed her companion's hand. "I'm sure your sisters are as glad as you to finally know what happened to your father."

"Yes, they are," Rita said before picking up the smaller box from the chair next to her. It was roughly the size of a coffee-table book. "Here." She handed the package to Zelda. "This is our way of thanking you for finding our daddy."

"Oh, Rita, you didn't need to get me anything," she said, grasping the package with both hands. She opened the box, expecting to find an art-related tome, but instead discovered a bubble-wrapped object. As she pulled it out, she felt a metal frame through the packaging. Though she had an inkling of what it could be, she refused to believe that Rita and her sisters would be so generous.

"Open it."

She carefully removed the bubble wrap, staring in awe at the object inside for several seconds before finally getting her voice back. "Is this really one of your father's pieces?" she whispered.

"Yes, it is." Rita's grin stretched from ear to ear.

Nestled inside the packaging was a framed watercolor of a girl standing on a bridge watching the sun rise. The clouds in the distance were painted in the most vibrant pink and purple hues Zelda had ever seen. She recognized the artist immediately; he was, after all, one of her favorite Dutch painters.

Her hands started to shake as her mind registered what she was holding. "Is this really a Jan Sluijters?"

"That girl sees a bright future before her, full of hope and promise. Like the one I see ahead of you."

Zelda choked up with tears, embracing Rita with one arm as she held the painting tight with the other. "Thank you so much. And all of your sisters, too." She released the older lady and wiped her face clean before clearing her throat, unable to look her in the eye. "Rita, you know this watercolor is worth a lot of money. Are you absolutely sure about this?" She wanted nothing more than to keep the Sluijters piece but didn't want the Verbeet sisters to feel obligated.

"As long as you don't go and sell it, then yes, all of us girls are absolutely sure," Rita said. "In fact, I have a little finder's fee for you, to make sure you aren't tempted."

Zelda was horrified. "Rita, this Sluijters is more than enough."

Rita looked pleased but determined as she shoved an envelope into the younger woman's hand. "This is what my sisters and I were willing to pay you to look for clues leading to any of our daddy's paintings. We sure didn't expect you to find them all!"

Zelda opened the envelope to find a check for five thousand dollars. "This is way too much," she stammered. She'd hoped to earn a few hundred dollars helping the Verbeet girls out, not thousands.

"Nonsense. You just told me you got into that master's program you were so gung-ho about. Now you won't have to worry about getting a job right away."

Rita had no idea how right she was, Zelda thought ruefully. She was extremely grateful and relieved that she'd been one of the twenty students selected for the museum studies master and couldn't wait for classes to begin. Only after she'd been accepted did she realize it would be virtually impossible to work and study full time, especially in another language. Reading and writing in Dutch still required a tremendous effort, though she was pleased to note that she needed her Dutch-English dictionary less and less. She knew it would get easier in time. This check, in combination with her savings, would guarantee her several more months of freedom, giving her time to settle into her classes and get used to the workload before having to think about taking out student loans or finding a job.

Zelda bear-hugged the older woman, squeezing her so tight that Rita squealed. "If there's anything else I can do for you or your sisters—anything at all—please let me know."

Rita pulled out of their embrace, readjusting her coke-bottle glasses before saying, "Well, we were hoping you could help us find out more about the lesser-known artists in my daddy's collection. Sure, several of them are considered important Dutch painters now, like Karel Appel, Jan Sluijters, and Charley Toorop. But others didn't survive the war and don't seem to be included in any art history books. It would be nice to know more about those other young men, whom my father respected enough to want to help. I know you're going to have your hands full with your classes and all, but if you get some free time, maybe you could check the local archives for us and see if you can find anything out about them."

"I think I'll be able to find the time," Zelda said with a laugh before tucking the check into her wallet.

Rita nodded, satisfied. "Well, young lady, you'd better escort me back to my hotel. I've got an early evening flight and lots of packing to do." It took her a few seconds to wriggle her pear-shaped bottom out of the wicker chair.

"What about your father's collection?"

"It's being bubble-wrapped and crated up, as we speak. I was honest enough with all those museum people to let them know they wouldn't be getting their hands on my daddy's paintings right away."

Rita gathered up her purse and her father's ashes while Zelda tucked the Sluijters back inside its box. "Did you know the Amsterdam Museum is paying to have them all shipped back to Missouri? Isn't that nice? That curator, Huub Konijn, has been such a tremendous help these past few days. As a matter of fact, he's the one who arranged to have the Sluijters boxed up for you. Funny, I got the feeling he didn't really like me when we first met. After that second meeting, he made me so doggone mad I thought about forging a letter from my daddy, naming the friend he'd stored all of his art with. Trouble was, I couldn't remember any of his real friends' names. Good thing I didn't. If I had, it would have muddled up our claim even more."

"I'm really glad you didn't," Zelda replied. Karen's fake documents had caused enough confusion. If Rita had forged that letter, Huub would not be helping her now, whether she was the rightful owner or not.

Zelda held the café's door open for Rita, chuckling softly to herself. Huub had indeed turned out to be one of the good guys, effectively lobbying the secretary of state for culture to expedite the return of all three hundred and twenty-seven paintings—including *Irises*—to their legal owners. Thanks to the documentation Arjan van Heemsvliet had enclosed in every crate, Zelda and the rest of the restitution project team had been able to locate all of the heirs within ten days. The artwork was now being readied for transport to destinations all over the world. Zelda felt good knowing Rita and her sisters were getting all of their father's pieces back, just as the thirty-seven other families Arjan once helped would, thanks in large part to her own unauthorized research and bullheaded actions.

"The only thing I'm taking back with me now is *Irises*. She just fits inside my suitcase. After all I've been through—heck, all we've been through—to get that painting back, I'm not letting her out of my sight again," Rita explained, as Zelda led them back to her hotel on the Museumplein.

Zelda thought of Philip Verbeet's own suitcase, sitting by Arjan van Heemsvliet's door, packed and ready to go to Venlo, *Irises* carefully wrapped up inside.

"And what are you going to do with this lovely summer's day, my dear?" Rita asked.

"I owe my friend Friedrich an airplane."

Rita looked over at her quizzically.

Zelda laughed. "Long story. I'm taking him shopping for model plane parts later today. He likes to build them from scratch." After that terrible day in the shed, she was happy to be able to do anything with Friedrich. Though his left arm was still in a sling, his broken collarbone had healed up nicely.

"Is it his birthday?"

"Something like that."

"Is he your boyfriend?" Rita teased, as they rounded the block and entered her hotel's tree-lined street.

"No, just a really good friend." Zelda knew she and Friedrich could never be a couple, with or without Pietro in her life. Somehow she'd finally been able to convince him of that during her stint as nurse and cook the first week after he'd been discharged from the hospital. But he'd proven himself a true friend, one she was quite grateful to have. And knowing they would never be romantically involved seemed to have relaxed Friedrich immensely, letting him enjoy his role as little brother to the fullest.

Once again she held the door open for Rita Brouwer, this time to the older lady's hotel lobby. They took the elevator up to her third-floor suite, generously booked for her by the Amsterdam Museum. As Rita laid her father's urn down on the bed, Zelda fidgeted with the box in her hands, unsure of how to say goodbye to someone who'd given her so much.

"Have a safe flight, Rita. I'll email you as soon as I find out more about those young artists you asked about," she finally managed, trying to keep her voice as upbeat as possible. She knew they'd stay in touch electronically, but Zelda doubted they'd ever see each other again.

"Thank you for helping us girls out. I'm already looking forward to reading your research updates." Rita grabbed her and hugged her tight.

Zelda pushed back and kissed her three times on the cheek, Dutch-style. "Thank you, Rita, for everything," she replied, softly patting the bubble-wrapped painting lodged firmly under her arm.

THE END

Thank you for reading my novel.

Reviews really do help readers decide whether they want to take a chance on a new author. If you enjoyed this story, please leave a review on Goodreads, BookBub, Facebook, or with your favorite retailer.

I really appreciate it! Jennifer S. Alderson

Acknowledgements

I am deeply indebted to Philip and Cherie—the earliest readers of this manuscript—for their constructive criticism, belief in this project, and encouragement to keep writing. Many thanks to my wonderful family and friends for being such fantastic cheerleaders. And much love to my darling son, Jasper, for being such a great kid.

The idea for this story was inspired by two actual events: an exhibition in the Hollandsche Schouwburg, *Looted, but from whom?* (November 2006 - March 2007), in which objects stolen by the Nazis during the Second World War were exhibited to the public in the hopes their owners would recognize and claim them; and a brilliant publicity stunt organized by the Bunker Museum Zandvoort on April 1, 2008, involving a German treasure hunter and priceless paintings buried in the dunes along the Dutch coast.

My own experiences as a student at the University of Amsterdam and intern at Museum Willet-Holthuysen provided the basis for Zelda's academic ambitions and work experience. Thanks, in particular, to Professor Ellinoor Bergvelt and internship supervisors Bert Vreeken and Nel Klaversma for happily indoctrinating me into the world of exhibition design and collection research.

All of the books, records, and historical documents I used as reference material while writing *The Lover's Portrait* can be found at one of these fine institutions: the library of the Dutch Resistance Museum; the archives of the Stedelijk Museum Amsterdam; the Rijksmuseum's Research Library and Print Room; the archives of NIOD: Institute for War, Holocaust and Genocide Studies; the Amsterdam City Archives; the National Library of the Netherlands; the Jewish Historical Museum's library; the Hollandsche Schouwburg: National Holocaust Memorial; the (now disbanded) library of KIT Tropenmuseum; and the University of Amsterdam's libraries and special collections. I am deeply grateful to the knowledgeable staff of all of these museums, archives, and libraries for so graciously helping a young American learn more about this incredibly complex period in European history.

I am particularly indebted to archivist Peter Kroesen of the Amsterdam City Archives for taking time early on in this project to share many interesting facts and obscure stories about Amsterdam in the 1930s and 1940s, such as the existence of the gay-friendly bar Café 't Mandje, real-life escape routes to Switzerland organized by various resistance groups, and the confiscation of occupied homes located around the Museumplein.

Three books were crucial in providing insight into the Dutch art market and standard practices of European art dealers during the 1930s and 1940s: *De Nederlandse Kunstmarkt 1940-1945* by Jeroen Euwe, *Roofkunst: de zaak Goudstikker* by Pieter den Hollander, and *Kunsthandel in Nederland 1940-1945* by Adriaan Venema. Two research papers, written in 1985 by then-bachelor student Rob Lambers, were immensely useful resources in understanding the kinds of exhibitions Dutch museums and galleries presented during the war, as well as how artists' collectives functioned: *Het Stedelijk Museum te Amsterdam tijdens de Tweede Wereldoorlog* and *Musea en Kunstenaarsverenigingen tijdens de jaren 1940-1945 in Nederland*.

The catalog for the exhibition *Westphaalsch-Nederrijnsche Kunst* (August 2, 1941 - September 14, 1941)—initiated by Reich Commissioner Arthur Seyss-Inquart, organized by the Nederlandse-Duitse Kultuurgemeenschap and held in the Rijksmuseum—explains why Hitler's Nazi regime considered Dutch citizens to be their cultural and linguistic "brothers."

The fictitious *Stolen Objects* research project and associated restitution process described in this book are based on the actual *Herkomst Gezocht* (*Origins Unknown*) project led by the Ekkart Committee. Their reports, published between 1999 and 2004, describe in explicit detail their research into thousands of unclaimed objects still in the care of the Dutch government and their efforts to track down potential claimants through international advertising campaigns and the aforementioned exhibition, *Looted, but from whom?*. The Ekkart Committee's reports and findings, as well as a description of the workings of the actual Restitutions Committee and links to its collection database, are available online in English via www.herkomstgezocht.nl/en.

There are countless books written about what Adolf Hitler considered to be "degenerate" art, as well as his plan to create a new mega-museum in Linz by stealing artwork he admired from private citizens, art dealers, and cultural institutions across Europe. I found these four books to be the most useful in understanding Hitler's motivations and the tactics used to realize his "dream": *The Lost Museum* by Hector Feliciano, *The Linz file: Hitler's plunder of Europe's art* by Charles De Jaeger, *Museums and the Holocaust: Laws, Principles and Practice* by Norman Palmer, and *The Rape of Art: The story of Hitler's Plunder of the Great Masterpieces of Europe* by David Roxan and Ken Wanstall.

In contrast, there is very little written about the plight of homosexuals in the Netherlands during World War II. Luckily I found two books containing a wealth of information that enabled me to better understand the challenges a prominent citizen and closeted homosexual, such as the fictitious Arjan van Heemsvliet, would have faced. These two indispensable resources are *Het vervolgen van homosexuelen voor, tijdens en na de tweede wereldoorlog (1911-heden)*, an essay bundle compiled by A. Dijkema and published by the Federation of Dutch Associations for Integration of Homosexuality (COC) in 1985; and the book *Doodgeslagen, doodgezwegen: vervolging van homoseksuelen door het nazi-regime 1933-1945* edited by Klaus Müller. To give my English readers a better idea of their tone, the titles of these two tomes can be translated as *The persecution of homosexuals before, during and after the Second World War (1911-present)* and *Beaten to death, silenced: persecution of homosexuals by the Nazi-regime 1933-1945*.

In 1995 the exhibition *Rebel, mijn hart: kunstenaars 1940-1945*, held in the Nieuwe Kerk in Amsterdam, commemorated Dutch artists who were killed during the Second World War. The exhibition catalog, written by Sem Dresden and Max Nord, explains how Jewish artists were affected by the rise of National Socialism in the 1930s, the ever-stricter rules created by the Reich Chamber of Culture, and widespread censorship. It also includes information about many of these forgotten artists' work and personal lives. This excellent resource helped me to understand the ordeals my fictional character, the up-and-coming Jewish artist Lex Wederstein, would have faced.

There is a wide range of literature available that recounts life in the Netherlands, and in particular Amsterdam, during the Second World War. I relied most heavily on three publications when describing the city in wartime: *Kroniek van Amsterdam 1940-1945*, published in 1948 by the Genootschap Amstelodamum and compiled by J.F.M. den Boer and Mej. S. Duparc; *Ooggetuigen van de Tweede Wereldoorlog in meer dan honderd reportages*, complied by Connie Kristel and Hinke Piersma; and *De bezette stad: Plattegrond van Amsterdam 1940-1945* by Bianca Stigter. The image banks of NIOD and the Amsterdam City Archives were also extremely useful resources when visualizing this era.

I am immensely grateful to my father-in-law, Jacques Derijcke, for sharing his many vivid memories of growing up in occupied Amsterdam as a young boy.

I would also like to note that this manuscript was complete before news broke on November 4, 2013, of the discovery of 1,280 paintings, once stolen by the Nazis and assumed to be lost forever, in the apartments of German citizen Cornelius Gurlitt.

As many of the resources listed above are only available in Dutch, it is perhaps important to note that I am fluent in the language—and have the government-issued certificate to prove it!

For the purposes of this story, I intentionally refer to a major earthquake taking place in Seattle in 2014, when in actuality the last significant quake to hit the Pacific Northwest—the Nisqually earthquake (6.8 on the Richter scale)—occurred on February 28, 2001. When it hit, I was working at Microsoft's main campus in Redmond. Zelda's experiences mirror my own.

Although I have done my utmost to ensure all of the historical facts, events, policies, and attitudes described within this book are accurate, any factual errors that remain are solely my responsibility.

About the Author

Jennifer S. Alderson was born in San Francisco, raised in Seattle, and currently lives in Amsterdam. After traveling extensively around Asia, Oceania, and Central America, she moved to Darwin, Australia, before finally settling in the Netherlands. Her background in journalism, multimedia development, and art history enriches her novels. When not writing, she can be found in a museum, biking around Amsterdam, or enjoying a coffee along the canal while planning her next research trip.

Jennifer's love of travel, art, and culture inspires her award-winning Zelda Richardson Mystery series, her Travel Can Be Murder Cozy Mysteries, and her standalone stories.

Book One of the Zelda Richardson Mystery series—*The Lover's Portrait*—is a suspenseful whodunit about Nazi-looted artwork that transports readers to WWII and present-day Amsterdam. Art, religion, and anthropology collide in *Rituals of the Dead* (Book Two), a thrilling artifact mystery set in Papua and the Netherlands. Her exhilarating adventure set in the Netherlands, Croatia, Italy, and Turkey—*Marked for Revenge* (Book Three)—is a story about stolen art, the mafia, and a father's vengeance. Book Four—*The Vermeer Deception*—is a WWII-art mystery set in Germany and the Netherlands.

The Travel Can Be Murder Cozy Mysteries are a funny new series featuring tour guide and amateur sleuth Lana Hansen. Join Lana as she leads tourists and readers to fascinating cities around the globe on intriguing adventures that, unfortunately for Lana, often turn deadly. Book One—*Death on the Danube*—takes Lana to Budapest for a New Year's trip. Can Lana figure out who murdered her fellow tour guide before she too ends up floating in the Danube? In *Death by Baguette: A Valentine's Day Murder in Paris* (Book Two), Lana Hansen escorts five couples on an unforgettable Valentine-themed vacation to France. In Book Three—*Death by Windmill: A Mother's Day Murder in Amsterdam*—Lana's estranged mother joins her tour to the Netherlands. Book Four—*Death by Bagpipes: A Summer Murder in Edinburgh*—will be released in September 2020.

Jennifer is also the author of two thrilling adventure novels: *Down and Out in Kathmandu* and *Holiday Gone Wrong*. Her travelogue, *Notes of a Naive Traveler*, is a must read for those interested in traveling to Nepal and Thailand. All three are available in the *Adventures in Backpacking Box Set*.

To sign up for her newsletter, follow her on social media, or learn more about her novels, please visit Jennifer's website: www.JenniferSAlderson.com.

Rituals of the Dead: An Artifact Mystery

Book Two in the Zelda Richardson Mystery Series

"Simply magnificent, filled with intrigue and suspense, and a lot of wonder!"—Amy Shannon, Amy's Bookshelf Reviews

"You will be on the edge of your seat wondering if Zelda will take one risk too many as well as wishing to discover what actually happened to Nicholas Mayfield. A thoroughly good read."—Lizanne Lloyd, Lost in a Good Book blog

A museum researcher must solve a decades-old murder before she becomes the killer's next victim in this riveting dual timeline thriller set in Papua and the Netherlands.

Agats, Dutch New Guinea (Papua), 1961: While collecting Asmat artifacts for a New York museum, American anthropologist Nick Mayfield stumbles upon a smuggling ring organized by high-ranking members of the Dutch colonial government and the Catholic Church. Before he can alert the authorities, he vanishes in a mangrove swamp, never to be seen again.

Amsterdam, the Netherlands, 2018: While preparing for an exhibition of Asmat artifacts in a Dutch ethnographic museum, researcher Zelda Richardson finds Nick Mayfield's journal in a long-forgotten crate. Before Zelda can finish reading the journal, her housemate is brutally murdered and 'Give back what is not yours' is scrawled on their living room wall.

Someone wants ancient history to stay that way—and believes murder is the surest way to keep the past buried.

Can she solve a sixty-year-old mystery before decades of deceit, greed, and retribution cost Zelda her life?

Available as paperback, eBook, and audiobook at your favorite online retailer.

Excerpt from *Rituals of the Dead*
CHAPTER ONE

August 17, 1962

"Dip, scoop, pour. Dip, scoop, pour. Dip, scoop, pour." Nick Mayfield's dried lips cracked open as he repeated his mantra. Just a few more inches, then she'll float as the survival guide had explained. He leaned against the t-shirt and bits of plank filling the gashes in the sides of the canoe, willing the stream of seawater to stop pouring in faster than he could scoop it out.

The sun was slowly descending, growing in size as it neared the horizon. Bands of pink and orange streaked across the sky, intensifying in color by the second. The new moon was barely a sliver. In an hour's time, he would be plunged into darkness. By then, he should be able to paddle back, he reckoned.

Nick squinted to orient himself, thankful he could see an emerald belt of jungle rising in the distance. He must be in Flamingo Bay, he reckoned, and not too far from land. Still, the expanse of blue-green water between him and the shore was vast. A strong wind tried to push him sea bound. Only the weight of the water and a few crates of barter goods still filling its hull kept the canoe in sight of land. Nick sighed. He was in for a long paddle back once his boat was seaworthy again.

Nick stopped scooping to reposition the jeans tied to his head, arranging the legs so that they covered most of his sunburned back. His thoughts turned to the eight rowers who had jumped overboard hours ago. Had they already made it to shore? Nick wondered for the hundredth time if he should have abandoned ship and swum back with them. Though his faith in his survival guide was unwavering, the water was rushing in extremely fast. The holes were too large to plug completely.

Nick gazed again toward the shoreline. He was a strong swimmer. He knew he could still make it to land if he had to, yet he wouldn't leave his boat unless there were no other options. His guide made clear you should never abandon ship until all attempts to save it have failed. It was the captain's code. Okay, the real captain had jumped overboard hours ago, but still. It was Nick's collection trip that went amiss and his supplies now bobbing in the waves close to his crippled watercraft.

Nick shook his head in disdain, certain the locals had given up too quickly. They all sprung into the water and began swimming as soon as they had discovered the first leak. If only they hadn't moved that bag of beads. Then the water wouldn't have filled the hull so quickly. Nick bashed his coffee tin onto the bottom of the canoe as he scooped, his irritation manifesting itself as Albert Schenk entered his mind. *That Dutchman should be here helping me,* Nick thought. His fever couldn't have come at a worse moment.

A few feet away, a gurgling noise made him jump. The second canoe finally took on more water than it could handle. As soon as the holes in both were found, he'd cut it loose along with the makeshift platform connecting them together like a catamaran. Nick's face paled as he watched its stern slowly rise until the canoe was perpendicular to the water's surface. The platform hung off it like a starched flag. Nick watched in fascination as it stood stock-still seemingly frozen in space and time before suddenly disappearing into the sea. Several large air bubbles broke on the surface, the only sign the boat ever existed.

Nick gazed down into the dark water and redoubled his efforts.

Inexplicably, a can of tobacco soon rose from where the canoe had gone under, and it bobbed next to him. *Its airtight container would make a useful floatation device,* Nick thought, resolving to keep it in sight. Almost all of his supplies had gone under as soon as he cut the second canoe loose. The rest he had thrown into the sea in hopes of making his boat light enough that the two holes in the stern would rise above the water's surface. Not that he had to worry about wasting supplies. He had plenty more stored in Agats.

Losing these trading goods was a minor delay, not a setback.

Nick laughed, splitting his lip further. Blood dripped down his chin as his thin bray drifted across the waves. *Just as capsizing and sinking was a minor irritation,* he thought, giggling again despite the pain.

Cracks of lightning tore across the broad sky. Thunder rumbled seconds later. The storm was closing in fast, Nick realized. He hadn't taken into consideration the storms that frequently whipped across the jungle. If the rain started soon, he'd never be able to get the boat floating enough to paddle back. Especially with only one oar to help—the rest had floated away in the ensuing panic when his rowers discovered the gashes in both boats' sterns.

As a second streak lit up the sky, Nick cleared his mind and focused on nothing but his coffee can. *Dip, scoop, pour. Dip, scoop, pour.* He had to survive—he was a Mayfield. It was his destiny to do great things, not die in the open ocean. *Dip, scoop, pour. Dip, scoop, pour.* And as every Mayfield knew, he had his destiny in his own hands.

* * *

Are you enjoying the story? Buy it now to keep reading!
Available as paperback and eBook at your favorite online retailer.

Death on the Danube: A New Year's Murder in Budapest

Book One in the Travel Can Be Murder Cozy Mystery Series

Who knew a New Year's trip to Budapest could be so deadly? The tour must go on—even with a killer in their midst...

Recent divorcee Lana Hansen needs a break. Her luck has run sour for going on a decade, ever since she got fired from her favorite job as an investigative reporter. When her fresh start in Seattle doesn't work out as planned, Lana ends up unemployed and penniless on Christmas Eve.

Dotty Thompson, her landlord and the owner of Wanderlust Tours, is also in a tight spot after one of her tour guides ends up in the hospital, leaving her a guide short on Christmas Day.

When Dotty offers her a job leading the tour group through Budapest, Hungary, Lana jumps at the chance. It's the perfect way to ring in the new year and pay her rent!

What starts off as the adventure of a lifetime quickly turns into a nightmare when Carl, her fellow tour guide, is found floating in the Danube River. Was it murder or accidental death? Suspects abound when Lana discovers almost everyone on the tour had a bone to pick with Carl.

But Dotty insists the tour must go on, so Lana finds herself trapped with nine murder suspects. When another guest turns up dead, Lana has to figure out who the killer is before she too ends up floating in the Danube...

Available as paperback and eBook.

Excerpt from *Death on the Danube*
CHAPTER ONE

December 26—Seattle, Washington

"You want me to go where, Dotty? And do what?" Lana Hansen had trouble keeping the incredulity out of her voice. She was thrilled, as always, by her landlord's unwavering support and encouragement. But now Lana was beginning to wonder whether Dotty Thompson was becoming mentally unhinged.

"To escort a tour group in Budapest, Hungary. It'll be easy enough for a woman of your many talents."

Lana snorted with laughter. *Ha! What talents?* she thought. Her resume was indeed long: disgraced investigative journalist, injured magician's assistant, former kayaking guide, and now part-time yoga instructor—emphasis on "part-time."

"You'll get to celebrate New Year's while earning a paycheck and enjoying a free trip abroad, to boot. You've been moaning for months about wanting a fresh start. Well, this is as fresh as it gets!" Dotty exclaimed, causing her Christmas-bell earrings to jangle. She was wrapped up in a rainbow-colored bathrobe, a hairnet covering the curlers she set every morning. They were standing inside her living room, Lana still wearing her woolen navy jacket and rain boots. Behind Dotty's ample frame, Lana could see the many decorations and streamers she'd helped to hang up for the Christmas bash last night. Lana was certain that if Dotty's dogs hadn't woken her up, her landlord would have slept the day away.

"Working as one of your tour guides wasn't exactly what I had in mind, Dotty."

"I wouldn't ask you if I had any other choice." Dotty's tone switched from flippant to pleading. "Yesterday one of the guides and two guests crashed into each other while skibobbing outside of Prague, and all are hospitalized. Thank goodness none are in critical condition. But the rest of the group is leaving for Budapest in the morning, and Carl can't do it on his own.

He's just not client-friendly enough to pull it off. And I need those five-star reviews, Lana."

Dotty was not only a property manager, she was also the owner of several successful small businesses. Lana knew Wanderlust Tours was Dotty's favorite and that she would do anything to ensure its continued success. Lana also knew that the tour company was suffering from the increased competition from online booking sites and was having trouble building its audience and generating traffic to its social media accounts. But asking Lana to fill in as a guide seemed desperate, even for Dotty, and even if it was the day after Christmas. Lana shook her head slowly. "I don't know. I'm not qualified to—"

Dotty grabbed one of Lana's hands and squeezed. "Qualified, shmalified. I didn't have any tour guide credentials when I started this company fifteen years ago, and that hasn't made a bit of difference. You enjoy leading those kayaking tours, right? This is the same thing, but for a while longer."

The older lady glanced down at the plastic cards in her other hand, shaking her head. "Besides, you know I love you like a daughter, but I can't accept these gift cards in lieu of rent. If you do this for me, you don't have to pay me back for the past two months' rent. I am offering you the chance of a lifetime. What have you got to lose?"

* * *

Are you enjoying the story? Buy it now and keep reading!
Available as paperback and eBook at your favorite online retailer.

CPSIA information can be obtained
at www.ICGtesting.com
Printed in the USA
LVHW050130300121
677807LV00002B/114